PRAISE FOR ANSTEY HARRIS' *WHEN I FIRST HELD YOU*

'Evocative, emotional and original, every word has been expertly crafted.'

—Catherine Isaac

'*When I First Held You* is a wonderful kaleidoscope of passion, love, grief and misunderstandings. Heartbreaking and yet hauntingly beautiful . . . A stunning book – one to read and reread many times.'

—Celia Anderson

'I loved this gorgeous, poignant novel about loss and love and how over time we are both broken and mended.'

—Sara Sheridan

'Compelling . . . A story of broken dreams and unexpected healing. You'll want to read this.'

—Sarah Ward

'This book has a very big heart. Full of hope and so beautifully observed.'

—Samuel Burr

For *The Truths and Triumphs of Grace Atherton*

'The real truth and triumph of this gem of a story is simple: it is one of the best and most gripping descriptions of heartbreak that either of us have ever read.'

—Richard and Judy

'Glorious on so many levels.'

—A. J. Pearce, author of *Dear Mrs Bird*

'Lose yourself among beautiful symphonies, the romantic cities of Europe and quirky characters . . . a triumph.'

—*Woman's Weekly*

'A powerful and passionate novel, awash with heartbreak but still an uplifting tale of friendship and rebirth. Five stars.'

—*Daily Express*

'Full of hope and charm.'

—Libby Page, author of *The Lido*

'A hymn to friendship, to getting back up and finding happiness where none seemed possible.'

—Katie Fforde

'Brilliantly and movingly written.'

—Dorothy Koomson

'Elegant and uplifting . . . I was both engrossed in and moved by this fabulous debut.'

—Catherine Isaac

'A moving, beautifully written, uplifting debut about mending broken hearts through friendship. The twists and turns make it impossible to put down.'

—Sarah J. Harris

'What a total joy!'

—Fanny Blake

For *Where We Belong*

'Incredibly moving and atmospheric.'

—Beth O'Leary

'Absorbing and original.'

—Katie Fforde

'Simply stunning.'

—Fionnuala Kearney

'Utterly enchanting.'

—Heidi Swain

The
House
of
Lost
Secrets

ALSO BY ANSTEY HARRIS

When I First Held You

The Truths and Triumphs of Grace Atherton (also published as,

Goodbye, Paris)

Where We Belong (also published as, *The Museum of Forgotten Memories*)

The House of Lost Secrets

Anstey Harris

LAKE UNION
PUBLISHING

Text copyright © 2024 by Anstey Harris
All rights reserved.

Published by Lake Union Publishing, Seattle

www.apub.com

Amazon, the Amazon logo, and Lake Union Publishing are trademarks of Amazon.com, Inc., or its affiliates.

ISBN-13: 9781662512575
eISBN: 9781662512568

Cover design by Emma Rogers
Cover image: © Plus69 © Lukasz Szwaj © KPG-Payless © Katie Thorpe © Helen Hotson © Andrey Danilov / Shutterstock

Printed in the United States of America

Dedicated with love to Paula and Robin, who ate stilton with a silver spoon and who taught me how to sing.

And to Maziar.

Chapter One

Rachel and I share a birthday. My mother stopped holding birthday parties for me when I was ten, but Rachel offered me part of hers from our eleventh onwards. She did it as graciously and as generously as everything else she's included me in over the last forty-something years.

Today's birthday is about Rachel. It's about me, too, in that I'm doing the speech, but she's centre stage.

'No ex-boyfriends,' Tim said. 'That's the only rule. Other than that, you can say what you want.' Tim is the kind of man who tells, rather than asks – which is why Rachel likes him so much and I don't particularly like him at all. There wasn't a part of this conversation where he asked if I minded doing this on my birthday, if that mattered.

'And I don't want to see it beforehand.' Tim looked at me. 'Surprise me, on the day.'

Just like that, the minutiae of his wife's big day are someone else's problem – there'll be caterers, and waiters, and me. Hired help, unpaid in my case.

I have been working on these words for three weeks – twenty-four-seven. At night, phrases of it go round and round in my mind like the lyrics of a bad song.

Tim didn't ask me to do this because he thinks I'm funny – or even reliable. He asked me because Rachel and I twist through one another like vines, each written through the other like a stick of rock. If anything, my best friend's husband thinks I'm a pain: expensive; time-consuming; all the things that move his wife's focus from him to me. But I'm her longest-standing human, just as she is to me. She has outlasted my husbands, my family, and I – now that her parents are long gone and Tim is going to be her only marriage – have been the same for her.

◆ ◆ ◆

It's irrelevant whether I've got it right or not now, because it's time.

It's today.

Happy birthday to us.

At two this morning, I took out the line about Rachel and me planning to spend our twilight years drinking ourselves to death while the sunset turns us to leather, funded by the money that Tim – and until recently, Terry – have left us from their life insurance. It's not the moment for it, or the audience: it's a private joke, for the two of us.

I picture Rachel's reaction to every line I've written. It will have to be just so: pitch-perfect for the audience and occasion. And if it were about anyone else, I'd be reading it to her over the phone, asking if it's all too much, too sentimental.

Terry, as predictable in divorce as he was slippery in marriage, texts first thing: the morning is still pink, new at its edges. It will be a long day.

You've got this, babe, his text says, as if he were an overfamiliar life coach.

This is not the week. Do not talk to me. It is not only the pressures of today that squeeze me from all sides: this was a bad week for our decree absolute to land and – simultaneously – a huge chunk of the equity in my house to be transferred to Terry's bank account. My retirement plans, even the sensible ones, have vanished overnight.

I'll be hovering in the background, Terry texts, and I can see his face as he does it, picture the tiny glint of gold from the only one of his teeth to not be perfect and pristine, tucked away at the side of his mouth so you only see it when he wants you to, when he needs the extra sparkle. *Beaming love to you.*

I don't grace him with a reply.

◆ ◆ ◆

'You look good, Jo,' Tim says when I get there. 'Very calm.'

Last night was the zenith of twenty-one days of insomnia. I look like I've been boil-washed.

'The dress code didn't leave much wiggle room,' I say. And then, because I don't want him to think I'm sniping, that he got anything wrong: 'Which was one less thing for me to worry about.'

'Are you worried?' He looks at me in his sideways squint, the one that gets slightly less appealing when he's been drinking.

I tell him, no, I'm not – me worrying will only make him worry – and I lean up against their slate-grey cupboards as everyone who counts as 'family' gathers in this small kitchen.

We're meeting everyone else there. Everyone here, including Tim, is even older than me. I need the wider party of Rachel's friends and neighbours, her work colleagues and old college buddies, to stop me feeling like this is it, like this lot are the end of the line and that I am numbered among them.

'You'd be her only choice, if I'd asked her.' Tim almost whispers it, as if he doesn't want anyone else – any elderly cousins or deaf aunts – to hear him.

3

I take the sponge out of the washing-up bowl and touch the end of my shoe with it. I've only walked from my little hotel room round the corner, but I've already managed to get dust on my outfit. A splosh of water dribbles from the corner of the wet sponge. It hits my leg and a dark bloom runs down my black crêpe-de-Chine trousers. I grab a piece of kitchen towel to dry it, and something white and fibrous comes off the kitchen towel on to my trousers. This would never happen to Rachel.

At five thirty this morning, as people driving to work became the sound of the cityscape, I removed a whole passage about how Rachel helped me leave Terry, how she listened – for hours and hours – and how her advice was always so accurate, how she'd got my back. Rachel was as invested in my leaving him as I was, and I couldn't have – wouldn't have – done it without her.

I look at Tim, straight and pale, his glasses clean and the lines of his suit sharp – no corners or caves or whirlpools – and I see, not for the first time, where I fit. I am the curve to his corners, the soft to his solid and between us we make the exact person Rachel requires. We are an exercise in build-a-buddy.

Tim makes a subtle gesture among the old ladies and the well-dressed cousins. A noise almost. And the relatives move as a tide towards the back door.

'She's here,' Tim says.

The hearse is exactly across the end of the drive, perfectly placed so that Rachel's coffin is in our eyeline as we walk towards it.

It is no more real than it was when we were inside, no more possible that my beautiful friend is dead, that her loud laugh and unmatchable cleverness are now a matter of record, of digital files and documents, of Super 8 film and old birthday cards.

I imagine the relatives already know that this isn't grief – this bleak catastrophe unfolding. Grief is longer and heavier than this. Grief likes Wednesdays and bus queues, a hijack in the most unlikely of situations. Grief likes to be close, and friends for years.

I anticipate that grief will entirely fill the space Rachel took up in my life.

Tim rang me when the results of her autopsy came home to him. A massive stroke. 'Out,' he said – his choice of words keeps repeating itself in my head as if it's the end of a night on the tiles – 'like a light.' Rachel has been dead for six weeks, the longest I've gone without speaking to her since I was eleven years old. Out like a light.

The abruptness of her death is a blast that overwhelms everything. Sudden death is a bomb exploding above you, blindingly bright and showering you with its fragments every time you close your eyes. My thoughts are still shocked, ringing with white noise and scattering around in panic.

The eulogy has been a way of ordering those thoughts, of trying to shepherd them. I don't dream any more – I haven't done for the forty-three days she's been dead – and sleep is a black emptiness, a muffled quiet. Rachel refuses to join me there, however hard I try to summon her.

When I attempt to see her face, pin down the memories of the two of us together, I only remember times that I've been cross with her, when she's been late to a meet-up or cancelled last minute because of work and, although these minor irritations were few and far between, they are all that come when I think of our long lives together, of all our days. I know my brain is trying to protect me, trying to shelter me from the awfulness of it all by convincing me I didn't really love her. But I did.

The eulogy is printed out and in my bag. I could, probably, do it from memory if I had to – and the vicar has a copy in case of disaster.

'It's called corpsing,' he told me down the telephone when he rang to tell me what a eulogy needed to be – how long, how tasteful. 'If you find yourself paralysed with terror—' He cut himself off, added, 'Or grief,' as an afterthought – as if he'd just remembered what his job was, what the day will entail. 'If you can't speak – or breathe – I'll take over where you left off.'

And he told me to project my voice to the two stone pillars at the back of the church – that way, my eyes would avoid any sudden surprises among the guests, and everyone would hear me, right to the back.

I thought about the vicar's posh military voice, the pomposity in it. I remembered the name Rachel called him when she and Tim first moved to their little village and started going to church as a way to fit in.

'You're doing what?' I said to her, laughing. 'Have you turned into your mother? Are you having a tiny sherry before you go?' And now she never will turn into her mother. She will never have time.

'I'll do it,' I say to the vicar. 'I'll be fine.'

And I am fine, if that describes getting the words out, in the right order, and only crying on the very last bit – taking deep steadying breaths to make sure no one missed my poignant punchline.

Rachel is in the coffin behind me. I presume her feet are pointing to my back, her head to the altar, and I realise I don't know what she's wearing, which shoes. I wonder if Tim made the choice himself, or whether someone helped him. Rachel had a lot of shoes.

As I leave the lectern, I reach out and touch the wood of the coffin. 'Bye, mate,' I whisper, so quietly that no one can hear it but her and me. This is the last time I shall be near her and, apart from the people who will carry her out and lower her into the grave around the corner of the church, I will be one of the last people to ever touch Rachel.

I try and smile at Tim as I settle back into the pew behind his, and he reaches back over his shoulder to squeeze my hand.

◆　◆　◆

At the reception afterwards, it is a matter of interest to all the mourners to find out who I am, why Tim asked me to do it, why he chose me to write the last tribute to Rachel.

There isn't much to say.

'My name is Joanna.' But they know that from the order of service. 'Joanna Wilding – so I sat next to Rachel Willoughby on the first day of secondary school, when we all lined up alphabetically.

'Until recently, I ran a business, importing bits of plastic vital to switches. But, actually, I'm going to retrain.' They aren't interested enough in me to ask as what, and that's good because I don't know: only old men ever ask about the switches or the change in legislation that turned them off. I am afraid of having to tell anyone that I don't know what I'll be when I grow up.

'That was wonderful,' says Rachel's Aunt Poll when she catches up to me. She walks with a stick now, in her late eighties, and her clothes hang from her, a drizzle of silk and gauze. 'You always were the most wonderful friend to her. And happy birthday.'

'I can't believe you remembered,' I say. 'That's very sweet.'

Poll is Rachel's dad's sister and she looks just like him, has the same double chin and heavy eyebrows as he did. Less bald, just.

I've always liked her enormously. 'It wasn't the best day to bury her really, was it?' she says.

'It's a busy time of year apparently.' I half-smile at her. 'And the bank holidays screw everything up; people are still away on their summer breaks before this. It was the same for parties when we were young.' Rachel's parties, with an extra cake.

'I wonder if you were born at the same time.' And I can see in Poll's eyes a memory of Rachel as a baby, the overwhelming iniquity of death in the wrong order. 'Did you ever ask your mum – or Rosie?'

We must have done once, but I don't remember, and it's too late now. Rosie is dead, reunited at long last with her daughter, and I haven't spoken to my own mother in nearly forty years.

'It must be brutal for you, darling. Let me know if there's anything I can do to help.'

'Thanks, Poll,' I say and give her a squeeze. I know she means it; the Willoughbys never offered anything they didn't mean.

Being accepted by Rachel's family was like a scholarship. At first, it was a melee of holding things wrong: conversations, knives and forks, beliefs – it was confusing and destabilising. But the teenage me knew that something had got me there, saw them collect me like they did the impossibly old dark oak furniture, the books and books of photographs going back to when photography began, the lavender-scented drawers full of Rachel's grandparents' clothes long after they had died.

The Willoughbys had confidence that comes with breeding, of being certain that they knew how to behave anywhere, from a subway tunnel to a funeral. The Willoughbys knew that money talks, but wealth whispers, and nothing fazed them. Rachel was born with it, that style and grace, and she still had years of it left to grow into.

When I was young, I thought we were equals. All credit to the Willoughbys that they hid how much we weren't.

'She was everything to me,' I say to Poll. 'Everything.'

'And that came across beautifully.' Poll wanders to the buffet table, squeezes in between a young couple I don't know and carries on talking. 'Your voice was jolly clear. I'm half deaf – and half daft – and I heard every glorious word.'

In many ways, this is like any other party – people discuss the food, how difficult it was to park near the venue, what house prices are doing. And occasionally they stop and remember why they're there and they bring themselves up sharply: go quiet or well up. Rachel is in all the conversations, but not necessarily in the words.

There is a little anteroom behind the venue where the caterers have left their boxes and empty trays. I go and sit in there with my empty wine glass, breathing out for the first time in hours, welcoming the silence. The eulogy impressed people – it impressed me. There were a few smiles, laughter bubbled round the church at a couple of points, but mostly I'd managed to make it speak of Rachel and what she meant to us all, in a universal sense: of the generous light inside her, and how it shone; of how we owe it to her, and the loss of her, to try and find something of the same to give to the world.

The wall of the anteroom is painted in a municipal nicotine-peach and I rest my head against it, confident that I won't dirty it or make it worse. I open my eyes when I hear someone cross the room, but I don't move or look. I need it not to be Terry, not today. Not now.

It is Tim who sits down beside me and takes a bottle of vodka from his inside pocket. No hip flask or decoration, just one of those flat small bottles from behind the counter at the supermarket: a quarter bottle, I think. This isn't a day for hip flasks. This is a day for hard stuff from the bottle, from an inside pocket.

9

He opens it and passes it to me, holding the screw top in his hand.

I swig without wiping the neck, like they do in movies, and give it back to him.

He does the same thing and puts the cap on. The metal legs of his chair make a quiet scrape against the wooden floor and he leans back against the wall next to me.

'Your words were brilliant. She'd have known you'd get it right.'

If we were friends, he'd add, 'I thought you'd fuck it up.' But we're not really, so he doesn't.

'I'm glad. It's a tiny thing to do in the great scheme of things. A last gift for her.' My voice squeaks slightly, and the pain in my chest that I'd been afraid would come during the eulogy starts to throb.

Tim doesn't say anything. From the main hall, chatter comes in on the air like ghosts.

I can smell the alcohol on the air between us, our sour breath. 'I surprised myself, if I'm honest.' There is a hollowness inside me, a change – a before and an after. The person I was with her and the person I am without her.

'Not real, is it?' he asks me, getting the bottle back out again.

I want to tell him that it is, that it feels so real my heart is on fire, that my insides have disappeared and I can't feel anything from the lungs down except a vast empty pressure. It's far too real to me. 'It's like a dream,' I tell him, for the sake of saying something. 'A nightmare.'

'There are school friends of yours in the hall.'

I make a gesture to him to pass me the vodka. 'Not my friends. Rachel's.' I didn't really have friends at school except Rachel – Tim won't understand the reality of that. The reality of walking home from the bus stop with Rachel and joy in my heart, spending the evenings writing letters to each other to swap in the morning or going for long walks by the canal. Then the daytimes again, when she became part of the popular group, the A-listers, A-graders, A-girls. And I was back to being a bit odd, a bit of an outsider.

'Karen Roberts.' Tim takes the bottle back from me, gestures to the hall with it; the open neck points towards the door. 'Rachel couldn't stand her.'

'Me neither. She was a rat at school. Worse now.' Karen Roberts was a deathly combination of boring and mean at school – no huge crime, there were lots of others like her.

But Karen weaselled closer to us, physically rather than emotionally. Karen went out with Rachel's brother, Tris, and that meant she was invited to tea, to birthdays, and to their cottage in Scotland for holidays. That meant she was everywhere I might want to be alone with him.

My teens were ruined by being in love with Tristan Willoughby. The decades that followed were all touched by it, shaped by it.

I've spent most of my life in love with Rachel's brother, with the corporeal radiance of him while he was alive and then – far more easily after he died – with his ghost.

And Rachel never knew.

Chapter Two

The vodka has given me indigestion – my throat is burning so hard it makes my eyes water.

'I'd better go back in.' I feel awkward sitting here with Tim: this is the longest we've ever spent on our own. Being together emphasises our loss.

I walk back into the main hall and find Poll, sit with her and share a plate of buffet food, try and calm my raging throat with sandwiches and dainty pastries: fat and white flour that will see my oesophagus scorch until daybreak.

'I'm glad Rosie and Duncan didn't live to see this day,' Poll says. Her eyes are rheumy blue, perpetual tears scooped inside the lower lid, a fold underneath her lower eyelashes that pleats away in wrinkles to the sides of her face. The sherry has added to her grief, allowed it to amplify and spill. 'Burying both your children . . .' She trails off; it's a sentence that doesn't need finishing. They were her niece and nephew, it must be dreadful.

Rachel's parents were great. Her dad worked hard all week and played golf hard all weekend, returning to jolly us up, cheeks red from the sunshine and the nineteenth hole. Rosie was elegant and tall, a willowy English teacher and the best of everything. They wouldn't have survived seeing their beautiful girl, their only child left, die.

'It's a mercy,' I agree, and think how hard it must be for Poll, to be one of the last ones left, to outlive your generation's children.

'What's your plan?' she asks me, shaking off the sadness before it engulfs her. 'From here?'

That question, the vodka, and the back view of Karen Roberts across the hall unseat me. 'Plan?'

'Tim told me about the divorce. I'm awfully sorry, dear. He seemed so charming, your last chap.'

I like to believe that I had suspicions about Terry as soon as I met him, scents of too-good-to-be-true, wafts of why-didn't-anyone-else-marry-him, but I didn't – I was as bowled over by him as Rachel was.

'He's honestly fabulous,' she said the first time she met him, when Terry had taken us to a tiny little Italian restaurant hidden in the middle of a city we thought we knew inside out and the staff had greeted him like family. 'He's the kind of person I've wished for all your life.'

Rachel and Terry laughed together like drains, rolled around helplessly and squeezed the last chaos from every joke, the very final moment from an observation. Long after the two of them had drunk me sober, they'd still find a reason we should all stay up, have one last thing to laugh about before we called it a night.

The only other person who had ever fitted into our dynamic like that, once upon a time, was Tristan. There were almost two years between Tristan and Rachel, but because of their birthdays, he was in the school year above us. It was an 'in' – Rachel and I could fancy all his friends, and he and his friends used us as a conduit to meet the girls in our year. It was only ever Tristan for me, but I played the game, pretended there were other boys.

Everyone else in our lives was like Tim – perfectly nice, but an outsider.

'Tim said he was going to talk to you about the cottage, about Clachan,' Poll says.

For a moment, I have a flight of fancy where Rachel has bequeathed me her family's country house, her great-grandfather's cottage tucked between the forest and the sea. Even her great-grandfather didn't need to live in it – it has been a holiday home for four generations.

'I suppose he'll sell it now?' I ask Poll. She's been going there for decades, just as I have, but the cottage doesn't belong to her side of the family – it came with Rosie, long before Tris and Rachel were even born.

Poll raises her finger to show me that she'll speak in one minute, when she's finished her mouthful of salmon. Rachel's local girlfriends have stepped in to sort out the buffet, giving Tim nothing to do except pay the bill, and they've done a great job. The salmon Poll is eating came curled like an orange comma, perfection against the pale green of cucumber and peppered with yellow lemon zest. Everything is elegant, tasteful, and just as Rachel would have wanted it. Just as I would have done it.

'He wouldn't sell.' Poll pats her lips with one finger, then another, and I know that I would have wiped my whole hand on my trousers without thinking about it if it were me, because that's who she and I are. 'But neither would he ever use it. It's so Willoughby-ed, it's a bit of a liability.' She laughs – she is a Willoughby, she knows what the verb means.

I know what she means too. I have grown up adoring the way its priceless portraits rub shoulders with knick-knacks from the local summer fete, where Wellington boots of every imaginable size clutter the understairs cupboard as if they've been breeding in there for years, grey and blind from a lack of sunlight. Emptying the cottage for sale will be like emptying that cupboard on an enormous scale.

Behind Poll's shoulder, I am keeping half an eye on Karen Roberts.

'And Tim hates the countryside.' Poll is incredulous at that.

Karen is holding court with a small circle of women and I recognise other netball team stars, science-class whiz-kids, clear-skinned all-rounders from school. They kept in loose touch with Rachel through university, afterwards too, but I never could stand them.

I've made poor choices in life: not going to college until I was in my thirties and even then not studying what I wanted to, not following my heart; marrying Evan while I was still a teenager and then, in a triumph of hope over experience, marrying Terry when Evan didn't work out.

There was a peculiar kind of feminism at our school. We were taught to despise anyone who married young, who dreamed of keeping a house and raising children – it's probably part of why I did it. We were encouraged to judge and deride other women's choices. But not being friends with Karen and the rest of that group of women is a choice I've never regretted.

Poll follows my gaze. 'I remember them,' she says. 'What a ghastly bunch.' She pats my arm. 'We always preferred you.'

I know they did. Losing Rachel is the last of my grip on the life raft the Willoughbys were to me, this crazy family – so overprivileged and, at the same time, so humble, so generous of spirit and such an asset in my life.

Poll and I are looking across the sea of people towards Karen when she turns round. She raises an arm, waves and sets out towards us.

I feel rather than hear the rush of air that is Poll groaning.

'I'm not fast enough on my pins nowadays,' she whispers as we steel ourselves to greet Karen.

'Bad timing,' I whisper back. 'I could leave you here.'

'Don't you bloody dare.' And she's all smiles as Karen stretches out her arms.

Karen hugs us both without really touching us. She makes lots of noises about how little we've changed, how sorry she is. None of it is true: Poll is a bag of bones, stooped and crumpled; I am a vision in ordinary – grey-haired, chubby, pale-skinned, with blueish semicircles of exhaustion under each eye.

'Terrible circumstances but marvellous to see you.' Karen looks past me and says, 'I didn't get to Tristan's funeral.' He died almost forty years ago, it's a strange apology to make now.

There is a silence as the mirage of him shimmers between the three of us, crosses time and space.

And then Karen reels off a precis of what her husband does for a living, of how successful their children are. It is almost a hymn sheet, practised into a little potted boast. There is nothing about her in it at all.

'Did you do the food?' she asks me. 'You used to be obsessed with cooking at school.'

'I didn't. We had caterers.' *We.* There is no *we* now. I look at my shoes to see if my dreams are underneath them, trodden into the floor.

'You were a walking bake sale.' She laughs. 'Always with a Tupperware of cakes or a batch of biscuits wrapped in silver foil.'

I don't tell her that I was trying to bake myself a family, to fill a painful house with the smells of other people's childhoods.

'Well, your eulogy was wonderful,' she says, when she's finished her mouthful of caterers' food. 'Did you write it yourself?'

The wind sucks out of my lungs; echoes of school ripple through me, reduce me.

'It was a eulogy,' Poll says, her voice cracking a little with irritation, with speaking so quickly and not having time to prepare her throat. 'Of course she did.'

Karen waves a hand in front of her as if she can dissolve her words. 'Absolutely, I mean, of course.' And then she looks right at me. 'It's just that at school you were, well, you know – cakes apart – you were a bit weird.'

◆ ◆ ◆

My mum had her first breakdown when I was twelve.

Everyone at the church she'd joined – we'd joined, it turned out – was just like her, all looking for the same kind of salvation. One that comes on Earth. The old friends and neighbours, the people who might have noticed things going wrong, had all disappeared when my dad did: divorce was unusual back then and they seemed to believe they could catch it, that if they spent time propping my mum up perhaps their own marriages would falter and flicker and fall apart.

When I got up in the morning, pulled on my nylon school jumper and tried to get my socks to stay up, I never knew which mum she'd be. And sometimes she'd be one mum for breakfast, and a different one for tea – a grey, weeping one, like a ghoul or a haunting.

Our house was neat and small, modern and open-plan. The walls were papered with fashionable flowers and swirls, our sofas were leatherette and conker-coloured. Everything looked bright and ordered. It was the perfect scenery for the chaos of her mind to stand out against.

School wasn't an escape – because of girls like Karen Roberts – but on the way there and the way home, I had Rachel, and through the death of pets and changing friends, through music and collecting records, on to posters and crushes and TV stars, she made it all alright.

I knew every part of Rachel, and she knew almost everything about me: she didn't know that, every day, I was waiting to turn into my mum in the way my mum turned into my gran – wondering when I'd go mental too.

Chapter Three

When I get to Rachel's house – Tim's house – the morning after the night before, he looks like someone who's just buried his wife. He is wretched, wrung out and soaked in grief.

I don't know what else I expected.

Tim shuffles backwards into the kitchen, ushering me in. He is wearing a crumpled blue dressing gown. His skin is taut and bristly. He looks ruined.

'Coffee?' He switches the machine on at the wall and I nod. I need it too.

Last night finished in a hail of singing and dancing, as if suddenly the mourners had had enough and switched tempo, dialled up to full party. We bellowed songs and staggered through tunes: we cried at the past, and we wept for the future.

The ritual is done, completed, and she is properly gone.

'I'll hang around until I'm sure I can drive.' I drank more than I normally would last night, a steady drip of socially acceptable anaesthetic for the soul. Today it brings its own pain.

Tim looks down at himself as if only just realising he isn't dressed. Under the robe, candy-striped pyjama bottoms hover over carpet slippers. He looks like an old man – I suppose he will be now. 'I'll run and put some clothes on. Make yourself some toast, whatever.'

I trail my fingers along the jars and tins in their pantry, lift the terracotta lid of the old crock pot that holds the bread. I think of all the meals she and I cooked together, over all the years that this was her pantry. I need to screenshot this kitchen, memorise these cupboards: Tim and I are being civil, but I have no reason to come back here after this. This will be the end of my visits.

'I want to talk to you about the cottage,' he says. 'Before you go. Rachel told me about your house.'

Writing the eulogy was a break from preparing my beautiful house to be rented. And that came about because I didn't listen to my inner voice and I did listen to Rachel – I married Terry and brought him into the business, and everything I owned became half his. In ten years of marriage, eight of them wrong and badly fitted but which had seemed like a good idea at the time, I went from solvent to drowning.

A stab of memory, a reminder that, at the beginning, Terry and I were so full of future, of planning. We even thought we might have a child, snatch a last-minute family from the waiting maw of the menopause.

Despite everything, despite his debts and his demands, I haven't lost my home permanently. But I have lost it for now. The only way I can pay the enormous mortgage I had to get to buy him out was to find a tenant for my elegant townhouse and rent somewhere smaller and cheaper for a couple of years.

The rent coming in is high enough to cover the mortgage and give me a small income while I look for a job. It saddens me, angers me, but it doesn't scare me: I've worked up from nothing before – I can do it again.

The clothes Tim comes downstairs in are crumpled, pre-worn. His grey T-shirt has a mark on the front and he pulls a jumper over it as he walks. 'The cottage. Clachan.'

'Poll mentioned you wanted to talk about it. She didn't say why.' And then I wonder what would happen if Rachel had actually left it to me, if she and Tim had so much money that another hundred thousand or two mattered so little she could give it away. But that's not realistic – they're well off, more than comfortable, but they're not obscenely rich.

I put two slices of elderly bread in the toaster. Crumbs and abandoned cutlery litter the oiled wood worktops, surface chaos. I clear away a smear of butter with my finger, look round for a tea towel to wipe my hand on. 'Do you want toast?' I ask.

Tim ignores me so I assume he doesn't.

'Rachel was having the cottage done up. Painting it out and so on,' he says.

I nod. She and I were excited about it: we made mood boards, collected pictures online and sent each other snippets and ideas. It's been hard to stop now she's dead. I still want to send her photographs of colours, links to curtain fabrics. It was our project, something to distract me, to help me rise from the ashes of my marriage.

'And then we were going to look at the whole thing: maybe rent it out a bit, maybe sell it.' He carries on talking as if I don't know more about what Rachel was thinking than he ever has.

She would never sell that cottage, I want to say – but it's his cottage now and what she would do is utterly and miserably immaterial.

He turns and busies himself with the coffee machine: I know how it feels to look at people when you're as raw as he is, when you need to turn away in order to breathe. 'It's the last of her family gone. The end of her mum and dad – her brother.'

Tristan was long dead by the time Rachel met Tim, nothing left of him but a stone to lay flowers at in the Auchlaggan kirkyard.

'And the last of her, of Rachel.' It's remarkably insightful for Tim, who had no time for our traditions and habits when Rachel was alive.

Clachan is not like my house. I think of the sweep of my stairs, the gentle rise with one hand on a dark wood Edwardian banister that ends in an original scrolled finial, the tall, thin windows at each half landing and the way they pour light down on to the climber as if you are reaching for heaven. The cottage is not like that.

Clachan has shadowed corners and low ceilings. It is surrounded by silent forest on three sides, and the vast silver sea on the fourth, rippling over umbral depths.

Clachan is under trees that whisper as you sleep, call out to you in creaking threats that one day they might fall, might point their twig fingers right through the glass and into your bed, scratch at your skin. It is at once heavy with joyful buoyant stories and pulsing with dark memories and painful ghosts.

'I know you don't want to go back there. I realise how hard that will be. But . . .'

His tailed-off sentence might have ended . . . *it would be good for you*, or . . . *it could help you put the bad memories to rest*. Or even . . . *you could stay for a bit, it would be cheap, rent-free*. All of these options float between us, all potentially true until he chooses what he is, actually, trying to say.

At Clachan, there are no next-door shops or neighbours, only brambles and bracken and the uneasy possibilities of hidden things moving around the undergrowth, hiding between trees and snaking through the dense dark. At Clachan, there are stars that twinkle like pinpricks in a velvet black sky and shells that wash up like treasure on the beach. At Clachan, if I didn't pay rent, I would have enough to live on, albeit frugally and not forever, without working.

At Clachan, I could regroup.

21

'It's yours,' he says, 'so you have to go back. That's what I'm trying to say.' His voice cracks at the end of the sentence.

I hear him, but I can't grasp the meaning. It must show on my face.

'She left you Clachan in her will.'

The coffee machine whirrs and chirrups like it's laid an egg.

'She made her first will before we even met – it was already yours. I assume it always has been, ever since her parents left it to her.' Tim passes me a small black cup, the top a speckled foam of crema.

Their perfect lives: their three-thousand-pound coffee machine. Their spare houses to leave to friends.

Out like a light.

He gestures to the milk jug as if this conversation is in some way normal and I shake my head.

'Some of that stuff in the house is very valuable, and some is junk. I have no idea which is which. I wondered if you wanted to move in – now, before probate – and sort it out. You'd be doing me a favour. The law is different in Scotland – it takes a long time before you can actually do anything with an inheritance. And you'll have to work round the decorator. That might as well be finished – it's all being paid for.'

Rachel has left me Clachan. Exactly half of my body screams that I never want to see the cottage again, that it's cursed and deso-late and the last place I ever want to set foot in, while the other half – wrenching and wringing – knows that it's the only place I'll be able to find her, the only place she'll be able to speak to me, and the closest thing I have to a family home.

It's too much to take in. Too impossible. But even while my brain still throbs and spins with the news, the house draws me like a magnet.

◆ ◆ ◆

Eight weeks ago, Rachel sent me an email. In it she said she had something she desperately needed to tell me, and on the phone or by email wasn't the way, that we needed to be together 'to talk about it', and she suggested a long weekend at Clachan.

I'd written back immediately, worried she was ill, that something awful had happened to her.

Her reply was quick, and smooth. Nothing to do with health, nothing to do with Tim. But she really needed to talk to me, to tell me whatever it was, and it could only be done in person.

It was out of character, the mystery. Rachel wears her heart on her sleeve – she's impulsive, ideas and news wriggling out of her, seeping through her closed lips, making their way to daylight through the pores of her skin.

My first thought was that perhaps she was going to leave Tim, or have an affair, shake up that quiet life. I've never understood how they work, how his long slow sentences chime with her bubbling overspill. I realise that his logical thought-through pragmatism gives her safety – but he can be very dull.

And she'd said tell me, not ask me. That made it, after a night of tossing and turning, throwing it around in my sleep, definitely something about her, not me.

If it was about me, concerned me, she would ask me, but she was telling me – so it's something I don't already know. But we need to talk about it, so it will change something in some way. Change me, even. Change us.

We typed riddles, backwards and forwards, but Rachel didn't budge. She would tell me at Clachan, when we were together, and not before.

◆ ◆ ◆

We were excited. We hadn't seen each other for months – my efforts at clinging on to my home and business had taken all my time, and Rachel hadn't stopped working at breakneck speed for years.

Let's make it a spa retreat, she'd said in one of her texts once we'd started organising the weekend. *Clean living. Sea swimming and good food. No booze.*

No booze? Is this Rachel Willoughby's phone? I'd texted back.

Seriously. Spring-cleaning my life. Putting a lot of things behind me.

She'd followed that with lots of kisses that we both knew pertained to whatever-she-was-going-to-tell-me, but I'd given up digging: I'd know in a week.

I had a problem with the arrangements. *Where do almond croissants fit in with the new regime?*

Central to our existence. I am not the kind of woman to deny anyone an almond croissant.

Bread? I didn't know how I'd do a weekend without.

I am not a monster.

Normally, I would arrive at Clachan with a car boot full of shopping – wine and treats, cheeses and crisps and indulgences, knowing that Rachel will have made an order for even more from the local shop. I would park as near to the cottage as I could, then look for the old silver wheelbarrow hidden in the undergrowth. Once all my bags and bounty were decanted into the barrow, I could set off through the sandy woods. It is how Rachel's family have arrived at the cottage since they first had cars.

Our usual weekends together are punctuated by Champagne as early as is decent, a little wine with lunch, and cocktails before dinner. One summer in our thirties, we laced smoothies with rum and sat on the beach until the sun crested the horizon, staggering and giggling back to bed in the pink daylight. There is no doubt that Rachel Willoughby and I know how to party.

It would do me the bloody world of good to have a weekend off, I told her. I've read the text over and over again, the last one I ever sent her. *It would do me the world of bloody good.*

◆ ◆ ◆

Everything about visiting Clachan is ritual. The circumstances of the rituals have evolved as we've got older, as things have changed, but essentially things work one way, and one way only – the Willoughby way.

As always, I went to the bakery near my house before I left, their very first customer of the day, while the shop sign was still set to 'closed' and the smell of baking was yet to be released on to the street. I bought us the almond croissants for Saturday breakfast and a loaf of artisan sourdough – I'm not sure if there is another sort of sourdough – to eat with our supper. I had a bunch of sunflowers, wrapped in brown paper by the florist and artfully tied with raffia. The flowers went on the back seat, next to my weekend bag. At the last minute, as a gesture to Scotland, I ran back inside to fetch my raincoat and wellies.

The cottage is an easy three hours from my house – a little more difficult for Rachel to come by train, but she was staying for a few days more than me to make the journey worthwhile.

I timed my journey to both miss the traffic and make the very most of a long summer day. I left home before 6 a.m., breakfast stowed away for us in the back. In front of me, the dawn cracked open the horizon like the portal to another world and I drove towards the leak of orange. Behind me, due east, the daybreak was a vivid flood across the sky.

With every mile, I shed stress like flakes of skin, as if the journey were whittling me clean. There is a magic to the oldest of relationships, a deep peace that comes from a lifetime of shared experience, of understanding the things that made us.

Terry had been nothing short of awful in the last weeks. In the aftermath of a divorce that he had created, asked for, and orchestrated, he was feeling lonely. His latest younger model had dumped him and he had suddenly realised that half my capital wasn't enough to buy a house when his credit was too poor for a mortgage. I'd memorised chunks of his bleating to recite to Rachel. She would hoot with laughter at his rationale, be suitably furious at his cheek. We would be the old team for a whole uninterrupted weekend, and it felt great.

I didn't realise what was about to happen, that I would never forget this weekend.

I pull off the motorway and drive due west for an hour. By now, the sun is high in the sky and fresh. It seems ungrateful to dull it with the sun visor, so I squint as I drive, letting it bathe me.

After a flurry of ever-more-unpronounceable place names, my memory takes over the route-planning, registering changes as the lanes become smaller: a forest sliced down and harvested here; a new house there. The sun sparkles through fir fronds and, when I slide my window down, the mole-brown scent of forest floor is unmistakeable.

The 'car park' is no more than a gap in the trees marked with a single supine log as a gate – always left open. The sandy circle has been made bigger over the years, but otherwise it is just as it was when I first came here, aged fourteen. A large area of compacted sand, with five or six paths running out from it like a delta. Each path runs into the forest and disappears into mountains of wild rhododendron – high as a house – or curls round rows of larch until it peters out under the pine needles.

I wonder if Rachel will have brought the wheelbarrow back or if she will have left it outside the cottage after she took her own stuff down. I peer into the hollow underneath a group of hawthorns: they lean in as if they have secrets, forest gossip for locals, things that I wouldn't need to be told if I didn't keep leaving.

There it is. Upside down to keep dry, the wheel pumped up and ready, the handles pointing towards me. I wrestle it out from the thicket, and my hair catches on the tight small branches as I bend low but not low enough.

This barrow is relatively new. We bought it from a local iron-monger's only twenty years ago and in Clachan-years that is practically yesterday. The barrow is a dull silver, with red rubber grips for handles that are starting to disintegrate. The one before had been Rachel's grandfather's – a huge rusted-iron thing that flaked all over whatever was in it. It was a nightmare to push and scratched our hands with its open-ended handles, but it was history, it was part of the fabric of Clachan, it was family. How well things work is never a Willoughby measure of worth: many things stay in circulation just because no one can remember a time without them.

The old barrow will still be here somewhere, underneath a heap of nettles or hiding in the shrubs at the back of the cottage. That is how this goes, everything and everyone who has ever been here becomes part of this fabric, this story. The Willoughbys have a huge visitors' book in the kitchen and they fill it in every time they come, every time anyone comes, with drawings and stories and a written record of things that happened here and might otherwise be forgotten.

'Births, deaths, and marriages – hatches, matches, and dispatches,' Duncan Willoughby used to boom, the volume turned up to disguise the pain of Tristan's voice having vanished from the entries.

It is always part of the first evening at Clachan, that Rachel and I sit down and turn the pages, looking for our younger selves, the records of the past. The book is unedited, uncensored – Willoughby life as it happened. I am the only person to know there is a page missing, soft serration in the margin of a history torn away.

The visitors' book is just one part of what Tim can't stand about this place – the old wheelbarrows, the lack of 'proper coffee', and the stinging nettles are among the others.

Rachel doesn't ever drive here: she gave up driving in her early forties and I applauded her commitment to the environment. Over the years, she has become friends with the local taxi drivers in the way she becomes friends with everybody. They are happy to collect her from the intercity train that stops twenty miles away, delighted to see her again. Most of them happily wheel the barrow to the cottage and back for her – the kind of thing that would never happen to me.

I am putting my stuff in the barrow when Tim texts.

Are you there yet? No word from Rachel yesterday. Text me when you get in, will you?

I text back that the satellite had probably not flown over last evening, but that I will try. Tim knows the reception is bad at Clachan – it's one more thing he hates about it and one more thing we love.

And then my nightmare begins. Present-day me tries to think back through every step, to see if there's a part where I could have shaken myself awake, a portent that would have turned me back to the car.

There is nothing unusual, no foreboding nor clouded sky nor single rook cawing into the warm waking woods. It is not the stuff of horror films, where doors are left unlatched or candles melt down to their stubs. It is bright new daylight, shining on dewy leaves.

I open the door as I always do, as every visitor does here, with a loud call to announce myself. I shout, 'Hallo,' letting the *oo* at the end ring round the hallway. Tradition dictates that we declare ourselves individually. It is a Willoughby thing, among all the others.

Rachel always makes the same arrival-whoops she made when we first came here, when I listened with my mouth open, a bewildered teenager. Her hello is a joyous scream, like an enthusiastic American at a football match.

Her dad used to rumble a low-belly repetition, a *woowoo* sound, and her mum, Rosie, inexplicably called out like a cuckoo. *Cuckoo, cuckoo*, whenever she got home with the shopping or back from walking the dog.

I shout my *hallo* again, but Rachel must be in the bathroom or out for a walk. I'm momentarily annoyed that she hasn't waited for me, and then too excited to be here, to be back. I go through the sitting room into the kitchen: Rachel is definitely in the house, as chaos reigns on every countertop. I pick up a family bag of crisps that has been knocked off the side, open, on to the floor. I scoop the stray ones into my hand and drop them into the bin, a habit. We are yin and yang: Rachel, queen of scattering, and I, her equerry – calm and ordered, with a place for everything. The same behaviour in anyone else would drive me mad.

The house is quiet. There are three silent centuries of history within its walls. We used to scare ourselves with its births and deaths before we walked up the narrow, windowless staircase in the centre of the house, waiting for the certainty of the creak on the fifth stair and jumping out of our skins when it happened.

The fifth stair creaks and I smile. I am back.

I put my case straight on to my bed and open it, the same bed in the same room for almost every visit since Tristan died. It is literally known as 'Joanna's room' as if I were an extra child, an annexe: as if renaming it could send in a human form to dislodge his ghost.

If Rachel isn't in the house, she will be down at the beach, already floating out on the warm waters of the firth. It is less cold than any other British water I've put my feet in; the Atlantic chill is pulled out of it as it leaks in from the Gulf Stream on its journey north.

The window of my bedroom looks out into the trees. The room has a sea glimpse: between the two tallest larches, where the edges of their higher branches touch, there is a 'v' shape of sand, incongruously gold against the forest. Above it, the sun glitters on the sea and blurs the edge of it into the sky.

I start across the landing to Rachel's room, to the proper sea view, to see if I can spot her bobbing about in the waves.

Beside me, the door to Rosie and Duncan's old bedroom is open. My eye catches a flash of colour that doesn't belong on the geometric shapes of its antique rug. It is an iridescent blue, as if a kingfisher has paused in the doorway, stopped to admire the exotic history of the carpet's pattern.

It is Rachel's dressing gown. Silk. Expensive.

Peeking out from the dressing gown, like a child's game, is her foot. Her toenails are lacquered red. Vivid. Her foot is the colour of a cloud, sulphurous, and blooming with the yellow of a storm.

I already know, in the split second before I push the door open, that she is dead. I know from the curve of her shoulder, the splay of her legs, the odd – uncomfortable – stretch of her arm. Her face is a wan dough, a matte facsimile of someone who looks a bit like Rachel. She is almost unrecognisable without the bloom of her cheeks, the fat pink of her lips, her animation.

Rachel has been gone so long from her body that her face has collapsed, hanging on her cheekbones and chin, tight and shrunken around her mouth like an old woman's. Her eyes are closed, the lids stretched taut over the orbs inside them. She is as cold as the floorboards, as lifeless as leather.

I drop to my knees to be near her, to comfort her, and take her hand in mine. It is not made of what her hands used to be made of: the texture is wrong, the resistance.

I remember a diving accident I saw once on a holiday beach: 'You're not dead till you're dead and warm,' the woman in charge shouted, blowing air into what I had thought looked like a corpse. That man didn't look like a corpse, it turns out. This spent carapace, this cocoon cast off by my beautiful friend, this is what a corpse looks like – as if she has been carved out of soap.

There is no warming that will breathe life back into her. She is dead and beyond cold, beyond temperature.

Rachel has gone.

I don't know what I did then. I know I kissed her: I know because every time I put my lips together, try and eat, touch my tongue against them, I feel the tallow of her. It is the only part of her I can bring to mind, the wax of her cheek against my lips.

The surprise of it, the simpleness – of it being so easy to be dead – eclipsed her life.

I have pieced together that I called the police, an ambulance, but I can't remember which of those I asked for and which was the suggestion of the operator. I know that they told me to commence resuscitation, to try and restart her heart, and that I said her poor body had been through enough – pole-axed backwards on to the floor, stiff-jointed and sorry from lying there all night.

'No,' I said. 'I don't want to hurt her.'

31

This is a tiny place and everyone knows everyone. The policeman arrived before the ambulance, although he had nothing to do but make me tea and talk about Rachel.

We sat downstairs in the sitting room and I looked at the preparation Rachel had made for our weekend. She had brought in logs but not piled them in the basket: they have tumbled across the carpet. The tartan blankets should be folded just so, one on each sofa, one for each of us, but she has left them in the crumpled pile she last used them in. The whirlwind of Rachel.

There were flowers in a vase on the table: short bright gerberas, orange, yellow, hot pink. I remember thinking, *Oh no, too many flowers, and all the wrong colours now that she is dead.*

My sunflowers were on the kitchen worktop, still wrapped.

They must still be there now.

My conversation with the policeman is clear in my mind. He knew Rachel, remembered Rosie and Duncan, said they'd been here all his life and that his grandmother had lived in one of the fishing cottages just along the cove when he was a boy. Inane, professional chatter designed to keep me from screaming.

I sat on the floor, on the dusty old Persian carpet with my back against the sofa, trying to warm myself from an unlit fire, and the policeman, with his young skin and speckled ginger stubble trying to meet round his chin, asked me about Tim, reminded me that everyone knows everyone's business round here.

The policeman's cheeks were blush-red at the tops, rosy with effort or stress. Vivid.

I thought of the polish on Rachel's toes.

'Tim is in Manchester.' And then, because words felt safe in the silence, normal: 'He doesn't come here.'

'Aye,' the policeman said. 'So he doesn't.'

Tim and I had lived totally normal lives for a night, maybe a whole day, while she was already gone. Our worlds carried on as normal even though she was missing, she had left.

And then the policeman asked me if I wanted to phone Tim, if I was the person to tell him. And that cracked a canyon across the world, a fissure that opened between the past and the future.

I wanted to tell the policeman that it's me, my fault. That this kind of thing had happened to me before, that I am the Jonah. But all the breath had left my body.

◆ ◆ ◆

I knew something was wrong as soon as I got home from school. From the street, before we even walked up the short slope to the garage door, to my house, we could hear the music.

Rachel had never been in my house when my mum was crazy. Whenever Rachel came round after school or on a bored Saturday, my mum was smiling, generous, trying to be funny. She cooked pizza from the freezer, she was normal, modern.

I had started to think that maybe my mum could hold it all in while Rachel was there.

'Is that coming from your house?' said Rachel. 'It's very loud.'

'Maybe we should go to yours,' I said. 'Maybe my mum's got friends there or something.' There were no friends. No one came to our house except the man my mum worked for in her office, who went to the same church as her and liked to talk about the day God first spoke to him as a shaft of light through their canteen window.

I always wanted to tell him it was just a shaft of light through a canteen window. I was too young to know that the sun can feel divine when you need a god that badly.

'Got your key?' Rachel asked. 'I'll wet myself in a minute.'

'Do I still smell of fags?' I stuck my tongue out at her; the tiniest circle of a mint clung to the end of it. We were going in, there was no way not to, and the last thing I needed was my mum smelling cigarettes on me while she was like this.

'My mum might be . . .' I started to say that she might be funny, or weird, or not herself, but the words died in my mouth.

'You're fine.'

Inside, the music was uncomfortably loud. 'We need to turn that shit off,' Rachel said. She walked across to the radiogram, lifted the stylus by its tiny hook and stopped the noise.

'I'm going to wet myself,' Rachel said again, already on her way up the stairs.

There were perhaps two seconds of silence before she screamed.

I think I knew what she had seen, what I would find. I think I'd known since before we got to the house, before I went out. I think I'd known all summer.

My mum's bedroom door was wide open. Rachel stood, silhouetted, and looking in. My mother lay across the bed, her limbs stretched out and her pink cotton nightie sodden with vomit. Her hair was wet with sick, and clear, sticky mucus hung from the corner of her twisted mouth. Her face was bleached paper, her eyelids livid purple smears.

'Val?' Rachel's voice was tiny.

I leaned down and touched my mum's hair. Normally, it was curled, stretched through a heated brush until it bounced into a bubble. Now, sodden with sick, it was much longer than I had realised, as if she had unravelled physically as well as mentally.

On the floor between the bed and the door were four empty pill bottles, translucent brown plastic, white labels. Their lids had rolled in different directions, as if it was a game.

Rachel's voice slid quietly into the silence. 'What do we do, Jo?'

'She's not dead.' I stretched my hand towards my mother's bare wrist, touched the skin then pulled back. 'We need to call an ambulance. Can you ring them?' Our phone was downstairs, in the dining room.

My mum's bed was a divan; little round balls held in flat brown cups replaced the legs. The side of the bed base was hidden by a frill of cream nylon, and a sliver of dark, a bedroom monster, hung like a living thing in the three-inch gap between bed and floor. I waited for Rachel, listening to her urgent words downstairs and trying not to think about monsters. I didn't touch my mother.

Val didn't die that day. I would keep returning to her, in an effort to find comfort, for five more years.

Chapter Four

I leave what is now Tim's house and walk out into a different world. I see the loss of Rachel everywhere, in every person, every object. I can't imagine I'll ever come back to this flowery little village that Tim and Rachel chose for its proximity to the train station, for their ability to get out of it.

I walk back to my hotel, to the car, acknowledging every separate thing I can never tell Rachel: the pockets of my mind, out of habit, are stocked with moments to share with her later.

Tim has given me Poll's number. I hope I can catch her before she goes back to London.

I didn't want to be annoying, she texts back, pleased to hear from me. *So I didn't ask for your number. Old people are such a wretched commitment.*

Her comment makes me smile. I instinctively keep myself free from emotional clutter in the same way Poll does, I know exactly what she means.

We've arranged to meet in the only coffee shop in Rachel's village. I don't suppose Poll will have a reason to come back here either.

'You know then?' she asks. 'You spoke to Tim?'

I nod. It is still too preposterous to say out loud.

'It's the right thing.' She leans forward and takes the sugar bowl, adds a heaped spoon to her coffee. 'It's no use to me or the other old goats. It belonged to Rachel and it's her decision.'

I can't drink any more coffee: I am saturated with it. The glass of fizzy water I ordered bubbles joylessly in front of me. 'Please – please – come up and see me when I get there,' I tell her.

'I will do that. You have to be careful at Clachan, to make sure the sadness doesn't overwhelm you – especially now.'

She's talking about Tristan, about the terrible darkness of his death, about the family having to hold his funeral in Scotland because he simply wasn't wanted in their home town, not even when he was dead.

'I have to go back, I need to.' There is more of Rachel to come. Somewhere in the cottage is whatever she was going to tell me, to show me.

'Tim said it's a mess, that there's a lot to do.'

I start to tell her that we have an interior designer, that the work is underway. But then I realise she doesn't mean that, and something stirs at the back of my mind, a memory that I've folded and packed and sealed away where my thoughts don't go.

When I left Clachan, the day Rachel died, I didn't even clear up my own things. The second police officer to arrive was a woman, and she picked up my bags, closed the bedroom windows.

I called Terry to help me get home, simply because the policewoman asked me if she could phone my husband and I'd said yes automatically, hadn't mentioned that we weren't married any more. But Terry stepped up: he took the next train and arrived inside four hours, ready to drive my car back. I waited in the village, in the quiet side room of the café where the policewoman had put me. It was barely lunchtime.

The keys are in my bag now and I can go whenever it suits me. Clachan has always been a source of solace, even attached as it has been to trauma. Rachel's dad used to say, 'That house is three hundred years old, you can't teach it a thing.'

The cottage has seen generations of births and deaths, waves of sorrow and loss, wars and celebrations. It hasn't changed since I was last there, but I have. Writing Rachel's eulogy has changed me: totting up our past and reckoning our history has changed me, and navigating this new world without her has changed me most of all.

'I'm already packed up – I've been living out of a suitcase for weeks,' I tell Poll. We are sharing a piece of cake, pushing our forks into it alternately, breaking off miniature icebergs of yellow, topped with a snow of icing. 'But I hadn't really decided what to do with myself. I thought I might take a few weeks' holiday, go to Europe or something. I didn't have room in my head to decide while I was writing the eulogy.'

'Keep in touch,' she says. 'My life is almost all in the past now, and there are fewer and fewer people who remember the cast of it, let alone the plot.'

'That's how I feel – and I'm only in my fifties.'

'You're in the shadow of a loss right now,' Poll says, one hand on mine. 'But you will learn to live with it. I was the same when Rosie died. It won't always be like this.'

Poll loses a moment to memories, and I think about the stories she and Rosie used to tell about when they'd first met and Duncan had still been away doing National Service. They'd climbed mountains together, jumped off cliffs, travelled through inhospitable countries.

'I never got her back, you know, after Tristan died.'

His death was like a forest fire, raging through the Willoughbys. And then, just as quickly, while its leaves and twigs still crackled, it was gone. Buttoned up. Consigned to history.

'In a sense, I think Rosie had been waiting for it for years.'

I look at Poll, confused.

'Tristan,' she explains, and at the same time starts rummaging in her bag. 'He was always on a path to destruction, set on it fast. Even before he was a teenager. Rosie knew it too.'

I shake my head. 'Oh, don't say that, Poll. Poor Tris – he had everything to live for.' There is so much in that statement that she will never hear, never unravel.

'It wasn't that. It was the way he was.' She wags one bony finger, the nail shaped and clean. 'He had the charm of the very devil, from when he was a wee boy.'

Poll leans towards me, earnest, and I see the reflection of the windows behind me in her eyes.

'The trouble was, no one ever said "*no*" to Tristan Willoughby.'

She has no idea.

I sit in the silence of my own house, on my own pastel sofa – handmade for me by a furniture-maker back when I had money. This whole room has been reduced to shades of vanilla; all the ceramics, sculptures and pieces of original art that I've collected over the years have been carefully wrapped and stored in the attic. They were the vivid personality of this place, setting off its understated elegance, but they're too personal for tenants and too precious to me. I've replaced them with more mainstream prints, neatly framed and inoffensive – just as the estate agent told me to.

This is one of my houses now. Once the probate goes through, barring legal complications, I will have two. Like Rachel did. The thought of two lots of council tax, of the second home tax due in Scotland, of double the bills when I could barely afford a single set, makes me feel dizzy with fear.

And then, just in case I have space to think, time to nurse my wounds and gather myself for this next chapter, the doorbell rings.

Terry has been kind over the last few weeks, texting to check I'm alright, occasionally ringing, although I haven't forgotten that he accepted my offer of paying for his train ticket when he came up to get me from Clachan.

'Whenever,' he'd said, his voice faux-soothing. 'I mean, whenever you're ready. You've got my bank details.'

I absolutely have his bank details: most of my retirement plan went in there. But I don't make friends easily and even when I do I find it hard to talk about things that really matter, things that hurt – so Terry was, even with hindsight and logic, the obvious choice that day. He is also the only person I know who would have let me pay the train fare.

And now he's standing on my doorstep. A place he hasn't been since he began the long process of wrestling half of it away from me five years ago. Legally, his position was shaky, nebulous even, but Terry has the tenacity of a dog and he would have kept on shaking me in his teeth until my legal bill outstripped the value of the house.

'He thinks you're richer than you are,' Rachel said when I showed her yet another letter from Terry's pet solicitor. 'Always has. Have you thought about sending him all your bank statements?'

'I've literally done it.' I had my head in my hands: it had become my default position.

'Marry in haste, repent at leisure,' Rachel teased me, and for a moment I was furious at her dull but financially perfect marriage, her clever choices. 'He has been a real laugh though – at times. I mean, he is hilarious.' She cocked her head to one side to convince me.

It made me feel better, just as it was intended to. I had had a reason to marry him. Rachel and I had both fallen for his daring, his sharply funny mind: I wasn't a complete idiot – or if I was, I wasn't alone.

Terry doesn't look like he'd be a hit in a crowded bar, but there's something about him that's irresistible. It was irresistible to a couple of different – and much younger – women while we were married and at least two more since. They're always gorgeous – always nice or interesting – but, like me when I was younger, gorgeous and interesting, they get bewitched by Terry for a while.

He is standing one step below me, on the threshold of the house, which makes me taller than him. His eyebrows are fuzzy and out of control above his tortoiseshell-rimmed glasses.

'What do you want, Terry?' I don't make any move to let him in.

'How are you?' He beams his widest smile, the one that shows the twinkling gold eye tooth in his top jaw. 'You didn't say where or when you were going – whether you've got a new place to go to. And I was on my way to the bakery round the corner, so . . .' He has a paper bag in his hand that he raises to his eye level and wiggles.

Instinctively, I bank the image to tell Rachel: Terry announcing his newly re-singled status by means of cake. And then I remember, like driving into a wall, that Rachel is still dead.

It is not the rustling of baked goods against paper that makes me let him in, it's the experience of knowing Terry, of knowing how long he will stand there chatting, how hard he will work at it.

I don't have the energy.

'This looks' – he struggles for the word – 'clean. Big, too.' He gestures around the half-empty sitting room.

I wonder whether to rise to his bait. 'It's how it got let out so quickly.' And then, because being Terry's victim doesn't sit well with me, I add, 'And I have plans. It's time for a fresh start.'

He changes face, swaps to Genuine Terry, the Listener. 'Are you OK, are you coping? It can't be easy and it's very early days.' As he speaks, he reaches an arm out to me, a familiar gesture that I have to steel myself against.

'Fuck off, Terry.' It is important to make my armour visible, rigid. 'I wouldn't be doing any of this if it wasn't for you and we both know it. I'd be mourning my best friend, in my own home, and at my own pace.' I sit down on one of the armchairs. The sides of it are high and narrow and leave nowhere for Terry to sit next to me if he tries.

'I'll get plates,' he says, changing the subject, and walks through to the kitchen.

I hear him clatter in the cupboard. The crockery there is not mine – it is a cheap set, fully matching, that I bought to dress the house for rental. 'Don't bother making coffee, you're not staying long.'

The plates are white and plain. Terry balances one on the arm of my chair. He has put three tiny macarons – pink, brown, and green, in the most appealing of shades – on my plate. They are jewels of colour, the antidote to my anonymous house.

'How are you coping?' he asks again.

'I'm numb for the most part, actually. Like it's all happened to someone else.' I put the almond biscuit to my lips, feel that touch of Rachel's skin, the wax memory. I open my mouth and bite to make it go away.

Terry sprawls across my sofa like debris. His legs are long and relaxed in front of him, stretching out into the emptiness that used to be full of my detail. 'It's going to be hard to reinvent yourself.'

I narrow my eyes at him, assess whether to let him speak or just kick him out now. 'I don't know what you mean by that?' It's a question, despite myself. I both do and don't want to hear what he has to say.

'Well, they're all gone now, aren't they?'

I've invited this, asked for it. Stopping him seems pointless; letting him carry on will flay me, but make me feel alive.

And because I don't answer, he adds, 'The Willoughbys.' Just for clarification.

'Has anyone ever told you you're fucking insensitive, Terry? Oh, hang on, yes – me, I have. Loads of times.'

'I mean that she was the last of the Willoughbys. It's over. All your Willoughby past, that part of you. You're going to have to do Wilding things now, Joanna things. Clachan and all of that, it's not going to be there any more.'

'I'm going to Clachan tomorrow, actually.' Wherever Terry goes, drama follows. My knee-jerk reaction to him has created a situation, one that I'll need to shock Tim with, one that I'll need to pack in a hurry for. 'Yes, first thing tomorrow – I'm all sorted. Petrol in the car, raring to go. I'm going to help Tim out with some stuff.'

It hits me like a train that if Rachel had died even a few weeks earlier, mine and Terry's financial agreement wouldn't have been settled, and Terry would own half of Clachan too. Even now I don't tell him the truth, guarding myself against his opportunism.

Terry has flecks of chocolate on his white T-shirt, on his chin. He eats with reckless enthusiasm, the same way he does everything else. 'You don't like Tim,' he says. 'How come you're helping him?'

'His wife died. I feel sorry for him.'

'I'll come with you if you want.'

'I couldn't afford it.'

He wipes his mouth with his arm, smiles broadly, sparkles.

Terry loved Clachan too. Rachel and I had to be strict with him about visits, to explain that it was our place and he couldn't always come with. We loved that about him too at first, that enthusiasm for something we both adored. Terry's parents were Irish and he connected quickly to the way the green forest surrounds the constantly shifting shore, said it reminded him of 'home'; a place he'd never lived.

43

'Fun aside, my darling, it isn't going to be an easy thing. Going back in there, I mean.'

When he's all concern and understanding, I wish that it were possible to be real friends with Terry. History proves it is not possible and that boundaries are the only thing that can possibly work to protect myself against him.

I am peeled without Rachel – and without my marriage. Skinned bare. What Terry says hurts because it's so accurate: I don't know this version of me, this fresh pink flesh, vulnerable and raw – as helpless as a newborn mouse.

The only thing more unimaginably gut-wrenching than opening the door back into Clachan is the idea of never seeing her again.

For the first time, I take no pleasure in the ritual of arriving at Clachan. The barrow is not in the thicket – of course it isn't; who would know to take it back there when I left? I shut the car door and stand in the sandy car park for a few moments, breathing it all in.

I came here for the first time the day after Val's suicide attempt. We didn't lock the car in those days, I remember, and I doubt there were seat belts in the back. As I had stood watching Val's shallow breath and her grey eyelids flickering translucent over her closed eyes, Rachel had rung her mum.

Rosie had been practical and efficient, full of life. I felt guilty for wishing she was my own mother, cheated that she wasn't. She helped me pack a bag and took me home to sleep in Rachel's room with her. My first week here was the start of their support; support that still ripples on, all the way to Tim handing over the keys this week.

I remember being so puzzled by this clearing, by the fact that anyone would leave their car in the middle of nowhere and decamp via a wheelbarrow, even more confused by the fact they liked it. And then, when we got to Clachan itself for the first time, I thought it was tiny and dark and that most things in it – sooty paintings of long-dead ancestors and sagging sofas with horsehair poking out – were broken or dirty.

I had only been on holiday in a static caravan: a tidy green and white village on a hillside with lots of other children knocking on the door to try and get me to play with them. Its doll's-house neatness was a million miles from this dilapidated cottage.

I cried on the first night, totally removed from my own life, part-Willoughby, part-stranger.

I aim my key fob at the car and the four corners flash orange as it locks. This is another time and another world, although there will be crying on this visit too.

My suitcases can stay in the car for now: I need to walk to the sea's edge, to remember how the land ends, peters away against the persistence of the water. I need to see the curve of the Earth on the horizon.

Dealing with Rachel's happiness, unpacked in her bedroom, will be poignant: clearing it away will be an acute pain. Rachel arrives with gusto, fills Clachan with a tornado of colour, a hurricane of smells: she has a potion for everything; a perfume for each day. The smell of her will be bubbled and bottled and scented all through her bedroom – even now – in a stark contrast to the dusty room where she died, musty with family photographs and Rosie and Duncan's quilted bedspread still in place, years since they slept under it.

I'm not ready for it, not quite.

Somewhere in this house is what Rachel was going to tell me: what we were doing next. Something significant that would alter our lives: that much was clear about her mystery.

From the car park, several paths lead off into the undergrowth, beckon me to leave the trail, but I know better – they're the ruts of fat, low badgers, scooping out runways with their tummies; the tracks of sharp-hooved deer, using the same route every time for a getaway until it's grooved into the land. Humans cannot follow them.

Once, Rachel and I found a prayer tree somewhere here, tied all over with scraps of coloured fabric and decorated with paper wishes, but, try as we might, we never found it again. It's somewhere in this side of the forest, but the chances of hitting the right path are so slim that we've been searching for it for at least fifteen years. I would love to tie a wish to its branches, ask it to give her back.

I walk, alone, through the forest. It's not remotely eerie or scary: the sun is still beating down on the foliage, daring it to go yellow, coaxing its oranges and reds into being. The summer is officially over and the colours of autumn lick at the edges of leaves like flame.

There it is – the first pale yellow of the sand, the diamond-studded sea behind it, and the estuary tang of salt water meeting mud, different to the sea smell anywhere else. The smell is its connection to the land, the acknowledgement of the rivers and burns that feed into it, the imprint of the cows and sheep and horses that graze on the damp meadows upstream.

The sea is as thick and grey as paint and so calm, it is like watching the skin of my belly when I breathe.

I sit down on a flat rock and take off my shoes. I chose trainers for the drive and for most of my packing. I have shorts, a couple of skirts, jumpers and T-shirts. But for the jeans and old shirts I put in to wear for cleaning, it could be holiday packing.

Rachel was raised with the idea that skin dries and fabric doesn't: 'It's just common sense,' she'd yell, backing out of the cottage into a hoolie of rain, a battering storm. 'Trousers will stay wet all day, bare legs will be bone-dry before you can say "Get into the pub and sit by the fire."' We wore shorts here most of the year round – in some spectacular rain.

Now I hitch the edges of my skirt into my knickers so that I'm free to paddle. A tiny blue crab scurries in front of my toe and buries himself deep into the sand to get away from me.

Rachel is everywhere here, her dried footprints across the rocks, her sandy body shaken clean at the water's edge. This landscape knows her as well as I do.

I saw her on my journey too. Every time I caught a clue of her from the corner of my eye, I forgot that she is dead: a woman in a traffic jam with the same red hair, the same awkward way of holding the steering wheel, peering forward with enthusiasm. At a service station, I saw the same little blue car she last drove, the one she bought herself for her fortieth and used less and less until eventually she gave it away. Rachel was never much of a one for selling things. She only really got rid of stuff when someone else might find it useful, might need it more than she did.

And here I am, without her, about to use something I need more than she does.

A gull smashes a shell against a rock, oblivious to me – not four feet away from him – and utterly focused on digging out whatever creature is hiding inside his prize. The bird taps the shell sharply, repeatedly, and the tiny noise is loud in this quiet cove. His wings are the oyster grey of the faraway sea and his belly clean white. His eye is a ring of beady gold.

The desire to turn round is a pulse inside me, to go back to – to what? I have no choice but to go forward.

The gull holds the shell down with its wide pink foot, webbing stretched like rubber between its claws, and wrestles the hapless gristle out. The shell drops away with the clatter of a flint spitting sparks and the bird tips back its head. Its beak opens and closes as it gulps down the prize.

I turn my head, away from the gull and the tiny death.

Clachan is unchanged. It contains so much of me and the very last of Rachel and yet, in this lazy afternoon sun, it looks the same as it ever did. Where it should bulge with secrets, glare with revelation, it is calm, it is silent, it is still beautiful.

Directly opposite the cottage, and standing proud of the water, is the ruin of St Lutha's castle: a yellow folly of stone that is no more than a boathouse once you're close to it but, at a distance, is a jagged jaw of crenelations and arrow slits. The island it sits on is a green and brown mass of birds' nests and undergrowth where otters slip and slide on and off the land.

At the right time of year, when the tide is in retreat and the sand is firm, you can walk to the island and picnic on the sandy shore at its far side, surrounded by birds who aren't scared of humans, and straining your eyes for dolphins and whales in the Atlantic distance.

Along the far edge of the bay is a row of cottages in different colours. They were all white – or sea-worn shades of it – when I first came here, but over the years the incumbents have moved on and their replacements in, painting the cottages in pastel shades of pink, mauve, and green. The one nearest to our section of the beach – still more than a quarter of a mile away – has turned egg-yolk yellow since I last walked on this shore. One road inland from the cottages is civilisation, the real world: the village, a shop, a pub and the small café where I waited for Terry.

It takes focus to realise that the bobbing lobster pot in front of me is a head – no one ever swims in this bay unless they're staying at Clachan. At first, I assume it is a seal, but then she stands – emerges from the water like Venus, wet hair like seaweed stuck to the skin of her shoulders. She is facing away from me, far enough away not to hear me if I call, close enough that I can see she is naked. The sun catches the line of her back and she dives forward, gone from sight into the waves as if she belongs to the sea.

There is no pile of clothes on the shore, no unpeeled swim-suit – the woman must have swum right across the bay from the village. I squint my eyes against the sparkle and try to find her, but she's vanished, behind the rocks or round the bend of the bay, back into the water she came from, back to her B&B or her holiday cottage.

In the pocket of my skirt, safely threaded on to the ring with my car keys, are the keys to both my houses: one that isn't really mine until after probate is granted, one that has tenants in after the end of next week. My whole life on one silver ring.

I sigh, swallow as if I can physically stomach my fear, and take the last steps towards the cottage.

On the outside, Clachan is a fisherman's cottage with a vantage point for the tide, small windows and a low ceiling to keep the warmth in and the damp sea fret out.

This isolation is still magical: the gulls behind me and the peep peep peep of oystercatchers picking their way across the pebbles are the only intruders. I check again for the girl, but she has gone.

The last time I was here, the world came too – an ambulance beyond in the car park, the local police officers clambering over the rocks and the strip of patchy grass that delineates the beach from the garden. A trolley that the paramedics wheeled through the shortest forest path to the house. I didn't stay to see it leave.

I crouch on one knee in front of the house to put my shoe on, change legs awkwardly and do the other. The sand is a fine film inside my socks and I curl my toes against the crunch of memories.

Chapter Five

During my teens, the Willoughbys were a sticking plaster. They didn't change my day-to-day life, but they were enough to stem the flow, to keep the wound – temporarily – from becoming life-threatening.

The fact that my mother knew Rosie a bit – not the same thing as approving of her – meant that my friendship with Rachel continued relatively unencumbered. Parties, pubs, nights camping in the woods, would all have been impossible if I hadn't been able to stay with Rachel – or if my mum had known I was doing them at all.

My exams had just finished: O levels that I'd ill prepared for. The last two summers had been a spiral for my mum and me since her suicide attempt, and the atmosphere at home was glass – slippery and brittle.

'I'm coming round,' Rachel hissed down the phone. 'In a minute. I've got such exciting news.'

There'd been a party the night before, a celebration of the clutch of sixteenth birthdays in our wider friendship circle. I hadn't been allowed to go, although I'd begged till I cried. Brother Davies, my mum's boss, who seemed almost a permanent fixture in our house by then, had been adamant about its sinfulness. Maybe his constant presence was supporting my mother after her near miss with suicide, maybe he was avoiding his wife. I didn't give either of them much consideration beyond the constant awkwardness of them praying in the dining room every time I walked in.

'It's so weird,' I told Rachel when she got to my house. 'Creepy. They have to hold hands and have their eyes closed and then off they go.'

'Show me,' she said, the mischief wriggling up inside her, giddy with excitement.

I sat on my bed, she on the end. There was nowhere else in the little room to sit. 'First, tell me what you're so excited about. And then we'll pray about it.'

We mock-shuddered at the idea, locking our fingers together ready for the séance, the heebie-jeebies of my mother's rituals.

I remember, with a shadow across my joy, that whatever Rachel was going to tell me had happened at Ken Steed's party. And I hadn't been there because my mum hadn't let me go.

'Jeff.' She puffed it out into the air of my room as if she could magic him here. 'Jones.' She let go of my hands, stretched her arms wide in freefall. 'Asked me out,' she concluded as she fell face forward on to the bed, on to my feet, my white school socks at a weekend.

Jeff Jones was in Tristan's year; they played rugby together. Tall, curly blond hair like a pop star, handsome as a pin-up. He and Tris Willoughby were the twin dream of almost every girl in our year, and the year above and the year below. And for Rachel – with her own brother as the other coolest guy at school – Jeff Jones was the prize, he was 'being recognised', he was the absolute pinnacle of cool.

'And we snogged all night at Ken's party. I mean all night. They had to prise us apart when the hall shut at eleven, when my mum came to pick me up.'

I was impressed and, at the same time, horribly left behind. I had never kissed a boy, let alone spent all evening in a wet embrace while people picked their way round us to the drinks table or giggled as they tried to get us to separate.

'My lips are puffy from snogging,' she said, pointing at nothing – no change – on her top lip. 'I look like Bette Davis. I *am* Marilyn.'

Everyone wanted to be a 50s film star that summer: Tris had nailed it with his soft quiff, slick with a hair pomade from a little white pot with black writing, so cool you had to go to London to buy it. He and Jeff wore their school shirts open at the neck, the collars flicked out, the knots of their ties over-fat and loose.

If James Dean had gone to a grammar school in Cheshire, he would have wanted to be Tris or Jeff.

'You have to pray for me.' Rachel laced her fingers in mine; we closed our eyes.

'Heavenly Father.' I knew exactly how to do it. Like a good letter, you had to say thank you first, then ask for what you wanted. 'We thank thee—'

'*Theeeee*,' Rachel said. We were high on her recitation of the party's events, my dizziness heightened by the anger I'd felt the night before.

'We thank thee for Jeff Jones, for his hair and his pointy shoes.'

'Brothel-creepers,' Rachel added, in case God misunderstood. 'And his drainpipes.' Jeff had long legs and tight – always black – trousers.

'We thank thee for his snogging ability,' I said, 'for his wiggly tongue and his wandering hands.'

Rachel laughed out loud.

'We ask thee to guide him bonkwards, that he and Rachel may soon be relieved of their sexual frustrations and their virginities.'

'Lousy virginities.' Rachel was heaving with laughter, bubbles of it making her whole body shake. Her hands were clasped together and her eyes closed.

I raised my face to the ceiling, made my voice as low and serious as Brother Davies'. 'Heavenly Father, we beseech you that they may have it off before the exam results come out, that she may be upon the pill and that they might—'

The noise was tiny. No more than the brush of fabric against a door frame, the lightest of breath. But it was enough that I opened one eye, looked over the hysterical tremor of Rachel's shoulder. 'Screw and screw and fuck!' shouted Rachel, kneeling up on the bed, her head thrown back and bleached streaks of hair falling across her face.

Behind her, Brother Davies stood in the doorway, his face granite with fury. He shook his head, his eyes looking directly at me and carrying every moment of my punishment, every atom of what I was about to lose.

'Amen,' I said, not taking my eyes from his.

'Filth,' he said. 'Disgusting and blasphemous.'

But I was carried away, I was with Rachel. We were floating on a sea of funny, of every moment this summer that had crawled out from under this choking cowl of religious sadness.

◆ ◆ ◆

We laughed and laughed until Rachel went home, until I dared to go into the kitchen, to see my mother's awful face, at once twisted with fury yet paper-white with disappointment.

'I always thought Rachel was such a nice girl.' My mother walked away as she spoke, looking anywhere but at me. For the rest of the summer, she found excuses to avoid Rosie whenever she called or to scurry off if they met in the street.

My exam results were awful, but this was before the days when anyone in school wondered what had happened out of school, what could turn a bright and able pupil into a failure, into a husk.

The easiest way to navigate August was to join my mother and Brother Davies in their odd little church: no more than rows of chairs in a village hall. I learned the words, got on and off my knees, sang the ludicrous songs in place of hymns.

Rachel and I wrote to each other every day – not using the house phone was part of my punishment – and Karen Roberts went to Clachan with the Willoughbys in my place.

◆ ◆ ◆

The house is made of stone and whitewashed. The window frames are a peeling blue, blistered raw where they need redoing, white oak – washed with salt – showing through the gaps. Each window sits in a perfect square of stone, painted sea blue, sky azure, in the local tradition. In Gaelic, they call the colour *liath*, a blue-grey that is sometimes the sea and sometimes the sky.

There is no tussle with the lock, no cobwebs or fairy-tale keepers hold it closed. Any ogres or beasts in here became real six weeks ago – they have done their worst.

There is an old settle in the hall – of the sort one might find in a church – to sit on and take off wet clothes and Wellington boots, and the pegs that line the wall are full of coats, as if the house were packed with people. These coats have been here for donkey's years, layered over and over, until eventually – once a decade or so – someone sorts them out. Sorts them out into the coats of the living and the dead. In this cottage, in this tradition, the coats of the dead stay on the pegs, and will be worn by someone else. A pressure wrapped around the back of my head says that these are my coats now, my walls, my door, but I can't listen to it, can't think about it. It is too much.

The silence is unnerving. I have to do it. I have to walk straight up the stairs and into Rosie and Duncan's bedroom.

I have to stand in the space where she lay – for at least twelve hours, apparently – and see that it is just an empty room, no ghosts, no surprises.

And then I have to search for whatever it is she wanted to tell me. I remember the chaos behind the closed sitting-room door, the jumbled muddle that Rachel left in the kitchen. Somewhere, under all her usual mess, is the answer.

I take a swallow of air as if I will hold my breath, as if I'm diving or stepping out of a spaceship, and I walk up the stairs.

The bedroom sparkles with the gold of late afternoon light. The sun has worked its way across to the west side of the bay and pours through the window. I can see each dot of dust on the panes, each tiny and overlaid cobweb where the spiders have come back, again and again, to reinforce their work. In the very corner at the top right, a chrysalis, woven tight and black against the oncoming weather.

I am startled by the noise of me exhaling. There is no danger here, just a sadness, heavy and real, in the fibres of the rug she lay on, wiped against the wooden corner of the drawers she scraped as she fell. The layer of melancholy is only visible to those who know. Without the history, this is a sweet room that catches the summer evening light, a room that anyone would be glad to sleep in. I think of the granite of Rachel's closed eyelids, the shade of her.

Across the landing, my closed door: a room that belonged to a lost boy, a room they moved another girl into like an exorcism. More unseeable mourning.

Everything is neat, tidied. Someone – I imagine the police or the ambulance crew – has made sure that the corners of the rug are straight, that the curtains are half open, half closed.

There is a trunk at the end of the bed – full of extra blankets, bedspreads for surprise visitors who might have to bunk in the sitting room – and on top of it is a large brown envelope, thick with stuffing. The envelope is square on the lid – it too has been tidied, but it is open at one end and its contents are poking out. I can see, even without touching it, the edges of folded paper, the thicker white corners of photographs.

This envelope doesn't live here. It doesn't belong. This bulge of words and pictures is full of things Rachel knows and I do not. I know before I even touch it that this envelope is the thing she wanted to share with me.

I reach out my hand, soft as a ghost's, and turn the envelope over. Rachel's name and address is on the front, written in a spidery, looping script, in blue felt-tip.

I know the writing from my first eighteen years of birthday cards, from notes to school to explain an absence, from shopping lists and Christmas present orders.

I am winded with shock.

I grab the brown envelope, upend it in the silence, watch as letters and photos and cards slither and spill across the rug.

All addressed to Rachel.

All in my mother's handwriting.

The top letter uncurls itself, reveals the words inside like a riddle, an enchantment – a trap.

> Remind her that you both loved him once – at
> the beginning. If he had you charmed too, she won't
> be alone in it. I remember how much you liked him
> when they first met. You were both fooled hook, line
> and sinker by Terry.

'He has been a real laugh though – at times. I mean, he is hilarious,' Rachel said to me when I was at my lowest, when we had come here for a weekend's respite from constant solicitors' letters and drunk-Terry ringing up in the middle of the night, repeating himself over and over. 'He had me wrapped round his little finger too.'

It was a scripted puppet voice, my mother speaking through Rachel's mouth. No wonder Rachel couldn't tell me, no wonder she wanted us to be together. How did she think that eye contact would make this any less of a betrayal?

My mother's voice plays soundlessly in my imagination, all of her words seeping into my memories. I did feel less stupid when we talked about Terry's once-upon-a-time charm and his party attitude, how he bought great presents and cooked us lavish meals.

Rachel had put her hand on my arm. It was only four years ago, almost yesterday, and I remember it exactly, remember what I'd thought it was. 'Come on,' she'd said, 'let's drive to town and get a takeaway, come back here and talk about all the times Terry was funny – and then all the times he was a wanker.'

We ate curry, greasy and hot. And laughed until Rachel got hiccoughs.

It was all my mother's idea.

I unfold the last third of the letter, look at the sign-off, the scrawl of a capital V for Val, and a cockeyed kiss. How she wrote to her friends back when she still had them. The top of the letter says, *Dearest Rachel*. It is an arrow through my dense heart and I'm surprised that there is enough of it left to injure.

And that's when I hear the creak of the fifth stair.

◆ ◆ ◆

I rock towards my feet, to half standing, vulnerable and caught out. Like a thief.

Standing in the door frame, reflected threefold in the dressing-table mirror beside me, is a girl.

'Hi,' she says, one hand on the door frame and the other by her side, holding her phone. 'You're Joanna, aren't you?'

She is somewhere in her twenties, maybe younger – I am old enough to have lost the ability to gauge youth. She has twists of wet blonde hair, rumpled and framing her face. She is a faerie. A mirage. Instead of clothes, she has a towel wrapped around her, tucked in under her armpits and separating her bronzed shoulders from her long brown legs.

'What . . .' It is the start of a sentence I can't finish, that has nowhere to go.

'I should have knocked,' she says. 'Would have, if I knew you were here. Your speech – eulogy – was . . .' She trails off and a bead of seawater drips from her hair on to her collarbone.

'Who *are* you?' The question comes out oddly – I hadn't expected to speak. The emphasised *are* makes it sound as if I'm asking who she is in the broadest sense, how she fits inside the cosmos. She is a mermaid come to land.

'Did Tim not tell you I was here?'

I shake my head, explaining my rash decision to come here, realising that I didn't even speak to Tim before I left – it's all too much. I bend and put the letters back inside the big envelope, thinking, as I sweep them, both how very many there are and that I should protect them from this girl, from the water dripping off her. And then I toss the envelope back on to the blanket box. I have no need to protect my mother.

'Tim didn't say anything about . . .' I gesture at her, raising a finger but not pointing, doing my best not to be rude, but furious inside at the interruption.

'I'm working here, decorating.' She drops her voice. 'I was working for Rachel.'

In my mind, I take my phone from my pocket, scroll to the right screen, text Rachel. My fingers twitch to do it and my eyes smart. I have come here to cry, but not like this. A heat rises in my stomach, seeps upwards to my face, my scalp.

'Tim did say. Sorry.' The decorator. Of course. 'He did.' And Rachel had too – before – back when I thought I knew everything about her, before the chasm of these letters stuttered open between us. I try a smile but I cannot imagine what it looks like on the outside of my face.

I move a step towards the door to get this conversation on to the landing, or downstairs, away from the letters and the questions. 'I knew the cottage was being decorated.'

The girl moves backwards on to the landing, starts back downstairs, leaving me speechless at the top. 'I'm Meg,' she calls back to me, for all the world as if we are friends.

This pile of paper is the closest I've been to my mother in almost forty years. On the day I needed her most, she gathered all her religious ire around her and used it as a battering ram. I was eighteen years old.

'You will be damned,' she screamed at me. 'You will rot in hell, where flames will scorch you and where demons will make sure you never rest again. It is a place of torture, where you will burn for all time.' Spittle flew towards me as she spoke but she was too incandescent to even notice it. 'Repent!' She lunged towards me – I stepped backwards quickly enough to never find out what she was going to do. 'You still have time to change your mind, to save yourself from sin.'

I didn't change my mind; the sin was mine alone and I carry it to this day. My mother never spoke to me again, nor I her.

But she wrote to Rachel. And from that cursive – jolly – 'V' and the 'dearest Rachel', I assume Rachel wrote back.

◆　◆　◆

I open the door of the bathroom, curl over the toilet bowl a second too late, and vomit squeezes between my fingers, soaks and splatters down the backs of my wrists as I try to hold it in. I move my foot back and kick the bottom of the door so that it closes to.

Rachel's betrayal sticks to my skin, green and yellow, stinking. Rachel's betrayal has pieces of my lunch in it, skins of chickpeas, chunks like soup. It is slime in the edges of my fingernails, it colours the half-moons of my cuticles yellow. Her betrayal drenches the front of my shirt and clings – acid – inside my nose.

I take a huge breath, a gasp, and the fumes of it burn my eyes.

The betrayal is everywhere. The worst thing she could do to me. The very worst.

And maybe it's karma.

Chapter Six

Everything I have held inside for six weeks has poured from my mouth and down the front of me.

The girl, Meg, is still downstairs. I am in the bathroom covered in sick. And my clothes are in the car, ten minutes' walk away on the other side of the forest.

My best friend was a liar.

I turn on the hot tap over the bathtub, push the black rubber plug into place while the water scalds my hands.

Rachel had this new boiler put in. 'If we're going to hide out there, we might as well make it comfortable.' Glee, she had said it with glee. That delight where money is no object and can buy you the thing you want, even if it isn't really something you need. Did she come to Clachan for a weekend's peace, strike up the new heating system, and sit down – cosy – to write to my mother?

For a moment, I imagine my mother here, walking along the beach with Rachel, and my knees threaten to give way. I sit on the edge of the bath: fifty-six, empty, soaked in vomit, and alone.

Meg knocks on the door and it moves slightly. She has the decency not to push it further.

'Are you OK?'

I know she can hear the bath running, my heavy breathing. 'Thank you, yes. I'm alright.'

'I've left a glass of water here, by the door.'

'I had a bit of a shock. Sorry. I'm alright.' I'm repeating myself. Apologising. She is working here – she is part of the Willoughby staff – and when the working day is done, she will go home. That is how it works.

The Willoughbys had a succession of help. Men, weathered and ruddy, who did the garden. They had names like sheepdogs do, short and one-syllabled: Dan. Bill. Wynn. Each one would work until his arthritis got too much or his son needed him to help on the farm or another reason as far from our lives as a storybook. They all went home after work.

I spoon bath salts into the water and watch them foam, turning the bathwater into seawater. We use bath salts here, always have. They sit in a tall glass jar with a Bakelite lid – it belonged to Rosie's mother.

The garden men had a cup of tea and a slab of homemade cake when they were working. Rachel and I would deliver it to them out in the garden as they oiled the mower or raked sticks up into a bonfire. They – again, like sheepdogs – never came indoors. There is still a garden man, shadowy and seldom seen, who cuts the grass and takes care of Duncan's rowing boat, hauls it up for the winter, floats it in the summer for no one to use.

Women helped too but they, for reasons the Willoughbys were born knowing, had to be called Mrs Something: Mrs Shapley. Mrs Thompsett. And one Rachel's mum called Mrs Doo-Dah, unless I misheard her.

Only Rosie called them by their first names: Maureen. Margaret. Peggie. But we kids didn't, and Duncan didn't. To this day I don't know how that worked, or how they all knew. It was like learning a foreign language only by speaking it.

And then there was church. We dressed up for it, we sang the hymns and put money in the collection. We bowed our heads at prayer time and shook hands with the vicar at the end – but no one meant it, no one believed in God. It was all about knowing how to behave. Pitching up to the local kirk, suitably dressed and scrubbed, was how to behave as surely as peeling potatoes for the lunchtime roast, which they never served before four.

The twisting grief inside me buckles, threatens to snap, and I peel off my sodden clothes and pour myself into the water.

I turn on to my front, letting my hair float like seaweed, and I blow bubbles under the water, feel them pop beside my ears. It makes a noise from childhood, from before everything went wrong.

◆　◆　◆

It took almost a year to clear my name at home after the blasphemy episode; eleven months before I was allowed to come back here with the Willoughbys. I saw Rachel every day at school, seven hours of normal, of safety. But I missed Tristan like a part of my body.

Rachel would tell stories of him, of what he and Jeff had done next, of parties and midnight swims and being brought home by the police. Some of the weekend tales involved Karen, but Rachel hadn't warmed to her any more than I ever would, and we picked holes in her all the way to school and all the way home.

I wasn't there while Jeff and Rachel fizzled away, only heard the tail ends of it at school, but virginities had been lost, pledges made and broken. Rachel had moved on to a sort of fledgling adulthood I still dreamed about, an adulthood I only heard about second-hand, an adulthood I was scared would pass me by entirely.

And when the summer finally came – at the end of the longest year – I was allowed back to Scotland, back to Clachan, for two glorious weeks. Everything about Scotland filled me with happiness, gave me a reason to keep going: the food; the house; the sea.

At the heart of it was Tristan with the sun shining like ice on his dark hair, that light in his eyes that said 'mischief', his outright joy at life.

◆ ◆ ◆

I had spent my sixteenth birthday in church, Brother Davies laying the palm of his hand – hot and huge – on my scalp to bless me. He held it there horribly long, horribly softly, while the rest of the congregation mumbled over me for this life and the next: asked that I be reunited with my family in the celestial kingdom – although, for me, that was a fate far worse than hell.

On Tuesday evenings, not that I told Rachel, my mother had me join a scripture study group with a few teenagers from the church – all purer of heart than me, and all spotty and pale. I thought it was God's way of keeping them from mating – although I had no one to say it to.

We would read through the verses of their alternative 'bible' while I looked around the room and wondered how many of them were doing what I was, eyes down and firmly on the prize.

But it was worth it for two full weeks away. Fourteen summer days of being trusted out of sight with Rachel; of sunbathing; of Rosie and Duncan giving us a glass of something with our supper and treating us like grown-ups; of cutting furry-stemmed and pink-flowered campions in the forest and arranging them in jam jars, presenting them to Rosie like they were bouquets from the most sophisticated florist's. We were, at once, children and adults, loving every second of passing backwards and forwards between the two.

It rained a lot, that first week – an interruption in my picture of childhood, that peculiar set of memories, curated so that they are all of sunshine or Christmas, nothing in between. Rachel and I spent the wet days in an ageless limbo: playing board games and drawing, rolling around the carpets like puppies, perfecting make-up and plucking our eyebrows.

The second week was Tristan's eighteenth birthday. He would have a supper party here in Scotland, a formal dinner in a restaurant with his godparents and the family friends, and a party in a hall attended by anyone who was anyone in the sixth form, along with Rachel and me.

'I haven't finalised the menu, Joanna,' Rosie said. 'I thought you might like to choose something. Maybe even make it?' She poked me in the side, teasing – she definitely wanted me to make it. Rosie marvelled at my creations, encouraged them even when they took up all of the surfaces in her kitchen and used up all of the food in her pantry. If they were inedible, she would exclaim in pretend French, dramatically waft the dreadful smells away from her, and get me to have another go. The privilege, although I didn't know it then, of being able to afford ingredients.

Being trusted with Tristan's birthday dinner was a whole new closeness.

'What's your favourite thing I've ever made?' I asked Rachel.

'Not the beefburger curry,' she said.

We were lying side by side on the beach, under the warmth of a sun that had only just made its way out of the clouds. This sea was almost silent, barely moving the pebbles beneath it. The water was as clear as glass, the browns and greys of the stones underneath round and smooth like sweets.

I moved my hand towards hers, swatted it like a fly. 'I couldn't find minced beef. You know that.'

'Still tasted like dog food.' She sat up, threw a pebble past her feet on to the sand. 'Cornflake tart?'

It was simple – a pastry case filled with cornflakes, covered in syrup and baked – but it worked. And when I'd last made it, Tristan had eulogised over it.

'And custard,' she added. 'The custard made it perfect.'

'You're a genius, Rachel Willoughby. What would I ever do without you? Not even any shopping required.' It wouldn't have occurred to us then that there was any other way of making custard than with the squeaky pale-pink powder that came in a tin and miraculously turned yellow as it cooked.

'Tris loves that tart,' she said, and I pretended that I hadn't realised, hadn't remembered with every beat of my desperate body for nights and nights afterwards.

And then, out of nowhere but the seagull cries and the shh of the waves: 'Do you fancy my brother?'

I let out a little gasp. It took a moment to understand that she hadn't been inside my head rummaging around in my thoughts.

'It would be disgusting if you did, like incest.' She threw a pebble the length of her body, and it skittered off her feet.

I foraged for words, tried to breathe calmly and stop my burning face from giving me away. 'He's got a girlfriend.'

Rachel rolled on to her front. 'He's going to chuck her. I know it. Before his birthday. Anyway, that's not exactly an answer.'

My skin fizzed with the idea, the hairs on my arms and legs prickled a giveaway. 'We'd know, surely, if he was going to chuck Karen.' Hope squeezed through my body.

'She's not here, is she? And Mum was doing the table plan for his proper birthday dinner and he asked to have Aunt Poll sat next to him. Mum on the other side, obviously. Not Karen.'

The idea that she could have carried this nugget from home to here, walked around with it for days without telling me, made me want to shake her. Instead, I focused on pretending I knew what a table plan was.

'He's not a nice person, you know, my brother. He's not nice to people.'

I pretend-shuddered with all the disgust I could muster. 'Then it's lucky I don't fancy him,' I said. Technically, it wasn't a lie: 'fancying' couldn't come close to the all-encompassing passion I had for Tristan Willoughby.

'Race you to the sea,' I screamed to cool off the red-hot half-truth spreading across my face.

◆ ◆ ◆

The summer evenings at Clachan go on forever; the warm wind is a smell I sometimes wake up to from a dream – even now.

Back then, we ate outside for Tris's birthday. We could have been in Italy, France. A chequered red cloth on the long dining table, heaved outside, and the best red wine splashing into tumblers, breadcrumbs littered across place settings. The tart was a triumph – unctuous and yellow, moreishly sweet. Rosie had talked me into cream instead of custard, to fit the weather, and that had made it sophisticated, crisply perfect.

And best, afterwards, giddy from wine, when Tristan had followed me into the kitchen – alone.

'Thank you so much for that,' he said, and I realised that he was closer to my face than he had ever been before, even in fun. His skin was smudged with brown – both tan and sand – and seven freckles in the constellation of my birth sign had appeared on his nose. 'You're really special, you know. I'm so glad my sister has a friend like you.'

All the big brothers I knew from books were like Tris: he could be cruel and teasing but he could just as easily be like this – tender, sweet. Rachel was too hard on him.

He leaned the extra couple of inches and his lips, soft and stealing as a tiny animal, brushed my cheek.

I was close enough to see each of his long black eyelashes.

'Queen of tarts,' he said and walked back into the hallway, laughing at his own joke.

I knew, instinctively, preciously, that it was something not to tell Rachel.

Chapter Seven

MEG

This is Rachel's best friend. She found Rachel, Joanna did, which must be the worst thing imaginable. No wonder she's so upset.

I creep upstairs with a glass of water. I can see her clothes in a heap on the floor through the crack of the door hinges and the side of her head – she's in the bath. I was worried she'd be collapsed on the floor or something – that was the real reason for bringing the water. But she's in the tub, having a howl. I'm all over that – baths, showers, they're good places to cry. I should try and get her down to the sea.

I loiter for a bit at the top of the stairs, wondering what to do, how to make it better. There are awkward situations and then there's this – a woman you've never properly met, crying her head off in a house that belongs to a dead woman, in the middle of actual nowhere. I have no idea what happens next.

I've left my phone downstairs by the sink so I go quietly back down, missing out the creaky step by supporting my weight on the banister rail. The other side of the stairwell is a long patch of pale beery brown where generations of people have held on to the wall with one hand and the rail with the other. And there isn't a paint in the world that will cover that much grease, that kind of stain: it might even need replastering. The history of hands.

I didn't know Rachel that well, we only met a handful of times, although we really connected. I know what her relationship with my dad was and I respect that. I went to her funeral for my dad's sake really, so no one would ask who he was, and because she trusted me with this job and that was kind.

My dad was adamant: Joanna knows nothing about any of it and I have to consider every word I say. It's going to be tricky, but I need this job. Boy, do I need it.

The first time I met Rachel, she and my dad were in Glasgow and I literally bumped into them on the street. I was still going out with Liam then: I knew it wasn't going anywhere but I wasn't ready to let my dad be right, so I persevered with Liam's boring conversation, his self-obsession.

I don't know who was more awkward of the four of us.

Rachel had a huge bag from a shoe shop, and a tiny paper one – tied with ribbon – dangling from her wrist. She saw me looking at it. 'The perfumier on Sauchiehall Street,' she said. 'They make it for you, bespoke.' She lifted the inside of her wrist towards me for me to smell and the little bag twinkled under the streetlights. 'I'm always looking for someone to go with. I can't really take your dad and I only come to Glasgow to see him. Maybe we could go sometime?'

'Good to finally meet you, Liam,' my dad said then, and I could hear the judgement in his voice.

Rachel obviously heard it too and she shot him a look, side eye, but he was too busy looking Liam up and down to catch it.

'We'd better go.' She looked at her watch, then turned back towards me. 'Your dad says you did a degree in interior design?'

I watch for the flicker of disappointment on my dad's face. I passed my degree with flying colours, but since then I've worked in shops and pubs, a stint as a cleaner. It's impossible to get a foot in the door, design-wise, if you can't afford to do an unpaid internship. It's one more way for me to disappoint him. I am his only surviving child: I'm supposed to succeed for two of us, for my poor little brother who didn't get to grow up, as well as for me.

'Ben showed me some of your designs. I love them.' Her smile was radiant – you say that about dead people, but Rachel knew how to smile. How to work it. She could have been a fairy-tale witch – the whitest white skin and red lips, long ginger hair down over her shoulders and not too neat but not in a mess. She just needed to carry round a blood-red apple. It costs a lot to look like that – and not everyone can pull it off. I remember at the time wondering what it must be like to be her, to have those powers. I expect Joanna is the same – when she's not covered in sick.

'I have a little cottage – down in Dumfries and Galloway. It's a mess, if I'm honest. I'd love you to take a look at it. How about next time I'm in Scotland seeing your dad, we meet there?'

My dad hates this kind of thing. He keeps his worlds separate, and there was Rachel mixing them up like paint colours. But I needed this gig – regardless of him, regardless of Liam – so I said yes to Rachel.

And we all went our separate ways on George Square – them off somewhere fancy for dinner, I imagine; Liam and me to the bus stop. But she meant it, Rachel, and the next time I saw her was here. Just her, me, and my dad. And she really did give me the job.

Joanna's been in the bath for more than an hour. Maybe I should offer her a cup of tea, or tell her that I'll go and get her bags from her car. She must have bags.

I decide on coffee, less like she's ill, and black, because then if she does have milk, I can go downstairs and get some. Fix it.

'Joanna,' I call through the door; the bathroom is silent now. 'It's me. Meg.' Idiot, she knows that. Unless it's me, the axe murderer. 'I've made you a coffee, it's on the landing.'

I leave the cup on the little green window sill at the top of the stairs. The window looks back towards the forest, across a single gnarly tree with no leaves. Its top half has seen so many storms that it points inland, like it gave up and bent at its waist. The spindly black branches blow like long twisty hair on a wild wind. It's a great silhouette – spooky but stylistic: it would make a great motif for a wallpaper.

This house will be my portfolio – the thing that gets me on the ladder and into the job that I've wanted to do since Mum first came into my room and asked me what colour I'd like to paint it. I think I was five. Bubble-gum pink and hyper-real orange aren't everyone's cup of tea; I don't think they were mine for long. But we learn from our mistakes.

Hand-blocked wallpaper is mad expensive to print, but I'm keeping the costs right down everywhere else and it would look insane on the stairwell. We'll see.

'I'm going out into the garden,' I call out. Maybe she wants to come out of the bathroom, get dressed, but she's embarrassed. 'Can I get you anything?'

'I'm fine.' Her voice is quiet but the bathroom has no soft furnishings, so the words slip off the enamel and carry on the steam. 'You can go now, honestly. Thank you. It's nearly six o'clock anyway.'

I don't know where she thinks I'm going.

Chapter Eight

Jo

I hear the front door go. Meg has left and I can get out of the bath. The skin around my toes and fingernails is puckered and the bath salts have left a film on my skin that sparkles on my arms when I push myself upright.

I pull the towel round me and walk across to Rachel's bedroom. My own clothes are still in the car and I'm going to have to hope Rachel has something stretchy in her drawers, something that I can get on. Rachel was always a willow, and I am definitely more oak. 'I wish I had curves,' she says in my memory, accentuating the positive in my strong legs, broad shoulders: always my cheerleader.

I push open her bedroom door. This is what I'm here to do, regardless of everything else. I am here to undo her from this place.

Rachel has always been untidy – a sloven, even – and she has always left a trail of hurricane chaos behind her.

The drawers are half open, except the bottom one, which has come completely off its runners and is lying, askew, on the floor. The mattress has been pushed off the bed so that the slats show down one side and the covers are heaped between the bed and the wall. I wonder what Rachel was looking for.

The hat boxes on top of the wardrobe – full of mementos and photographs – are on the floor, upended. Rachel's life is in piles by my feet.

The little china dish – which has, of course, been in the family for hundreds of years – on the dressing table is full of her rings. Her earrings are scattered across the burr walnut, no longer in pairs but all present and correct. Her necklaces drape from one corner of the mirror, clearly valuable and within arm's reach. No one has been in here but Rachel. This is her own chaos.

The second drawer down is T-shirts. I pull one out, shake it unfolded. It wouldn't cover my belly button – and that makes me think of Meg, think about what I've decided in the bath: that she'll have to suspend her project while I'm here. Even if it means Tim has to pay her for longer, I can't do the things I'm supposed to do while a decorator moves around, and I can't recover. I need silence like never before.

I find a big yellow tee that Rachel used to wear for a nightdress and shrug it over my head. It smells of her: of heavy perfume, of washing powder, of the faded lavender papers that line the drawers here. There is a pair of pale-grey tracksuit bottoms in the next drawer down: too warm for this late summer but fine to get me to the car to collect my own clothes.

I look at myself in the mirror, braless and pale: diminished, somehow, by the day.

There has always been a stack of jumpers in the built-in cupboard in my room. The bathwater has left me cold, and I cross the landing to go and get one. My room is not as I left it. There are someone else's things on the bookcase, toiletries on the dressing table. There is a pile of folded clothes on the chair under the window and a row of coat hangers on the curtain rail. Linen clothes hang from them, in stripes and spots, swirling patterns. It's obvious whose clothes these are: whose make-up; whose books; whose washing on the floor.

The decorator – Meg – is living here. I take out my phone to call Tim, then I think again. I need to call him sensibly, tell him I'm here. He doesn't need this on top of everything else.

The jumpers stay in the cupboard: I'm too cross to step over someone else's detritus. She has made my bedroom out of bounds, colonised it. The envelope of letters is still in Duncan and Rosie's room, spilling with secrets, savage yet irresistible. There is an energy, dark and magnetic, that comes from inside. I need to get out of the house and breathe.

I will have to get my clothes out of my suitcase, dress properly, before I can confront Meg: I look like I have heard the bin lorry in the street and grabbed someone else's clothes to go and haul the trash out.

At the bottom of the stairs, I remember that my trainers are upstairs by the bath, that there is sick on the toes of them.

There are flip-flops, trainers and Wellington boots under the coat rack in the hall. I know that the withered silver-and-black trainers fit me, slip on to my feet without being undone.

Meg is in the garden to the side of the cottage – between me and the forest path. Even if I'd wanted to put this off until my tits weren't bouncing around in a flimsy T-shirt, I can't.

She is sitting, her knees drawn up, with a large sketch pad on her knee. Her subject is the sea-blown hawthorn – green and puckered with lichen – that stands at the edge of the garden, marking the line between seashore and forest.

I am too old to sit like that: my back would ache, my thighs would cramp. I have forgotten how it feels to be that strong and supple. She looks untamed, part of this wild garden.

'Meg.'

Meg looks round, smiles. She is clearly relieved that I haven't gone off the deep end, slit my wrists in the bath. 'Are you feeling better?' she says, her hand stilled on the page, her pen hovering above the white paper. 'I was sketching the outline of this tree. It's amazing. Magic.'

'We used to call it the witches' tree.' I can't help myself. 'Because of the way the hair flows out behind it.'

'I thought the exact same.' She beams. 'I'm using it to make some wallpaper for the stairs. Block it on.'

'Meg, I don't quite know what's going on here. Your things are in my bedroom.'

'Oh,' she says. 'I'm sorry, I didn't know that was your room. It was empty and I could see the other one was Rachel's and . . .'

We both know she means she didn't want to sleep in the room where Rachel died.

'I didn't realise you were staying here at all.' I drop my hands to my sides. And then I suck in my stomach, tighten my muscles, because this is confrontation and I am not dressed for confrontation. My mind flashes back to Terry – to furious rows in practically every state of undress, in every room of our house. Ludicrous situations that I'd make Rachel laugh with later, once the hurt had subsided.

Meg puts the lid on her pen. 'I'm staying here. It's part of the deal, the job. It would be pretty impossible otherwise.' She crosses her feet in front of her and stands up. She doesn't put her hands on the ground, just rocks forward and stands, unfolding skywards, like a yoga flow. 'Rachel sorted it all out with my dad: he said it would still be OK, even though . . .' And her voice trails off.

I need my clothes. I need underwear. I turn towards the forest, my hand in the pocket of the sweatpants to stop my car keys falling out. 'I'll deal with this when I've got my stuff. But you can't stay here, Meg. You really can't. Things are different now.' I am practising the words, rather than saying them to her.

I almost sound like Rachel as my voice growls through the undergrowth at an invisible Meg. 'This is my house. You can't just wander in as if you own it. This. Is. My. House.' I don't know if I'm rehearsing to convince Meg or me.

All the way to my car, all the way back with the barrow, dropping bags and going back to pick them up, all the time a thought flies and flutters around my head like a tiny blue bird.

When I catch it gently in my hand, my fingers around its rapidly beating heart, the thought is saying, 'Who even are you?' And I don't know whether it's talking to me or to Meg.

◆ ◆ ◆

I'm exhausted by the time I drag everything to the cottage. This is a job for two: I haven't always done it with Rachel, but I've hardly ever done it on my own. I go up and down the stairs with my bags, an armful of coats, a small box of shoes. This is more stuff than I've ever brought before: this is moving in.

Meg is in my room with the door shut, shouting down the phone. I hope it isn't Tim she's talking to like that. I hover outside the door, long enough to hear her bellow, 'Dad!' with absolute frustration – it isn't Tim.

I pull Rachel's mattress back square with the frame and sit on the end of her bed. Her horrible old doll, a greasy strawberry-blonde made of felted wool, is on the floor. I hold the doll in my hands and stare into her grey stitched eyes. She saw what happened here, she heard what Rachel said as she emptied shelves, pulled stuff out of cupboards. 'What was going on, Rach? What were you looking for?' I ask the negative space of her.

I swallow my tears down, tuck them away with the panic of a life spiralling.

Meg won't be able to get home tonight: I would imagine she lives a long way away – her accent suggests Glasgow – and there was no other car in the car park. Clachan is hard to get to or from by public transport, I've never even called a cab from here: Rachel was in charge of that.

I knock on the door of my bedroom.

'No,' she shouts, then – 'Sorry, Joanna, not you. I was on the phone. Come in.'

Meg is sitting up on the bed. She is wearing a pair of the striped linen trousers and a tiny yellow vest. Her shoulders are bony and golden.

'We need to have a chat about things, about your work here.' It dawns on me that the only 'redecorating' Meg has done is to appropriate my room as her own. 'When did you start?'

She swings her legs down to the floor, puts her phone on the bedside table. 'I've been here four weeks.'

She started a month after Rachel died.

'It was already arranged, and there didn't seem any point in not starting.'

There is a fury building inside my head. Tightening, crushing, voices that say, 'This is how it always is for you. Nothing ever turns out right. Nothing is ever good.' For a moment, I'd believed that maybe things would work out, that I would find my space to grieve and the financial safety to be myself. Instead, as ever, I've rushed in half-arsed. I've failed to plan and I didn't think to let anyone know I was coming.

I want to tell Meg, *This is* my *house and I belong here.* But I rush away before the words and the tears leak out.

◆ ◆ ◆

In the kitchen, I make coffee loudly and angrily. Coffee grounds scuttle across a work surface that was – before I started – far cleaner than usual. Everything I touch in this kitchen is a memory, attached to Duncan's booming voice or Rosie's firm kindness. It's technically mine, or about to be, but it all belongs to the Willoughbys, no matter where they are, and, mindful of that, I grudgingly clear up after myself. I flatten my fingers across the wooden beading at the edge of the countertop. It still feels like a mistake.

Maybe drinking my coffee under the watchful gaze of the family portraits will sort it out, avoid me having to ring Tim about Meg, about my gatecrashing her job and the house being too crowded. The sitting-room doorknob is a slippery brass, dented and dulled. It feels good in my hand, something I can trust.

The Willoughbys on the wall are the only thing recognisable in the sitting room. And even they have moved.

Only one of the rugs on the floor remains, circular in the centre of the room and revitalised. What was once a bleached-out pattern of worn maroon is a burnished red, bright with its pattern of trees picked out in cream and blue. Beneath and around it, the floorboards burn and glow like the evening sun, sanded and bright, varnished with a lacquer that looks like wet syrup in this light.

Every knick-knack and oddity, every faded book spine, has been given a space of its own on shelves that line the back wall, top to bottom and side to side. No two pockets in the shelving system are the same and it gives the air of a museum, of a collection one should study and value, a cabinet of Willoughby curiosities. The shelves themselves are a matte moss green, a shade that is popular this year but might not look out of place in a stately home.

I turn around, twice, a three-sixty tour of this new room. It belongs in a magazine. On the hexagonal table is a display of objects, inviting the viewer in to examine them. A tall carved lamp-stand with a pleated gold shade watches over a cluster of crystal decanters in different sizes and a stuffed red squirrel in a glass box. The wall behind the table has been painted a clean light oatmeal, and then decorated with six antique china plates held on with little clips. The plates are intricate pictures in red, gold and blue and balance perfectly with the freshly cleaned rug.

On the other walls, the family members gaze down from their frames: some ornate gilt, some wooden, in all sizes. But now the paintings have been grouped together, balanced, each shape complementing the one beside it, leaving space for a little one or leading on to a strong oil in a heavy and complicated frame. The paintings look at me in a way they never have before, their eyes bright and focused. And I realise that generations of soot and dust that fogged their view is gone.

Everything is still here: old wounds; childhood; the port in the storm that this place has always been to me. But now it is more, it is equipped for the future. Just as Rachel moves away from it, Clachan opens another epoque, another version of itself. I sit down on the sofa and the need to tell her ricochets around my empty heart.

Meg knocks lightly on the door and opens it simultaneously.

'Do you want me to move out of that room? I can. I didn't know it was yours. I'm really sorry.'

'Was this all you?' I gesture round the room. A spring in the sofa nips at my hip; the reminder makes the new room even better. 'The shelving?'

She nods. 'I built it. But I discussed it with Rachel, she chose the colour.'

I nod. I can picture the magazine I saw the original in, place myself on my own sofa texting a photograph of it to Rachel.

'Apart from materials, I haven't bought anything. It was all here.'

I reach out to my side and pick up the squirrel in his glass box. 'I haven't seen him before.' His bushy tail is paler than his russet body, sandy-coloured, and his little paws have been squeezed together in front of him round a dusty hazelnut.

'He was in the shed.'

I nod and put him back. 'How did you get the job? If you don't mind me asking. She'd – we'd – been talking about getting someone in, but I didn't know she'd found anyone. You didn't say how you know Rachel.'

I am looking at Meg when I say it and I see her drop eye contact, as subtle as it is. The pause before she answers is a few seconds too long. A few seconds of secrets. Of complications.

'She is – was – a friend of my dad's.'

'The dad you were shouting at earlier.'

She looks as if she isn't going to answer, as if she's annoyed that I listened. 'Yes. Him.'

'And how—'

'I can move out of your room. I'm happy to. But . . .' Meg looks at her feet. The second half of her sentence is obvious, but she says it anyway. 'I can't move out-out – I haven't got anywhere else to go. I can't invoice Tim till the end of the job and, I'll be honest with you, I'm absolutely broke. Rachel did say I could stay here while I did the work.'

'I totally understand.' I feel for her, I really do. I want to tell her about the grieving I have to do, about the envelope full of letters and photographs that I haven't even started on yet. About the parts of Rachel that are missing. 'The thing is, Rachel left me the house in her will.' I am compelled to add detail, to make myself sound less entitled. 'I holidayed here with her as a kid. All my life, actually. And I'd hoped to be here by myself now, take some time to be sad.' I don't want to bully Meg out of a job, but I am too old and too broken for a house-share. 'What about your parents?'

'For a start, I'm twenty-five. And I haven't lived with my dad for a long time. And' – Meg is looking for words, turning ideas in her mouth to find the right ones – 'my mother doesn't live with him. She has addiction issues.' She looks down at her feet, as if she's betrayed a confidence, said something shocking.

'I'm so sorry.' I feel terrible, even though her home life is no more my fault than mine was.

'Do you have another house? I don't mean to be rude. This is your second house, second home?'

Meg thinks I'm like Rachel. Why wouldn't she? She thinks that Rachel's best friend lives the way Rachel did, the same charmed life and lack of worry. She doesn't realise that I know exactly what is in my bank account to the nearest pound, and that my tenants' first payment will catch my mortgage and council tax by a whisper, that any delay would see my account in the red and my bills bouncing. It makes me feel sick.

When the probate goes through, the responsibility for Clachan will be added to that poor bank account. I honestly have no idea how that will work.

'It's rented out.' That's all she needs to know. 'It has tenants in.'

'Sorry. I'm just trying to find a solution.' Meg fiddles with her hair, tucks it behind her ears.

She sees me as a Willoughby, with the trappings of a Willoughby, the confidence and privilege. But Terry was right and I'm not one, not really.

I was a lifelong satellite to a family who no longer exist. The only witnesses to their way of life, their ebullience, their very existence, are this house and me.

Chapter Nine

The last days of the summer I spent here with Rachel and Tris were as blue and perfect as any I can remember. There is something about sun, for teenagers, that unravels them, takes them back to simplicity.

We ran everywhere on the beach: walking was never enough. We ran to dry ourselves, we ran to be first in the sea, we ran laughing into the forest to light illicit cigarettes.

And then Tris decided we should go to the island.

'We take a picnic, row out there while the tide is high, then stay on the island all day till it comes back in and we can row off again. Twelve-hour castaways.'

Rachel gave him a look that would have withered lesser men. 'Except we could walk back when the tide is out, so, actually, not castaways at all.' The sun had been up for hours before us, and she held her hand over her eyes to shade them. The island was a silhouette, edged in filigree.

'But even if we go now' – I looked at my wrist, at the wide white stripe where my watch had been all summer – 'the tide's going out.' I pointed at the damp band at the edge of the sea, the bubbles of white foam popping on the sand. 'And it's already half ten. It'll be almost dark before it's deep enough to row back.'

'Don't be a chicken. You're on catering, Wilding.' Tristan spoke like a sergeant major, and I scorched at the thought of his mouth on my skin.

I hacked chunks from the solid brown loaf Rosie had made yesterday; took ham and tomatoes from the fridge, a packet of biscuits. I searched the back of the cupboard for crisps but, as I suspected, there was nothing there but a long, thin packet of breadsticks – no one else I knew had even heard of breadsticks. The box was bent and slightly flattened. Into the picnic it went. I burrowed my hands as deep as they would go into the back of the pantry. The rewards were a tin of olives, speckled with oily dust, and a jar of quails' eggs in some sort of liquid. Chances were they tasted the same as hens' eggs, only smaller, so I made a twist of salt from a paper bag and buried them in the basket. It was an audition I couldn't afford to fail.

I topped up the squash bottle with water so that we had the whole bottle of lurid orange drink, saccharine sweet, to take with us.

'Hurry up, Wilding,' Tris shouted, knee deep in the water and holding on to the wide wet rope at the rowing boat's stern.

'I haven't got my swimming costume.'

'There's no time.' He held his hand in a stirrup and I put my foot in it to heave myself into the boat. 'Skinny-dipping. That's the way to end a summer.'

'If you weren't my brother, maybe.' Rachel shook her head in disgust.

'Shut up, Rachel. Or don't come with us.' He stood in the water behind the boat, both hands on the back of it.

'You shut up,' she said, but she looked away from him and out at the sea.

Tris jumped into the boat as if it were the easiest manoeuvre in the world and it rocked gently as he took up the oars.

◆ ◆ ◆

Rachel and I sat at the pointy end, our backs to the horizon and watching Clachan fall away from us. The optical illusion of the sea made it seem so far, another world. In reality, the ocean floor was only a metre or two below us – if that – and the distance could be walked in twenty minutes across the wet sand once the tide was fully out.

Tristan had ditched his T-shirt and was rowing with his top off. The turn-ups of his long navy shorts were dark with seawater.

'Look!' Tris yelled, so loud it made us jump. 'Oh my God, look!'

Across to our right, where the bay widened out into the sea, was the bent black fin of a basking shark. The sun cut a bright stripe across the wetsuit-black fin tapering into the water over its back.

I wasn't as excited as Rachel and Tristan. I was afraid of sharks.

Their genes weren't afraid of anything.

'It's a bloody miracle,' said Rachel, her arm round me and squeezing my shoulder. 'My dad will be so jealous we saw that. They can't hurt you, they don't even have teeth.' She widened her own mouth, her lips obscuring her teeth, and gummed my arm.

Tristan leaned to his left and dug the oar deep into the water. 'Let's go round the far side,' he said, and the boat, as if by magic, turned towards the huge black shape of the shark. 'We won't bother him, but let's land on the jetty and see if there are others.'

The island had been a smugglers' stop a hundred years ago, where boats parked up in the night to swap barrels of brandy and tobacco, protected from the elements by the castle ruins. I thought of us smoking all day on the island, no one to see or stop us. If only we had brandy too.

The jetty ran up to a long stone slope and that, in turn, led to the ruins of the castle. No one came here but us – we were certain of that. There were never remains of fires or beer bottles strewn about. Presumably the local teenagers had easier places to hide away, better party spots.

The jetty always made me nervous. Its broken black posts and wobbly boards had to be haunted. 'Let's just row up to the beach and sploosh in, pulling the boat.' Rachel and I had only ever done it that way.

But Rachel wanted what her big brother wanted, keen to be friends again, and he rowed round to the far side of the island where there was nothing but deep wide water sparkling between us and the horizon.

Tristan reached up to the end-post of the jetty, flung the rope around it and pulled it taut.

My side of the boat banged against the boards, and they creaked their objection.

Tris was stronger than Rachel or me, and his legs were longer. He put one foot on the deck, the sun catching the dark hairs on his shin and thigh, and heaved himself upwards. The lines and sinews of his calves stood out with the effort and he swung on to the jetty.

Rachel stood, barefoot, on the plank seat across the boat and it rocked alarmingly.

'Rach!' I said. 'Stop!'

'It's fine,' she said, and wobbled the boat twice from side to side to prove it. 'This old tub is as wide as a table, it's not going anywhere.'

Tristan hooked her out of the boat; she stood upright on the jetty and I passed the basket of food up to her. Tris took his cigarettes from his pocket, lit one and exhaled the smoke into the clear sea air. Behind him, the square tower of the castle shimmered and billowed in the vapour.

Rachel leaned down to pull my arm.

'No, don't. I'm fine – I'll climb out.' I didn't want her to realise how heavy I was, how ungainly compared to her. I wouldn't be skinny-dipping, even if they were going to; my off-white knickers and stretched grey bra would have to do, my T-shirt a shroud over it all. The sun was hot enough to dry it all in seconds anyway.

I put one foot on the side of the boat and both of my hands on the edge of the dock. I straightened my leg against the boat to push myself upwards and curled my fingers into the wood of the dock for purchase. The edge plank bent towards me: where the rusty screws had been moments before, there was nothing but tiny black holes. There was a loud *crack* and the edge of the jetty sheared away. The pain in my head was a fleeting smash as I tipped head-first into the sea and my face hit the side of the boat, but it was the pain in my back as I plunged upside down against the rough splinters of the jetty that set my entire body on fire. The top of my nose threatened to split open with all the water inside it and I thrashed and thrashed, trying to find up.

The very last thing I remember is opening my eyes and my mouth, and how much it hurt when the searing grey water poured into my throat.

I woke up in sections: different parts of my body emptying of water at different times. The pressure in my chest was unbearable, suffocating, and I gasped, my arm hitting out at the weight across me.

'Oh my God, oh my God.' Rachel was on her knees, sobbing, her hands over her face. 'You're alive. Oh my God.'

Tristan rolled away from me – I saw him go out of the corner of my eye – and he lay, palms up to the sky and silent, on the rotten black planks of the jetty.

'Fucking hell,' Rachel said, and I could see the red blushes of how hard she'd cried blossoming on her cheeks. 'I thought you were dead.'

She threw her body over mine and I was grateful to feel the warmth of her.

'Put this round you.' Tris had picked up a towel. 'Can you sit up?'

'You were dead,' said Rachel in gasps. 'Actually dead. You'd stopped breathing. Oh, Christ, I was so scared.'

Tristan put his fingers to his lips. Shook his head a little at her. 'We have to get back to the shore. You need to go to hospital, Jo. Can you sit up?'

Seawater bubbled up inside me and flowed, green and yellow, from my mouth. I couldn't stop shaking and the cold, despite the glaring sun that hurt my eyes, made my teeth chatter.

Tristan wrapped the towel round me, sat down beside me on his haunches and put his arms around it to hold it on. 'You're in shock, Wilding. That's all. You're perfectly alright but you're in shock.' He enveloped me with his arms and rubbed my back through the towel.

I could barely hear; my ears loomed and echoed, full of water. I leaned into Tris, half conscious, letting my useless arms and legs hang.

'We couldn't find you. Rachel dived down, she pulled you out. You were under the jetty.'

Rachel was rubbing my legs, trying to get some life into them, trying to stop the shuddering jabbing into every one of my muscles. 'And Tris knew how to do . . . how to—'

'Expired-air resuscitation,' he said. 'We did it at rugby camp. Never thought I'd use it.'

I stayed with Rachel while Tristan rowed the boat to the sloping beach on the land side of the tiny island. He bounded back across the island to half-carry me back to the boat. 'You'll be fine, Wilding. We're nearly there.' His voice was soft, coaxing, and I stood, trembling, at the edge of the sea.

I tried to walk into the water to get in the boat but, as my feet touched the first lacy edge of a wave, my body went into a rigid panic. My knees clenched together and I screamed, my hand flapping and fluttering around me. The warm indignity of fear trickled down my legs.

I had no control over my reaction at all.

Tristan splashed back through the water and scooped me up into his arms. 'Put your hands round my neck.' And he carried me, like a groom going over the threshold, out to the boat.

I kept my eyes tight shut until we got to the shore, and Tristan waded through the ebbing water back to Clachan, pulling the boat behind him.

Rosie put me in a warm bath, called the village doctor. I spent the evening swaddled in blankets, lying along the couch like a baby waiting for a bottle.

Rachel, diving like quicksilver, with the grace and ease of the shark, had found me – dragged me to the surface. And then Tristan had blown his own air into my mouth, breathed life back into me from his lungs. I owed them both my life.

'That was all your fault,' I heard Rachel hiss at Tristan in the hallway. 'You had to row round to the wrong side of the island, even though you knew it was dangerous.'

I could see shapes of them through the gap in the hinge side of the door, see them moving around each other.

'I didn't hear you try and stop me. Quite the opposite, actually.' His voice was low, threatening. 'And if you say anything to Mum or Dad about it, I'll make sure they know it's your fault. All your fault.' He dropped his voice lower and I strained to hear him.

'And you know who they'll believe.'

That night I dreamed of Tristan's lips, the fullness of his mouth. And, in the darkness, his tongue, darting and flitting like a minnow.

Chapter Ten

It is only eight o' clock. The evening of an exhausting day, stretched so far that it feels like deepest night. Everything has been emptied from the car and I'm lugging the last two moving-in carrier bags. I've moved backwards and forwards through the forest, always taking the quickest path in case of wolves dressed like grandmothers and wondering which part of a fairy tale I'm in – whether I'm the witch, the wolf, or the frightened little girl.

I round the last edge of the dense trees where the leaking colour blooms above the bay. The sun, with its bottom-most edge just touching the water, is directly opposite me and rolls out a widening spool of gold that dusts the clouds with peach.

I have been thinking of the hardest, saddest parts of Clachan. This is the mechanics of my mind that protect me from the loss of Rachel, protect me from the fear of this empty house that I can't pay for. These horrors – like my doubt in Rachel – are protection, making me believe, for a moment, that I don't love it, and her, with all my heart.

I have forgotten that when I get up at four or five o'clock to tiptoe across the landing for a wee, I will see the sky crack and the first blue threads of day weave through the fur of night. I have forgotten that Rachel was the most devoted of friends, that she listened for a whole life as I reeled off my latest disaster, my next crisis.

I've shut out that as the autumn properly unfurls, I will see the earliest skein of pink-footed geese come honking back from Greenland screeching their arrival and filling the sky with sound. Storms, calm, wilderness and busy skies: everything has a beauty here. *Remember that*, I tell myself. Remember.

I go up to Rachel's room as quietly as I can, swear under my breath when I am betrayed by the fifth step, swear because it's me being stupid, because I knew how to avoid that like I know how to cross the road.

These are still Rachel's sheets. I haven't dreamed of her and maybe sleeping in her scent will make that happen. A dream is better than nothing: I just want to hear her voice.

My supper is a cheese sandwich, packed with salad, and a bag of crisps: the kind we ate in the playground, in the pub, in the past. Wax food, like everything I have eaten since she died.

I have added two tomatoes, cut in half and bright as poppies against the white plate. This is all stuff I had packed in the car, a supper for one. It took all my efforts to churlishly offer to share it with Meg.

'I'm good, thank you.' She was in the dining room, a polythene dust sheet like a curtain over the door so I could only see her silhouette behind it. She had a brush in her hand and her long, lean arms made a shadow puppet monster. 'I'm going to keep working for a bit, then I'll stay out of your way. Is that OK? I won't disturb you?'

My bones are too tired to explain to Meg that her being here at all disturbs me, that scraping or hammering or banging won't matter at all, that the damage is deeper than that.

Up here, this room is so Rachel: the ugly doll; postcards of faraway places stuck into corners of the pale old watercolours that have been here since before she was born; her make-up and lotions that I have picked up off the floor and put back on her dressing table. A gallery of her life.

There have been so many conversations in here – things I will never talk about again because only she knows, because they only matter to her. Because only we were there when those things happened: codes and shorthand and jokes. We have talked and whispered and shouted and laughed in here. I hope she brings that noise to my dreams.

I chew the sandwich but much of the pleasure in eating has been gone this last month. Food no longer fills the hole in my belly – that is where my grief lives now, a little burrow it has hollowed out for itself. It has annexed and exiled me so totally I no longer have access to all the parts of my body.

It is time to brave my mother's letters. The fat envelope is on the duvet beside me. I wipe my fingers on my outstretched legs and open it.

The first thing I pull out isn't a letter: it's a photograph.

I lost contact with my mother when I was eighteen. And because of that, I left all the pictures of me behind. When you're still a child yourself, you can't know that there will be value in these photos one day, that they will be the prompts necessary to remember. When you are still a child, you don't yet know that you will forget some things and misremember others. Even the picture of my mother in my mind is only what I think I know: I have no idea how accurate it is. She will be old now, frail.

The picture is square, edged in white like photographs were back then. I am standing, awkwardly, in my school uniform, my new bike beside me and my fingers curled round the handlebar grips. I'm a shy child, coy in the camera. I got that bike for my birthday, so it would have been the summer before I went to secondary school. 'Before I even met you,' I say to Rachel.

I pull a few more photos loose: me with my grandmother, sitting on her knee and beaming up at her. She died when I was ten and now I think about it – now her face jogs my mind – that must have hit my mother very hard.

Me as a baby, fat round cheeks and no hair, propped up like a bean bag on a round carpet and our cat, still a kitten, rubbing his head against my soft cheek. I loved that cat. We'd had him all my life and it was so hard to be without him when I first left home. I used to feel guilty that I missed him more than I missed my mother, but as an adult I know that it's hard to have a fundamental disagreement with a pet.

There is something quite magical about these pictures – some of them I remember posing for or looking at when they'd been developed. The rest are of strangers I know are me and mine.

My mother – who I only ever think of as Val, have done for years – is exactly as I remember her.

And then I start reading Val's letters to my best friend. The form is indelibly etched: start with thanks and go on to the things you'd like to ask for. Pray like you'd write a letter. Write a letter like you pray.

The timeline is jumbled, the letters are randomly stacked in the envelope. After a few, reading about my struggle to keep my house, finding a few paragraphs of how I had started my business – bought the tiny factory – I start to shuffle them into date order. There are two a year, sometimes three, and the last is only weeks before Rachel died.

> I am so glad you have found Ben. We are nothing without hope and I thank God you have found yours.
>
> We all deserve the chance to be washed clean of our pasts – that's what faith is about. Change is always difficult, but God will be beside you.

It is never too late to start again. I will keep
you both in my prayers.

The sandwich in my hand wilts on to the plate. I read the single page again. And again. The whole letter is about Rachel's new life, about Ben who she can trust and can talk to, and about how hopeful Val is for it all.

It doesn't mention Tim once. It doesn't mention me.

I am across the landing in two strides.

'Meg.' I open her door without knocking, my voice as cold as my crawling skin. 'Is your dad called Ben?'

Chapter Eleven

Meg

It takes me by surprise. When she first arrived, I was totally ready for the questions: how did you get here? What's your connection to Rachel? All the rest of it. But she'd moved off that, she was all about how long are you here for and when are you leaving and I thought she'd gone past it, forgotten.

So I'm all out of balance when she asks me about my dad, just like that – totally out of the blue and standing in my bedroom in her pyjamas.

I don't answer. I mean literally don't answer, because there aren't any words and an answer won't come. I talked to my dad about what to say and all of that, but that was then and this is now and nothing we talked about fits into this question. My dad and I aren't even speaking in any civilised way.

'Yes.'

Joanna has her hands on her hips and she fills the little doorway: I don't have a choice but to answer if I ever want her to leave. 'Ben's my dad.' But I don't know how she knows. I don't know what she knows.

Maybe Tim told her.

Don't offer any information, my dad said. *Don't assume anyone knows anything. Just wait and respond.* So I'm waiting and responding. My dad likes a bit of mindful – and so I'm practising now, breathing slowly and carefully. Not rushing into anything, even though these are not my secrets to keep. My face hots up a bit at the unfairness of that.

Joanna opens her mouth to speak, changes her mind, and turns round. The door slams shut behind her.

I need to text my dad, tell him what just happened, ask him what to do next. The little numbers on the top of his screen say he's not online, that he hasn't been for a few hours. My dad is strict about his phone use – never upstairs, always switched to silent if he's doing anything else at all. It wasn't like that when Rachel was alive – for a while back there, I could get him any time of the day or night.

I sort of spoke to him yesterday, if you can count that as talking. He ranted, and I tried to defend myself.

What the heck is going on? was his opener. My dad likes to reserve his swearing for special occasions. Big guns, he likes to say: use them as ammunition, not punctuation. If you overuse them, they lose their meaning. So he says things like 'What the heck?' when he really means 'What kind of unholy clusterfuck is this?'

My dad pulled himself up by his bootstraps – another direct quote. Direct quote imprinted on my mind like a scratched record, I've heard it so many times. *So many fucking times*, I say to myself, just to annoy him.

I've closed up my flat, given back the keys, and put my head in the sand about my credit cards. I knew they couldn't find me here and that would buy me a bit of time to start sorting it out, chipping away at them – at least at the arrears. And then, when my dad rang, I remembered that little box you have to fill in, the one you can't get the card without ticking. The one that says 'any other addresses within the last five years'.

And I realised that everything I've hidden from him, practically since I started uni, had just arrived at his door in neat envelopes.

So that was yesterday's parental communication. It did not go well. Plenty of volume. It had that going for it.

My phone vibrates and I see that it's today's communiqué. A text from my mum. Although she won't be as furious as my dad: I don't think he's ever had those kind of letters – threats of repossessing furniture, of bailiffs – even in all her years of chaos.

Thinking of you, miss you. And always love you. Mum xxx.

I often wonder what goes through her mind to make her text. Has she set an alarm on her phone? Is she high, loaded? Has she spoken to my dad and heard about my latest disaster? Does she think, oh, perhaps I'd better get in touch with my daughter, let her know I'm still alive?

My name's Meggie and my mum's an addict, I would have said if I'd ever gone to the Families Anonymous meetings my dad wanted me to. I've had lots of counselling to understand that it's not my fault and neither is it a straightforward choice between drugs and me – it is, by the way, a straightforward choice – but it's still changed me. It's changed us – my dad too.

My mum being an addict was what set him on this route, what brought Rachel into his life, and that is how I ended up here. And I'm happy here – finally, usefully, happy. Until yesterday, I'd had a brief reprieve from the constant barrage of debt letters. I haven't got space to start dealing with my mum on top of all that. She is going to have to leave me alone. But my dad, I'm not going to be able to avoid speaking to him now that Jo knows I'm here.

Given how few times I met Rachel, she knew a lot about me. Rachel talked as if she was sharing everything with me and that, directly, made me share everything with her. I ended up, very quickly, telling her things I've never told anyone: not friends; not boyfriends. Certainly not my dad.

Our second meeting about the cottage was just the two of us. And I don't know if she did that on purpose – if she wanted to get to know me better, or if she just wanted rid of the brittleness that infects my dad whenever I'm around.

I toured the cottage open-mouthed. It didn't take long: two floors; four rooms upstairs, three beds and the bath; three downstairs, although the kitchen runs the width of the house and could easily be two rooms. All the time, I was thinking about my portfolio, about how it would look if all these ideas came off.

'I want to keep the history.' Rachel was clear about that. 'But I want a contemporary vibe on top of that. And then' – this was an afterthought – 'I want it to be timeless so that we don't have to do it again. I don't want to interfere with it too much, stoke up the ghosts.'

I have a client. A real live client. I am not a pot washer or a waitress. I am not cleaning offices. I am in the middle of a forest, talking to my glamorous client.

'My family is deep in the fabric of this place.' She ran her fingers along the arm of the sofa, as if she could slough them off it and on to her skin. 'Precious memories,' she said, and there was a twitch of tension at the corner of one eye.

Rachel's fillers were immaculate. You could see she'd had work – even the best of genes don't do that to your late fifties – but you couldn't see where. Her forehead and face still moved enough to let the pain out, give her away.

It wasn't like a normal conversation, where you work at the thread of something buried and it slowly spools out, creeps from its hiding place.

This was just open, honest. Not like any conversation that has ever taken place in my house, my family home.

'My brother died too,' Rachel said. 'And then, like you, I was suddenly an only child.'

Chapter Twelve

Jo

I watch her from Rachel's window. She is in the sea, washing away the day, washing the colour – quite literally – from her body under a moon that paints everything ivory and picks out the details in alabaster relief. It's not dark yet but the moon has definitely taken charge of the sky: the sun is slinking – tired – along the sea.

I walked away from our conversation, back to the letters, to sifting through my mum's words to Rachel, looking for hidden meaning in her sentences, trying to fix together the pieces of a giant jigsaw puzzle. And I only have half the pieces. I wonder what was in Rachel's letters to my mother – more detail, I'm sure, than it's possible to put together from my mother's answers to her.

Rachel and Ben have been together for almost three years, if I take the gap between the last letter that doesn't mention him at all and when my mother first mentions him. My mother speaks of the two of them brightly, earnestly, and in tones that don't chime with the woman I remember, with her judgement and hellfire.

My mother is ill, terminal. I'm not surprised. I put down my glass and spell out the numbers on my fingers: she is eighty-four. Old by any measure. Eighty-four and coming to the end of a long, embittered life. I search around inside myself to see if I am sad, but I don't have access to my feelings about my mother. I walled them up years ago.

In the middle distance, Meg pushes herself out of the water like a fountain. Just as when I first saw her, she is swimming nude. It is the kind of thing that makes me realise how buttoned up I am, how full of missed opportunity. Even if I could get in the water, taking my clothes off would be a spectacularly uncomfortable idea.

'You'll have to work around the decorator,' Tim said when we talked about me coming here. This can't be what he meant – living with a stranger in a tiny house.

I think about Tim, whether he knows about Rachel and Meg's father. In one simple phone call, Tim could unravel this whole thing, strip it down to its complete innocence and explain. Or he could be devastated to find out that his late wife, who he worshipped, was having an affair.

The only thing I can be certain of is that the relationship with Rachel and Ben isn't *nothing*, isn't something casual or painless.

And I know that because she didn't tell me.

I have left Clachan behind, albeit temporarily. Already my feelings about it are knotting and clotting: the place where my demons snarl from under the floorboards, but, simultaneously, a sanctuary like no other. I don't know why I thought this visit would be any different.

Because I thought Rachel would be there. Intangible, ephemeral, but everywhere in the tiny cottage, filling it with smells of her, memories of her. My knuckles tighten on the steering wheel and I drive west, to the nearest town, to catch the supermarket before it closes.

I called out to Meg that I was going and did she want anything – although it was only courtesy, I don't really want to do her shopping. She needs to use up what she has in the house before she leaves, although we haven't sorted the details of that exit.

Maybe Meg will go and I can make order of my sadness, organise my grief into boxes and bags and things for the charity shop. There will be a simple explanation for the letters – written out in black and white – and they will be defanged, defused. Some of my life will be restored.

Rachel and I always use this same supermarket when we're here. At home, this would be an express store, a slightly bigger version of a corner shop. Here, it is the biggest store for miles around.

I pick up a pot of olives, look at them in my hand and smile. I tell the absence of Rachel that there are olives here now, that next there will be sushi.

There is no sushi. Instead, there is the warm, round face of the man at the till, his voice typical of the area, some of his words impenetrable. *Yin*, he says, instead of *one*, and I wish that I did too.

He chats to everyone in the same hearty way, expects everyone to respond, to share their day.

Please don't ask me, I think as I push my shopping towards him – shopping that is largely wine. Please don't ask me how my day is going, or am I having a good one. I look at the box of eggs on the conveyer belt, imagine the vacuum crack they'd make as they hit the shop walls, the cling of yellow yolk to paint and posters.

'And how are you?' he asks me. 'Here on holiday?'

I don't know if wine, eggs, olives, salad, risotto rice is holiday shopping, or if it's just that he doesn't recognise me and knows everyone here.

'Kind of,' I say, while the jagged edges of my trip hurt my head with their grinding.

'Anywhere nice?' He uses short prompts to wriggle my story free.

'A cottage on the coast.' That's all it is, whatever happens there. 'Near Auchlaggan.'

He stops passing my meagre shopping through the reader and looks up at me. 'I've an auntie who stays down there. Two doors from the shop.'

This isn't news: in this part of the world, everyone knows everyone – their history, their relationships, sometimes even their secrets. 'Stays' in this part of the world means 'lives'. His auntie lives on the bay.

'It's a beautiful spot,' I say, and I take a chocolate bar from the rack beside me to avoid having to look at him.

He swipes it through, turns the little screen to show me how much my shopping comes to and where to tap my card. 'A wee break there will see you right,' he says, as if he's a soothsayer, a witch. 'Food for the soul.'

There is a beep as my card goes through and his welcoming face turns, like a lantern, to the next person.

Back in the car, I examine myself in the rear-view mirror. Do I look like someone who needs a break somewhere nice, with food for my soul? I move my face about, wiggle my jaw, open my eyes wider and then wrinkle them tight. I don't look any different to when I arrived: tired, middle-aged, and with a faint something about my eyes that says my heart is broken, probably dead.

Inside the supermarket, the happy cashier goes about his business and the shoppers collect their groceries. How do they go on, as if nothing has changed, when Rachel has gone? The helplessness of it is huge inside me, the pressure of being totally unable to fix it.

For lunch, I have cooked store-bought tortellini, floated them in a browned butter flavoured with pale sage from the garden. The sage has darkened as it soaks up the oil, crisped into flakes.

'Meg.' She is hard at work – I assume – behind her gauze curtain. 'I've made lunch.' We need to talk and it may as well be over food, with something gentle between us to soak up the harshness of the words the way the sage has soaked up the butter.

'Blimey, Joanna,' she says when she comes into the kitchen. 'I usually have toast. Or cheese and crackers.' Her smile is genuine. She moves one of the pine chairs out from the kitchen table and sits down. 'I didn't expect this.'

'I'm Jo, really. Hardly ever Joanna.' I reach forward, push the round white plate towards her. I topped the leaves with lemon zest and the yellow is quite beautiful against the almost-black of the sage.

I concentrate on the first mouthfuls, assess the quality of the pasta, bite through the filling. I look at the view out of the window, the hoppings and flittings of the bird table, and get ready to speak.

'Do you have an actual contract?' It's a low blow, but I need the space to stand on the beach and scream.

'I do. More a scheme of work, really. It's on my computer.' She knows I didn't expect this, and there is the slightest note of triumph in her voice. Meg makes a face to show me how delicious her unexpected lunch is, waves across the top of it with her fork.

'And Rachel signed this?' I nod towards the bowl of grated Parmesan, motion it into a no-man's land between us.

'Rachel, and then Tim. I'll get it down in a bit and you can have a read through the thread. It's all in emails, very clear. All agreed. Tim has the emails too, he was cc'ed in. I was going to make myself scarce the odd weekend she wanted to come here: if she needed time with—' She stops before she names him.

'If she and your dad were coming here?'

There is a long pause. Only after she has exhaled with a long, expressive sigh does she speak again.

'Please don't ask me about my dad and Rachel, Joanna – Jo. It's not for me to talk about – none of my business. And you're stuck with me. Really. I don't have anywhere else to go just now.'

'I've got a lot of stuff I need to work out.' I am not going to give her detail. 'And believe it or not, I don't have anywhere else to go either – for the time being.' I also – it occurred to me last night, like a noose tightening around my life – have no money to pay for anyone else to do the cottage up. I have neither the desire nor the resources to do it myself, and Tim is meeting all Meg's bills.

I literally can't afford to stop her.

'But we really need to talk, OK? Sit down and chat properly? Set some rules.'

Meg nods and it is agreed: for now, we are housemates.

I'm sitting upstairs with my coffee, out of the way. The photographs are sifted out from the letters and spread in front of me on the covers. The micro-short skirts of the early 70s, my sailor-suit swimming costume with a white pleated trim, old ladies in plaid skirts and thick tights who were probably fifty: it is the stuff of another time.

I am old enough that my friend has died of natural causes. I am older, on our next birthday, than she ever got to be. I'd all but forgotten the long and intricate past of these pictures: people; places; pets.

I wonder where Val is now, who she is. I know her address – only a few miles from where we lived when I was a child – but I don't know if she's in a home or a mansion or a hostel. It is a home for the elderly, my phone's street map tells me, and I search for information about it.

My mother was a civil servant, a clerk in the coroner's court, and a single parent – she never had much money. The home looks alright, nice even, from its website. I don't know why I care.

I have read the most recent letters but there is a limit to how many of them I can read at one time. Each one is a reference to my life, a perverse diary I didn't know I was keeping. There are reports of my worst times, accounts of days that I've been lucky enough to forget: reminders that make my head pound. There is still a great deal of 'God bless you' and keeping people in her prayers in the letters, but the more fundamentalist moments – the ones I suffered as a child – seem absent. Maybe my mother has dialled back on that crushing immutable belief that everything is ordained and constrained by God, that His entire agenda is wrath and punishment.

Everything that happened at Clachan years ago, events that literally shaped my life – took what it might have been and moulded it into the shape I have learned to live with – none of it would have happened if she'd just been on my side.

If she had just held on to me.

I tried as hard as I could to fit in with Val's picture of the perfect daughter. I knew that the more I did it, the looser her restrictions would be. I became ever more isolated at school by spending most evenings and all day on Sundays going to meetings and services. Rachel knew where I was when the rest of them were at all-night beach parties that ran on to Sunday morning, or going to the pictures on a Wednesday evening, but she kept my secret.

At times, the Tuesday youth group was almost bearable. Some of the kids there were funny and, if I tried hard and forgot myself, I could make it work for everyone. I felt for those teenagers, growing up in a world that their parents were pretending wasn't there: it must have been nigh-on impossible. A couple of them were in my school, in the years below me, although I barely acknowledged them out of church – I couldn't afford to. My own position at school was perilous: I had only hung on to my sanity because of my association with Rachel and the honorary cool that bestowed upon me. But now the last exams were done and people were partying, spending a summer of last hurrahs before they parted for good in September.

While they partied, I was sitting in the cold village hall with a glass of squash. My mother's church forbade even the simplest of cultural rituals like tea and coffee – 'The Bible says hot drinks are vexatious to the soul, Joanna,' my mother would tell me every time I begged for a cup of tea.

Rachel, and everyone else I knew, was experimenting with cider, beer, even vodka. I had weak squash, the cheapest sort, in scratched plastic cups.

I was surprised to see Brother Davies in the tiny kitchen of the village hall, although he was becoming a semi-permanent presence in our house. My mum had recently added supervising me at the youth club to the list of things we might do together – which had previously sat at zero.

'I just thought it would be nice to do something you actually like. To do it together,' she said.

I couldn't point out to her that I didn't actually like it, but her presence there showed me – ironically – that I could like it less.

We teens were sitting in a circle, the squash had been handed out and drunk, and we were discussing a play we thought we might write for a competition with some of the other teenage congregations at some of the other weird churches. No one but me seemed to notice that the whole drama festival was a conspiracy to marry us off, a cattle market to introduce us to similarly curtailed and covered-up young people.

'Ahem.' My mother stood awkwardly in the circle. 'Brother Davies has something to tell you. A very important message about something awful that you all need to know.'

Brother Davies pulled a chair from the top of the pile. Its metal legs scraped in reluctance. He motioned for two girls to make a gap for him: Ann and Emily. They were wispy, frail girls, sisters, faintly coloured and quietly spoken.

'I've come to talk to you this evening because Satan walks among us.'

What's new? I wanted to ask him, and felt my cheeks sizzle as I thought of the boy I'd snogged last weekend – a rare escape to a party while my mum thought I was at Rachel's – of how he and I had clung to one another as our hands explored.

Tristan Willoughby haunted my dreams and fuelled my days, but I was still looking, still attempting to find someone to stand in for him. Try as I might, I never fancied the same boys who fancied me. They always came up short compared to Tristan. So I kissed the frogs, the toads, and hoped for the best, and no one came close.

'An awful thing happened this weekend, to one of our own.' Brother Davies was sombre.

The more pallid of the two sisters, Ann, blushed slightly – it suited her.

'Sister Ann was walking home from a church meeting last Friday evening, along the path by the canal—'

I knew it – it was a pretty horrible and stupid place to walk at night; bushes and scrubland on one side, the murky black of the water on the other.

'—when Satan stepped on to the path in front of her.'

I watched the girl's face, trying to see how his account chimed with hers.

'He went to grab Sister Ann, and he meant to assault her. She could smell the brimstone and the evil on him.'

Ann looked at the floor. Her modest long-sleeved top was a pale buttercup yellow.

'But Sister Ann knew the Lord would not abandon her. As the man grabbed her, Sister Ann pushed her Bible into his chest and shouted, "Get thee hence, Satan! By the power of Jesus Christ, I repel thee!"' He looked at the wide-eyed circle. 'By those words, Sister Ann was saved. Satan returned to the shadows.' He sat up, raised his chin with pride. 'Jesus Christ will walk with you whenever you need him. This is proof that he will keep you safe, wherever you are, as long as you walk his path of righteousness.'

I couldn't bear it. 'Stop. This is nonsense, Barry.' I knew that calling Brother Davies by his first name was tantamount to sacrilege, but I couldn't play along any more. 'That wasn't Satan. Ann, you know that, don't you? You know that was a man? A horrible, vile man? You saved yourself, Ann.'

'What do you think—' Barry Davies was apoplectic, but I didn't let him finish.

'You saved yourself, Ann, and good for you. But that wasn't Satan.' I was standing now. 'This is all wrong. All nonsense.'

I could see from the slump of her shoulders that Ann didn't believe Brother Davies either.

My mother was striding towards me from where she'd been watching at the hatch of the kitchen, but I carried on. 'Don't walk by the canal, or anywhere else that might be dangerous – dangerous because of men, not because of Satan.'

My mother grabbed me from behind. 'Get out,' she hissed into my ear, her nails pinching the skin of my arm. 'Get. Out.'

It left me balanced on a tightrope. Rachel, Rosie and Duncan were on their way to Clachan. They'd been visiting family on one of the tiny islands far north of Scotland and out into the sea. They would get to Clachan, where I would join them, the day after tomorrow. I couldn't risk my mother grounding me, locking me in. If I wanted to get away before my mother got home, it would mean sleeping in the bus station.

Tristan had been on a sailing expedition for almost the whole summer. I had a vision in my mind of his bronzed skin, of the way the work would have muscled his arms. In my picture of Tristan, he was always wearing a snow-white shirt, rolled up at the sleeves and half open at the chest so that it told the story of his outdoor summer, of the sea spray and the wind and the pitching waves. It was the 1980s; any boy worth having had to be part pirate.

The ship was going to return to dock via south-west Scotland, pull into Kirkcudbright harbour with its rigging and its voluminous sails, for Tristan to disembark – for Tristan to come to Clachan.

I could leave early. Change my bus and train tickets and leave in the morning. The only real difference would be that I'd need to hitch from the station to the house with my suitcase: Rosie or Duncan wouldn't be there to pick me up from the station. The key to Clachan would be underneath the stone dog by the front door, just as it had always been. No one would be there and no one would object.

I made up my mind and I took control of the situation. I ran home as fast as I could, packed before my mother had even rinsed the orange squash from the plastic cups, and spent the night on a bus station bench, pretending to be on an adventure.

I'm puzzled, rather than alarmed, by the email. Her name, despite her teasing when we were at school, doesn't scare me now.

From: Karen Roberts

Subject: My apologies

Mail:

Hi Joanna

I've been chewing myself up about the way I spoke to you at the funeral – there's no point pussyfooting around it. It's been on my mind night and day since – I was being a bitch. There's no excuse.

I'm sorry I lost touch with Rachel: I feel bad about it now – of course I do. And I was being a bitch to you because you hadn't. Because the two of you were obviously still as tight as you were at school. Deep-seated jealousy and insecurity I didn't know I still have and that I'm not proud of.

The last time Rachel and I met up was a disaster: Rachel had come in on a red-eye from the States and she'd clearly been drinking all night, all the way home. We met up for brunch but I ended up calling my husband after an hour, in floods of tears. He told me just to leave her there, so I did. That might have been the wrong thing to do but I couldn't handle her.

Rachel and I didn't really speak again. Not properly. Christmas cards, that was pretty much it. Obviously I regret that now, but I didn't know it was a problem.

Anyway, sorry I was rude, it doesn't cover me with glory. There was no excuse, especially under the circumstances.

Best regards and massive apologies,

Karen

The child in me never expected anything but rudeness from Karen. My home life meant that I was different, fair game for – I understand now, as an adult – her own insecurities, but it had never occurred to me that anyone could be jealous of me. Her email came to my work address, to my silent little factory with its pale-blue wooden doors shut up: she must have looked me up online. I do the same thing and look at my life laid out there, a life so inexorably changed.

I'm glad Karen emailed, and equally glad she didn't leave it with a hanging invite to get together in the future, to pretend to be friends. I could reply, tell her that I understand how she came to lose touch with Rachel, let her know it's OK – but I'm not going to.

The version of Rachel that Karen met from the plane was hard to handle, even for me.

'Sometimes,' Rachel told me one morning after a late one here – a debrief from our normal lives – when she'd crawled from her bed looking like death itself, 'I have to buy and sell Third World Debt. It's part of my job to keep a system going that kills people. Starves millions of children.' And on those days she would get home, shut herself in her study, and drink a bottle of wine without coming up for air. She'd phone me and talk in loops – about anything but what she'd done at work – worn-out stories that went round and round and back to the beginning as if she'd never told them before.

Tristan always featured. The same story, as if there was a switch inside her that went on at a particular point of drunk. As if I could breathalyse her emotions.

I lean against the headboard and think about those times when the lid came off, when the pressure inside her rose to unbearable levels and she sank into her wine like a circus high-diver, landing in an impossibly small pool that couldn't save her.

I can picture Rachel sitting on this bed, her legs crossed and her hands over her face. She always said the same thing, as if I'd never heard it before, as if it were a one-time confession.

'I borrowed my mum's car, you know. The day before he died.' And the sobs would come to a boil. 'There was something wrong with the brakes, a grinding, a spongy feel. Something not quite right.'

And then she'd take her hands off her face, look right at me as if unloading this guilt would make it stop – and it would, until the next time. 'I was busy – I don't even know what with. And I forgot to tell my mum. I didn't tell my mum that the brakes were going and Tristan wrapped himself round the war memorial.'

That wasn't the worst of it, not for Rachel.

'And I never told them, Jo. I never told my mum and dad that it was my fault. I never confessed.'

I always wondered whether she had, whether she'd been this drunk in front of Duncan and Rosie once, had told the same circular story and then forgotten, starting again at the beginning as soon as she got to the end – just as she did with me. In every other aspect of her life, Rachel hid it well, the belief that she'd killed her brother.

My own reaction to the loss of Tristan was mostly silent; very little made it to out-loud. I had a space for my own secrets. And I hid them well.

Chapter Thirteen

MEG

When I was a wee girl, my mum used to tell me the story of the selkie. It was one of my favourites. A farmer fell in love with a magical woman of the sea. He'd seen her on the shore, walking down to the sea's edge and shedding her human skin – folding it neatly on the sand. Then she'd slipped into the water in seal form, graceful and sleek.

He captured her by taking her seal skin – hiding it in his little house that I imagine looked very much like this one once did. She bore him ten little half-selkie half-human babies before, one day, she found her skin in an old chest and escaped into the ocean, never to be seen again.

I don't think my mum meant it as a metaphor, but it's a story I think of often now that I'm so close to the shore.

Twenty-five isn't too old to pretend, I've discovered. I fold my clothes neatly on the beach, sometimes twice a day, and as soon as I'm in I am that selkie, returned to the waves, free from the shackles. When the shock of the cold has worn off, I dive, head-first, my arms flat against my sealskin sides, and I leave every bit of dry land behind me.

My mum never explained – and I never asked – what happened to the ten half-selkie children. What happened when they got up in the morning and cried for their breakfast, but their selkie mother was swimming: their selkie mother had escaped.

I do own a swimsuit, but it's upstairs in my room. And I don't think Jo's the sort to mind. She minds me being here – but I don't think nude swimming is part of that.

I totally appreciate how she needed to be alone – still does really – and it's so good of her to muddle on around me. I think there's a lot to Jo – layers. She looks very thorough, as buttoned up and proper as my dad, but she talks as if she has a past full of mistakes.

I don't think she notices how much her eyes tear up when she's talking about Rachel – maybe she's got used to it. Yesterday, it made me feel sorry for my dad. He's lost Rachel too and, given everything, it must be extra hard for him.

In a moment of weakness, I texted him. A moment of thinking that he probably misses her in the same way that Jo does, that way that she has of drifting off – still speaking – into their memories. If my dad is doing that too, he's probably doing it alone. And that made me sad.

So I texted him this morning, seemed like a good idea at the time. Short, simple, although I spent a long time thinking about it, about what to write. I don't want to open up the row, have him lecture me about my debts, about how completely fucking dumb I've been. But silence is worse. I've grown up like that since I was six, since William died and everyone in our house stopped talking about him – everyone stopped talking at all.

My dad's shoulders are broad, and it was him who signed up for his relationship with Rachel and all that, but for a second there – earlier – I kind of missed him.

117

I was thinking about you. About how much you must miss Rachel and be sad about it. You can always talk to me. Xxx

Anyway, that bloody backfired.

He was delighted to hear from me, clearly. So delighted he's coming down tomorrow. Driving two hours to see this daughter who has let him down in every other way but is still emotionally adequate when it comes to listening. That's what he said, more or less – popped the bubble of sympathy I had for him with one badly worded text.

Thanks so much for your support, Meggie. I'd love to talk to you – I miss her very much. I'm off tomorrow, how about I drive down and take you out for supper? Or we can go for a walk – or both, make the most of the last of the long days and walk to the pub for something to eat? Love you, Dad.

◆　◆　◆

Oh, Christ on a bike. I walked right into it. I have no way to say sweet-Virgin-Mary-and-mother-of-saint-fuck-I-didn't-mean-it.   I was just being nice: nice like he's always wanted me to be.

But now I'm having supper with Dad, and going for a walk, because I walked into a trap.

I think of Rachel, of her laughing, her sparkly eyes. *It's your fault*, I say, and imagining her laughing at me makes me laugh, and then it makes me sad, and I shake it all off myself and put my overalls on. Let's get on with it.

I've almost finished the dining room. Tucking myself in here to try and keep out of Jo's way, and having the last of the light evenings to work into, means I'm smashing it out. I can't paint once the outside light starts to fade but there's much more to do than that.

The dining room looked like the others when I got here, literally turned upside down. There were books right across the floor, in a cascade, a stack of steps. It didn't take a detective to understand that they'd been in piles. There must have been books on every surface, piled high on the bureau, covering the sideboard. Maybe they were even all over the table. They're lovely books, not readable really – tiny print and pages thin as silk – but they make a beautiful theme for the room so I've saved them all, put them neatly in boxes by colour. Pale sage greens, bleached orange and ashen yellow. The leather ones are red, mostly, mottled and swirled and all ancient history.

Where I've made the sitting room eclectic, this room is going to be formal. Super measured. I made the sitting room's shelves to have tiny shelves and long ones, pockets and boxes and elongated spaces, horizontal and vertical. These are going to be uniform, floor to ceiling along the back wall and nothing on them but books. No wonder no one has tried to do anything before – getting timber delivered and barrowed through the woods has been its own challenge. There has been a lot of maths involved.

I've selected the pictures for here carefully. They all – although it's not obvious in the beginning – are to do with Rachel. She talked about books a lot – gave me some good recommendations – so this room is my memorial to her, on the quiet. I'll tell my dad, because he'll like it. And now, I suppose, I'll probably tell Jo too.

There are a couple of pictures of Rachel as a child – one as a teenager, and one when she's small, a really old photo that looks like her but can't be because it's a hundred years old at least, and two oil landscapes that say *The Peak District* in slopy black letters on the gold frames. That was near where she lived, when she wasn't here. 'In reality, I pretty much live on the train to London,' she told me. 'Or to my lifeline in Scotland.' And I know she meant my dad, as well as this cottage.

The wall isn't straight – walls rarely are, especially somewhere this old. So I've built a frame behind the shelves to give them maximum strength. I stick two fingers up at my Product Design lecturer, who said I didn't turn up often enough. The frame is ramrod straight, flawlessly strong.

The plaster is ancient and came off in lumps when I touched it. So I put my headphones on and got on with the business of sanding the flakes with a forensic gentleness, hoping as little as possible crumbled. I don't have a plasterer to fix it for me – and I don't have the budget to get one in.

I spend the morning touching up and finishing: this afternoon, all I will have left to do is dress this beautiful room – return the books to shelves, rehang the curtains, put up the pictures.

At lunchtime, sticky and stuffy in my overalls, I go outside and walk down the shore. I am the selkie, trapped in this skin, and I unbutton the coverall, plaster dust all over my fingers, sticking – despite the mask – to my tongue.

Ten seconds later, I'm in the water, free and clean, cold and fizzing. I look back to the shore in case someone should be considering stealing my human pelt, but why would they? Who would want a pile of dusty old clothes, when they could have this: white horses of foam and diamonds of sun on water?

I roll and float and wash off the work. When I walk back out, Jo is standing at the cottage door – she makes a gesture of rubbing her tummy and I hope to high heaven she means she's made me food again.

◆ ◆ ◆

Jo made the bread – she says it's easy and she'll teach me, but we'll see about that. There is an oval plate full of things to top it with – eggs in a spicy mayonnaise, pickles and leaves, olives and salty cheese.

'Do you always swim nude?' she asks me, literally out of nowhere, while she's putting slices of tomato on her sandwich.

I choke on a crumb of the bread. 'No. Yes. I mean—' I break off to cough. 'I didn't – I hadn't. Not before I came here. But I just tried it one day because I was here on my own and no one could see me and, frankly, I couldn't be bothered to go back indoors for my costume. And it was the best. You should try it.'

She sort of nods, in a way that says she absolutely wouldn't, ever. I can't understand how people who live by the sea aren't in there every day. What a waste. Another slice of this bread and I would sink like a stone: I take one anyway and load it up.

'I had an accident,' she says, and her eyes do that miles-away thing. 'Here, actually, a long time ago. I'm really afraid of the sea. I never go in beyond my knees.'

I don't know how to answer that. I want details – the gory part of me wants to hear the story that is so awful she can't go swimming forever after it. But the adulting part of me doesn't think I should put her through it.

'And I'd really struggle with the clothes-off. At my age. I'm not keen.'

'I don't see it as clothes-off. It's just that wee bit when you get in and out. And going in doesn't really matter because people can only see your behind, and that's not so' – I have to think about it for a second – 'public.'

Jo laughs. 'Your arse isn't public?'

I'm not explaining myself well enough. 'It's not as public as a full frontal, I mean. We've all got an arse and they might be bigger or smaller—'

'Or hairier or saggier,' she helps out, and I avoid adding the *eww* that might hurt her feelings.

'Yes, that, but essentially it's just a bum. They're all the same. So wading in doesn't count, not really. It's just wading out that's a bit nude. But that's not really any different to when you're getting dressed and you realise the bus is going past your bedroom window, but you really can't be bothered to cover up just to move a couple of feet and grab your jumper. Know what I mean?'

She's proper laughing now, her eyes screwed up tight. 'Flashing? You mean you flash innocent bystanders?'

'It's only a glimpse. Come on.' I need to defend my reputation here. 'Surely you do that occasionally.'

'I love how normal you think that is,' she says. 'Make sure you never change.' And then she is quieter, serious. 'My last marriage was a bit of a body confidence-kicker, if I'm honest. Hurling fat insults was one of Terry's first lines of fire in an argument.'

I'm so sorry I've made her talk about this. The air has whistled out of her and she's slumped like a deflated balloon. I can't imagine someone like Jo, someone so solid, so in control, letting a man talk to her like that. 'That's awful. What a horrible man.'

'I guess he was just looking for weapons,' she says. 'And I had those handy for him, ready-made. I had my own – pretty vicious – arsenal that I hurled back. I was easily as mean as Terry, don't worry. I'm a bit ashamed of myself now.'

Jo is strong and well built. You can't see health, I know, but if you could, I'd imagine it looks a lot like Jo, like someone who could carry things, walk far, hold her own if attacked by a bear. That's how I think about my own body – my thighs aren't small, my six-pack is hibernating under the cutest dome of wobble – and it should be how she thinks about hers. 'There's a lot of shit talked on social media,' I tell her. 'But at least parts of it make us aware of the way society has groomed women to think. There are hundreds of memes that disarm those subliminal messages. Maybe not disarm them, men will still throw them – but ideas that give you armour, show you it's not true. And once you can see what bollocks it all is, how the patriarchy weaponises shape and size, it's a lot easier to deal with.'

I'm in my stride and I illustrate my point with my sandwich, holding the edges of it together as it wiggles emphatically above the table. 'The average man – pretty ugly, bit chubby, dumb-AF – how many times a day do you think he thinks about his weight? Or how many calories in his coffee? Even while he's wolf-whistling out of the window, or offering diet advice, or brushing by a colleague's bum when he needs to get past her – do you think he's thinking about his belly fat or his droopy arse? Is he fuck.'

I'm chewing and eulogising, on a roll. And it takes me a minute to realise she's crying. 'Oh my God, I'm sorry. There's me banging on about microaggressions when you – oh, my God, I'm sorry. What can I do?'

She wipes her face with the paper napkin scrunched up by her plate. Blows her nose loudly enough to make us both smile. 'It's fine. It's not you. I cry whenever I stop concentrating on not crying. I don't sleep much since Rachel died.' She wipes her finger under each eye.

I hadn't realised she was wearing make-up until a little of it slid off under each lower lid, tattoo deltas of black that crinkle in the folds of her skin.

'I'm a bit tense.' She laughs and it comes out as a snort in her nose. 'Slightly manic.'

'It's my fault. Threatening you with naked swimming and making you remember your ex. After you'd made me such a nice lunch, too. And flashing you on the beach, full scary frontal.'

'You carry on with the streaking – it's very healthy, and don't let anyone tell you otherwise.' She points a finger at me for emphasis. 'And Terry's harmless, he doesn't bother me now – and as I said, I gave as good as I got. I don't care about it.' Jo pauses to put one more olive in her mouth. 'The worst thing that could happen to me has happened. And it turns out it was nothing to do with Terry.'

It's too awkward, too heavy for me. It makes me realise that the air has closed in around us, sticky and fully of insects. My arm is dotted with little black thunderbugs.

I think of the selkie skin – of how you can't go back to the water until someone gives you yours back. My change of subject is clunky and obvious, but I think Jo wants it as much as I do: 'I've been drawing the selkie,' I tell her, and I pull my sketch pad out from under the table.

'How can you have?' She looks puzzled. 'I thought Duncan made her up. Rachel's dad, he used to see the selkie here.'

'Everyone knows about selkies in Scotland.' It might be a generalisation; my dad would point that out. 'It's folklore. Wouldn't she look beautiful on wallpaper, with the hawthorn witch representing the land?'

My selkie sketches are better than I thought they could be. The seal is shimmying her skin off, a human form rumpled and wrinkling around her hips and tail. Her bright eyes are facing forward and there is a patch of light on her head that shines. Black and white, simple.

Jo's thoughts are far away, lost in the distance of memories. 'I thought it was a Willoughby thing. We used to pretend to be seals, Rachel and me.'

'It was my mum's best bedtime story. And we'd look for her whenever we were at the seaside. Especially if we saw a pile of clothes on the beach.' I'm knocked off kilter by real sadness: sudden, clean and sharp.

Jo's grief has worked like a mirror: reflected my own so brightly it hurts my eyes. The perfection of the surroundings, the food, the blooming rolling sky, it all pinpoints everywhere I've gone wrong.

It's been obvious to me since I got here, since I paused to draw breath and think.

I pretend to my dad that I still have the horrible boyfriend he hated – who I might never have gone out with at all if he hadn't criticised when I very first met him – to give my dad a focus, so that he doesn't dive any deeper into my life. And it worked until those letters arrived. Now we are going to have to talk and I am like the swan, calm and graceful above the water, paddling with frantic feet below it.

It's not just my dad's disappointment that hurts me, makes me feel bad about myself. If I'm adult and honest about this, those letters remind me that I've criticised my parents for so long, it's impossible to tell them when I've gone wrong. That's the kicker.

Chapter Fourteen

Jo

The bus north left first thing: I queued up to get on while it was still dark. It was cold with the sun still firmly down, the dew of the morning settling on my coat and bag. The bus station was a hub for drunks and misery – everyone who had choices was on the train.

I thought about going home but my mother had made it very clear how she felt. In the tiny kitchen of the village hall, she had wagged her finger in my face, our lips so close together I could see her tongue moving, pink, behind her teeth. There was too much saliva in her mouth and it bubbled like foam at the edges of her gums.

My mother's vision of what would happen to me in purgatory was the kind of thing I would recite for Rachel, perform with actions until we were holding our sides laughing and its sting was disarmed, muffled. But Rachel was on a Scottish island, two ferries away, and I was on a grubby bus, leaving the dark city streets in search of the motorway.

My mother had told me how high the flames would lick and how long it would hurt for: *over my cursed head* and *forever* respectively, according to Brother Davies, whose voice I could hear inside hers even though we were alone in the musty little kitchen. 'At least I'd be warm,' the bravado inside me muttered and rehearsed to tell Rachel.

It didn't make it any less painful, turning Val's madness into a performance, a comedy of insanity, but it was a way to get it out. Without the caricature I made of her, the spectre I built from Brother Davies, I don't think I could have told anybody at all – and that would have been so much worse.

I hadn't realised that it would take a whole day to get to Clachan by public transport. It was so easy with Rosie or Duncan driving. My hitching, that I'd decided on in a moment of wild boldness, became a drizzled walk almost all the way back from the train station, the dark creeping behind me and malevolent shapes hiding in the edges of the forest.

I'd almost burst into tears when a barn owl swooped white and moonlit across the road in front of me: jumped out of my skin and then realised with a crash how alone I was. The next set of headlights, weak in the driech, belonged to a car driven by an old lady. She took me right to the Clachan car park and set me down with my rucksack.

'I wish I had a torch to give you,' she said, peering into the gloom of the trees. 'It's *awfa* dark in there.'

We're stuck here, Meg and I, marooned together. And even if a rescue ship sailed by, neither of us could afford the ticket to get on it.

Cooking has always been a good way to channel my emotions, boost my confidence. I'm good at the alchemy of it, daring and optimistic. I became dented during the Terry years. Dented by life: by the rejection that comes with any kind of miserable relationship, by the feeling that there ought to be more, that I ought to be doing something else. I feel it again today – for the first time in a long time – that fledgling fluttering inside, those humble wings of discovery.

Meg knows more than I do about Rachel and her father: feeding her is a sure-fire way to disarm her, work my way into the secrets. Feeding her is something I can do well, and having someone to cook for nourishes my own soul.

I stack the dishwasher and wipe down the work surfaces. Rachel had a new kitchen put in not long after Rosie died – it's a little out of fashion now, but it's clean and solid. In our hours of plans for Clachan, we were going to revamp it with new doors, but otherwise its white tiles and wooden worktops are timeless and more than serviceable.

There is a positivity nestling inside me, as if I have let out some of the pressure. It was nice talking to Meg, it was helpful. It is good to talk.

I have other friendships outside of Rachel, but none of them are so effortless, so easy. Now I wonder if I should make some calls, catch up with some work colleagues, old neighbours, people whose company I really did enjoy but who didn't know all of me – who never would.

It is impossible to stay cross with Rachel, even for being dead. On the odd occasion I have been annoyed at her – when she's cancelled at short notice, or no notice; when she's been too hungover to eat the breakfast I've made – it always passes the second we speak. I give in to her as soon as she looks at me, earnest and twinkling, squeezes me tight and apologises – when she pings back to life or good humour like a storm blew through and left a day washed clean.

I go back upstairs, to my task of sorting the letters. I am starting to understand them: both how they came to be and what they mean. I know with a deep connection that they are Rachel's secret – the one she was going to tell me that weekend.

She was sorting her whole life out: putting her affairs, literally, in order. She was going to tell me about the letters – or they wouldn't have been here – and then, inevitably, she would have told me about Ben. He is mentioned in every letter from the last three years: it would be impossible to reveal one without the other.

The ugly little doll has been sitting beside me while I've gone through them, a companion. And we've chatted, she and I. It is easy to talk to an inanimate object and have the answers rumble back from deep within me as if I already knew them. Her pale-blue eyes are never startled by the revelations, her tiny O of a mouth never changes, neither widens nor narrows, in judgement. I like her, despite her waxy sheen of a thousand fingerprints.

After a weekend with me, getting used to hearing her new life out loud, to bringing it out of the shadows in her own voice, Rachel would have gone back to tell Tim. Poor Tim.

The doll knows it, and I know it.

Tim and I have never been close: he thinks I'm a bit of a liability, childish. He's never said it to me, but he really hasn't had to. The lectures before Rachel and I go anywhere – dressed up as fun, as a joke, but a clearly transparent list of how Tim thinks I should behave, the kind of trouble he believes I should avoid. He's patronising to his core, but he doesn't deserve this, and I hope he doesn't know. There can't be much worse than losing your wife twice.

Rachel was press-ganged into the letters, press-ganged by that Willoughby way of doing the right thing, behaving properly. It is a relief to know this, that she fell into it by omission, by not telling me the first time. And that first time was while she was grieving her own mother's death, after the earth-shattering loss of Rosie.

Back in the day, when I first left home, Rosie started writing to my mother. It makes total sense. It was the way she was brought up, to help those less able or – in my mother's case – more deranged.

I imagine Rosie felt it her social duty to be a thread between my mother and me, to try and heal the fractures so that I could one day go home, even if just for the odd Christmas.

I cross my legs, lean back against Rachel's headboard. Reading about my own past, these things I would rather forget, is tiring.

One of Val's earliest replies to Rosie was after I married Evan. I was twenty years old, living in a single-room flat and trying to recover from my childhood, the abandonment of my father, the madness of my mother.

Rachel was away at university, partying hard but studying harder. Our lives had separated like the zipper down the back of a ballgown: Rachel meeting the people she would end up working with, dazzling and international, confident and powdered with money, while I pretended to be a housewife, waiting to get pregnant in a tiny little rental and living on air. That version of me feels like someone else now. I can't imagine being that limited, that diminished – it is a relief to know that I have grown out of it. I wish I could hug the girl I was, whisper to her that things would get better, bigger.

I'm so pleased she's married. It's a shame the ceremony was so small, but how wonderful that she's found someone to love her.

Even from miles away, uninvited and hearing about my marriage second-hand, Val managed to belittle it. It helps though, it makes it clearer – as if I didn't already recognise the panic with which I married the first time, the need to find someone who could love me after everything that had happened, and how ruined I was. The letter makes it even clearer that I didn't imagine Val's obsession, that her need for me to be someone else was real.

These reports are third-hand: Rachel to Rosie, Rosie to Val, and then on to what I'm reading here – Val's interpretation of what Rosie said. It's a whole other way of looking at my life. It doesn't read as pathetically as I thought it would.

And then Rosie died, after many years of correspondence with Val – the strangest of pen pals – a twice-yearly habit of decades. I have read the letter that Val sent to Rachel, offering her condolences, assuring Rachel that the mother she adored was 'in the celestial kingdom' and 'resting with Jesus'. The desire to tell me she said that must have almost burst Rachel.

And I wish she had told me, before she replied, before she entered into the exchange that she couldn't find a way out of. Now, in her care home, Val has all the details of my life, my history. What I thought I'd withheld from her, my only means of punishment, she has had all along. She can chat to other residents about her daughter without ever having to speak to me – to say she was sorry. As if she'd been the perfect mother and raised a perfect daughter.

Bits and pieces of Val's life come out in her letters to Rachel, and I try not to be interested in how she is now, who she is now. I'm reading to find out about Rachel, I tell myself, not my mother, and anyway, I only have her letters to Rachel, nothing from the other way round. I only have half a story. I'm not incurious about Rachel's letters, about what she might have written about me – but they were never mine, and I'd have no way of getting them anyway.

It is warm up here in this room, and the sun is a yolk-yellow glow against the window that throws gold shadows into the corners of the room. I stretch my legs out in front of me and flex my toes.

My mother had a framed print of a prayer on our sitting-room wall, no family portraits for us.

The only line I remember from it was something along the lines of how, despite everything, this is still a beautiful world. It works for me now, looking out on to the flat sand, the empty beach. With the tide out, it is drying into a crisp landscape of scuttling crabs and marooned seaweed.

A world that will be submerged and secret again within hours.

Chapter Fifteen

Meg

Does it count as a lie, what I told Joanna? That I swim to relax, to feel good about myself, body-confident. Not a word of it is true. I swim so that I can't think, can't hear.

You have to be smart in the sea, switched on and with-it. You have to be thinking about the currents, the wind, about how far you've swum and how far you have to go. I try and do a kilometre a day, measuring it on my smartwatch. I can't measure it by time because one day it'll take me half an hour to get to the island and back, the next day an hour. Everything shifts here.

Stupid smartwatch: I bought it on credit, before anyone else had one. It's outdated, outmoded, but every penny I paid for it is still racking up interest. On and on, day after day, the watch gets more expensive and more worthless. Schrödinger's stupid smartwatch.

So when you're in the sea, when you're concentrating on your breath and your stroke and going in the right direction, you can't think about anything else. Specifically, in my case, I can't think about the giant fucking cock-up I've made of the last few years.

I am here to escape, to get away from the memories and to get away from the realities. My dad will be here this evening and that will bring both.

I haven't seen my mum in a while. That's an easy way to say *just over a year*, a way to say it without feeling like a bully, like I'm punishing her for something I might forgive in other people.

I last saw her when I was going out with Liam, the boyfriend my dad was right about. I was staying at his, but I'd forgotten my toothbrush. My flat was the other side of town, it would have been crazy to go all the way back, so we stopped at a chemist near Liam's. It was a shitty bit of the city; the hipster bars and doughnut shops haven't got all the way out there yet. It's yet to be *discovered*, apart from by all the people who live there.

The good side of Liam -- the only thing of merit about him, I twigged before too long -- was that he really cared about the environment, glued himself to roads on behalf of all of us, climbed up gantries to get the media to think about oil consumption. It turned out that isn't enough to base a relationship on, but this was before I realised that.

I asked the chemist if they sold bamboo toothbrushes and she stepped out from behind the counter to show me where they were.

I saw my mum out of the corner of my eye, that kind of deep recognition where someone doesn't have to speak, or turn round, where you know them just by shape, by the way that they move. And I pressed myself back into the gap between the toothpaste display and a round carousel of toothbrushes in case she saw me.

'Just behind you,' the pharmacist said, bewildered that I wasn't looking in the right direction.

I muttered a reply, as quietly as I could. 'Thanks. Thank you.' And my skin prickled all over.

'Are you—' Liam stepped towards me, worried. His voice was loud in the shelves and packets of the shop.

I put my finger to my lips, flashed him a warning with my eyes. I shook my head and moved to the other side of the stand.

'Let's go,' I hissed at him. I looked round once before we went, just to check she wasn't watching, and then I walked, as fast as I could without attracting attention, until there was a park, until I could slip unnoticed into the peace of the trees.

'Are you alright?' Liam struggled to keep up.

'That was my mum.' Even saying it made me feel shaky.

'Who was?'

'There was a woman in the pharmacy, at the counter. Long dark hair and a cream-coloured jacket. Smart-looking.'

He shook his head, long hair in white dreadlocks on his shoulders and down his back. Liam didn't notice her – and that's what she would have been going for, she would have been trying to look completely unnoticeable, unrecognisable, as she went from pharmacy to pharmacy, shop to shop. I shouldn't have to know that's what she was doing, that her hair, make-up, clothes, were deliberate, but I've been dragged in with her enough times – I worked it out.

'You know how they always ask you all the questions in a pharmacy when you want painkillers? What else have you taken? What do you want it for?'

'Aye.' Liam laughed, stretched out a hand to me to calm me down. 'Thommo always says, "It's fae ma sair bawbag." And then they go bright red.'

It wouldn't be long after this that I realised Liam was every bit as annoying as his best friend. 'Well, they're asking for her – because of people like her. She needs a lot of pills to get the level of codeine that is her "zero", her normal, but they'll only sell you one small packet at a time. She goes all over the city.'

I sat down on a bench, planted my feet square on the floor, my elbows on my knees and my head in my hands. Across the park, children shouted, dogs chased each other.

'She works in the theatre, or at least she did. Looking after people on tour and sorting stuff out for them. She used to take me to all these shows when I was little.

'And we used to go backstage, walk all over the sets like we were in the plays. It was brilliant. But there were loads of things that went wrong.'

And I didn't tell Liam what went wrong. Our relationship never got deep enough, wide enough, for me to trust him with that. It is too hard, this bit, the fact of my family.

I remember the little marmalade kitten vividly. I remember his smell, his sound. The way his tiny needling claws, rhythmic like a sewing machine, punctured my skin. I remember minuscule jewels of red blood on my white arms, although it didn't hurt at all.

It was a warm day, the sunshine of the past, and my mum was crashing around. I knew then – I was almost fourteen – that I should stay out of her way, wait until later when she returned to normal. I knew – even though we didn't talk about it – that it would pass. My dad told me all the time that it was not my mum's fault. My mum pretended it wasn't happening.

She was jonesing. Feeling physical symptoms of her withdrawal. My mum needed a codeine fix.

The kitten was sitting on the kitchen work surface; I had been on my way to lift him down. My mum reached out an arm – I could see the sweat clinging to it like oil – and opened the kitchen window.

He was gone, the little ginger kitten, before I even registered that he'd moved. Straight through the kitchen window and into the front garden. From the front garden, it was a few inquisitive steps to the road, and he got there just as I ran and opened the front door.

Seeing the kitten, squashed, his flattened body stuck to the warm tarmac, was the worst moment of my life. His tiny lifeless claws protruded from his soft feet as if his reflexes had tried to save him.

It was ten years ago, but I've wondered every day since then if something similar didn't happen to my brother. If my mum was looking for drugs, preoccupied. If she was shaking or overheating or being sick somewhere, when he died. I don't remember the same things about William – how he smelt, how it felt to touch him – I was only six. One minute he was asleep in his carrycot next to my mum. The next minute, he was dead.

No one had heard him go. No one tried to stop him.

But I remember the same full stop, the same shock. The same slapped world of silence afterwards.

I put my face in the water, hold my breath, and I swim as fast as I can.

Chapter Sixteen

Jo

I'm making breakfast. It's simple, tortillas soaked in egg, a salsa of tomatoes, coriander and chilli. There is a green lime on the side, waiting to be squeezed over the finished dish.

At home, I would grab a piece of stale bread, jam it in the toaster and look for something miserable but convenient to put on it. At home, I would be cooking for one. It is still a bittersweet thought, sucking the lime, to remember that this is my home.

The differences between this and the home I built for myself are vast. This house is short and solid, mine is tall and thin. My house backs on to a bakery, an off-licence, a row of gentrified and charming shops where I know all the owners by name. The back window of Clachan looks on to the forest, that edge where the darkness starts, where the sunshine is sucked into the trees, absorbed by the mossy ground. In front of the forest, the patch of green garden is strangely still, static, and it only takes me moments to realise there are no birds. No rustle of shrubs or sudden flutter among the trees. The kitchen window is open and the world is silent but for the distant rumble of a car way out on the road.

I slow down my looking, fairly certain of what I will see if I concentrate, if I half-close my eyes and let the shapes loom from their camouflage.

There he is, on the ridge of the shed, a silhouette against the trees. He turns his head towards me as if he hears me thinking.

The sparrowhawk waits with death concealed in his lemon-yellow claws, prophesied in his bright gold eyes. He is magnificent, terrifying in his beauty.

All around the forest, birds and animals hold their breath.

The clatter of the letterbox makes me jump, the reminder that life goes on. The sparrowhawk judders into flight, scared off by the postman. I imagine robins and wrens breathing a sigh of relief, looking out from their hiding places and living to fight another day.

Tim and I have talked about the bills. We had to: he needed to make sure the law was followed to the letter; I couldn't afford to pay them anyway. Until probate is granted and Clachan is officially mine, Tim – and Rachel's estate – remain liable for the bills. I couldn't even protest that I should pay them, just in case Tim said yes.

The first money from my tenants comes in in three days: it will be just in the nick of time.

I walk towards the door, still holding a tea towel, wiping my hands. There, on a doormat that says 'Welcome' in faded black letters, is a stack of mail.

'Open it all,' Tim had said. 'And only send me anything you really have to. I'd rather you dealt with it from here on in.' He managed to say it in his robot voice, no feelings either way about the house his wife had given away, about the contents of her mail, her privacy.

I think about it as if Rachel is coming back, as if she will be annoyed that I opened her mail, that Tim said I could.

Rachel isn't coming back. My appetite for the breakfast slides into the grief vortex I carry inside me.

I flick through the mail. A guarantee renewal for the cooker hood. An electricity bill.

And a third envelope addressed to Rachel, handwriting that makes my legs weak, my mind spin.

Her very last letter from my mother.

◆ ◆ ◆

I remember how it felt to drown. The colour of it, the crushing brown that darkens as you thrash through it, white bubbles foaming into your eyes. The smell of it, the stench of the salt and the sea-mammal scents and the suffocating sting inside your senses.

The taste of it: vomit, acid, salt, and water, water, water. Dissolving you as you try to find upwards.

They say drowning is a peaceful way to die, that a euphoria comes from oxygen starvation. All I remember is the pain, the way I wished my lungs would split, would let the water into every cavity, stop it from stretching my body to bursting.

If there was a euphoria, maybe Tris sucked it out of me as he pushed the air in. Maybe he popped it as it was rising through the stem of my brain. Maybe Rachel snared it when she pulled me free of the broken jetty, kicked back to the surface.

I remember how it felt to drown, standing in the shaded hallway of Clachan, looking at the spindly spidery version of my mother's writing on her last letter to Rachel.

My fingers shake as I open the envelope, unstick the glue that she licked just yesterday or the day before. Days where Val is still alive and Rachel is not.

How real my mother feels to me suddenly. How pointed her absence.

I don't know why it hadn't occurred to me that Val wouldn't know Rachel had died. It is like a circle, on and on, she didn't know that Rosie died so Rachel had to write and tell her. Now she doesn't know that Rachel has died – but there it ends: I will not be that messenger.

I take a deep breath, prolonging the time before I read the letter, before Val enters this quiet hallway.

Dear Rachel

Thank you very much for coming to visit me. I can't tell you how good it was to see you as grown up. You haven't changed at all. I know people say that, but I would have recognised you anywhere: you look just the same.

It was wonderful to meet Ben, thank you for bringing him. I know that God is watching over you both as you move forward into this new part of your life.

There are no surprises here with my health. The nurses are doing a wonderful job and, as you know, death has no fear for me. When you get to this age, almost everyone you love has died. And I know that my saviour waits for me with open arms.

It is because of that, of the judgement I will receive when I sit at His feet, that I needed to tell you about your brother. I hope you have recovered from the shock – I can't imagine that was easy to hear. It was wrong to let what he did go unpunished.

Everything Tristan did on this Earth will have been forgiven in God's love. He is safe in God's arms – as we shall all be.

By the time you get this, you will have made the changes you needed to make and everything will be new and fresh. Starting over is one of God's greatest gifts. His capacity to forgive is infinite. Everyone you love will be happy to know you found the strength to rebuild your life. Ben is a good man and a wise one: listen to him and you will get through this.

I know that Jo will understand why you didn't tell her – and she will be so happy for you.

I imagine this will be my last letter to you. Everything takes much longer nowadays and the medication they have me on, although wonderful and effective, makes it hard to concentrate.

Good luck, dear Rachel, God speed. I hope you have the answers you needed. We all make mistakes.

Yours in Christ
Val

It was wrong to let what he did go unpunished.

I wish – for the thousandth time – that I'd never told her, that I'd never turned to my mother in my hour of need. And then, after decades of secrets, she decided to tell Rachel anyway.

Rachel died knowing that I'd lied to her. She died before we'd ever had a chance to talk, for her to hear my why, my how. My when.

All the things I've imagined over the last few days, all the solutions to why she wrote to my mother, how she lived this double – triple – life without feeling the need to tell me: that was just the shallows, that was the knee-deep edge of the water I walked in. Deep below the surface were the things I should

141

have told Rachel, the things I thought I would never have to share with her.

Last night's dream comes back to me like a wave. Last night, a sleep I shook off only two hours ago, I dreamed of Rachel for the first time since she died. Last night feels like a lifetime ago.

We were in an amusement park and Rachel dared me on to every ride.

'Come on the Big Wheel.' She walked backwards towards it, her hand outstretched.

A man by the ticket booth looked at both of us, smoked a cigarette with his forefinger and thumb around the butt of it, the ember glowing orange into his palm. 'That's Ben,' she said, and he narrowed one eye, stared at us. His face was stubbly and his mouth chapped and dry. He licked his top lip then drew heavily on the cigarette.

The buckets of the Big Wheel were ladders. Clean steel ladders that hung, vertical, in mid-air. Rachel stepped on to hers and I hung on to mine, my hands vibrating with fear.

'We have to say some prayers for Brother Davies,' she said, and laughed. Her head tipped back and her long red hair flew in my face. The machine creaked and whirred and started inching forwards, upwards. The music below was 80s pop from a speaker that rattled and failed against the open space.

The Wheel reached its west point and my ladder swung upside down. I clung to it, screaming, as the wheel turned and the world disappeared below me. Rain and sleet rushed against my face and I pressed my heels hard against the rungs. My toes slipped on the wet metal: there was no purchase, no way to stay on against the force of gravity.

Every time I looked at him, I saw Ben lick his lips, and every time he licked his lips his tongue flickered as he simmered and morphed, as his face cleared and he became Tristan Willoughby.

◆ ◆ ◆

I'm done. I left the letter on the bottom stair – more courtesy than it deserved – and I came outside.

I don't want to stay here, uncovering detail after detail of Rachel's life, layer after layer of the masks she wore. Finding out more and more about the ways in which we have hurt each other.

At some point today, I am going to call Tim, ask him questions. If I have to tell him about Ben, then so be it. None of this is my responsibility.

If I am to stay here, to use Rachel's gift in the way she intended, all of these things must be unravelled – before they unravel me.

I walk into the forest beside the house. I let the badger trails and the deer paths take me, making my footsteps as soft and quiet as I can. Sharing my space with a roe deer, a twitching red squirrel, a vivid striped chaffinch, would calm my soul. I go lightly: this is their forest and I am only visiting.

I follow the seashore until the woodland beside me gets thicker and more dense. The sea is on my right and I walk between the trees, away from Clachan.

Under last year's leaves is a soft layer of the year before that. I let my feet scuff the layers up, turn them over to the sunlight. The rot and the compost and the peat: the worms and the soft white maggots, the rolling out of an ecosystem, it is the peace we all fit into. I inhale deeply, rise on to my toes, hold the calm forest inside me.

Part of me wants to call her name, to see if I can magic her into walking beside me, and then we can talk. She can explain everything, as she meant to: starting with Ben, moving on to my mother, and ending – as it always does for me – with Tristan.

We can sit on a fallen log beside the path, side by side and staring at nothing, at everything – motionless so long that we start to see the movement in the branches, the twitching flits of tiny birds. Her voice will be soft, sweet, and she will think hard about her words, twisting her bottom lip with her top teeth as she does when she's thinking.

'I'm sorry, mate,' she'll say and then stop as a woodpecker rat-tat-tats bullets around the forest. 'I was going to tell you. And I have now, I sort of have. Most of all, I'm sorry about my brother. And everything it cost you.'

'I'm sorry I didn't tell you,' I'll say, and I'll be happy to finally talk about it with Rachel, to be free of the secret that has nailed me down for a lifetime.

'We all have secrets, don't we?' she'll say.

Our voices will be soft on the wind of this forest, the pine breeze. And then, as we sit longer, as our bums numb on the moss-covered log, as twigs and knots make our seats uncomfortable and something starts to niggle beneath the skin, I'll remember. I'll remember that Val hoped Rachel had found the answers she was looking for.

And that I don't know her questions.

Chapter Seventeen

MEG

I had a good day: my swim cleared my heart and made me stronger. When I got back to the cottage, I took stock of what I'd done so far in the dining room and – boosted by the smell of the sea on my arms and the ache in my legs that says my muscles work – I felt proud of myself. I'm proud of what I'm doing here and how well I'm doing it. Maybe – I allow myself this stretch of the imagination – I can extend this sense of order, of accomplishment, out into the other bits of my life. I can phone the credit card helplines, start making a payment plan. It would give me something to tell my dad, a way of trying to move on from his horror of debt. It is my debt, and mine alone, but I know it throws him back to the poverty of childhood, to not being sure where the next hot meal will come from.

The dining room is stunning. Finished except for the old leather books on the shelf. I'd put them in without organising them, just to have something to show Jo. I thought I could go back and organise the colour more later – they're not set in stone and I'd love them to graduate through the faded shades of orange and green. But I wanted to get it all done, completely finished, before she got back from her walk.

I thought she'd like it.

I thought it was beautiful.

Jo calls out as she comes in. *It's only me*, or something like that. And I hear the front door slam behind her.

'I'm in here.' And then I think better of that, of all my hard work. 'Hang on.' I put my foot behind the door to stop her from pushing it open. 'Wait one sec.'

I tidy the last of the cardboard boxes, push them back through the kitchen door, and pick up the few bits of paper that have drifted on to the floorboards. I didn't touch these boards: they were already an even dark oak, shiny from years of waxing and softened by the scraping of chairs, the dropping of food.

I turn the lamps on in the corners – although it's broad daylight – straighten the fold of the faded velvet curtain in its tie-back, and I'm ready.

'On three,' I say and stand in the centre of the room, ready to surprise her. 'One, two—'

She opens the door and steps in.

Seeing someone in the room in flip-flops and cut-off denims reinforces how formal it is, how elegant.

'Ta-da!' I open my arms wide, splay my fingers.

She opens her mouth to speak and then stops, freezes on the spot.

Jo begins with the joy of spring, eyes wide and her face lit in surprise. Then, as her eyes take in the wider picture, the colours and shades, the books along the back wall, a broad grin of summer, fresh and warming. The room looks so much bigger, so much more welcoming like this, but it is still – fundamentally – what it was, a melee of pieces, a soup of memories and antiques.

Jo's expression darkens, fails slightly as it moves to autumn. And then winter, the full crushing avalanche of hard cold, of ice snapping and screeching, of a spider's web of cracks forming underneath both of us.

'No.' She says it softly, says it as she walks across the room like a puppet. And then again, louder. 'No.'

'Jo, are you OK? Don't you like it?' I'm a bit hurt by her reaction – this room is gorgeous. 'I think it's fantastic.' I say it and then I realise it doesn't matter what I think.

Jo is clutching her stomach, her arms wrapped around herself as if to stem a stab wound. 'No,' she says it again and I can hear that she is crying. She keeps walking, a somnambulist; her eyes are wide open but totally expressionless.

She is frightening me.

As if to correct short-sightedness, Jo peers at a picture of Rachel. Rachel is young – maybe six or seven – backlit by a halo of gold light and grinning from ear to ear. There is a doll, soft-bodied and homemade, tucked into the crook of her arm. I thought it was beautiful. I thought it was so like the person she grew up to be.

'What's wrong, Jo?' I touch her arm and she jumps out of her skin, gasps.

She doubles over and I wonder if she's having a heart attack. She isn't speaking with words now, just making horrible wounded noises and struggling for breath.

Jo curls down on to her knees, her arms still wrapped across her, her head down.

'Shall I call an ambulance?' I ask. I don't know what to do. 'Do you think it's a heart attack?'

'I can't breathe,' she whispers. She makes a stuttering choke in her throat, waves her hand in front of her face in panic. 'Can't breathe.'

I am crouching beside her now, my arm around her shoulders, and I can feel the tension, the way her lungs are stuck – frozen. The rest of her body shudders with the effort of trying to inhale.

'Is it asthma, Jo? Do you have asthma?' I am pulling my phone from my pocket, hoping that this is one of the bits of the house that has a signal.

She takes a deep urgent breath and almost screams with the pain of it.

'I'm ringing an ambulance, Jo. Try not to panic.' I look at my phone – no signal. I stand and run through to the kitchen. Behind me, I can hear her gasping for breath.

Someone knocks on the front door. Knocks again. I shout 'Help!' before I have even got there. 'Call an ambulance!'

The person lets themselves in, opens the dining-room door.

'Dad, help her, please. Oh my God.'

My dad crouches down to Jo. 'What happened?' he asks me, calm and level. He tips Jo into a sitting position against the wall. Pushes her feet up towards her bum so her body makes a 'W' shape.

'Where is the pain?' He is speaking to her, but he is looking at me. 'What happened?' he asks again.

'She just fell on the floor. Stopped breathing.'

Dad moves himself directly in front of Jo, speaks right to her face. 'Are you choking?' he says, and her eyes flash wildly as she shakes her head. 'Do you have an existing condition that has caused this?' His voice is slow. Normally, I would be irritated by it, but in this room, against the terrifying background of Jo's laboured breath, my dad's voice is perfect, comforting.

'We haven't met before, Jo, but I was at Rachel's funeral. I'm Ben. Midge, I want you to go to the kitchen and get Jo a glass of water. And see if you can find a paper bag anywhere.'

Jo tries to breathe in, but there's something there, something stopping her. She flaps her hand, up and down, wild with panic. The noises she makes are terrible, the noises of someone dying.

'Dad, please. Help her.'

'Now, Megan.' Serious, his doctor's voice. 'The water. And a paper bag.'

I barrel through to the kitchen. On the chopping board is a bag of tomatoes – I recognise the brown paper from the local shop. I empty them on to the floor. 'I've got a bag,' I shout.

'Bring that first,' says his disembodied voice. 'Then go back for the water.'

My dad makes a fist around the neck of the bag, scrunches it into a circle inside his thumb and forefinger. 'Jo,' he says quietly, 'I am Rachel's friend Ben, and I am a doctor. You're having a panic attack. It's perfectly alright and it won't hurt you, but it can feel very serious. Very painful and frightening.'

Her head jerks up and down with the effort of trying to catch her breath.

'Try and blow into this bag.' He holds the back of her head in one hand, his palm cradled around the base of her skull, and he brings the bag up to her lips. 'Here, try and exhale. Don't worry about breathing in, just blow into the bag and your diaphragm will do the rest.'

His voice is so quiet, he could be talking to a baby bird.

'The water, sweetie?' He looks up at me and smiles, winks one eye. 'Jo's going to be fine.'

My hand is shaking as I hold the glass under the tap. I'm scared of chipping it against the spout, shattering it in the sink.

I take the water in and hand it to my dad. Jo is holding the bag herself now; it is slightly inflated, as if she has trapped a tiny ghost in it. Her cheeks are red and purple, the rest of her face a plastic beige. The sound of her breathing is horrible but it is an exchange, she is able to breathe in and out again.

Jo twists her chin up, turns her head to look back at the picture.

The little Rachel smiles, one tooth missing at the top left of her mouth and her tongue poking into the gap.

'No,' Jo says quietly. 'No.'

Chapter Eighteen

Jo

Rachel's eyes bore into me from the photograph. Just as on that night, it's the innocence of them, the all-round open trusting that makes me sick to my stomach with guilt, with responsibility.

These are stories I have never told, things I have barely spoken about at all to anyone, and yet I hear myself say them to the tiny Rachel, to the greasy doll on her lap. I know Ben can hear me, and Meg. But the first words of my secrets have started to spill, and I can't stop.

I shouldn't stop.

◆ ◆ ◆

'Stop being pathetic,' I said to myself as I walked through the dark forest, my bus ticket screwed up in my pocket, the whole horrible journey a distant warmth compared to this. 'This stuff only happens in fairy tales. It is not going to happen to me.'

And I kept on walking, braver than I'd ever been before, brave as someone who could travel this far alone, hitch a lift from an old lady. Every corner was a heart-stopping moment, every creak and twig-snap certain death. Twice I tripped on tree roots and my duffel bag of clothes hit me from behind as I fell.

'No,' I kept saying. 'I will not be afraid.' But I was terrified, the whole way.

When I got to the edge of the forest, the moon had risen over the bay. I gasped at the stripe of moon rolling out to meet me on the water, the jagged castle ruin a silhouette lit from behind.

The moonlight was bright enough to walk to the front door as if it were day. No ghosts, no monsters, just the house – its windows and door like a broad smile.

There was one light on in Clachan – the cleaner must have been here to get things ready for the Willoughbys – and when I lifted the little stone dog by the door, no key.

Someone was inside, someone had taken the key and put it in the back of the door, where it should be if anyone was home. My heart leaped and I confessed to myself, without words, how scared I had been in the dark. I wasn't ready to be alone.

'*Helloo.*' I called out my Willoughby greeting as I opened the front door, without a hint of embarrassment.

'*Ho-laah!*' Tristan.

The door to the sitting room opened, a slice of yellow light flooded the hallway, lit my feet.

'Wilding.'

Tristan had been sailing all summer. His hair was its usual dark, in this light as black as a crow, and his skin was dark with the weeks of work, taut from the hours of rigging and pulling in sails.

'Tristan Willoughby.' My voice held steady, didn't let me down. 'Of all the bars in all the world.' Walking past wolves and bears had made me bold.

'For fuck's sake, Wilding. Is that supposed to be *Casablanca*? Do you mean "Of all the gin joints, in all the towns, in all the world"?'

I'd had one chance to be cool and I'd blown it already. He was at university, living away from home, and I was – until a few weeks ago – still a sixth former, still wore school uniform. We could be as far away from home as we liked, but that chasm of an age gap wouldn't change.

'Are you hungry, Wilding?'

And I realised that I was so ravenous, so completely starving, that I'd even eat in front of Tristan.

'I'm so hungry.' I said it like a confession.

'Good,' he said and walked through to the kitchen. 'A picnic? In the moonlight?'

'Why are you here, Tris?' I stood behind him, still holding my duffel bag.

'I could ask you the same thing, Wilding.'

The fridge was full of food. The shopping must have been delivered for Rosie and Duncan's arrival tomorrow. Tristan took out a paper bag, laid it on his hand. He pulled out strip after strip of the strange wafer-thin ham with its petrol sheen – stuck to itself in translucent sheets – that Rosie had delivered from the deli. He sawed thick chunks of bread from a fresh loaf on the side, gestured to me to butter them.

'Do it so I can see my teeth marks in it,' he said, sounding just like his father. He stowed the sandwiches in Rosie's basket, the one we'd taken to the island that day. I wanted this to be the most perfect evening of all time. 'I'll get my costume on,' I said and left him in the kitchen, took my bag up to Rachel's room.

When I got back downstairs, I'd changed into my shorts and swimming costume, pulled a crisp white shirt of Rachel's over the top.

Tristan was in the hall, carrying the basket. He'd added a bottle of wine and two glasses to the midnight feast.

I could barely breathe.

'There was a postcard waiting for me, for us. From my mum.' He pointed to the table by the door, to the picture of a seascape, green cliffs and yellow sand, an absurdly small dun pony in the foreground looking towards the camera. 'My idiot sister broke her arm. Had to have pins put in it. They won't be here till at least the day after tomorrow – so they won't miss this.' He pointed to the wine bottle, its cork already loosened and pushed back in. A little was missing, already drunk, and the liquid lay at a slant across the shoulders of the bottle.

'But they are coming?' We had planned this all summer, Rachel and me: our last, glorious holiday before we left for uni. She was going to Durham, and I was going to catering college in a far less romantic two-bit town by the sea but with the dream of being a real chef at the end of it. It would be our last – golden – hurrah before we were pulled apart.

I had spent the whole summer dieting. I'd tried everything, starting from Easter: hi-fibre, farting my way through the exams; then the one where I had to substitute two miniature bowls of cereal for two of my meals each day; most recently the grapefruit diet – where I ate only grapefruit and, when the acid in my stomach got too much, sicked up a yellow paste that swirled and curled in the lav like a goldfish.

It had been an obsessive, weird time, but my belly was flat and my thighs more like Rachel's than they had ever been before.

'How does it feel to look like a normal person?' my mother had asked when she walked out of her bedroom and found me looking at myself in the mirror at the end of the landing. She thought gluttony was a sin – of course she did – and her church kept its women whippet-thin and obedient, even if their natural temperament or body type was nothing like.

I didn't answer her, but inside I was proud that she'd noticed, delighted that my mother thought I looked like everyone else – at last.

Going along to her church meetings over the last year had led to more babysitting jobs than I could actually do. These people had five, six, seven kids, who needed someone to say their prayers with them while the parents were out finding more friends for Jesus, more funds for the church.

The babysitting money had been a game-changer. I spent a significant chunk of it on my swimming costume: it had a racer back and was tight against my skin, like fish scales. I hadn't been in the sea since the accident and it made me feel confident again to have this swimsuit, to feel so sporty and sleek in it.

I unbuttoned my shorts on the beach, the sand like a sheet of pearls in the moonlight. I wriggled them off and folded them. Put my towel round my waist, excited that there was enough fabric left over to tie at the side – the year before I'd held it closed with my hand as I walked to the sea, my thighs chafing with sand where they rubbed against each other. This year I was a catwalk model.

Tristan threw his shirt behind him and ran for the surf. He howled at the moon and flung himself forward into the foam of the waves. He surfaced, whooped and yelled at the cold, then struck out from the shore, his lean arms cutting the water.

I walked to the edge, let the bubbles and foam collect around my toes. The sand pitted and puckered and I was calm. The wide band of moonlight ran right from the horizon to my feet, bathed my ankles in jewels and connected me to the stars.

Nothing this beautiful had ever happened to me before. We were new people, we were Hemingway characters, Waugh's company, Fitzgerald's ravishing protagonists. We were wild and free, unworldly.

◆ ◆ ◆

'Come on,' Tris yelled.

I think he was prepared for me to be scared; it made sense. And it was kind of him to try and jolly me through it.

'It's not that cold when you're in.'

I walked slowly, without looking back. I moved one pebble at a time, slow as a chess piece, from spiky shell or slippery rock into the next soft patch of sand – for my footing, to make sure I had my balance. There are boulders under the water at Clachan at high tide. Once the sea goes out, they are nothing but rock pools, full of trapped crabs and wafting anemones, but under the water they are hurdles, stumbling blocks, sharp traps for the incautious. I didn't want to trip on one, to feel my face getting nearer the water as I put my hands out to save myself. The thought made me shudder.

A wave slipped the water level up to my knees – just for a moment; it sagged back down immediately afterwards. I curled my toes deeper into the sand, looked down at my distorted feet, the black rocks under the water.

I sucked in a breath, shouldered my courage, and let my hands drop to my sides. One more decent step would take the water over my knees.

'No.' The word shook out of my mouth, stuttered into the moonlight. I stopped walking forward. 'No,' I said again, not to the sea, not to Tristan. I said it to – and for – me.

My *no* wasn't an apology or a confrontation. It wasn't an excuse or a shame or a skeleton in the cupboard. It was me, it was my decision, it was my considered opinion of the water, of what might come next.

'You OK?' Tristan bellowed from further out.

I read the words on his lips, rather than heard them. 'I am.' I gestured with a thumbs-up – and then a wave of my hand, a dismissal. 'I'm not coming in,' I said, even though I knew he couldn't hear me. My feet moved backwards through the clear water.

He waded through the shallows, flopped down next to me on the sand. 'I thought you might feel like that. It's why I splashed in – I thought there'd be less pressure on your own. You have that independent streak.' For all his bravado, all the outer bluster, Tristan could be piercingly kind, mostly when you least expected it.

I smiled at him, not anxious or defeated, and surprised at myself for that. 'It doesn't matter. I'm just not going in the water, that's all. No big deal.'

And Tristan accepted my decision without question. More than that, he accepted it as an adult choice – he didn't focus on my fear or make me a coward. He straightened his towel and lay on his back, sunbathing under a cold moon. 'It's not all that anyway,' he said. 'I've got sand shrimps down my pants.' And we lost ourselves in giggles.

I shook the sand out of my costume on to the antique rug in my room and stood with my towel in my hands, watching my own body in the full-length mirror. It was thrilling to have Tristan in the opposite bedroom, no one else in the house – to know that if he opened my door he would see the whole length of this new sleek me, however fast I rushed to cover myself.

My mother and I were not a naked family. We took every measure to protect our bodies from being seen by each other, by anyone – locked doors and long dressing gowns, covers pulled up or curtains drawn. My mother wore special underwear, distributed by the church: knee-length shorts and a T-shirt to make sure they all knew the lines that 'modest' lay between.

Here, I moved across to the window, stood against the low window sill level with my thighs and my entire fresh pink self obvious to anyone walking around the bay. As naked as a baby. Immodest.

I put on my wrap-around skirt and my new white holiday vest-top and went downstairs.

Tristan's eyes went straight to my chest, automatically and before he had a chance to check himself, to correct his mistake. It made him cough and clear his throat and I realised I should have worn a bra under the vest-top: I hadn't because all my bras were grey, washed out, and the straps would have showed – unsophisticated – on my shoulders.

For the first time in each other's company, we were embarrassed.

'Shall I make some hot food? Some supper?' Tristan was notoriously always hungry, and I wanted to change the subject. He hadn't meant to look. When I glanced down at my own chest, I realised my nipples – round and poky – were mapped out in fine detail by the herringbone weave of the vest, glaring at him like headlights. I wanted to apologise, and Tris – Tris looked at the floor as if he wanted it to swallow him.

I pulled Rosie's apron from the hook, wrapped the string twice around my waist and tied it at the front as I'd seen Rosie do with floured hands. It did the job: it covered my breasts, and Tristan was able to look up again.

My face was roasting, the humiliation hot enough to pull at the skin around my ears, tighten it across my cheeks. I needed to change the subject, move things back into that magical world we'd had on the beach. Before I'd failed that Willoughby test.

The shopping had been delivered – and put away – for the Willoughbys' holiday. I realised that if I married Tristan, if I became a Willoughby, I would live that way too. I would read my shopping list over the telephone and someone would make it find its way to the shelves of my kitchen.

I thought of my own mum, of the frozen pizza we shared before the fateful youth club, of peeling the polystyrene disc from the bottom of it and laughing about the first time we had one, when Mum cooked the polystyrene base too. Our last supper.

My mother would be appalled that I could cook supper after midnight, but Tris and I were at Clachan – we were playing by Willoughby rules.

The basket on the side was full of eggs. 'Have you ever had a soufflé?' I asked him.

And at last, I knew something he didn't, had an edge of finesse on him. I knew it was risky, and I'd only made it once, but these eggs would be the freshest and nicest: straight from village hens to Rosie's kitchen.

Tristan pulled another apron out of the drawer, set to as my commis, grating cheese and chopping nuts.

'Chop them very finely. The mix has to have something to climb up round the side of the ramekin, otherwise it'll sink.' I touched his finger as I showed him how to bring the knife down and he turned and looked at me.

It took my breath away. My mind was so hot and fogged I thought the eggs would never beat, that the egg white would sense the fever inside me and sink in shame. None of that happened.

We talked and laughed for the whole time it took to make and eat the food. We sat opposite each other in the dining room like a married couple.

'You're going to make the most amazing chef,' Tristan said, and I thought my heart couldn't be more full.

Tristan took another bottle of wine from Duncan's collection in the corner of the kitchen. It wasn't even that Duncan wouldn't notice: he genuinely wouldn't mind. 'As long as you enjoyed it, drank it with food,' Tristan said in his father's voice.

We took the wine into the sitting room after our supper. I'd made the cornflake tart that Tristan liked so much and our bellies were full, our bodies tired. We played cards until we were exhausted and I was the happiest I'd ever been. Our wine glasses left sticky circles on the dark oak table.

We went up to bed at the same time – almost three in the morning. Tristan used the bathroom first, coming out to the landing for just a moment to stare at the sea while he cleaned his teeth.

I mistook the sound of him opening the door for his being finished. This time the embarrassment was mine, the awkward intimacy of seeing Tris in his blue-and-white pyjamas, of how much they made him look like a little boy from a storybook.

'I'm sleeping in my parents' room,' he said. 'There's a bat in mine, got in through the window.'

I knew the protocol: leave the window propped wide open, the bat would make its own way out if left alone. The treasures of living in the forest.

When I came out of the bathroom, Tristan called my name. 'Jo?' through his closed door – a question.

I didn't answer at first, not sure what he meant. Was he checking it was me? Did he need something?

'Jo?'

'Yes.' Ambivalent.

'Come in here a sec.'

I was still wearing the vest – I had decided to only wear it as a pyjama top from now on. When I'd pulled on my flowery pyjama bottoms, I'd felt like an American film star: they were the only people who wore vests to bed instead of nighties or pyjama tops.

I stood at the end of Rosie and Duncan's bed, my arms folded over my chest and my heart thumping so loud he must have been able to hear it.

'I thought you might want a hug,' he said. 'In case the whole getting-back-in-the-sea thing is a bit much in the dark.'

I had spent years daydreaming about something I couldn't put my finger on. Now I knew it was this. This whispered shadow.

Tristan lifted one corner of the covers. 'Slide in,' he said.

And I did.

◆ ◆ ◆

Tris made a space for me in the crook of his arm and I lay against him in the moonlight. I remember that the top of the tiny mullioned window was open but that the room was thick with heat.

We were both trembling.

There was no preamble, no small talk or questions – Tristan leaned his face down and kissed me. His lips were dry with toothpaste but his tongue was wet and soft.

I kissed him back without a moment's hesitation, without the smallest thought of Rachel. I had left her on the landing, put her away as I turned the doorknob with my hot hand, my guilty fingers. I ran the same fingers, my flat palms, across Tristan's chest, mirroring – with far less experience than him – what he was doing with mine.

His hand worked down between the elastic of my pyjama bottoms and my skin, wriggled round my hip and hitched them towards my thighs.

I turned on to my side so that he could get them down.

And then, as suddenly as she'd vanished, Rachel came back. My wordless mantra of *what she doesn't know won't hurt her* became my mother – staring at me – saying *be sure your sins will find you out.*

I grabbed the side of my pyjama bottoms with my hand, moved my hips backwards a little to put space between us.

Tristan's face was pressed against mine and his words were warm on my neck when he spoke. 'It's OK, Jo. Shhh.' And his hand went back down on to my belly.

Rachel loomed back into the darkness of my imagination. 'My brother isn't a good person.'

'We can't do this, Tris. It's all wrong.'

He kissed me again and I tried not to kiss him back.

'I can't.' I reached a hand out of the bed, snapped on the little bedside lamp as if light could defuse this.

'You know what a prick-tease is, don't you?' Tristan's voice was bitter, but he kissed me after he spoke. It felt deliberate, as if he was giving me time to think about the words.

I closed my mouth but his tongue snaked between my lips and my body ached for him, ached to do the thing I'd dreamed of for so long. The thing I'd turned down from all the other boys I'd kissed, because none of them were him.

It was like drowning again.

He rolled me on to my back with one flat palm on my shoulder; the fingers of his other hand made me tingling and breathless.

'No,' I said. And this was the other kind of no. The one I was used to. The one that meant nothing because no one listened to it. Beside me, the photo of little-girl Rachel on Rosie's nightstand beamed that gap-toothed smile, radiated innocence from the halo rays around her.

Tristan manoeuvred himself, tipped his weight from one hip to the other and on to, into me, and I said it once more. I said it in that quiet voice that no one took any notice of, the one from my house, from school, from my mother's church. A useless, pointless, no – barely more than a whisper. 'No.'

I turned my head away from Rachel's big blue eyes and let the tears drop silently on to the sheet.

I said it again, mute. The word silent even in my own head. 'No.'

Chapter Nineteen

MEG

I'm in the kitchen. Dad has sent me to make coffee – Jo doesn't like tea – like the spare part in a film. In the dining room, next door, I can hear their quiet voices.

Dad speaks for a bit, low and calm. And then Jo says something – short, hard. More crying.

I've made the coffee stronger than normal, and put just the tiniest bit of sugar in it. Hopefully not enough to taste, but enough to pick her up a bit, stave off the shock – although I don't know who's more shocked, her or me. I didn't expect today to go like this.

When I go back in with the coffee, she's sitting in a dining-room chair, her head in her hands and her elbows resting on the edge of the table.

My dad is next to her – a respectful distance away, close enough to jump back in if anything goes wrong again.

I'm not sure what to say to her – it's a horrible story and horrible because it still happens all this time later, happens to people I know, to my friends. I know my dad will tell Jo that it wasn't her fault, that she didn't do anything wrong – that neither naivety nor changing your mind are crimes.

My dad is in charge, and I feel like an amateur, butting in.

'Do you want me to take the picture away?' I ask. Apart from making coffee, it seems like all I can do. 'Put it up in the attic?'

She looks up. Her eyes are puffy and pale, her skin blotched purple and pink, but she tries a half-smile. 'That's kind,' she says. 'But it's a beautiful picture – and it's her fault less than it's anyone's.'

Everything Jo says reiterates that she thinks it's her fault. That saying no wasn't enough to stop him. I have a million things to tell her, I want to pick her up and shake her free of it all, but this is not the time.

'Jo?' There is a part of this I keep coming back to, that I can't get out of my mind. 'What happened afterwards? The next day? How did you get home?'

She reaches out to the picture, gestures for me to pass it to her. I look at my dad for a *yes* or *no* and he nods the smallest *yes*.

Jo fiddles with the back of the picture, slides the catch off it and opens it. There, folded into a perfect square, is a piece of paper.

'I didn't want to throw it away,' she says. 'It felt like a curse to take it out of the house. It's the only page that anyone has ever torn out of the visitors' book. I used Duncan's razor blade, right into the spine of the book, so that no one would see it.'

She passes the folded square to me, without opening it.

The room is thick with the memory of her meltdown; her gasps and sobs are still in here. It makes me want to open the windows as wide as they will go.

'Open it.'

I unfold the page. It is like top-quality cartridge paper, you can see the tiny bulges of pulp on its surface. Just as Jo said, the left edge is a perfect straight line, razor-sharp.

Without looking at the page, Jo starts to speak.

Silly Rachel broke her arm
Swinging from the trees.

So Rosie and Duncan had to stay
In the Outer Hebrides.
We spent three days marooned here,
And nowhere else to go
But Clachan took good care of us,
Tris Willoughby and Jo.

She gives the sort of shallow laugh that means she doesn't mean it at all. 'Did I remember it right?'

'Word for word.'

She reaches out her hand for the page and I give it to her. She traces the little drawing, coloured in with pencils, that is clearly a cartoon of her and Tristan in the kitchen.

'He was almost twenty-two when he died. Just a couple of years after he wrote that. He wrapped his car – Rosie's car – round the war memorial in the middle of town.'

The room feels as if it might explode.

'But, in true Tristan style, that wasn't enough for him. He took three other young people with him. Rosie and Duncan never recovered. Part grief of losing their only son, part guilt for the deaths of his passengers. We lived in a very small town – the loss was profound.'

I can see my dad doing that thing where he thinks about speaking and chooses not to – he makes a weird shape with his mouth, like he's tied it up to keep it silent.

'I'm going to go and see what there is in the kitchen,' he says. 'And cancel the table I'd booked at the pub. I hope that's OK?'

Jo lets out a long breath when my dad leaves the room. He has taken the paper bag with him, and her water glass. I don't know whether he's refilling it or removing the evidence – my dad always has an agenda.

'Afterwards,' Jo says. 'Afterwards, he curled up beside me and went to sleep. And in the morning' – she looks awkward, fishing for the right words – 'we carried on as if we were a couple. For the whole three days until Rosie and Duncan and Rachel turned up. And by then I thought he was my boyfriend and that it was what I wanted. I mean, I did want it. I was obsessed with him.'

She gets out of her chair, walks across to the window and stares at the beach. It is clear that she's looking for ghosts out there – maybe she sees them.

'And then when they got here, once we'd all written on Rachel's plaster cast and heard all about their trip, he came into my room while Rachel was downstairs. "That was a bad idea really," he said. "And awkward too, if my family knew. Rachel would be mortified." And I said I agreed with him. That it was a bad idea and we shouldn't do it again. It was such a shock, it was like being stabbed.'

Beyond the window, the top corner of the castle ruins stick up from the island like a tooth, a fang.

'And you never told anyone? Not even Rachel?'

I imagine her working backwards through the memories. Her brow knits tight with the weight of it. 'I told my mum.'

'Weren't you worried that he'd do it to someone else?' As I say it, I want to swallow the words, choke down the fact that I've just made her responsible for his actions. I squeeze my nails into my palms in fury: angry at him, angry at me. 'I shouldn't have said that.'

'We were kids,' she says, like she didn't even hear me.

My skin prickles. They weren't kids. They were five or six years younger than I am. Old enough to vote, to drive. To have kids of their own.

'He was old enough to force you into something you didn't want to do.' I put it there, let it hang in the air above the table.

'But I did want to.' She looks right at me when she says it and I'm a bit shocked. A bit wrong-footed. 'I wanted to lose my virginity to my best friend's brother and I got into a situation that would make sure it happened. If he was old enough, I was too.'

Maybe this is generational. Maybe women her age accepted the whole *boys will be boys* thing, maybe the voices of the straight white men around them were so loud they drowned out anything else. I'm losing control of my words: I want to explain male privilege, consent, but it's all strangled – tied up inside the hundreds of things I want to tell her.

She puts one hand up towards me, palm flat. 'Meg, I know you're trying to help, but I've barely talked about it before. Not to my husbands. Not even – especially not – to Rachel. I can't do this – not right now.'

I go to apologise – not to climb off my high horse, but to tether it up and park it for a moment – but she's still speaking.

'Why am I talking about it now? What's the point of talking about it now?' she asks no one. 'What's the point, when Rachel's—' Her eyes fill with tears and she stops talking. Jo's fingers weave through her hair and I notice the wrinkles on her knuckles, how her skin seems more tightly drawn than it did before, her nails pale.

'It's part of the grieving process.' My dad comes back in from the kitchen, wiping his hands on a tea towel. 'My specialism was psychiatry, once upon a time, if you want my credentials. I left a long time ago. It's important to get all this stuff out, even if it doesn't seem relevant, important for the stages of grief.'

He smiles at her, in charge for now. He talks about food and space to think and the weather.

For once I'm glad he's there, glad he's so bossy.

Chapter Twenty

Jo

I'm stupefied that I told them – confused as to where it came from, poleaxed by why. But it fell out of my mouth and went into freefall once the first knots unravelled.

I look at him – at Ben. I look at his short grey hair, set off by brown eyes under blondish eyebrows. I look at his broad shoulders, his loose blue jacket, the bump where his nose had once been broken – a fault that makes him more interesting, more lived-in. Ben's face is, by anyone's standards, handsome. But he's more than that – he's large and kind and interested. He is gentle and refreshing and measured. He is so many things that Rachel and I would have put together if we were building our perfect man.

He is all of it.

And the first thing I think is – however churlish, however unreasonable – how dare you, Rachel. How dare you not be satisfied with your wonder-job and your beautiful house and your immaculate collection of clothes.

I take a step away from her in my mind, the cold of us not being friends any more catching the edges of my face.

How dare she not think that she had enough. Tim was dull, but he was her very specific choice. Her salary, her holidays. Even the cottage her parents left for her – an extra house in one of the most beautiful spots in the world.

She had me.

How was this whole world of excess, of privilege, not enough?

Suddenly, I don't know her any more. And what I do know, I resent with a fury that borders on rage.

Why was none of this enough for Rachel when it was so much more than I have ever had? When she even had my own mother standing up for her, taking her side and listening to her.

Tears sting like sharp claws behind my eyes.

Ben's hands were strong and calm on my shoulders. His voice is soft; cultured, yet kind.

I can see how he impressed my mother.

And I hate Rachel for it. Hate her for always having it all, for being so perfect, and then for that not being enough.

And now I can't listen to Meg talk about it, however hard she tries to help. All I can hear is the white-hot fury inside me, my indignant pulse thundering in my ears.

'I'm sorry,' I say to Ben. 'I really can't eat anything. I'm going to go upstairs if you don't mind.' I need to be away from him – from someone else in love with Rachel, from the memory of her irresistible charm.

And of course Ben says he doesn't mind, of course he asks all the right questions and says all the right things. Because Rachel always gets the best of everything.

Me – I started with nothing, and I went downhill from there.

Upstairs in my room is the Willoughbys' visitors' book. The record of everyone who ever stayed here – what they did and where they went, cartoons and signatures and funny little jokes that mean nothing to outsiders, and everything to those who were there. It tracks the births and deaths and marriages – the changing friends and new babies. My first marriage didn't last long enough to include holidays, so Evan never came here – but Terry has written in it many times.

I brought it up here this morning to start writing an entry for now, for Rachel's death and the end of the Willoughbys. For everything that will mean to Clachan.

I sit on my bed with the book across my knee. I know what I'm looking for. I sweep the pages back and the years go with them. I see our handwriting deteriorate – a life in reverse – from elegant grown-ups to the fat, round writing of our teenage hands, festooned with love hearts and extravagant circles on the letter *i* and for full stops.

I go past the barely visible razor-edge of the missing page. Past the guilt I felt when he died and his parents would have given anything for one more moment of him, one new piece of Tristan, and all the time his silly poem, his sketches of the two of us, were hidden in the back of a photo frame beside their bed. Beside our bed.

Somewhere between the two sets of handwriting, between then and now, is an entry with no drawings, no colour. It is one of two short, sad entries written the same way – twelve years apart. The last of the Willoughbys.

◆ ◆ ◆

I had no one else to ring but Rachel.

'I'll only be two hundred miles away,' she'd said when she left for university, three months before. 'And I'm taking my mum's car for the first term, until I find somewhere proper to live.' The Willoughbys being the Willoughbys had meant that a family friend was putting her up for the start of college, in an annexe attached to their house, so that she didn't have to cram into a damp halls building with people she didn't know and quite possibly wouldn't like. It meant Rachel wasn't eating dehydrated food from plastic pots, and walking through grubby streets and alleys at all times of the night. But it also meant she had a phone. And I called her, when there was no one else who could help me.

I didn't tell her what had happened. We'd stopped telling each other the truth by then: Rachel didn't tell me how amazing college was, how her brain and her social life were growing, and I didn't tell her the reason why I was suddenly too timid to go to catering college after all, too syruped in failure to spread my wings.

I didn't tell her anything – except that I had to have an operation and that I wouldn't be allowed to go home by myself. I imagine she waited for me to tell her and, when I didn't, she assumed I didn't want to talk about it. It is a feature of the British upper classes that they rarely talk about their health, that they consider doing so extremely gauche.

Rachel wasn't my first port of call. I told my mother first. I asked for her help.

We'd been teetering towards a relationship again, Val and I, just before I realised I was pregnant. She wasn't ready to have me home, or I wasn't ready to come back – I forget which – so I'd been living in a bedsit for a couple of months. It was a grotty bedroom in a shared house and the landlord never cleaned the bathroom – it wasn't anywhere anyone would choose to be, but it was warm and dry and, mostly, private.

I had been to see the doctor and taken a pregnancy test. A week later, I went back for the results – praying to be wrong, to have a tumour or some kind of life-shattering cancer. Anything but be pregnant.

'Congratulations,' he said, knowing full well from our conversation last week that I wanted an abortion. 'You're going to have a baby.' He sat back in the chair, laced his fingers through each other across his taut pot belly. He looked further on than I was.

'I can't.' I was trying to make myself sound brave. 'I have to have an abortion.'

The doctor was everything I thought he'd be, everything I feared. Abortion had only been legal for thirteen years: it was clumsy and surgical and, hardest of all, judged brutally – especially by those who'd never need one.

'No one will know, will they?' I asked him.

'Someone will have to,' he said. 'This is a serious procedure – you're four months gone. You'll need someone with you afterwards.'

I was scared – beyond scared, I was terrified. I had never been in hospital in my life, let alone had a general anaesthetic, although a girl in my primary school class had died of one in the dentist's chair.

The doctor was emphatic that I couldn't be alone the night I came out of hospital.

'I don't live alone,' I said. 'I'm in a shared house.'

He looked down at my notes and back up at me. 'You need to be with someone.' He raised his eyebrows. 'What about baby's father?'

I wanted to tell him that there was no such person as 'baby', that there never would be, never could be. 'He's not—' I paused. I knew what Tristan was not: interested; available; responsible. None of those were things I could tell the family doctor.

The GP shook his head. 'Your mother?'

I suppose it was the fact that he'd met her, knew her, and still thought that she'd step up and help me that made me go home and ask. That, and utter desperation.

◆ ◆ ◆

My mum had cooked for the two of us. Meat stew and dumplings. It was a gesture – my favourite dinner when I was young. It tasted of the time before we stopped loving each other.

'I need your help, Mummy.'

She put down her knife and fork. 'I'm a bit short at the moment, I'm afraid,' she said – as if being broke was the worst that could happen.

On my plate, gravy thickened as it cooled, slid translucent from a slice of orange carrot. The puckered pock marks of the dumpling stared at me like a thousand tiny watchful eyes.

Whether it was suspicion or intuition, witchcraft or the pull of our genes, I didn't have to tell her.

The blood drained from her face until she was the same colour as the dumplings. Her fingers began to shake and the cutlery ting-ting-tinged against the edge of her plate. Her lips moved in prayer, rapid and possessed; the end of her tongue darted backwards and forwards like the serpent himself.

She had waited for this moment every day since I started my periods, dreaded it and fantasised about it – prayed over it and been haunted by it.

My mother began to stutter out half-words like bullets. Syllables popped out of her mouth and burst, unable to manage in the open air.

'Ho—'

'Th—'

'When?'

'Bu—'

And then, because it was all that really mattered: 'Is he going to marry you?'

I shook my head. I couldn't look at her. She'd been right – every outfit she'd hated, every magazine she'd thrown away, every friend she'd said was trashy – she'd been right about all of it. Because here I was, full of alien, growing a baby I couldn't want, growing a baby made of Rachel's brother.

'Get on your knees,' my mother said. She pushed her chair back and slithered to a praying position, all one movement, graceful.

I lumbered backwards, knocked my chair back against the wallpaper, folded forward on to my knees with my head on the floor.

'Heavenly Father,' she began, and I wondered what she would thank Him for today.

The breath squeezed out of me and for the first time I was fully conscious of the mass inside, pushing my organs out of place. I didn't dare lift my head.

On the other side of the table, her prayer began. She thanked Him for the food, for the weather, and for bringing me back to her on my knees.

I curled my head up, looked through the table legs at her face. Her eyes were closed and her hands were held out to her sides, palms upwards, holding hands with angels only she could see. There was an expression on her face that I struggled to translate, despite having her words as signposts.

It was vindication. She was acquitted.

Her suspicions had been right-and-proper parenting. She had known I'd turn out like this – heap shame upon our house – and now I had.

The thing she'd waited for would arrive in five months' time.

I pressed my forehead against the floor and listened to the litany. I had no choice.

I concentrated on breathing in and out, only aware of the impediment inside me, and tried to blot out my mother's wailings.

And then it changed.

175

Val went back to the early part of her prayers. She returned to the gratitude, to thanking God for the blessing of this baby.

I uncurled from the floor, raising my head and opening my mouth in horror.

God had spoken to her, it transpired, in this, her hour of direst need. He had reminded her of the missionary he had sent to her house the night before. A young man desperate to marry and – most conveniently – to return to his own country, far across the sea, with his bride.

My mother had been rescued from the desert – regardless of what that young man might have thought about marrying a woman he didn't love, about raising another man's child – and she was frantic with relief. She would pack me off to America with a missionary and his cuckoo baby, and soon God would bless us with countless other babies to take the sting out of this one.

'I'm not having it, Mum,' I said. 'I'm having an abortion on Thursday.'

That was how Val and I came to separate. There was more: insults were hurled, and names called. That was the day the curses and the accusations and the violence of words hurt so much more than any other part of the abortion – we didn't have the compassion to use the word *termination* in the 80s, to downgrade the shame and the blame.

Val's hands rained down on my back as I lay, curled over a mass of cells I hadn't ever intended to protect. Her palms were open and ineffective – unless the only reason for hitting me was to stop herself from exploding, from bursting into flames on the floor next to the dining-room table.

I put up with it until my mind steadied, until my brain clicked back into place and started working.

She didn't resist as I got up and unfolded myself from her life.

I stopped at a call box and I rang Rachel's landlady: we arranged that I would ring back at 7 p.m. when Rachel was home, when Rachel would calmly and efficiently write down the address of the hospital, the approximate time she would need to collect me.

'It's fine,' Rachel said. 'I'll spend the day with my mum and you ring me when you think they're letting you out. We'll go straight to Clachan, be on our own. For as long as it takes.'

Rachel was as good as her word. I stayed in the hospital for one night after the abortion, then she was waiting in the car park – bags packed with treats and flowers – as I blinked my way out into the daylight on the Friday. We drove straight here and she never asked me what the operation was.

'Women's troubles' covered it. Tale as old as time.

◆　◆　◆

The entry is brief. Rachel's handwriting in black and white.

> *Rachel and her darling Joanna were here from Friday to Wednesday. We didn't swim in the sea or walk to the pub. We spent four precious days sat by the fire, together.*
>
> *Clachan, as ever, took care of us.*

And we'd both signed it underneath: hers, the flourish of her name with a pointed two-triangle star on top of the L; mine, small and quiet, an apology in letter form.

I leave my fingers splayed out across the page: it's not the first time I've seen the sad little entry since then. It sticks out for being quiet, for having no illustrations in the pages of colour and cartoons and landscapes and doodles.

And so it's easy to find the next black and white page. The one Rachel wrote when I drove her here. When Tim rang me to tell me the news and to say that he'd never seen her so sad. When Rachel rang me a few days after it had happened, when it was all done, and asked me to bring her here.

'I didn't think it would go like this,' she said, still pale and quiet from the surgical process that had been necessary to remove the last of her longed-for foetus. 'Usually, I set my sights on something and it happens.'

I was driving but I sensed her head turn, felt her gaze on me.

'I've always got everything I've wanted. And that makes this feel like a bit of a punishment – for taking things for granted.' She cleared her throat, tried to jolly up her voice, Willoughby-style. 'But I do know it's only a first attempt, that there'll be loads more opportunities and we can try again.'

I had known this visitors' book entry was similar: I hadn't realised it was the same – that Rachel reproduced her words exactly. That she had always known what my operation was but, at the same time, had known I didn't want her to ask, had trusted me to be too smart to sleep with her brother.

That one miscarriage turned out to be Rachel's only pregnancy. And the space where children might have been, where we both had imagined them in our lives, became a silence that neither of us visited. We talked about everything – or so I believed – except children.

Now I realise we didn't talk about mothers either.

Rachel and her darling Joanna were here from Friday to Wednesday. We didn't swim in the sea or walk to the pub. We spent four precious days sat by the fire, together.

Clachan, as ever, took care of us.

I look around this room, at the same old furniture, the metal handle on the window cockeyed with age, at the sky view with the barest glimpse of sand beneath it. It has always been here for me, this place. An island to drag myself on to – out of the water and safe from the sharks.

It is as close as I have ever had to a family home.

I close the book, pull up my big girl pants, and go downstairs.

Meg is in the dining room, rearranging the books. They start at green, the gold lettering highlighted by the sun, and move through pale creams and peaches. The orange and red are still in a stack by her feet, as if she is preparing the sunset.

I chew my thoughts before I speak. I don't want to sound as if I'm accusing her father of anything: it's certainly none of her business and she is as unwilling a participant in this as I am, but only Ben, now, knows what was said when Rachel went to see my mother. Only Ben heard what my mother needed to tell her.

In the middle of my panic attack, as I relived the experience of my lungs filling with water, of losing consciousness under the crushing pressure, I realised something. I realised that the way I feel about death has changed.

Wherever Rachel is, I will be there too eventually. She has made a path for me, just as she always did, and whether that turns out to be the road to Valhalla or a still and silent blackness, or even – how we'll laugh – my mother's celestial kingdom, Rachel is there and one day I will follow.

We will be together again.

And I don't want to be angry with her when that happens. I have to know her truth to understand mine.

Ben has slipped away home, agile, refined. No need for an awkward farewell.

'I need your dad's number, Meg. I have to talk to him.'

Chapter Twenty-one

When we first had mobile phones, I loved talking on the move. I would ring Rachel from the car, on a walk, in the gym. She would call me from the shops, the swimming pool changing rooms, the executive loos at work.

Over time, we morphed to texts, to the pith and wit of brevity – tiny messages that made the most of anything funny we had to say. My phone files only go back so far, but I've read and reread her messages to me – wishing she was beside me so that we could dissolve laughing at the past, at the people we've glanced by, who've crossed our paths.

The text habit stuck, and I still find text messages so much easier than phone calls. I enjoy being able to reply – sharp and to the point – coming away from a conversation without the *esprit d'escalier* of all the things I could have said given a bit longer to think.

Once, many moons ago, I ended a text argument with Terry by writing 'Fin' as a one-word text. I'd forwarded every twist of the row to Rachel and, after my triumphant and emphatic sign-off, she messaged me back.

You know he won't get that, don't you? You know he's just scratching his balding head and wondering where in the string of texts it mentions fish.

Everything I do lacks that debrief. Nothing is properly funny any more.

I texted Ben, rather than calling him, when Meg gave me the number. And as I did it, I imagined Rachel's eyes behind her dark glasses, her mouth twitching with laughter as she sent a rapid-fire reply – always sharp, always the best kind of imperious.

My text gave nothing away. A request to meet, to talk. I didn't say whether it was about him or me, but he's an intelligent man; he'll have an idea.

His reply took a few hours – that could have been the satellites over Clachan, or it could be that Ben had better things to do.

The Burrell Collection. I hold a lot of meetings there. Does that work for you?

It did and we arranged a date and time. Meg was pleased I was driving to Glasgow: it would work for both of us – I'd give her a lift to see the people she needed to catch up with, and she'd give me directions to the museum.

It felt strange to leave Clachan this morning – to lock the door after what seems like months but is only three weeks in the house. I was looking forward to the busy anonymity of a city.

Ben is already in the café when I arrive: even from our single meeting I know there is no chance he would let me be first. His greeting is polite, non-committal, and he gets up to fetch me coffee and a cake, waves away my offer of money.

'I want to talk to you about Rachel,' I say.

His face is unreadable. 'I realise that,' he says, and his blankness, his lack of reaction, makes it hard to navigate a response.

Around us, people meet one another for coffee, a woman at the next table sets up a laptop and starts to type, schoolchildren mill noisily into the foyer.

'Have you been here before?' he says.

'I've not actually been to Glasgow at all.' It seems crass to tell him I've never visited his home city, that I've ignored it in favour of the flashy tourist spots of Edinburgh.

'We like it like that,' he says, and almost-smiles. 'We have some of the finest art collections in the world, and you don't have to look over other people's heads to see the pictures.'

I had to cobble together a city outfit this morning, from things that have been folded in the drawers since I arrived. I am wearing earrings, make-up, a return to the things I used to take for granted. It is hard not to see them as an imposition and yet I wasn't ready to go out without them. I touch my right ear, check the silver butterfly is still tight on my earring.

'When you've finished your coffee, do you want to look at some of the collection?' he asks.

It is oddly intimate, the sort of thing you might do on a date, but I know – and so does he – that it will make conversation easier, less intense.

'I'd like that very much.'

The cake is flecked with raisins and flashes of carrot: it is soft and moreish and I concentrate on that rather than being in a strange city with Rachel's boyfriend while I know the landscape of her husband's life so well I can imagine exactly where he is right now. I wonder if I can imagine what Tim is thinking: is it the same as me, where every taste and smell, every sight and sound, somehow translates into loss and is deadened? It is as if there are corners to each experience that we can only wriggle into if we explore them with that person, corners that will stay dead and unexplored now.

Ben has the same cake. He eats it with a spoon, as if it is pudding. 'Good, isn't it?' he says.

The real subject rolls and boils beneath the table, threatens to upend it, but we sit and smile politely, sip at coffee, wipe cake from our mouths. He looks far calmer than I feel but then there is something of Rachel in him – with him. That impenetrable confidence, the surety.

The gallery is vast. The outside is an ornate red brick with a huge wing of glass. The inside has cool polished stone floors. 'It's not all Scottish,' he says. 'There's Monet and Bruegel and Gauguin, but we'll head to the Glasgow Boys – there's something you might like.' He stands up, takes a messenger bag from the back of his chair and puts it over his shoulder, across his chest. 'We can talk on the way.'

We start through the galleries, for all the world like everyone else in this building – friends or colleagues, a couple. The connections between us are both fragile and laden.

We are walking past gallery entrances, down the opulent spine of the building. Our chatter is polite, weather and road works and light, surface-level only, politics.

We slow down: Ben is scanning the frames, looking for the picture he wants to show me.

And then the little bell that was ringing in my mind brings me back to what I'm doing here, what I'm supposed to be thinking about. 'How did you meet Rachel?' I ask. I don't ask if he brought her here; it is quite obvious that he did. I look ahead of me, down the gallery, to see if I can catch a glimpse of her red hair, see an echo of her from another time.

'We met in Scotland.' He doesn't look at me when he says it.

I resist the urge to say, 'It's a big country.' We both know his answer is deliberately obfuscating.

'You went to see my mother,' I say instead. 'I'd like to hear about that.'

He stops in front of a picture. 'Here,' he says, and if he heard me, he shows no sign of it. 'This is what I wanted to show you. It's painted by Flora Macdonald Reid.'

The picture is smaller than most in the room, and mounted in a gilt frame. The colours are bright and instantly engaging. Lime-green leaves and a rich liquorice black, and everywhere gold, amber, copper, all the shades of sunshine. It is a view from one side of a bay, looking out at an island – just beyond detail – through the edge of a forest and across a flaxen beach. The wet black rocks below the surface and the effect of the rippling clear water over them is exactly how I see my toes when I walk through the edge of the sea at Clachan.

'Is it Clachan?' I ask. 'Is it painted from the house?' I move closer to the picture to see how the brush strokes become the stems of leaves, how dots and puffs and lines become integral parts of the rocks and the sea, how it burns with light as if the canvas is pinpricked and lit from behind. 'It's so beautiful.'

'I showed it to Rachel last time we were here,' he says. 'Just after I'd been to Clachan for the first time.'

I want to ask him how long he's been going there, to try and tease out clues before I ask the big question. But he has more to say.

'It's painted down the coast a bit. At Kirkcudbright.' He spaces the syllables out, pronounces it correctly as mostly only the Scots do. Ker-coo-bree. And I think of the first time we went there from Clachan, of Rachel howling with laughter at my trying to say it.

Ben continues. 'There was an artists' community there – the Glasgow Boys. They're very famous – the women among them were just as talented but less renowned.'

'Plus ça change,' I say.

Again, he goes on as if I'm inaudible, as if he is alone with his memories of Rachel, of telling her about this picture. 'It's not the same wee island you see from Clachan, but it could be – bar the castle.'

He stands back and stares at the picture. 'She's been my favourite painter forever. I wanted to call Meggie *Flora* but Wendy didn't like it.'

'It's a treasure.'

He nods. He sits down on one of the long benches in the centre of the gallery, right opposite the picture.

I sit next to him. From here, the painting is like looking through a window in the cottage. The light, the movement of the sea, the soft wind nudging clouds across the blue sky: it is all there.

'Why did you go and see my mother?'

He doesn't hesitate. 'I went with Rachel. To support her.'

None of my questions answered.

The room is large, it has the potential to echo, for words to bounce from the glass roof light, against the pictures, to the marble floor. I drop my voice. 'What exactly is your relationship with Rachel? And how long has it been going on? I need to know, Ben.'

For a moment, there is no sound at all in the great hall. As if every punter, every painting, is holding their breath and waiting for his reply. He doesn't move, just stares somewhere between the middle distance and the picture.

In my head, I start to count. I will give him to ten. Then I will ask again.

On eight, he speaks. 'My relationship with Rachel is private.'

'But you went to see my mother.' I whine the *my* like a demand.

'I know how this must feel and I apologise for any pain it causes – and I acknowledge that pain must be considerable. But, again, it was Rachel's wish to go and see your mother.'

He crosses his legs and I think how expensive his leather trainers look, how well matched he and Rachel are. Were.

I can see how the two of them would work in this gallery: surrounded by the beauty, the priceless paintings, the clever people who come to look at them.

'I know you're in an awful position, Jo. Your grief must be unbearable.' He stops there – finishes before he makes me some kind of offer, compromises on what he's willing to share, to explain.

The silence feels wrong, but the pause grows and stretches and swells and becomes everything.

'I'm in the dark here.' It's exactly where I am – untethered and floating, completely unable to get any purchase, to find my feet. 'Everything I thought I knew was wrong. The person I've been closest to my whole life had secrets from me.'

He's listening. The walls are listening. The silence is almost alive around us. Nothing and no one moves.

'And the worst of all of it – what she does with you is her own business – the worst of all of it is visiting my mum.' I can't speak about her in the past tense; however hard I try, Rachel flings herself back to the present. I cannot let her go.

He leans forward, his elbows on his thighs, his hands in front of him. 'Rachel needed me to go with her, and I went,' he says.

It annoys me, him telling me that like he knew more of her than I did. But I hold my breath, suck down the knee-jerk reaction.

Facts are facts – Ben knew more of her than I did.

'The only thing I can suggest is that you talk to Tim. Start with him. And then, I don't know. See how you feel – whether you want to talk to your mother about it.'

It's the last thing I expect him to say. 'Tim knows?'

The filter comes down again. It starts with his eyebrows, a settling, relaxing. Then his eyes – still bright – stop moving, and it becomes impossible to see where his gaze is actually focused. His mouth is non-committal, the line of the Cupid's bow impassive, his bottom lip full, wide.

He picks up his bag and it's clear that he's leaving; he's done here, and I can continue my day, enjoy the gallery.

'Why did you agree to meet me, Ben? If you weren't going to tell me anything.'

'I have told you what I can,' he says. 'But that doesn't include what you wanted to hear. And I am, genuinely, sorry about that – but it's not my place.' He does up one button across the chest of his jacket. 'Thank you for putting up with Meg, and for taking care of her. She obviously – genuinely – enjoys your company very much.' He raises one hand in a half-wave as he walks away.

I sit quietly with the paintings for a while. A tour party comes through, led by a slender woman with grey-brown hair. She stops by Flora's painting and talks about the artist, mentions – as Ben did – the imbalance of the men and the women. She talks about the coastline, describes a view I see every day. I look at her audience – city dwellers, tourists, students – people for whom Clachan and all its privileges are something you find once or twice a year on holiday, if you're lucky.

My back starts to ache from sitting upright on the leather bench. I went to a yoga class every week when I lived in the bustle of civilisation. My life here is more about strolling and cooking, eating and reading. My core strength has suffered as a result. I think about doing yoga on the beach in the mornings, downward dogs with Meg beside me, parallel warrior poses on the sand. It's my imaginary picture of Clachan, my made-up image – as two-dimensional and fictitious as a painting.

There is a huge ceramic collection at the heart of the gallery. Normally I'd be fascinated by the opportunity to see the history, other people's skills and habits, but I'm hot and uncomfortable. My skin prickles with the stress of it.

I go back out through the huge vaulted hallway and into the fresh air. There is a fine drizzle today – as if sunshine is something magical that only exists at Clachan, an enchantment that breaks if I try to leave. I breathe the wet air deep into my lungs.

I drive into the city suburbs, park on a side street, and get out to explore the artisan shops and the little cafés. This isn't dissimilar to my own real world back in England: the bakeries and florists' shops nestled among long, dark shops selling phone cards and hookah pipes.

There is a chai house with a plastic menu stuck in the window, a short, slightly dog-eared list of my favourite foods. Inside, the tables are clean Formica, the chairs stuck down like a fast-food restaurant. I order and choose a booth near the back, somewhere quiet to think.

'Start with Tim' is easier said than done. I've known Tim for well over twenty years. I first heard about him on a weekend in London that Rachel and I had been planning for months.

We still shared a hotel room in those days – twin beds and one bathroom. It wasn't the money – Rachel was earning very well by then, even if I wasn't, and she loved to share her absurd salary, to spend it on things we enjoyed. We were about ten years older than Meg is now, and we thought we were decrepit; the twin beds and talking in the dark made us feel like girls again.

Our trips always started with Champagne, breakfast, lunch or dinner. It was Rachel's way of spoiling me, of kicking the whole trip off with a level of luxury we'd do our best to keep up for the whole time we were together.

Afterwards, I'd go back to my studies, to the degree I should have done at eighteen, and when that was all done, to paying the mortgage that would have been so much smaller if I'd done it in order, at the right time – like Rachel had. I'd shelved my dream of being a chef: that belonged to youth, to carefree times. In the end,

I took Business and Hospitality Management at university because I needed a proper job at the end of the course, one that paid the bills. I told myself that one day I'd be in a professional kitchen, that I could move sideways from management to cheffing. Instead, I moved into a tedious in-and-out export business. 'It pays the bills,' I told Rachel, and kept on trying to convince myself.

'Tim works in the same building as me, but a floor above.' She popped the cork and I held the two white mugs from the coffee table underneath the foam. 'Where all the really clever people are. And he knows Nick, who I play squash with.'

And I nodded enthusiastically, well versed in all the city traders, all their hobbies, how they interacted with Rachel. 'Cheers,' I said, eager to get going, to put real life behind me for forty-eight hours.

'We were in the lift, coming back up from the squash courts, and I was a total mess – hair everywhere, sweating like a pig, and Nick introduced us.' We'd taken the first sips and Rachel topped up the mugs, urging me to drink up. 'We can get another one – or cocktails. Let's do cocktails – have you ever had a French 75?' It was the 90s – I would have been the only person she knew who hadn't.

'He emailed Nick, Tim did, to say he fancied me. I mean, really, like as if we were still at school. My mate fancies you, that kind of thing.'

And she told me how they met up, where they went for dinner, how exciting and suave it had all been.

'He's a bit older than us. And it really showed. He knows stuff.'

I raised my eyebrows and poked her in the side with my finger.

'Not that sort of stuff.' She drained the mug. 'Stuff about wine, food. He's been everywhere.'

Rachel had been everywhere too – her travels after university were a list of postcards and impossibilities to me, of wishing I could be as brave.

'Anyway, I want you to meet him. This weekend. Would you mind? He wants to take us out for dinner.'

I remember minding awfully, but feeling babyish about it so not saying anything.

Tim, it transpired, had booked us a restaurant beyond our wildest dreams, one run by the newest in a group of chefs-cum-celebrities, people tying in books and television with cooking and fine dining.

Tim turned out to be nice enough; and he did, just as Rachel said, know lots of things about lots of things. But where she found it awe-inspiring, I found it a bit patronising – even dull.

Back in our twin beds that night, quite drunk and very happy, we were back to ourselves – by ourselves – again, chatting in the dark, words bouncing off the ceiling.

'You would tell me if you thought he was boring, wouldn't you?' she asked.

'Of course I would,' I said. Although I never did.

As he got older, Tim added controlling to the boring. Once they'd been married for a few years, after the miscarriage, he always offered to book ahead for our meals, chose where we went – controlled how much Rachel spent.

And he always made it my fault: *Make sure you behave, Joanna*, he'd say whenever he dropped Rachel off at mine or at the station if we were meeting up to go away together. 'Don't get wasted before lunchtime.' And he'd make a joke of it, pretend he didn't really mean it.

But I knew full well Tim would never have said it if he didn't really mean it – he didn't waste words, wasn't generous even with them.

We've got on better since Rachel died, in the few interactions we've had – all about bills or contracts or direct debits.

We're not competing for Rachel any more, that's all, and he has no need to show me, constantly, how much more grown up he is, how much more mature.

The young girl behind the café counter brings out my order. It's the kind of food I don't know how to cook, and that always tastes better somewhere like this, somewhere desi. There is a squat bronze pot of chickpea curry, a huge yellow omelette that has probably been deep-fried, and flaking golden breads to eat it with. The chai comes in a paper cup, steaming and spicy, a green cardamom pod floating on the surface.

Tim wouldn't eat this food. He'd pay ten, twenty times as much to eat something slightly less good in a restaurant with fancier lights and cleaner tables, to be served by waiters who nod and bow and call him 'sir'. We're very different people, he and I, neither of us wrong, neither of us bothering anyone else with our lifestyle choices, but very different people.

I picture Rachel as if she were sitting opposite me, straddling the two worlds – his and mine – with grace, being able to bend and blend so that she fitted in anywhere. *The common touch*, her mother used to call it. That gift of being absolutely comfortable with anyone.

'You can't just stagnate,' she'd say. 'You only ever regret the things you don't do. Never the things you do. And you should do one thing every day that scares you.'

And then I'd say that that was bollocks, and that things that scare you often lead to your death – or at the very least, ex-communication from all of those who love you – and she'd raise her glass at me, or her chai cup or whatever she was holding, and those dancing brown eyes would dare me, would push me on.

So I text Tim. I'm going to ask him.

Chapter Twenty-two

Meg

It's so nice to be back in Glasgow. I love what I'm doing and definitely where I am, but it's great to be among all these people, all this activity. It's nice to kick back and chill and, as much as I feel sorry for her, to not be in the same house as Jo. She'll enjoy tonight too, the house to herself until I get back tomorrow.

I start with my granny. She is old school, not a modern granny who does aquacise and holidays in Vietnam. My granny knits, and smokes in the garden with her neighbour at the back – although she thinks we don't know – and you can't say you like your mug or a picture or her cardigan because it'll be in your bag when you go home.

My granny makes tablet, whenever I come to see her. My English friends at uni had never had it; they used to fall on it, devour it, crunching on its brittle sweetness.

The tablet is on the kitchen top, squashed into its tin as harmless as fudge and yet, somehow, twice as sugary. I'll do my best at it, but there'll be loads left. I'll take it back to Clachan and see if Jo knows what it is.

'Your mam will be pleased you came to see me,' Granny says. She is beaming, so pleased I'm here – I should come more often. 'She was in yesterday to take me for my messages.' She means shopping, but all the old words are part of my granny, part of her charm.

I make a non-committal noise and then surprise myself by, 'How was she?'

'Aye, grand. She's got a new show coming into the theatre. A big musical from London, and she said she'd take me. We could all go.' She never stops trying.

My dad's parents died so long ago I only know them from photos. And my grandad too, my granny's husband. She stays here, by herself, surrounded by friends and neighbours who all pop in for coffee – it's always coffee round here.

'Maybe.' I didn't know my mum was still working. When I last spoke to her properly, she was on gardening leave – taking some time to sort out some issues. And I know she hasn't sorted them out because I saw her in the pharmacy, in her 'blending in' clothes.

'Tell me about the job,' my granny says. She has a photocopy of my degree certificate up on her sitting-room wall. It is in a gilt frame, and it sits next to my mum's, *BA (Hons) Theatre, Film, & TV Design*. It's never occurred to me before that I did a similar course, have gone into a similar job. When I was a kid, my mum just worked backstage, putting actors in the right place, finding equipment for costumiers, booking accommodation for the cast of a visiting show. But when I was a kid – at least, from when I was old enough to remember – my mum was already broken, no longer the person she'd been before William died.

I think of my little brother a lot when I'm here. There are photos of the two of us everywhere, mostly me sitting with him squished on to my knee, gripping him round his tiny waist so he didn't slide off. The big one, next to the degree certificates and in the same frame, is me in my first year of primary, my first school uniform, a big studio portrait by those people who come into school and do all the children. My parents – it would have been my mum then, my dad was always at work – had timed it so that they were there to throw William on to my knee. That same gripping hold, just as the picture was taken.

I imagine there being two of us now, when I've let everyone down, when the last person my dad thought he could rely on went down the Suwannee too. If I had a brother, I could have told him all my woes – a problem shared is a problem halved. He might even have been imperfect too. But, looking at this picture of him, I truly doubt that.

He has blue eyes, perfect skin and the whitest blond hair. I did too when I was a baby, before my hair turned to this blend of mouse and straw I have now. I don't carry a picture of him, I didn't have one to show Rachel the time we talked about our lost brothers. Maybe that made it easier for Rachel: she didn't like her own brother much and maybe that would have been really hard to say if she'd seen William's sweet face.

Rachel and I were sitting outside the house, side by side on the old blue bench that faces the sand. My sketch pad was between us and we were doing the tricky bit, talking about money, the budget for the job.

'Honestly, your plans are cheaper than anyone else. The recycling and reusing is so on-brand as well.' She waved her hand at me, waved away the money, and her enormous diamond engagement ring caught the beach light. 'I've been asking around, talking to friends about what they paid. You're ridiculously cheap. I'm more than happy with this and I'll add a bonus to the end of it to try and make your prices realistic. That is part of running a good business, you know.'

I remember trying to imagine how it must be to have so much money you tell people you need to give them more than they asked for.

We had a bottle of wine on the rickety table between us and Rachel poured me another glass. I took a picture of it on my phone, of the round glass stretching the sand behind it into a curve, of the yellow wine making the bottom of the sky pale. The glass is in focus, the beachscape behind it almost abstract. When I looked at the photo later, on the train, I could see me in my peaked cap reflected in the glass, the shape of Rachel and her big hair sunlit beside me.

'I've got no one to fight with over it,' she said. 'There's only me left, and I'm lucky enough to be able to afford what I want – the key to happiness.'

I remember wondering if it really was.

'If my brother were still alive, it would be different.' She drained her glass, put it on the table and framed the beach again: I took another photo. 'He was a very mean boy. Unkind. The sort who pulls wings off flies – only Tris used to pull one wing off so that they were doomed to buzz round and round in circles on the window sill. This would be his party shack, I'm sure of it. I wouldn't get a look-in.'

She picked up the bottle again, topped up her glass then upended it over mine, finished it off. 'I don't believe he'd have ever changed. It was our whole lifetime. The relief when he left for university was immense, of not having to look over my shoulder to see what he'd do next. My poor parents.'

And she showed me the photograph in her purse, the tattered photo-booth picture of a beautiful young man. His eyes sparkle with character, his face animated with holding all that personality inside. His smooth hair is black and has a line of light across the fringe where the flash is reflected.

'He was beautiful. But so dangerous,' she says. 'He didn't deserve what he got, nor the others in the car. But—' She shrugs her shoulders, stares out at the waves and the island beyond it. 'But it was a relief to be free of his demands.'

I must have looked worried – Rachel jumped in with an explanation, a correction. 'People have worse, I know,' she said. She ran her fingers through the front of her hair, lifted it free of her unlined forehead; her fingernails were a perfect red. 'It wasn't anything sinister. Just, everything I had – toys, hobbies, even friends – Tris had to make them his. And he was so much more charming than me, the absolute charm of the Devil, he always got what he wanted.

'I didn't use to talk about him at all. Never. But since meeting your dad, things are a bit different.'

And I remember thinking then about William, his fat toddler thighs and squishy cheeks, the way everyone adored him. My brother was very different to Rachel's, but it's only now that I realise the loss of him was the same kind of explosion inside our family.

◆ ◆ ◆

My granny comes into the tiny sitting room with the inevitable tray of tablet. She has cut it into fat oblongs, stacked it up on a plate like a dentist's worst nightmare. 'I made your favourite,' she says.

It hasn't been my favourite, or even in my top ten, since I was about twelve, but there is no need to tell my granny that. 'I have a friend, where I'm staying, who will have never tried this,' I say. 'Can I take it home?'

Her face absolutely lights up with the honour of it, of her hard work going off to Dumfries and Galloway to my little cottage project.

'And, Granny, do you have a spare photo of William I can take home with me?'

'You can take any,' she says, and her eyes fill with the loss of him, nineteen years on. 'Although . . .' She looks up at the big, ghastly picture on the sitting-room wall, its brown and gold paper mount distracting a little from my missing tooth, my blue-rimmed glasses. There is a mark on William's T-shirt, a tiny stain of lunch, of life. Even in all these terrible circumstances, it is an awful picture.

'Not that one,' I say and squeeze her arm. 'Let's find another, something smaller.'

And we sit and go through the albums – laughing at memories, smiling at the beautiful little family. My mum is the spit of me, so young and a bit more beautiful than I am. My dad looks like a boy – goodness knows what patients must have thought when he rocked up at their bedside.

I try and remember the four of us together.

I try and remember us happy.

Chapter Twenty-three

Jo

It is evening when I get back to Clachan. It is the first time I have been in the house alone since I arrived, bar Meg's swims, and I appreciate the walk through the forest, the quiet, the absolute peace of it. It fits well with the city, yin and yang. Tiny bugs flit across the path in front of me, occasionally landing on my arm or my leg, but benign, not biters.

It feels as if I have been abroad, somewhere entirely foreign, and now I am back to this wood full of buzzing bird food, back to navigating the forest by recognising trees, the rings of their bark and the dips of their branches. Now I am back to being part of the landscape.

Knowing that no one will come here allows me to breathe in the silence, tasting it as it slips down. It's delicious.

I throw myself on the sofa, swing my feet up and on to the armrest at the far end. It feels decadent, welcome. There is a message from Terry on my phone – it arrived while I was driving and I've forgotten to check it.

Call me. Xxx

It's deliberate, that lack of detail. Terry wants me to wonder whether he's had a terrifying diagnosis, a car crash, or simply can't remember what brand of washing powder is best for his T-shirts. But Terry is in my old world, where I used to belong: I know those landscapes too and part of me misses them.

I summon the satellite gods – by walking into the kitchen – and call him.

'Great to hear your voice,' he says. 'It's been too long.'

Terry is so good at forgetting we're divorced. He can almost make me forget too.

'I've been busy. I went to Glasgow today.'

'Best curry in Britain,' he says. Food was a language we always had in common.

'I found that out. What do you want, Terry?'

He pauses, and a fleeting moment of me still cares about his health, his happiness. Then the shutters of the last few years roll down over the feelings, wrap themselves round me like armour.

'I want to come and see you. I'm sure you must be lonely.'

'I'm not, as it goes. I'm not even here alone.' I think about giving him the romantic trope of stumbling across the decorator in situ, leaving out that she's a twenty-five-year-old woman. 'Meg, the interior designer, she's living here too. Do you mean you want to come and see me because *you're* lonely?'

He laughs. 'Damn, you got me.'

In the back of my mind, Rachel says, 'He's sexually incontinent, do not let him in.'

'Rachel wouldn't like it,' I say, and I physically look for her in this room, see the wisps of her everywhere, ghosts of us cooking and laughing.

'Rachel adores me. Always will. You know it.'

It touches me that he talks about her in the present tense.

'She thinks you're a wanker.' I could elaborate, but we have put the brutal past behind us, buried it for the time being and – although I'm poorer – I'd rather have this truce than be fighting.

'I miss both of you,' Terry says. 'I miss being married to you and Rachel.'

I have started clearing out one of the kitchen cupboards while we talk, marvelling that a food processor this old can still have its original box and all its gadgets. 'You wish you were married to both of us.'

'Oh, I was, believe me.'

I pull out dozens of old yoghurt pots, cleaned out and neatly stacked. The labels are an exercise in nostalgia. The cupboard reaches round the corner of the units, it goes on and on.

'Everything I ever did had to be examined by the pair of you.'

'Maybe you shouldn't have done it then.' He did a lot of things.

I find a beautiful set of farmhouse mixing bowls, three of them that fit perfectly inside each other: eggshell brown on the outside, white inside, the edges crimped with a recurring pattern. I put them on the pile with the food processor – the yoghurt pots are on the 'bin' pile, although maybe they should go to a museum.

'It went through you, down the phone line, and some hours later I'd get Rachel's take on it back out of your mouth. And that was gospel. Fact. Once the two of you had discussed it, everything you thought I thought, believed I'd done, was absolute certainty.'

'Have you been drinking?' But it's true, there were times when we jumped to conclusions, filled in the blanks without giving him a chance to explain. We got carried away occasionally. 'Anyway, if you hadn't given us the rope, we couldn't have hanged you.'

'That's fair.'

Terry's ability to take criticism has always been disarming, always been his saving grace.

'Can I ring you back tomorrow?' And then, while he's still talking, I end the call, lay my phone on the floor by the yoghurt pots and pull out the biscuit tin.

It's a big tin, stamped gold and blue in a swirling pattern. Like everything else in this forgotten cupboard, it is older than I am. It has lost its lid but even if it hadn't, the stack of tiny bottles inside would stop the lid from going on.

I rest my hand on the top, feel its crunch like the seashells they were once made of. The lids are all off, sharp-edged in the bottom of the tin. The hollow noise of the bottles against each other grinds under my fingers.

These are the miniatures of spirits that they serve in the first-class carriage of the train Rachel takes to Clachan. The labels are bright and modern, the tops in primary colours like the buttons on a child's coat. I've been on that train with Rachel, seen her charm the staff into giving her extras, popping them into her bag for picnics or the opera – anywhere a miniature bottle of gin or whisky might come in handy.

I push my fingers to the back of the cupboard, surprisingly clean given how long it must be since it was emptied. I sweep the bottles forward to the edge.

When I've got them all and emptied the biscuit tin, it fills a carrier bag to bursting. Hundreds of tiny bottles, mostly vodka when I look at them all, and hidden. Every one of them drunk. Tucked away with her family's history, in the darkest corner where no one will find it.

◆ ◆ ◆

Tim invited me to their house – his house – for coffee. Formal, a date and a time. He takes pride in his coffee machine: he used to tell anyone who would listen about the beans and the roast and the grind. It's easy to see that even that has lost its shine, that the joy has gone from his simple morning alchemy.

'I miss her every second of every day,' he says to me, as if he is discussing the weather, the direction of the wind. It's not an explanation he needs to make – his loss is etched on his face like a lino print, deep wide grooves of grief, inked up with loneliness.

I want to tell him that I feel the same, that flavours are less intense, that noises are flatter and monotone, that I never sing now – not even when I'm driving – but I don't have the same right to grief as he has. I have lost my witness, my confessor; Tim has lost the person whose breath syncs to his in the night, the heavy presence on the pillow that shifts and moves with the rhythm of his sleep.

I have lost my connection to the past, my fantasy future, but Tim has lost today, and yesterday, and tomorrow. He has lost now.

'I don't know how you manage.' I mean it. I wish I could hug him, but we are not those people, he is not that man. And anyway, he wants Rachel to hug him, no one else; he wants her to throw her arms around him while her face does that Rachel thing of total joy, like a lighthouse beam. He wants to hear her laughter gust into his ear, her breath warm on his face.

Nothing else will do. For him, as for me, she is irreplaceable.

'Have you gone back to work?' I ask him.

'I had to,' he says. 'I was starting to smell.' It's an unusually human thing for him to say, as if he has to identify his own feelings now that Rachel is not here to point them out for him. 'And it does help to fill the silence.'

That's it, the small talk is done. There is nothing more to say unless we talk about her, about the things I'm here to say. I feel for him, but there is no other way.

'I'm losing her,' I say. 'What's left of her. The more I find out, the less I know.'

And he nods as if he understands my code, the short, bleak words that describe loss.

'You knew she went to see my mother?'

'I knew.' He is the old Tim again – holding back, distributing facts, letting Rachel out piece by piece so that he has her and I don't.

I shrug at him, aggressively, like a teenager wanting to say, *And?*

'You knew she wrote to my mum? All these years.'

His turn to shrug – exaggerated, mirroring my behaviour. 'The letters went to Clachan.' And then he narrows his eyes and says it. 'But we didn't have secrets.'

I want to yell at him, I want to fill the kitchen with screams of *yes you do, yes you do*. To tell him that I was at an art gallery with Rachel's secret yesterday. That he is real and solid and – oddly – aloof in that same uptight way Tim is. That they would probably get on.

That she has – had – a type.

I don't say anything for a moment: Ben is hurtling through my mind like a helter-skelter, I can't stop the thoughts long enough to find the least hurtful, the kindest. If there is a kindest way to hear that your late wife was having an affair.

I decide to make it about me; that's something Tim will understand, at least. 'I feel like I only knew a piece of her, like an iceberg. That nine-tenths of her were buried.'

The coffee machine makes a triumphant hiss.

'And every day, another bit breaks off and hits me.'

He turns away from me, looks out of the window down their long, immaculate garden, where arbours and statues peek from glades and nooks, where the lawn stretches like carpet, out and out.

On the work surface, a bottle of whisky is pushed back against the wall. Next to it, a half-drunk red wine, the cork replaced with a silver stopper. Tim used to be religious about clearing away bottles and booze, wiping down the worktops with a 'goodnight' flourish before we'd even got to the bottom of the bottle. The sunlight catches the amber of the whisky bottle; gold notes dazzle in it.

And there it is, hiding in plain sight. The reason Tim was so careful about clearing up at night, so involved in what Rachel and I did when we were away together, about what we bought ourselves in restaurants. So many of Rachel's decisions, her round-and-round conversations, swim in the bright bronze of the bottle. 'Tim.'

He looks at me.

'Was Rachel an alcoholic?'

The words hover in the air like a banner behind a tiny plane, shimmering across the stark clean kitchen.

Tim used to like to spread out his stories, drip-feed them so that his audience was captured by politeness, unable to move until he'd finished. He didn't realise how annoying it was, how boring. But that's not what he's doing now; this is genuine – he is going slowly because these are words that are going to tear his insides to pieces on their way up.

'I thought it would die with her,' he says. 'I thought it was over.'

He takes a huge breath, shudders it out.

I sip at my coffee, just to have something to do in the heavy air. To feel the too-hot liquid on my lips, to feel anything that isn't Tim's pain.

He presses his forehead on to the window in front of him, stares at the garden without looking. 'I thought I'd buried it all—'

There is a silent *with her* at the end of his sentence, too hard to spit out.

'Why did she go and see my mother? What did Rachel want?'

'I honestly don't know that, Jo. We didn't talk about it. I knew she was going, that's all. And I knew it was about Tristan, about the past. Your mother wanted to tell her something about her brother.'

He opens the back door; the outside world floods in and I realise how stale the air is in this kitchen, how still. The idea of Rachel knowing about Tristan without me having a chance to explain, of my mother telling her what I'd done, wraps itself round me – makes the air more stifling, despite the breeze.

Tim is still talking. 'And all the talking about the past was about her future. About the decisions she was making – about moving on, fixing things. I had to leave her to make all those choices by herself. I had to.'

And then he says it, says the thing that I came to hear but, simultaneously, can't bear. 'You'd have to ask Ben.'

The word, the idea, falls like snow in this bright summer place. The colours in the room stand out like a painting, intensified by the silence, by the cold: green apples in the fruit bowl; the turquoise lampshade hanging above the dining table; the deep red of the rug beneath my feet. It is the most silent I have ever been in this house: Rachel wasn't built for silence, didn't encourage it.

Tim moves, lifts up the lid of the coffee machine as if burying himself in banality will solve this. He snaps it back down, presses buttons, and it whirrs into action again like a hammer drill in the taut stillness of the room. 'You've met Ben by now, I presume?'

I start to say that I have.

'Then you can ask him – he went to see your mother too. He went with Rachel.' Tim sinks into a chair, leans on the dining table.

I expected to see his humanity when I came here, to be moved by how broken he is, but this is something else. He is hollow.

'Ben won't tell me anything. Nothing at all about Rachel.'

Tim half-smiles, a wry, wrung-out grimace. He reaches backwards, takes the coffee the machine prepared, and I get the idea that this is what he does all day, dose after dose. 'You want another?'

'I'd be bouncing off the walls.' I take the chair opposite him, make more eye contact than we probably ever have. 'You have to tell me everything. Rachel was going to – she told me she had to tell me something.' I stop there. Tim doesn't need to know she was leaving him. Some things are better left with the dead.

'I know, she'd planned it for a long time. But in the end, she couldn't wait. Didn't wait.'

I'm totally lost. My body is stable, anchored in this kitchen, this site of a hundred parties, a thousand hangovers. But my mind is dragging in and out like the Clachan beach, everything I know tumbling and turning like pebbles under the pull.

'Rachel was trying to stop drinking for as long as I've known her, Jo.'

Tim never liked our drinking – he never said so, but it was obvious in his every gesture. Even when he paid for the Champagne, for the cocktails, it was always an obvious attempt at stopping us there, counting our drinks.

I try to remember that he is a man whose wife has died, a man who has lost the person who filters him to the world. That he used to think things and Rachel would explain them to him, catch his thinking up to the modern day, make him intelligible, palatable.

'But I drank alongside her, every time. I drank as much as her.'

'No, Jo, you didn't. You drink a lot. You're a heavy drinker. We all are. It's not the same thing. My wife was an alcoholic, and only started to make progress in the last three years. Since she's been seeing Ben.' He tucks his head down into his hands so that I can't look at him. The top of his head is almost hairless. 'He did what I couldn't do. He helped her to deal with it. Almost.'

His voice is tiny as he says, 'But it killed her in the end. As she had been told it would.'

I knew her, I want to say. *I knew her and she died of a stroke. I know she died of a stroke because I found her.* It was Tim himself who delivered the diagnosis to me over the phone, read me the terrible heartbreaking conclusion of the post-mortem. She died of a stroke.

But I don't say any of it because a flicker book of pictures is whipping through my mind – image after image of us stopping for a quick glass of wine, toasting with Champagne in coffee cups, tinnies on a picnic. I don't say any of it as my mind struggles to find a picture of her without a drink. Of us – in the last few decades – without a drink.

Her face half obscured by a miniature paper parasol, a foamy froth on the top of the huge glass, bright plastic colours of a seaside resort, of late nights and sangria.

Us, lying on our backs, staring at the stars and planets. Telling stories to one another and passing the bottle back and forth. Laughing.

A table of empty bottles, of spilt drinks and broken glasses. A picture that says, 'It was a great night. We had a ball.'

'I don't understand,' I say, and he looks at me.

His face is full of sympathy.

'She's been seeing Ben for three years – three and a half. And he'd really helped her, almost got to the bottom of it. She'd decided to stop. Once and for all.'

A booze-free weekend, she'd said in her last text. *A spa experience.*

'It was the thing that really gave me hope, that she'd decided to tell you the truth. It was a first. The rest of it had gone over and over, she'd promised to give up a million times – for her sake, not mine. But she was always ashamed of you knowing before – of letting you down.'

He clears his throat, squeezes his eyes tight together as if to stem tears. 'I wanted her to stop for her, not me. We both knew it would kill her in the end. There are very few elderly alcoholics.'

I think of Duncan, Rachel's ruddy, happy father, broad and belligerent, dead at sixty-two.

'She died of a stroke.' It is almost a question; I am wondering whether I didn't know Rachel in death any more than I knew her in life.

He nods, sips his coffee. Incongruous and for a moment, as his lips touch on the taste of it, normal.

'Ben was working through a plan with her, a controlled detox.' He looks down the garden again, as if he can see her walking towards him, long legs silhouetted through a summer dress, her hair tucked behind her ears and flowing on to her shoulders – a Renaissance model made flesh. 'But she, being Rachel, did it her way. By herself.' He swallows and the tears appear in his eyes, escape his control. He pinches the end of his nose with his fingers. 'She knew the statistics, the dangers. But she is Rachel, and she does things Rachel's way.'

He has shaved recently, his chin and cheeks are clear of stubble. His clothes are clean. Everything else about him has rotted, wilted.

'But she had a stroke.' One more try at this not being true. One more try at not having been a collaborator, an accomplice.

Filling our water bottles with gin and tonic for the village flower show when we were staying at Clachan – making it a yearly adventure, an annual joke.

Caffè corretto on a cold day on the top floor of Harvey Nichols, looking at our shopping, smelling the perfumes the floorwalkers had sprayed us with. Brandy in our coffee because it was raining. Laughing, always laughing. Laughing and drinking and laughing.

A ski chalet, halfway down a slope. Glühwein and schnapps to warm us up. Pretzels, studded with rock salt, to soak it up before we skied on. Everyone else around us doing the same thing. Everyone.

'I matched her drink for drink, Tim. Every time.' It is a rebuttal, not a confession. He is wrong.

I knew her best.

'Why Ben? Why could she only do this after she met Ben? Why not me, or you? I don't understand.' Did Rachel need another person in her life to be able to deal with her problems? I can see how she might struggle telling Tim, but she and I shared everything. 'Was she leaving you, Tim?' I hope this isn't the first time he's considered it. 'Were she and Ben building a new life?'

He makes a strange noise, a pale, twisted version of a laugh. 'Ben isn't her boyfriend, Jo. He's her therapist.'

And then, into my wide-open mouth, set with surprise: 'Ben is a drug and alcohol specialist, an addiction counsellor. Best that money could buy.'

Chapter Twenty-four

'It happened gradually. It wasn't a problem as such – affecting work, friendships, our relationship – until the miscarriage.' He is speaking gently, cradling her secrets for her, not for me, holding her story close into him to keep it safe. 'She'd had a couple of glasses of Champagne after a big deal, you know how it works.'

And I do, despite doing low-paid jobs my whole life, despite never playing in their league: you'd be surprised what I know about the trading floor, about wheeling and dealing, about stocks and derivatives.

But I didn't know my closest friend was an alcoholic.

'She was barely pregnant, and she'd drunk next to nothing. But she couldn't shake the guilt when we lost the baby – no matter what I said, no matter what our doctor said. She convinced herself that two small glasses of wine caused a miscarriage.' He lets air out through his teeth, as if all the bad can be blown away.

'And after that, she didn't want to try again because she had had a drink. She didn't want to try again until she was sure, certain that she wouldn't wreck it. It was a conversation she had with herself – and with me – month after month. It crucified her.' He stares down the garden again. 'She put it off until—'

'Couldn't you stop her?' It's a stupid question and it comes out badly, comes out like I think it's his fault. 'I mean, couldn't you tell her that you wanted a baby, too? That she had to stop for that? For you?'

'I loved her,' he says. His words are plain with sadness, pure. 'I didn't want to force her into anything. Her pain was extraordinary.'

Am I sad that she didn't share it with me – or angry? When did I lose half of her, when did part of her disappear?

'We didn't talk about children. It was the one place we never went,' I tell Tim.

It was a loss we shared, a common denominator. I believed it was the thing that meant that, fundamentally, we were always there for one another, always available. I thought we didn't talk about it for me – to save me pain. Now I know we didn't talk about it for her too.

'I drank with her, Tim, literally with her. I know exactly how much she had, always.'

He shakes his head. 'You didn't.' He reaches an arm across the table, doesn't quite let his hand touch me. 'That's how it works. When you shared a bottle of wine, she'd already had a couple before you started. Or spirits. When you went to bed, she would be drinking in her room. That's what happens. Her suitcase, her handbag, the back of cupboards.' He looks right at me as if he's going to tell me something awful, something condemning. 'The cistern of the loo.'

'Every time she *failed*—' He makes quote marks in the air; he didn't believe Rachel was a failure. 'Every time, it wound her back in, it tightened. Like a noose. Each time she fell further down, the knot got tighter. Strangled her.'

'I can't believe I didn't smell it on her,' I say. I have failed my friend, every bit as much as she failed me and worse.

'Perfume.' He cocks his head slightly, as if he is following a ghost scent, as if a trail of her has floated across the kitchen. 'She picked her perfumes carefully – her brands. There are particular ones that a lot of alcoholics wear: strong, alcohol-based scents. Calvin Klein is one. When you smell booze, they'll lift their wrist, show you that it's the perfume. Had me for years.'

I think of all the tiny bottles strewn around her room in Clachan: the designs, the shapes, the smells. Her trademark collection of scents and extravagance.

'You don't need to know all the tricks, Jo.' He puts his head in his hands. 'There's a lifetime of them.'

Tim opens a little paper box on the table. Inside, tucked in tissue paper, are tiny biscotti. The brand stamp on the tissue is the same as on his coffee machine.

In the back of my mind, Rachel laughs. *Look at him*, she says. *Great poncey pillock*.

In the back of my mind, I think of many things we said about Tim.

How we criticised him for moaning about how long we'd been in the pub.

How it puzzled me for decades that he'd warn me not to take risks when she and I got on a plane, boarded a train to a holiday. I am no risk taker, I was shocked out of that a lifetime ago. It amazed me – angered me – that he didn't know that.

How we moaned and giggled, she and I, that he always went to bed like a boring old man when we wanted to dance till the small hours came rushing at us, rubbing their sleepy eyes and begging us to stop.

Tim offers me a poncey biscuit and I take it.

'Her new life,' I say. 'She asked me to come and stay at Clachan, and she was going to tell me about her new life – it's in her letter from my mum. Her new life was giving up drinking.'

Silence – he knows this. It's no surprise to him.

'She went to Clachan and she stopped drinking. Cold turkey. Ben begged her not to do it. She promised she wouldn't. And then she did. Rachel went to Clachan and stopped drinking. You want it all?' he says. 'It will hurt.' He has the voice of experience, heavy, flat.

I nod.

'The stress on her body – the stress of the withdrawal – it was overwhelming. It caused a massive brain haemorrhage.' His voice is soused in grief. 'Ben had warned her, he'd shown her endless statistics, studies. And she had promised both of us that she wouldn't do it. And then she did.'

I think myself back into the room she died in. I am back at that event with a forensic eye. I am a different person now. I am a detective, a seeker.

I am open to the truth.

I see the toe of my sneaker on the landing. I am a bird's-eye view, a documentary camera, watching every moment of what happened, looking for the tiny details. To the left of me, her bedroom. Perhaps I did see this in real time – perhaps I have forgotten, or perhaps my brain didn't let me understand it.

I see the mattress pushed aside, the space underneath it where a flat quarter bottle might hide. The drawers are jagged as rocks, the shorts and pants and jumpers turned upside down. There is a space in the front where a bottle of wine might lie, horizontal, a short, round dimple between socks that would take a can of beer.

The wicker bin is on its side, the paper and cotton wool balls and tissues thrown across the floor as if to squeeze any drops from them.

When I roll back time, when I understand what I'm looking at, I watch myself walk into the sitting room with the police officer. I see the understairs cupboard, ransacked, bottles smashed and undone and the smells of creosote, paraffin, path cleaner. The components of a bomb – but none of them drinkable.

And then my film goes – frame by frame – back upstairs, to the one room she didn't touch, the room where all the bad things happen. I imagine how her hand reached out to lift the lid of the blanket box, how – given time – she might have rooted through it, maybe even found a bottle of whisky, a miniature of vodka. And that very thing that killed her might, in that instant, have saved her. Outside, the stretch of calm sand – yellow as joy – glittered in the sun.

'It was why no one asked if there'd been a burglary.' It is a dawn; my brain has kept this hidden under blankets, coddled against the dark. 'Because she did it all.'

Tim nods, such a small movement, so hard to acknowledge the horrors of that day. 'She was looking for a drink, for her stash. There would have been stuff hidden everywhere normally but she'd intended to quit, she'd got rid of it all when she got there. She meant it.'

He explains that the taxi driver messaged him – full of anecdotes of all the funny journeys they'd had together, all the laughs. We are all in that place: we were enchanted by her easiness, her spun-gold light.

But there was more unravelling inside the driver's message.

Rachel had called the driver back, an hour after he'd dropped her at Clachan, and she'd asked him to drive her to – of all places – the tip. She had a suitcase with her, old and heavy – pasted with the stickers of bygone travel, bust airlines. And he'd helped her heave it into the hopper at the tip, joked with her that it was full of bottles because of the clinking and the sliding of glass.

And her lifeline dropped into the crusher.

'I tell myself,' Tim says, 'that she must have felt like the most powerful person in the world in that moment. Cleansed and triumphant.' He clasps his hands together, the poncey biscuit box beside him describing their lives, the veneer of perfect, of luxury, of extra.

He starts to cry as he talks, easily and gently, letting the tears fall. 'I tell myself how proud she must have been of herself that day. That she walked around Clachan – swam, lay on the beach, the things you people do there – and she was on top of the world. She had won – climbed the mountain. And it gives me comfort that that's how she spent her last day – believing that her life had opened up in front of her again, that it was all for her and she could do anything.'

Chapter Twenty-five

I swear that Terry has a homing instinct for misery. That there is some kind of call, audible only to bats and lowlife wretches, that fills the night sky when I'm miserable. Whenever Terry sees it, he scrambles into action.

I am almost home when my mobile flashes on the car dashboard display and I realise that call has gone out.

I'm doing it again, thinking of Clachan as home. It is a sudden realisation that there are new people washing up at my sink in my real house, that there is another woman or man walking up the stairs, trailing their hand along my beautifully restored banisters. It won't ever be my real home again, not even if I move back in.

Clachan offers me a different sort of home: restorative; magnetic. Clachan is a fairy tale, a magical refuge of castles and alchemy and poisoned red apples, and at the same time – I acknowledge out loud what I have always known – a place of secrets and enchantments. Clachan is a place made by – full of – humans, past and present, right and wrong. But I don't know if I can stay there – if it will ever truly feel mine.

Clachan belongs to the Willoughbys.

◆ ◆ ◆

Terry is always the wrong thing to do. He is the kind of man who seems like a good idea in the evening, who can woo you and wine you and win his way into your heart. And then with daylight comes the dreadful reality, the enchantment wears off and the real Terry appears.

I press green on the screen.

'You didn't ring me back yesterday,' he says instead of hello.

It's uncanny, the way he does it – always has. Or maybe, like a fairground fortune-teller, I find the something I need to talk about when Terry rings with the opportunity. Maybe, when it comes to Terry, I'm just suggestible.

'It's tough,' I say. There'd be no point lying, he'd hear it in my voice. It is amazing that a man so thick-skinned and un-self-aware can be so perceptive when he wants to. That's the key: when he wants to. 'What's up?' There's no point pretending that he doesn't have an agenda.

'Absolutely nothing,' Terry lies. 'But you've been nagging away at my head like a canker.' Sometimes he pretends to be as Irish as his mother was. This is one of those days.

I am in the smallest lanes, right near the Clachan car park – if I'm lucky, my signal will give out in a second.

'So . . .'

He has his 'adventure' voice on, the one that he uses to pretend he's twenty – or thirty – years younger than he is.

The pressure hammers in my head.

'. . . I jumped on the train to come and see you.'

Why, oh, why didn't I just ring him back yesterday. Or even this morning.

There is so much to try and understand. I need to talk to the shadows, listen for Rachel's story on the waves while Meg is still in Glasgow.

I press the red button and cut off the call – maybe Terry will think it's the signal, maybe he won't.

I pull into the sandy car park around three o'clock. At this time of year, this is the hour that the sun starts to burn at Clachan, as if it needed the whole day to summon up the power, all morning to warm the wide sky. On the way back, I stopped and did a big supermarket shop – food for Meg and me for a couple of weeks, bar some fruit and veg, which will come from the village shop. Cooking and feeding Meg will be my contribution to the work going on here, my way to find a temporary purpose. I text her from the car park, before the signal gets unreliable.

When your dad drives you back tomorrow, both have lunch with me, ok? Xxx

And then Ben: *I've spoken to Tim, as I'm sure you know by now. Will you stay for lunch tomorrow so we can talk? All best, Joanna.*

I load the shopping into the barrow, heavy things at the bottom, my overnight bag squashed in beside them, and then the light stuff on the top – fronds of coriander wobble from their pot as the barrow's wheel bumps along the sandy track.

There is no wine in my haul of food. I bought tonic, but no gin. Fizzy drinks, but no beer.

I push the barrow through the wild hawthorn orchard. The sandy path slips through the trees and there are wide patches of grass either side of it. The hawthorns are low and spend much of the year leafless; it gives the grass underneath a chance to grow, to see some sunlight.

Their trunks are bent like hags against the wind, curled over in its force and set there, gnarled and spindly with twigs like pointing fingers. The motif of the hag-trees and the selkie that Meg has chosen for the wallpaper is poignant – beauty revealing what lies beneath, slipping aside and letting the craggy, the sharp, the dangerous show.

I talk to Rachel in a low voice as we walk back towards the cottage. We laugh about Tim's reliance on the coffee machine as an expression of human emotions, although this time we laugh a little more fondly, with less criticism. She teases me for my alcohol-free shopping, calls me a chicken, and I explain that I'll no doubt drink again but that – for now – it is too tainted, too tinged with sadness. And she reminds me of all the Champagne, all the fizz and fun and the travel and the meeting people and the gales of laughter. I smile at her and we walk the rest of the way in companionable silence.

I don't ask her why she didn't tell me, don't force her into that corner. The only reason that comes back and back at me is that she thought I wouldn't cope, that she thought I needed her strength, depended on it, and I'd be lost if I even suspected she wasn't rock solid.

It leaves me empty, that thought. It leaves a selfish wound that will not heal. That I spent all my time moaning about Terry, or money, or another of the myriad injustices my life was pepper-sprayed with. And all the time she was killing herself, a slow suicide while she wished for someone to notice, for someone to stop her.

◆ ◆ ◆

I unpack the shopping, put it all away neatly – pushing the image of the kitchen cupboards to the back of my mind. I know that I saw this kitchen devastated – that I saw smashed crockery and white powdered flour and tin cans that had been kicked and rolled across the floor. That I had seen the things that live under the sink strewn in desperation: leaking bottles of lurid green cleaner; bin bags scrunched like dead crows.

It makes me wonder if I wiped the carnage from my mind because – deep inside me – I knew that Rachel had done it.

I put some of the shopping aside. A collection of objects Rachel would recognise. A glass bottle of tonic, flavoured with elderflowers. A green cardboard punnet of strawberries. A bread roll, crisp and flaky, brown on the top. Yellow cheese, one big bubble of air in its side like the cheese from a mousetrap. I point it out to her and she pokes her invisible finger into the hole, grins. This collection goes into the wicker basket we used for picnics. I add firelighters, matches, top the whole thing with a red-and-white tea cloth from a bundle I brought down here a few years ago when I realised the ones we had were too threadbare, too ragged.

Terry came with me on that trip, not Rachel. He and I were still married by a thread – in a roller coaster of punishment and reward, up and down and brutal and kind and breath-taking and deathly slow. I texted Rachel every detail of it. And I never once asked her how she was.

I pick up the basket and head for the beach.

One of the things I love most about Clachan is the front door. It is as old as the house, has never been replaced. It is weathered and pock-marked, dimpled by the seasons, with the sanding of winds and waves. It has a tiny diamond of handmade glass at eye level that gives you a distorted view into the hallway, a fairground idea of what's inside. And the same thing works as you leave: the outside world reduced to an abstract painting, yellow ground, blue sky, a blur of grey or brown or green where the sea connects them. If I were an artist, that's the piece of Clachan I would paint.

I close the door, step across the brief scrubby grass to the beach. I negotiate the boulders and the rock pools, watch the colour of the stone darken from grey to black as it gets wetter, as I get closer to the sea. On the sand, I flip off my shoes, leave them upended near the rocks.

And I sit, as we have always done, on the flat, sandy patch in the middle of the bay's swoop. If a drone flew over, I would be perfectly central in the arc of the shore.

I have put the basket down next to a flat scallop shell.

'Look for a tiny Venus,' Rachel says. 'She'll be scurrying around starkers, wondering how she got here, what to do now she's born.' And I examine the sand, dig around in it, looking for the shrimp-sized goddess, her panicked arms and legs as she buries herself and her nakedness.

From the trees behind me and the sea in front of me, there are bird calls everywhere – squeaks and shrieks and clicks and chirps. It feels good to know that hundreds or thousands of tiny eyes are on me, that I am in the middle of them, part of this shore.

For a moment, I cradle my phone in my hand, think about calling Terry back. I think about a problem shared being a problem halved. Nice Terry – and now we're not married he more than likely would be nice – would be understanding, a listening ear, all kindness and support when he hears about Rachel and what really happened.

I imagine inviting him here and him sleeping in my bed, the twofold comfort of someone to reach out to in the dark and the life-affirming properties of sex.

'Do it,' Rachel says. 'He's fun, funny. And sex is always a good idea.' She leans back on her elbows, hair scattering on to the sand; the flax-yellow ends mix with the diamonds of crushed shell, sparkle in the late light.

I blink my eyes tight to make her vanish. I'm not going to call Terry. I'm not going to call anyone, not going to share what I know about her. I can grant her that dignity at least.

It is getting cooler, even though the sun is golden across the sky. The horizon bubbles and boils with colour. This will be a sunset that fills the pale grey evening.

I work hard for twenty minutes, leaving a frenzy of footprints in the virgin sand: here and there and scattered, like the tracks of a sea otter. I collect large round rocks, too big to be called pebbles, and arrange them in a circle just above the tideline. They are easy to find, the tumbled remnants of many fire pits before this one. I collect driftwood in all sizes, pulling a long branch – wild as antlers – back to my fire behind me, snapping off its dried and salt-washed ends.

I take the firelighters out of the basket – *Cheating*, the Willoughbys call across the sand, all of them, and I laugh back into the wind, smiling. It only takes two matches to get the fire going, and I pile my sticks on.

This is a pyre for the sadness. It is a beacon to mark this spot, this moment in time and place. It is for Rachel and me. We will never be finished with the questions, the knotted past, but we are finished with pain.

In the bottom of my basket, I have folded a blanket: a green tartan travel rug, fringed at the edges and bobbly with age. I sit cross-legged by the fire, the blanket around my shoulders, and I sing.

I sing the filthy rugby songs that Duncan taught us, raising my tonic bottle at just the right moments, punctuating the song with swigs. I sing the hymns Rachel and I learned at school, standing side by side, Wilding and Willoughby, bellowing out our favourites.

I sing the songs that coloured our teenage years, romantic and heartfelt, moody and dramatic, although I've forgotten most of the words and any of the order they go in.

I sing out – at the top of my voice – on to the foam-speckled sea.

The songs are my offering, to tell her that the hard times are over: that she can travel across these waves, this beach; dance in this endless space. She is free.

The last light seeps across the sky, the colours rippling through orange and pink and red. My beach fire, blue and green at its very core, orange and yellow at its tips, leaks into the sunset, matches it colour for colour.

In the shallows, in a pool of apricot light, I see a black ball. At first, I think it is a human head and then, as it disappears beneath the water and surfaces again three metres away, I realise it is the seal. She watches me, wet fur and beady black eyes reflecting the peach and pink of the sky.

The seal stays in the shallow water of the bay, sometimes close to me, sometimes nearer the island. Sometimes I can see the silvered stream behind her as she moves silently through the water, other times she just appears – like magic – having travelled like quicksilver in the darkness.

I think of the selkie: of the grace and elegance of the coerced woman once she is returned to her proper form. I watch the seal for at least an hour and, whenever she surfaces, she watches me.

The fire starts to putter and die down. It is too close to autumn to sit here all night, the ancient blanket not long enough to cover my legs and my feet. I gather my party back into the basket and turn to go – to go home.

I raise one hand to wave as I walk towards the house. I wave goodbye to the swimmer, the proof – if I had needed anything more than the scorching sunset, the distant stars that are popping from the night sky now darkness has fallen – that Rachel's skin has been returned to her.

About ten minutes after I get in, there is a knock at the door. On any other dark night, miles from anywhere and all alone, I would panic. But I think back to my putting the phone down, to Terry's inability to take no for an answer. I know the beast.

'Where've you bloody been?' His hair is jutting out at angles; he runs his fingers through it when he's stressed. 'I've been ringing for hours.'

'I was on the beach. I didn't take my phone.' And then, because it's Terry and he sometimes needs an emphasis: 'Why would I?'

'Because I was on my way to see you is why. Because I've sat on a bloody train for four hours and then had to walk from the fucking station using my phone as a torch. It's on two per cent,' he says, as if I've worn his phone out and it won't ever work again. 'If it had run out, I don't know what might have happened. I could have been hit by a car.'

'Only if I'd gone out looking for you,' I say, and long to tell Rachel how quick and smart that was.

'It's ten past eleven,' I say. Terry has made huge assumptions here – that I'd be awake, that I'd be alone. I remember that, not an hour ago, I danced on the beach with a flaming brand held above my head.

Behind him, the moon winks through the bull's-eye glass of the door, makes its way indoors.

'It is late, I'll grant you that. But Clachan is always further away than you think. Especially when no one comes to get you from the station.' He steps towards me, brushes my cheek with his lips. 'You look fantastic. Sun-kissed, windswept.'

I think about my dance, my howling songs. He wins, Terry always wins. 'Come on, I'll make you a coffee.'

We take the coffees into the sitting room, and he is blown away by the changes. 'It's like something from a magazine – or off the telly. Where you think, I don't actually know anyone who lives in a house like that. Talking of which, what is going to happen to it? Are you going to live in it?'

I shrug. 'I don't know yet – I'm making some plans. They're, um, nascent.' Nascent was a bad word to use and the child Terry and I didn't have settles between us on the sofa. Neither of us speaks for a moment, acknowledging the space it doesn't take up.

'There's been a lot to get used to. Stuff I didn't know about Rachel.' That is as far as I'm prepared to go. 'Not bad stuff.' Because although it was for her, it wasn't for me, for our relationship – it was just a fragment of her, not all of her. 'Not that bad.'

'You never could see Rachel's feet of clay.' He leans back, raises his arm so that it runs the length of the sofa back, uses it as an excuse to squeeze my shoulder. 'She could do no wrong in your eyes.'

'What's that supposed to mean?'

'Just that. It was a mutual adoration society – neither of you prepared to imagine, for one second, that the other had a single fault.'

I fidget, curl my legs up underneath me. It is not as warm in here as it was outside by the fire. 'Sounds like a group I'd pay good money to join.'

'Anyone would.' A hand snakes across the cushion, lands – affable – on my leg. 'What an absolute perfect set-up, to be the hero of someone who is your hero. It was enviable, I tell you. Everyone should have that in their lives.'

I don't move his hand – the human contact feels good, warm and safe. 'I doubt I was Rachel's hero. But she was mine.'

'It was as mutual as anything could be. The envy of anyone who glanced past it.' He points at me with the hand that isn't moving up my thigh. 'And I say glanced past it because no one could get in, there was no room for a third party there. Not me, not Tim.

Total commitment, warts and all. It was annoying sometimes. But mostly, it was enviable. Everyone should have that.'

He has relaxed while he speaks, we both have. I am sitting on the sofa with my ex-husband, in the same familiar position we used to be in while we watched TV, listened to music, started the niggling rows that would eventually become pearls of discontent in our lives.

Nothing else is the same. The nagging doubts, the looming suspicions that were part of everyday life with Terry have gone. The ache to make him love me has spent time mellowing: it has matured and fluttered quietly away. And that changes everything.

'Are you tired?' I ask him.

Terry is hard-wired to take advantage of a euphemism. 'I think I am,' he says.

I stand up and trail my hand towards his.

He squeezes my hand as he gets up. We are almost the same height, Terry and I: he has a couple of inches on me at best, but he is thick-set and muscular – and mortal.

On the landing, Terry goes to open my bedroom door.

'That's not mine any more.'

He looks surprised.

'Long story,' I say. I put my hand on the brass doorknob of Rachel's room, but it feels wrong. I don't want to take Terry in there – that room is still the place where Rachel and I are unfurling, finding our new edges.

I open the airing cupboard, take out a thick wedge of bedding. 'Duncan and Rosie's room,' I say to him and kick the bottom of the door open before I can change my mind.

When you decide to have casual sex with someone you've slept with hundreds of times before, the unromantic tasks – making a bed, putting a quilt in a cover – are things you already know how to do together, prerequisites that need no explaining, no directions.

The dance of tucking in corners, shaking out pillows, without bumping into one another becomes almost electric. The middle-aged foreplay of crisp ironed sheets.

I smooth the white sheet across the mattress with my hand and I know that this is going to be a cleansing, a ritual banishment of all the awful things that happened in this room.

Rachel and I are even now; we both kept the secrets we needed to.

There is no consent to question in this room tonight, no commitment on either side. I am the one making the rules, the decisions. There is no surrender in this, only a reaching out and a taking of what I need – from someone happy to give it.

Chapter Twenty-six

We wake up later than I'd intended. My pillow smells of woodsmoke from my hair.

'Shit.' I shake Terry awake. 'We need to get up. I'm cooking lunch for friends.'

He rubs his eyes. 'That was a rude awakening. Not even coffee?'

'No.' This isn't the first time I've slept with Terry since we broke up for the final time. It's always been like this – transactional, no commitment on either part. I wasn't sure it was particularly healthy, but Rachel dismissed that out of hand.

'Whatever makes you happy, babe.' She laughed like a drain every time it happened – every time I rang her the next day, shame-faced and probably hungover. 'Just remember your solicitor who you're paying through the nose for when you could have chatted it out on the pillow.'

'I need the solicitor for the other Terry,' I remember telling her. 'He's two fucking people.'

He still is, but I have the good one here right now. More importantly, I am sending him home.

'This view is amazing.' He deliberately includes my naked back in his comment, which we both know is really about the window. 'Why haven't we slept in here before?'

'Reasons,' I say, and the ghost of Tristan wavers faintly before disappearing completely. 'And Rachel died in here.'

'Bless her,' he says, and means it. He loved her deeply too. 'Maybe we've, you know, breathed a bit of life into it.'

'Your charity knows no bounds,' I say, and laugh as I drag him out of bed. 'Now get dressed and bugger off.'

I leave him to shower and go downstairs to start the lunch. I'm surprised to find I'm still singing.

◆ ◆ ◆

There are gaps in the things I know – the things I understand – and Tim has asked Ben to talk me through what he can, the mechanics of it at least. Tim assures me – in a very Tim way, in a very formal email – that Ben will not discuss anything Rachel told him, that their client-therapist relationship still holds after she has gone.

This lunch will be the start of that chat, of opening what doors we can.

I am looking forward to the clatter of Meg coming back. I have a purpose with her, and a time frame. I have someone to share joy with.

Yesterday, I washed Rosie's old tablecloths from the bottom drawer in the kitchen, and they are still waving like a carnival from the washing line.

I have wrestled the garden table out of the shed and done my best to de-cobweb it. It isn't fooling anybody – it is nine-tenths insects and very little wood, but it will do for now and we won't be able to see it under the tablecloth decorated with tea roses and swallows: so ancient it is back in style again.

Twice I've shouted upstairs to Terry to hurry-the-fuck-up. Twice, he's yelled back that he's nearly ready and to chill out.

Reasons I am not married to him are rolling quietly down the stairs and settling at my feet.

Fuchsias bloom by the back door – out of control and monstrous, taller than a human but livid with drooping pink flowers. I clip a thick handful of them and put them in a jar in the centre of the table. I try not to lean against the table as I set it – one hard shove and it would go. The kitchen chairs are squashed around it and hopefully they and our own knees and laps will act as enough of a prop for it not to fall down during lunch.

I step back towards the sea, take a picture of the little set-up on my phone camera: conscious that I was – automatically – going to send it to Rachel. Instead, I store it, close the camera and keep it in the photo files for me – for a dark day, for when it rains.

Lunch is potted shrimp, fragrant with white pepper and mace, a treacle soda bread to eat it on, and a watermelon gazpacho bold with all the colours of summer and piquant with chilli. I have made a salad that looks simple and thrown together but hides emerald gems of asparagus tips and edamame beans under the lettuce leaves and fronds of rocket. For pudding, there is a lemon cake, sharp and sweet, dusted with white icing sugar. I am cooking to impress but I don't want to look too deeply at that, at the nagging worry that Ben knows everything there is to know about me: that Rachel has told him every ugly secret I ever told her.

Lemon cake probably isn't enough to make him forget.

Terry and I have only just left to walk to my car when I see the shape of Ben and Meg on the path ahead. Instantly, I wish I'd taken a different route – or got Terry out earlier, even made him walk back to the station. This is an explanation I don't need.

'I'm so sorry, guys.' I'm behind schedule and flustered. 'Everything's half an hour out of sync. Meg, Ben, this is Terry, my ex-husband.' I'm certain Rachel will have told him who Terry is, how ragged the ends of our relationship are.

'How do you do?' says Terry, jumping in before Ben has a chance to speak, taking control of the meeting and shaking his hand.

Ben smiles at him, completely unfazed, and I remember that Rachel's counselling was about her, not me.

'We'll be half an hour. I'll just take Terry to the station. Everything's ready.'

Behind Ben, and just out of his eyeline, Meg gives me a wink and a subtle thumbs-up.

I glare at her, at her unequivocal assessment of the situation. I pull Terry by his elbow and walk away as fast as my flip-flops allow along the sandy path.

We chat in the car. It's a sunny day but there are clouds – almost without shape – leaching the colour from the sky here and there. The sunlight acts differently on the clouds, glows white wherever they drift. Terry and I talk about the setting and the forests and how gorgeous it all is. But something is different between us, something has changed – an enchantment while we slept. A transition.

By the time we get to the station car park and Terry goes to kiss me goodbye, it is real, over.

When I say goodbye to Terry, friendly, warm, I realise that Tristan Willoughby wasn't the only ghost declawed and disarmed last night.

◆ ◆ ◆

All the way back, I think of phrases I can use to ask Ben what he knows, twists of sentences that will trap him before he realises, snares to snap information and drag it back towards me. 'Why my mother? What happened there?'

Ben is in the kitchen when I get back. 'Ah, sorry,' he says. 'I hope you don't think this is rude – I was just getting a coffee.'

I wave my hand, a gesture that says to go ahead, *mi casa es su casa*, and he turns back towards the kettle.

'I hope we're not interrupting,' Ben says. 'With your ex-husband, I mean. I hope we didn't scare him off.'

My cheeks burn with the distinct feeling that Ben is fishing, and my palms are suddenly clammy. It's been a year or two since my last – daylight – hot flush, and it's a terrible testament to my life that I think this is menopausal before I think it could be sexual attraction. 'Terry was going anyway.' I leave it at that.

Meg breezes in like a wind from the sea. 'It's so good to be back.' And she squeezes me, a hand on each of my arms, her head leaning in towards my shoulder. 'The city is great, but this is greater.'

'When it's not raining,' I say. But even when it's raining there is a delight to sitting in the warm and dry, watching raindrops blur the beach and the gulls – limitless – lifted by the gusts. I feel bad, overprivileged. 'It is really great.'

Ben sits well in this picture of seaside-perfect. He is more casual than he was in the gallery. He is wearing shorts, khaki and ironed, and a long-sleeved white shirt with the cuffs rolled up just once, neatly. He has swapped his expensive leather trainers for expensive leather flip-flops. His legs are thick with dark hairs.

'We call this look *beach boyfriend*,' Rachel would say – has said over the years, about men dressed similarly.

I pass him the tray that I've stacked with glasses and a water jug, try not to brush his hands in the act of it in case my smouldering skin combusts. 'Thanks,' I say and my voice crackles at the edges.

Ben looks at me with sympathy, assuming it is the loss of Rachel that has strangled my voice.

My inner Rachel laughs like a drain and cheerleads me with a few spicy words. 'Back on the horse that threw you?' she says. 'Look out, world.'

'I brought some flowers,' Ben says. 'To say thank you for looking after this one, and for lunch of course. But they're in the car.' He puts his hand to his forehead, a gesture of frustration.

'It's not that warm, they should be alright until we've eaten. And then we could go for a walk anyway?' I make it a question, and will him to understand that I mean just him and me, that I need to ask my questions.

'Perfect.'

'And I need to swim,' Meg says. 'I've dehydrated, I'm almost a landlubber again.'

'Don't swim naked while I'm here.' Ben shakes his head at her.

'I wish I'd never told you. Anyway, I have a full sealskin that I put on to keep warm. And become a seal for the day, obviously.' There is a glass of wine in front of her, a biscuit-yellow fizz.

'Don't drink that.' Perhaps there is a voice, a tone, that those who have almost drowned can use. 'Alcohol and swimming is an absolute no.'

She looks at me, her head pitched down so that she can gaze past her eyebrows – stern. 'Are you picking him up by osmosis?' she says, pointing to Ben, but she puts her fingers on the bottom of the glass, pushes it away.

There are clouds out to sea. Puffs and billows that look as though you could touch them, stuff them into your mouth so their spun water melts like candy floss. The shapes are random: a stretched-out swipe of white here, a crocodile there.

We eat with our eyes crinkled against the sun. The atmosphere is light, friendly. Three people who are happy to be here.

I offer Ben a second slice of cake. His enthusiasm for the first one was impressive: I have always enjoyed people who truly love to eat – who really appreciate what I have made for them, how long it took, how much of me is in it.

'Maybe I need to walk first. In fact, definitely. If I stay here, I'll grow roots.'

I can see him rooted here – his toes gnarling down into the earth, the mossy grass clutching his ankles and turning him into the landscape. He fits here better than Terry might; I don't know whether that's his accent making him sound as if he belongs, or his genes that are made of this place, this country.

'Sounds good. I'll get my shoes.' I have walked barefoot to and from the cottage with the food, savouring the feel of the tiny patch of sea grass, blue-green and sharp against my feet, contrasting with the flat cool of the flagstones in the hallway.

I have a small row of shoes in the hall now, underneath the hat stand-cum-coat rack that still groans with the weight of the Willoughbys. I run my finger along them: too tight; too hot; just right. My just right is a pair of old canvas sneakers, pale orange with wear and almost through at the toes. I push a couple of umbrellas to one side, squeeze in underneath the coats to perch on the bench and put my shoes on.

I pause at the door, look into the bull's-eye glass and fuss my hair in the warped circular reflection. I am wearing an old-fashioned tea dress, and sneakers with no socks: I feel young and floaty, improved.

I might as well get it over with.

'I thought you were her boyfriend.' It is the first thing I say as we step off the beach and into the forest. It seems appropriate, it seems like a confession I need to make.

Ben smiles. 'That was pretty apparent. And a not unreasonable conclusion.'

It is an absolution of sorts, and we walk on in silence. Ahead of us, a jay perches on the branch of a tree, his slate-blue wings vivid against his pink breast.

'What is that?' says Ben. 'I didn't know we had birds like that in Scotland.'

There is a blood-curdling screeching from the other side of the path. 'A jay, and that's the other half. Mrs Jay – or Mr Jay – asking where he's gone and why he's standing so close to the humans.'

We walk further into the forest, following the dappled gold that catches on the copper beech leaves, sparkles on the trunks of silver birch. It makes sense to walk out first then come back via the car park, collect the flowers on the way home.

The quiet of our feet on the generations of soft pine needles, the soft forest floor, makes us part of nature. When the first speckles of misty rain patter through the leaves, we don't break our pace; the drizzle is so light it is barely damp.

'Do you know Rockcliffe?' he asks me. 'Just up the coast?'

I tell him that I do, that I've been there many times.

'I went there on holiday as a wee boy, every year. I think most of Glasgow did. I have so many memories connected to this landscape.' He's lost in them for a moment.

We chat for a while about the landscape, and he is easy company. We are both waiting for the conversation to begin.

We turn and walk up the side of a burn, dark peaty water flowing oh-so-gently through a shallow trench, overgrown with moss at each side.

Ben decides he's found it, the moment. 'I can't talk about Rachel's thoughts, you understand. It was a professional relationship and everything she said to me is confidential.'

I nod. It has been hard to understand Rachel's need for silence, to shut me out of this, her terrible pain. But I am starting to get it – most of it – starting to know that we all have things we keep hidden.

'I'm surprised I can love her so much when I didn't know her. When she kept so much from me.'

Ben watches his feet on the path. His silence is clearly deliberate.

'I do, though, I do still love every part of her.' The words leave a track of tightness in my throat.

'Good,' is all he says.

I have thought long and hard about this limited amount of time I have with him, about the questions I can – and can't – ask. 'Obviously, I want to know about Rachel and my mother.'

He maintains his calm silence. The space for my words is enormous. Above us, a high canopy of green moves gently, telling me shhh. But there has been enough shushing, enough swallowing of secrets.

I listen to the forest for a moment, to the blunt echo as our feet fall on the soft moss and sand floor, to the birds screeching and singing. If I hold my breath, I can hear the rain weaving through the leaves.

'I don't have any memories of the Willoughbys where they weren't drinking.' It dawned on me last night, a realisation – just as I slipped into sleep – that this didn't start with Rachel, that her parents died young too, even though they seemed so old to us at the time. 'Even Rachel's grandad always had a tumbler of whisky on the go.' I only met him a few times; he died in his sixties, but I can vividly picture the inch of liquid in the bottom of his glass, the smell of it permeating whichever room he was in.

When Ben speaks, it is as if he is rewarding me for making the connection, for working part of it out on my own. 'Permanent happiness is not a normal human condition,' he says.

There is a pause where he lets the phrase sink in, lets the rhythm of my feet land on happiness and human. Repeated.

'But we're led to believe that it is.' His voice is quiet, fits the pine needles and the light-green moss that covers the branches like fur. 'And there are certain personality types, people, who are tied up in knots by that. For a lifetime.'

'I hate to think that she wasn't happy.'

He doesn't commit to this. Doesn't even shrug. 'How much do you know about alcoholism?'

I've been looking online, reading the websites of support groups I should have been part of while she was alive. 'I've started reading.'

'May I?' He is asking if he can explain, if it is patronising to add to my research.

I know how far away from the truth internet rabbit holes can take you: I'd far rather hear it from him – I'd rather it was said here.

'Firstly, you need to understand addiction. When we think of addicts, of addiction, we're mostly thinking of people who aren't able to access the thing they're addicted to.' He leaves that trademark gap for me to imagine.

I think about my go-to picture of an addict – desperate, miserable, and nothing like Rachel with her bright skin, white teeth, her sparkling, active mind. I nod; there is no point pretending I thought otherwise.

'But many people live perfectly well with addictions – even in situations you wouldn't expect, like heroin. If you can afford your addiction – in terms of money, time, and health – the chances are that even your closest friends will never know. The problems come when we can't access the thing we need. That's when people find out. I'm simplifying,' he adds. 'Generalising. But please don't feel like you weren't listening to her, weren't watching out for Rachel. Addicts, in general, learn a lot of skills to hide their problem.'

'But she came to you. She trusted you.'

'That's my job. We became very good friends, insofar as I can be friends with a client, but it was a professional relationship.' We turn on to another path without consulting one another, weave deeper into the trees. 'It can be much easier to talk to someone when you pay them to listen.'

He raises one hand as he talks, slightly bends his index finger as if to trace the thread of what he's trying to say. 'Have you ever seen one of those quizzes in a newspaper or online – they were big in magazines in the nineties – that say *Are you an alcoholic?* and then list a load of questions, of scenarios?'

I nod. Memories arise of Rachel and I asking each other, working through the list, of feigning shock and horror when the quiz decided that we were, in fact, alcoholics – although I'm still convinced that neither of us was back then.

'Those quizzes were adapted from questions we actually ask, scales and measurements that we use. But completely out of context. When we ask, in addiction support, if you drink alone, we mean: "Are you so changed or challenged by alcohol that you avoid family or friends, or aren't comfortable out in public?"'

I think of occasional trips with Rachel where her bravado was out of control, facing up to leering men on the Tube, flirting with stag dos or rugby club trips. I'd envied her – wished that I had her daring.

'The quizzes ask if your drinking has ever led to you missing work – but they don't mean did you stay in bed one Friday because your hangover was so bad. They mean, "Did you ever take two months off to try and get your drinking back into a manageable place?" And by *manageable*, obviously, we mean *hideable*, *disguisable*.'

Rachel, flying alone to Bali for a six-week spa. Rachel taking time off after breaking her ankle and using it to 'regroup'. And sometimes, times when I'd thought Tim was in control of her or that their attempts to have a baby might have secretly started again, just being out of reach – being *off*, being un-Rachel.

He breaks his stride slightly and my eyes drop to our feet, to the dichotomy of our shoes. His are clean leather flip-flops, mine are off-white canvas, sneakers that have been tarnished with summers here, with seawater and beach tar, with soil from the garden. I didn't notice the drizzle stopping but it has gone. The sun is a colourless glow through the leaves.

'I'll just say this now because it's a personal crusade.' He smiles at me. 'Forgive my zealousness. We have a hierarchy of addiction in this country – along with an enormous problem. We don't see the heroin addict begging outside Tesco as suffering from the same condition as a millionaire whose drug is fine wine, vintage everything. We think of people addicted to prescription drugs as somehow cleaner, less desperate. But addiction is addiction, no matter what your drug. The same condition.'

'An illness.' I say the words for him: words I want him to say about Rachel. Words that will forgive my inattention, everything I've missed.

'That's the debate. Is heroin use an illness? Or a lifestyle choice?'

'Before' – there's no point lying to him, and I feel as if he'd know anyway – 'before, I would have said lifestyle choice, but Rachel didn't choose this. This is something that happened to her – like an illness.'

We have stopped at a crossroads in the forest. The junction is bigger than usual – a loggers' path, wide enough for their rumbling lorries to drive through laden with trunks.

'Which way?' he asks me.

'I've never been here before. These paths are bonkers. You choose.'

He sets off to the right, in the direction that should be towards the sea if my internal compass is working.

240

'Did you get into this line of work because of your wife?' I ask. I don't know if it's rude to let him know that Meg told me, to blur his worlds.

'I had to find something less personally consuming – and damaging – than psychiatry. This is an area that I can have successes in – full recoveries, new lives.'

We are silent while we think of the failures and the losses.

And then I hear it. Tiny bells from a fairy tale, hollow ringing chimes of bamboo percussion. The sounds are completely incongruous, wild on the wind.

I step towards the sound, Ben following when he hears it too. And then it is in front of us. Just there, as if it has been waiting all these years. Patient and solid.

Our prayer tree. The crazy dream that Rachel and I found so long ago.

It is smaller than I remember, a twisting beech tree rather than the broad and ancient oak of my imagination. But this is definitely it.

The tree is festooned with joy, with fragments of gladness, scraps of glee. It is the happiest thing I have ever seen, tied with mirth and memories and prayers. Wishes and poems droop from it like ripe fruit, rags and patches and ropes climb around it like vines.

The tree flutters and flaps, a fiesta of colour among the green. Someone – or many someones – has spent years tying tiny flags of bold red, blazing orange and bright yellow through its branches. The twigs are heavy with gold brocade, looped round and round, twisted and tightened like bewitched ivy.

I have found the prayer tree.

It is absorbing enough to forget that I am even here with another person. I only remember when Ben's hand moves towards mine, when he curls his fingers through my fingers so that two people can see the tree, so that it is a dream I share with another human being.

We stand and take it in, bewitched.

Eventually, I drop Ben's hand – it feels completely natural both to hold it and to release it. I reach up and turn a piece of paper, flying nearest my face. The writing has long since faded, as if the wish disappeared after being granted. Next to it, from a gnarled branch lumpy with fungus, the golden threads of an embroidered square catch the sun. 'Here lie my dreams,' the stitches spell out. 'The best of me.'

There are dots and stripes and emblems. All manner of fabric has been used here. And everywhere, way above arm height, way into the tree, short ribbons of material are tied – like tags – round twigs and branches.

The years of work in this tree make me feel my heart in a way I haven't for months now, make me feel three-dimensional again. There are faded yellows that have leaked into the sun, greens that have dissolved in the face of spring showers, blues that have frozen into ghosts.

Ben takes a piece of red fabric in his hands, pulls it closer to read it, then extends his arm again. 'I didn't bring my glasses.'

It is a tiny embroidered lantern, picked out in gold on the red fabric. The words 'Be the light' are stitched underneath it in miniscule writing.

'Beautiful,' he says, when I tell him. 'This place is something else.'

'I wonder if Rachel ever left anything here. If she ever asked this tree for help.'

His face is impassive; he wouldn't tell me, if he'd embroidered it for her himself.

Instead, I talk about the tree. 'Do you think it's alright to read other people's wishes? Their private offerings to the tree?'

'I don't think it's alright, I think it's imperative.' He straightens up, visibly interested. 'The prayers and the writings are here for us to channel our collective strength in the direction of the person who's asking.' He shows me a piece of white cloth; it could have been torn from a work shirt, a school shirt. *Help me*, it says in big black letters, drawn with a marker pen.

Neither of us wants to voice the possibility that Rachel wrote it. It's not her writing – or her style.

'If you were the person who left this,' Ben says, 'I think part of why you're leaving it is for someone else – a complete stranger – to send you love, some good wishes into the universe.'

It's such a strange thing to hear from such an ordered man, such a cautious person.

'And do you believe in that?'

'The power of collective consciousness?' he asks.

'If you like. The power of prayer.' I think of my mother's unhappiness. All the prayer in the world didn't help her, didn't shore her up.

'I think it's all we have,' Ben says, and he pats the trunk of the tree like he's telling it to rest.

Our friendship is growing like a living thing between us, creeping along the forest floor like ivy, seeping into cracks like moss.

'Cup of tea?' I ask him, needing something prosaic, mundane, to ground us.

'More lemon cake?' he asks, as if it's a bargain.

We walk in near silence to the car, overwhelmed by the dark wood and the secrets it keeps.

Ben's flowers are the essence of summer, crisp blue statice and long stems of lavender. The smell is warm and hopeful.

'Good choice,' I tell him and try to ignore the fact that our hands touched for a fraction of a second longer than they would have before.

We have walked to the curve of the bay when Ben says, 'There is one person who can tell you the stuff I can't.' He takes the eggshells we've tiptoed over to make a lovely sunny afternoon, tips them on to the path and dances on them: 'Your mother knows everything – as far as I can tell.'

The thought of seeing my mother after thirty-eight years, the idea of walking back into that glass house, that ice palace, makes me shiver despite the warm westerly breeze and the smell of seaweed drying in the sun.

A tiny brown lizard flicks its legs and tail and skitters across the toe of my shoe. It pauses, stock-still, to keep predators confused, then flashes back to life, disappears in the yellow scrub beside the path.

'I'll do what I can to help you.' Ben looks ahead, closes his eyes against the shine of sun on sand. 'I'll come with you if you want. Same as I did for Rachel.'

There is a startling series of beeps and chirrups with a flurry of messages: Ben must have stepped under the path of the satellite. He takes his phone from his pocket and scrolls with one finger.

'Fuck,' he says. 'I'm going to have to go. It's my ex-wife.'

'Everything OK?' I ask, although I can see from his face that it isn't.

'She's in hospital. Accidental overdose.'

'Oh my God. Do you want me to get Meg, drive her up?'

Ben shakes his head. 'Wendy's being looked after. It's actually a step forward – it's very hard to access any help if you're not in a hospital. At least now she can be assessed, get some in-patient care. But I have to be there to make sure they know what they need to.'

'Do I tell Meg?'

'Thanks, yes. But Wendy's truly not in any danger. Accent the positives, if you could.' Just as he turns to walk back to the car, Ben moves across the few feet of space between us, kisses my cheek. 'Thanks for everything. It's been a beautiful day.'

Only when he's out of sight do I realise the rain has started again.

Chapter Twenty-seven

MEG

Being back in the sea is a joy. I have to find a way to make this my doorstep, to live somewhere with a front garden made of water. I dig my nails into my palms when I think of the money I wasted – I wish I hadn't done it. Liam had wanted us to travel, to see other cultures and understand them. Now I understand that travelling on credit is just a holiday, no different to someone's parents paying for their gap year: you have to work and support yourself to make something real, to properly experience it. I'm getting more from my weeks here than all those eco-lodges and guided tours with Liam.

My dad's not daft. When he stops being distracted by Jo and our inevitable showdown happens, he is going to remember those trips I made. And he's going to realise that Liam – just as he expected – didn't pay his share.

It would be cheaper to move somewhere like this than stay in the city – cheaper and more beautiful – but I'd need a job. This place is rural. Short of selling ice creams and pulling pints from May to October, there's not even enough work for the locals. What I've saddled myself with is the need for an extra income. If I didn't have any debts, I could live here on next to nothing. But I'm an idiot, and I do.

I push my face into the water to squash the misery out of my head. I feel the stretch down my sides as I slice an arm ahead of me, pull back through the water and propel myself forward by my own strength. It is harder swimming in the sea than a pool – easier to float because of all the salt, but harder to get through it, to get where you're going. I concentrate on powering my legs, starting the kick at my thighs, not my knees.

This swim is meditative, and I suppose that's what makes it so addictive. I'm trying not to think about when I've finished my work at Clachan, about what I'll do then, but there are holiday cottages up and down this coast, in every bay and on every clifftop – I might not approve of them being empty most of the time, but decorating them would be a way to stay here.

As my hands – fingers slightly splayed, knuckles straight – carve the waves, I think about places I can advertise, ways to get my services out there, to let people know. I want to stay for a good long time. Maybe forever.

For now, with Jo's bedroom as my base, I'll make the most of it. Squeeze the best of every day like my granny does. My granny talks about 'tonics' – anything or anyone that improves your life is a tonic: a holiday, or a friend or seeing a wee dog in the park. My granny has been a tonic for me.

I've brought the picture of William back here, found it a frame – one of the huge stack of empty ones leaning against the wall in the loft. I'm going to keep him by my bed and acknowledge him every day. I already feel less alone for it.

This side of the channel between the cottage and the island is a tricky patch, a junction where the tides from the sea meet the currents of the firth. I switch to breaststroke to make sure I catch the right channel, get through safely.

The view isn't as lovely as it was – I swam into light sparkling on the water all around me. Now, it's less picture postcard – the drizzle has started again and everything is one colour, the waves, the sky, even my hands if I look underwater.

The seal is sudden, she is no more than three metres in front of me, making full eye contact so close I can see the water on her long whiskers. I almost gasp out loud.

I'm not sure what to do – I know she isn't aggressive, we've come close before, but I've never been quite this close to her. I tread water while I think, moving my feet underneath me as if I am climbing stairs.

There is a grey line underneath the stark white clouds to the right of me, across the bay. Swimming in summer rain is a beautiful thing, but not this rain – this promises to bring the worst of Scottish summer and I need to get out of the water.

While I am thinking, and making as little movement as possible, the seal bobs her head about. Without warning she rises out of the water, easily as big as I am, and crashes down in front of me. The splash is enough to send me backwards and I turn on to my front and swim as fast as I can towards the shore.

It is a ten-minute swim at this speed, or at least it would be if I could maintain this pace. Breathless from the original shock of it, as well as the pressure of swimming, I take a pause to see where she is.

Next to me, further out this time, too far for me to touch her, the seal lies in the water: her grey back above the water and her nose bobbing up and down from air to wave.

I move.

She moves.

I turn back towards the cloud, the rapidly widening band of rain – I'm testing her.

She appears in front of me, between me and the island, and again rises to her full height – lands on the water in front of me with a smash. I can smell her fish breath, her sea skin, as she lands. I am showered with the water she displaces.

The seal is herding me, there is no doubt about it. Every time I turn towards the island, she gets between me and the skyline, leaps towards me without ever quite connecting, but making it clear who's in control. When I do as I'm told and head back towards Clachan, she swims along beside me, half in, half out, her wet back shining in the sea and the rain.

I swim on, reaching the shore before the rain really starts – just as the seal would like me to. I'm planning how to tell Jo – which bits to act out and which bits to leave till the grand finale, my big *saved by a seal* moment.

But then I see her leaving the trees and coming towards me and I know straight away that something's wrong. That this is not the time to tell Jo, that I – terrified now – must wait for her to say something to me.

She meets me halfway down the beach, my towel in her hands.

'It's OK,' she says – but her face says otherwise.

I will her to tell me, just so I can breathe. If I don't breathe, nothing is wrong. It isn't my dad, my granny – my mum.

'Your mum's had a bit of an accident.'

My heart leaps in my chest, then crushes me from the outside in. It feels as if someone has their hand inside me, is squeezing my life out through the gaps between their clenched knuckles.

'She's fine, and your dad's with her. Well, he's on his way. But he's spoken to her medical team—' She stops herself, backtracks. 'Her doctor. He's spoken to her doctor, and she's not in any danger.'

'What sort of accident?'

Jo swallows, coughs a little to clear her throat.

I have grown up with this language, but she has not: she isn't used to it. 'An overdose?' I ask.

'An accidental overdose. Your dad said you don't need to come – it's all under control and she's safe.'

'Will you take me?' The train will take hours. I need to be there. This is why the selkie sent me back to shore – to be with my mum.

'Go and grab a shower. We'll leave as soon as you're ready.'

It's almost dark when we get to Glasgow. The rain has made it darker earlier than normal and the streetlights as the motorway cuts across the city bleach Jo's face out.

We haven't spoken much on the way. I told her about the seal, and she said how nice it was and that I should maybe contact one of the local TV shows. And I said that that was probably beyond uncool and we laughed a bit, but neither of us meant it.

I am thinking about all the things I haven't said to my mum, about the way I cut her out of my life.

And Jo doesn't have to tell me that she's thinking about Rachel and how she wishes she could have made this dash for her, perhaps even saved her.

I'm scared to speak in case she says it out loud and I don't know how to answer her. I text my dad every twenty minutes or so, but his replies are loose: positive but non-committal. He knows how to write a text like that, both personally and professionally.

He has texted me the address of the hospital and I plug my phone into the dash of Jo's car so that we have the directions. We will be there in eight minutes and I feel sick.

I try to think about the seal, about her guiding me away from danger. About how huge she was when she needed me to respect her, when she towered above me in the water. I think about telling my mum the story, of her wide brown eyes, of how hard she would laugh. I think of all the women I've wished were my mum – a couple of Dad's girlfriends over the years; Rachel, of course; and now – Jo.

I think of the photos at my gran's house, the degree certificates on the wall, her obvious pride. I like – even love – all the other women because they're each great in their own way, but they're not my mum.

'You want to talk about it?' Jo asks. We are in the city now and the streetlights are a rhythmic pulse through the car.

'Now you ask.' I look at my phone. 'When we've got six minutes left.'

She looks at me, smiles. 'Precis,' she says.

'How did you stop talking to your mum?' I ask her.

'She let me down. Didn't take my side. And I just walked away.'

I don't say anything, my mind is a loop of memories, of conversations. I've always felt that my mum let me down – from the day she let William down when she should have been watching him. Only now, with four minutes left till I see her and the gnawing worry that she might die, I can't remember – apart from the little ginger cat who she cried over and apologised for and never got over – the other times she let me down.

Please, I whisper to no one, *don't let anything happen to her*.

Let me have another chance.

It's more of a clinic than a hospital. I wonder if it's private and my dad has arranged for her to be here instead of somewhere where she might get less care. For all the years they've been separated – everything she's put him through – he does still love her. He does, as he constantly reminds me, still respect her.

I text my dad to tell him we're here and he comes through to the reception almost immediately.

He looks like he's aged ten years since we ate lunch on the seashore outside Jo's house.

He's not old, my dad, as dads go. Fifty-two. Younger than Jo, although you wouldn't know it from the way he goes on. Jo is much freer. I feel guilty for thinking that; maybe she hasn't had as much to cope with as he has. I reach across the gap between us, hug him really tight.

'Is Mum alright?' I ask, my voice that kind of quiet that doesn't want to know.

'She will be.' He kisses the top of my head like I'm still a baby, reaches out to Jo and touches her arm. 'Thanks, Jo. That was a long drive.'

She shakes her head, she means *It was nothing, it was all I could do*.

'Do you know what happened?' Jo asks. She steps back as she says it, as if there is a line on the floor and she's worried she crossed it.

My dad lets go of me, but keeps me right by him. 'She tried to stop. Unsupervised. Use some nonsense from the internet to wean herself off.' He waves at a doctor down the hall, gets his attention. 'I'm not criticising her,' he says specifically to me. 'It was a valiant attempt, but not the right one.'

He walks away for a moment, towards the other doctor, and they speak in mumbled doctor voices while Jo and I stare around the glass-walled foyer, gawp at the flowers on the reception desk.

'I'm busting for a wee,' I tell Jo and go in search of a loo. It is as squeaky clean and white-walled as the rest of the place. It is quiet and cool in here and, at the long run of pristine basins, I splash my face with water, take deep breaths.

In lieu of giving myself a physical shake, I splash more water on my face, straighten my spine, and make some decisions.

My dad is sitting in the corridor with Jo when I come out of the loo. There are no other patients around, no buzz of crises or doctors in panic.

'What is this place?' I ask him.

'It's a specialist clinic. State-of-the-art, with a waiting list as long as your arm. Your mum accidentally bumped herself to the top of it. Result.' He stands up, hands in his pockets. 'Is there anyone you want to call? Liam? He's very welcome here if that's what you want.'

I half-laugh. 'Liam and I aren't a thing any more. I kicked him into the long grass months ago, but I didn't want to tell you – didn't want you to be right.'

He's not even cross. And he doesn't laugh it off. 'Sorry, I can be a bit of a know-it-all.'

He's a horrific know-it-all but I'm not going to spoil this moment, this peace.

'I made some mistakes,' I say, and he resists bringing up the bailiff's letters, the threats to his home. 'Granny said something the other day.' And I pause because it will hurt him.

'Granny said, "It's only been nineteen years. They haven't learned to live with their loss yet." And it made me feel so awful, made me realise how big it is. That I never stop to imagine what it's like to be you two.'

Dad takes my hand and we move down the corridor a little, sit underneath an enormous coconut palm. It feels like a high-end airport lounge, an oasis in the chaos.

'When you lose a baby, you don't process – immediately – that you've lost so much more than that: you've lost a child, an adult, their children. It's not until you see your other child grow and develop and become their own person that you really start to understand what was lost.' He leans forward, his head in his hands.

Behind him and a way away, I can see that Jo is getting coffees for us, arranging biscuits on a plate.

'We don't have a reason William died – we never will. Sudden Infant Death Syndrome. He was asleep next to your mum – in his little carrycot – and his heart stopped. It nearly killed us, your mum and me, but we couldn't die because we had you. And we underestimated the impact everything had on you.'

'I thought Mum was on something. I thought it was like the kitten.'

'We should have made sure you understood. I was a bloody psychiatrist, for God's sake. Cobbler's children,' he says, and exhales the sadness of William's little lifetime. 'The drugs your mum battles with were prescribed to her when William died. I should never have let it happen, but I didn't know how to deal with all our grief. Yours, hers, and mine.'

'I'm sorry about the bailiffs, Dad. About the debts. I know it's not what you wanted, and it was stupid. I regret it every day.'

'It matters so little, Meg,' he says. 'I know it seems huge now, but it matters so very little in the great scheme of things. There is so much time to put it right and I should have told you that instead of shouting.' He puts his arms around me. 'We have the privilege to be able to sort it out. I'll ring round with you, and we'll sort it out. No one died.'

The lights in my mum's room are dim, the curtains pulled against the city nightscape. She is half-sitting up in bed, against white pillows that are almost luminescent. Her long, pale arms are over the covers and by her sides, as if she hasn't the energy to move them from where the nurses had put them.

'I'm so sorry, darling,' Mum whispers into the shadows, and she doesn't say whether she means for now, for this, or for all the years we've wasted.

I take one of her hands in mine, squeeze her damp palm. 'It doesn't matter. It's all history. I'm sorry too.' And I perch on the side of her bed, shoogle myself in until I'm beside her, lying against her shoulder. Physically, we are almost the same size now – she's slightly smaller than me – but she feels like my mum again.

Our voices are soft and we talk in the half-dark. No one comes in, no one disturbs us. The things we say are private, sometimes wordless, but they will go on and on.

When my mum falls asleep, I kiss her and creep quietly back to the bright lights of the corridor, to my dad and Jo.

They are sitting side by side on a row of otherwise empty chairs. Their heads tilt towards each other and they are dozing. I sit quietly nearby – with myself; it feels wrong to wake them.

My dad opens one eye and looks over. He smiles at me, hollow but hopeful.

'It's like suddenly realising you're an adult.' We're in the car; Jo is driving us back to Clachan.

I'd have stayed with my mum if she'd wanted me to but she's going to do a couple of weeks of assessment, to get started on her treatment. So when Jo offered to go and get my clothes, I said we'd be better just both going home.

'Worst of all is one thought that keeps going round and round in my head.'

Jo doesn't speak: she has enough baggage of her own to let mine roll without stopping it, bless her.

'They both dealt with it in their own ways – no judgement.' A car zips past us at crazy speed, disappears into the night, and we both whistle through our teeth. 'And I blamed Mum for all sorts – cut her right out. But the person I punished the most – literally on a daily basis – was my dad. The actual person who'd stuck around to take it. How does that make any sense at all?'

Jo taps one finger on the steering wheel. 'Human nature. But he's a good man, and he loves you, you can move on from it.'

We don't talk much after that. I suggest a podcast – about seals – and Jo's more than happy to agree. I think she's had enough of our family for one day. It's two days now, actually – three o'clock in the morning and almost twelve hours since we left home.

The walk from the car is beautiful; the moon is a silver disc in the sky, far bigger than it should be, and the forest is full of the sounds of those who are not sleeping. When we step out of the trees on to the beach, we both gasp.

The bay is a painting. The sea is as thick and grey as soup; the beach looks as if it has been dipped in lead. There are no colours except every shade of silver imaginable.

'It's even more magical at night, isn't it?' I say to Jo as we walk across the bay to Clachan, and my resolve to stay here – or somewhere like here – deepens.

'It never fails to give you whatever it is you need at that moment.' Jo opens the front door, bends to scoop up the post that arrived – as slow as everything else round here – late in the afternoon.

When she turns to face me, her face has the same bleached ghostliness as the rocks outside.

Chapter Twenty-eight

Jo

I should have realised this was inevitable. That if I didn't tell my mother Rachel was dead, there was always the chance she would write again. This is how Rachel got into it in the first place, after all. And even if I had decided to live with it – to push the idea of Rachel and my mum to the back of my mind and ignore whatever it was they talked about – that's over now.

> Dear Rachel
>
> I hope this finds you well, and I hope that your new life is going exactly as you planned. This is just a little note to let you know that I moved to hospice care yesterday. The staff are wonderful and can't do enough for me and they are experts at managing all that needs to be done. I have a room to myself, with a garden view, and I am not afraid.
>
> I wondered if you would pass on a message to Joanna for me, one way or another. I want her to know that I love her, even though I wasn't always right in what I said and did.

I hope you have reached peace with your brother and found room in your heart to forgive him: just as I hope Joanna finds room to forgive me.

In God's love
Val

It is quarter past four in the morning; the gulls are about to sense the day beginning and start to call. I am wired.

I flap a hand at Meg. The gesture says I'm fine, not to worry, to go to bed. 'Mothers,' I say, and shake my head at her.

In the kitchen, I open the back door and shake the lunchtime tablecloth out into the last of the night. I fold the cloth into four by holding the edge under my chin and the corners in my outstretched hands. My mother and I used to fold bedsheets like this.

There were moments where we were happy. It is undeniable. There were pale yellow primroses in terracotta pots that I painted with huge flower motifs for Mother's Day; we cooked together – her making sure the pastry never got higher than my fingernails, keeping the butter and lard cold and solid; we read stories from big hardback books that had made their way from her own, uneasy childhood. We did things that were calm and normal and everyday.

Before Tristan Willoughby, before I tested her faith as a parent and her faith in her God.

I cannot begin to think about forgiveness: despite tonight's warmth, its hopefulness. It does not extend as far as my mother, her sudden need to make peace while death breathes down her collar.

I catch my reflection in the sitting-room window. I could be her, just as I remember her. This is her face, these lines and wrinkles are the contours of my mother a little older than when I last saw her. I don't see a monster. I see two women – almost strangers – tangled and smudged into this one.

I am like her on the outside, but I am completely different within.

Not the same, but similar.

'Jo?'

Meg is standing in the kitchen doorway. 'I just looked that moon up,' she says, and holds her phone aloft as if I can see the information from here. 'It's a supermoon, really special. Do you want to come and drink hot chocolate with me and watch it for a bit?'

I've made proper hot chocolate, melted Peruvian dark chocolate into warm milk. I've added cream, grated two different chocolates over the top. Last minute, I tossed five marshmallows into each cup: some things can be too poncey, I think, remembering Tim.

Meg and I are sitting side by side in this mercury landscape, both of us turned pearly white by the moon.

I let a handful of sand trickle from my palm to the floor. It glitters as it falls. Fragments of shell sit on top of my sifted fistful, tiny treasures – miniscule parts of this beach, this world. I resolve to open my eyes to it all, to try and remember the jewels, the beautiful moments.

Meg lies down on her back, staring at the stars.

'You never see as many stars when the moon is bright,' I tell her. 'Nature's light pollution.'

'It controls us all, doesn't it.' Her hands are spread out beside her.

'It controls the tide. And people used to believe we went mad with the full moon – hence *lunatics*.'

She turns her head towards me, and her stare is momentarily withering. 'I do have the internet, you know.' And then she smiles, her teeth almost blue in the light. 'I think this is a truth moon – everything that's happened with my mum, your mum writing to you – to Rachel.'

I stare out at the sea, at its inevitability, the darkness below its silver surface. 'Could be.'

'And I have something I really need to tell you,' she says. 'Now seems like as good a time as any.'

Life has taught me to brace myself when I hear those words, that what comes after someone has spent time brewing, mulling over things they're going to say to you or tell you, is never good, never what you want to hear. If it was to your advantage, or to make you happy, they'd just tell you.

'What you told us – what Tris did to you.'

There is a pulse of tension that ripples across the beach. I half-expect the sea to furrow with it, send up a wave – white-capped – through the soup stillness. Nothing happens, no demons rise from the deep. I wait for her to speak, despite how much I wish she wouldn't. Without Tristan Willoughby, this beach is perfect, this night, this moon.

'It wasn't your fault.'

I don't agree with her, so I don't say anything.

'Have you seen the meme about the cup of tea? It's on social media – I think it was on TV too?'

'I haven't.' I lie down flat, remove myself from her line of sight and press the small of my back into the sand. 'Do I want to?'

I would give anything not to have shared this memory, to be able to catch it – still wriggling – and push it back into its box. This story is the thing that makes me vulnerable again, when I have decided to be resolute. But I know Meg will not drop it.

She can't hear my pulse quickening and my heart fluttering up and down in my throat. I swallow and wait for her to speak. I can do this. I have done worse.

I close my eyes tight against the sky.

'So you ask someone if they want a cup of tea, right?' Meg says.

Beyond our feet, the sea rolls in and out, the only sounds the gentle decompression of the sand below it, the swoosh of the water's rhythm.

'And they say they do want tea. But then they take a sip and they don't like it – or it's scalding hot. OK?' She pauses, questioning me.

I don't answer, but I let her carry on.

'The person can stop drinking the tea any time they want, can't they?'

I stay silent.

'Maybe it wasn't your idea to begin with. They asked you for the tea. Maybe they absolutely demanded that you make it, but by the time you gave it to them, they're wasted and they can't sit up straight or hold the cup properly without spilling it down themselves and getting burnt. Or they're asleep.'

She raises one arm and waves it in my direction to check I'm listening. 'Jo?'

I sense the shadow of her arm across my face and open one eye.

'Or maybe they asked you – like, really adamantly – for mint tea, but when you made it and gave it to them, they say they don't want mint tea and they want a proper teabag. You wouldn't pour the tea down their throat, would you? See where I'm going? You might be annoyed – urgh, all my effort making tea all fucking evening – but they don't want it. And that's that: you can't make them drink it.'

I answer without any real words. Something tiny and sand-dwelling crawls from the dark on to my face and I sit up suddenly, blow it away from my lips, brush it from my cheeks, although it's already gone.

'Are you OK?' She sits upright too. 'God, I'm sorry if it upset you.' There is a sudden panic in her voice, the voice that was so confident talking in riddles just now.

'It's a fly.' I mime sweeping the fly from my face.

She nods, exhales loudly with the relief that I'm not having another panic attack.

'Go on,' I say gently. I have grasped her point, but I'd like a few more moments before I have to discuss it with her.

I turn on to my front, on my elbows, and start to stack pebbles on top of one another. They are smooth and round and refuse to stay where I put them. The stones make little grating noises as they slide off one another – it reminds me of being a child.

'So we can all agree that if someone doesn't want a cup of tea, or if it's not safe for them to drink it – if they're asleep or pissed or something – they don't have to drink the tea. It makes it clear that it's OK to say no anytime. Even if you stop drinking it halfway through.'

'I get it. Thank you.' She is doing her best and, for all the situations she has described, her analogy is utterly apt. 'But I don't think that's what happened with Tristan.'

Meg clears her throat in a dramatic manner. 'I'm just going to say this, OK?'

Only the sea speaks.

'I think that you mixed up the idea of having sex with Rachel's brother with what he actually did to you. And now you blame yourself for something that was – definitely – a sexual assault.'

She stops short of the other word – the word that has always loomed in the shadows – and I'm glad it stays unsaid on this quiet beach.

Chapter Twenty-nine

I was knocked sideways by my mother's condemnation, by what she wanted for me. I had wholly expected her conviction that I would burn in hell, but I'd been fool enough to think there would be some gap in her rage, a sliver of humanity where she cared about me, about my distress.

'Who is it?' she said, spat out into the kitchen. 'Who is the father? You don't even have a boyfriend.'

She was in a spiral, spinning round the kitchen as if she was possessed. Her hands flew at her face, and she chanted under her breath: curses disguised as prayers.

I pushed myself back into the corner of the dining room, tried to be as small as possible. I kept my hands in front of my face in case she flew at me again.

But she wasn't after me. Her hysterical dance, her hopping from one foot to the other, reaching out her arms – palms up – was to attract God. Or maybe the Devil. It wasn't about me.

Eventually, her hands came to rest on the silk-leaved book. She fell to her knees in front of me, her eyes rolling with the sheer madness of it all. She tried to read me passages, prayers, that promised damnation, but I couldn't hear her words, only a bubbling, droning delirium.

This wasn't like other mothers, scared of what the neighbours would say, worried about their family's reputation. This was her punching my ticket to Hades.

I slid down the wall, curled like a piece of luggage into the corner.

'Who is he?' she wailed. As if he could come and remove his seed, as if somehow that would be acceptable where an abortion wasn't.

'He isn't anyone.' It was true. He wasn't anyone I wanted to tell, anyone I could phone and explain what was happening here, how I had ended up.

It incensed her. She brought her face down to mine, livid and purple with rage. 'Who. Is. He?' She separated out the words in case the demon that had possessed me was foreign, in case it needed her to speak slowly. 'Do you even know his name?'

She knows who Tristan Willoughby is, she's commented on his driving when he's come here to collect me with Rachel – *too fast*. She's read his name in the local newspaper when he's scored tries and goals and wickets for the school, for the county – *flashy, so flashy*. She's seen that long black fringe, that wide, white-toothed grin, his open-necked shirts – *who does he think he is?*

'I said "no".' I can only whisper it. Saying it out loud will make it true and that is even more frightening – untenable – than where we are now. 'I said "no", but he did it anyway.'

She doesn't pause, doesn't stop her praying and chanting, isn't even shocked by what I'm saying. There is no sign that she even heard me until she says, 'Why were you there?'

'What?'

'Why were you in that situation in the first place?' She sees a verse in her book, crows at having found the exact one she wants, at having her opinion ratified by the prophets. 'Why did you put yourself in a situation where Sin was inevitable? Why were you there?'

I cover my face with my hands. I can't answer her because it was my fault, because I kissed him, ran my hands over his taut body, gasped with pleasure at what was happening to me, to us. I can't answer because I wanted him to, right up until I changed my mind.

She zooms in again; I can see the sparse grey hairs of her eyebrows, sticking out at angles, amplifying the effect of her crazed eyes. 'You wanted it, didn't you? You wanted a man to do this to you. I bet you were drinking.'

We were drinking. I think of the sticky rings of wine on the old oak table. The ritual where we'd thought we were grown-ups, sharing a bottle of wine before bed. Bed.

'It was Rachel's brother, Mum. It was Tristan.'

And then, in the quiet that descends while that soaks into her, while she tries to decide who is most to blame, most guilty, I try again.

'I said "no",' I say, but each time I say it, it is quieter, it has less weight and less conviction. Each time I say it, it is less true.

Each time I say it, I fade a little into the wall.

I couldn't tell Rachel, when she came to collect me from the hospital, about the conversation with my mother. Conversation, accusation, humiliation.

I couldn't tell her anything without telling her everything. She was my best friend. But even with the flaws and the secrets and the loyalty of the Willoughbys, she wouldn't have been my best friend after that, after I had sex with her brother. After I couldn't be trusted to be alone in a house with him.

And Rachel was all I had.

And because I didn't tell her about Tristan, I couldn't tell her about my mother's wretched curses, and because I didn't tell her that, I couldn't tell her about realising it was all my fault and – because I couldn't tell her that – I couldn't tell her the worst thing, the last thing. The consequence that has stayed with me all my life.

And that's why it feels like cleansing my whole insides, like letting a coil of tumours and twists and poison free from my body, to tell Meg.

The nurses were kind. They were all women, no doubt they had all seen this a thousand times, seen it since the dawn of time.

The doctor was female too. She spoke softly, gently, clearly aware – as I was – that this was a gynaecological ward, that I lay between beds of women losing babies they'd wanted, undergoing procedures in order to save their own lives, or losing their wombs. And here was me, behind a curtain of striped fabric no thicker than a page in my mother's Bible, talking to the doctors about my choice not to have one.

The guilt almost stopped me. Might have, except that the guilt at what I'd done was stronger. I deserved the punishment of being pregnant. I could stay still and quiet and accept it – or go through with this.

As I was wheeled into theatre, the first men appeared. Scrubbed and gowned, white-masked and anonymous. One of them was the anaesthetist, responsible for putting me out, keeping me alive. And I don't know if it was him, or the other man, the one who would put his hands inside the wound of my body, the one who would take out this cluster of cells, who said it. But I heard him speak, loud and clear.

'Let's make sure this never happens again, shall we?'

And it never did.

Chapter Thirty

MEG

It is a seminal night – I think that's the phrase for it.

We're sitting a little apart. And that's good, it stops me from touching her – for now. I can see that isn't what she wants. She is lost there – in the past, in all that trauma, and I can't physically pull her out of that.

But I am my father's daughter. I have been patronised and counselled and examined, merely for wanting a glass of orange squash: analysed for what I'm watching on telly; interviewed about how late I go to bed over the course of my entire lifetime.

'Do you really believe they did that?' I ask her. 'I know what you heard must have been incredibly alarming, but those men weren't alone in the theatre. There were nurses there, other people.'

And I wait, give her the space my dad would. The sea laps quietly and an early gull skits low across the surface. My stomach growls inappropriately and I hope Jo can't hear it.

'I took so many risks,' she says, and pokes at the fire with a twig she is holding. 'Over the years, I've lost count of the number of times I had sex without contraception, not just with my husbands. Nada.'

I count the seconds of silence; they grow huge and loud, beat like blood in my ears. Just as I think I'm going to have to burst it –

'Not so much as a late period. Logically, I know that what I think can't be true, but emotionally, I wonder if I've convinced my own body. Every thinking part of me knows the medics were imagining their own daughters, commenting on how I needed some support, some family planning advice, but—'

I nod, but I say nothing. Not yet.

She looks at me. The moonlight, or maybe the story, makes her look young.

'Some punishment, eh?' she asks me.

'You can't be punished for having a termination – it's not a crime. People do it every day. It's your right over your own body. Your body, your choice.'

'I don't mean for the termination,' she says. 'I mean for having sex with my best friend's brother. In Rosie and Duncan's house, in their bed, when they trusted me. It was a different time – sex was still taboo, people were getting used to abortion being legal, everyone was judgemental. The only thing that hasn't changed is that it's still the woman's fault.'

She has believed this for forty years, believed it's all her fault. And her mother reinforced that.

'That wasn't sex, Jo,' I say quietly. The dark drips over the rock pools like water, the waves have receded into the distance and all we can hear is an emptiness, a lightless silence where spoots tunnel downwards, where oysters open and close, spitting out water and propelling themselves through the sand. The predators are sleeping on the land, in nests and burrows, and the weaker, slower animals are kings of the night-time beach.

'It wasn't sex, Jo, it was—'

'Don't say it,' she says. 'Don't call it that. I gave up the right to call it that by deciding to do it again.'

'Choosing to have sex with him didn't change what had happened. What he'd already done.' I settle on words she can manage. This is about making her as comfortable as I can – not about me. Inside, I am raging against the patriarchy, against the fact that these stories never stop happening. That forty years later, friends of mine still find themselves compromised, assaulted, raped. All the words we can choose from. All perpetrated by men.

'Did you ever think of telling him?' I ask her.

'Never.' She is quick to say it, firm. 'It would have made it so much worse. Tristan—'

Along the horizon, the slightest smear of orange licks at the edge of the world. It is a blur, as if the sky is made of torn paper.

'Tristan was a difficult person, Meg. Not just this, other stuff too, a sort of disregard for other people, a cruelty even, occasionally. And telling him, him rejecting me, it all would have ended up with Rachel knowing about us – and she thought the sun rose and set in Tristan.' She scuffs something in the sand with her foot. 'We all did.'

Fuck. I don't know what to do here. I know what my dad would do, but that's because the law demands it, asks it of him. No one bought my confidence, paid me to keep their secrets. The glow is spreading up the sky, leaking like ink into the moonlight. Soon the whole world will be awake.

'Not Rachel, Jo.'

She looks at me, waits for more. A black cormorant stands on a rock, his jagged wings out at angles.

'Rachel didn't feel like that about her brother.'

'Is this something your dad told you?' There is anger in her voice.

I crouch down in the sand like an apology. 'Rachel told me. She said she hated him. That he spoiled everything she ever had.'

Jo leans forward, touches her toes. Then she rolls to one side, inelegantly, and gets to her feet. 'I'm done,' she says and walks back towards the house.

The cormorant sees her and, with one glance towards the crowning sun, flaps his way silently out to sea.

Chapter Thirty-one

Jo

'Val is all ready for you.' The nurse is chatty, animated, as if she's dragging me in before I get a chance to change my mind.

My mother's manipulation spears me.

'It means she knows you're a good person,' Meg said to me in the car on the way here. 'She trusted Rachel to tell you she was dying, and then she knew you'd come. That's OK.'

I didn't reply for the sake of looking churlish, but my mother used the words *hospice* and *sorry* in the space of a few sentences: how could I not come?

There are so many things she could be sorry for. At the end of this corridor, its windows floor to ceiling, I am about to find out which one it is.

The nurse walks slightly in front of me, calmly but quickly. There is a sweet scent in every part of the building, sticky like lilies or daffodils. 'She's seen a couple of people from her church, but . . .'

It feels like an accusation.

'Here we are.' She opens the door of the room and there, minuscule in a large pale-green armchair, is my mother.

I thought that not being in our old house – the place where our everyday turned from funny and sweet to the claustrophobia of her illness, and back again on a sixpence – I thought that not being there would make this painless, would allow me to believe that I'd imagined or exaggerated my teenage years.

On the coffee table in front of my mother's chair is a white plate full of those little square cakes covered in icing. On the top of each pastel-coloured cake – I know from my childhood that they come in a box of six – is a small dome of buttercream, covered in icing. I know the taste and smell of them without having to lean in. Without having to pick one up.

And next to the cakes, a statement. Her two black-bound books, her Bible with its dog-eared cover, supple creased leather. And the other book on top of it – not quite parallel – the one that is peculiar to her religion, the silken sheets and strange tales.

'Hello, Joanna,' she says.

Her voice has barely changed. Her face has folded in on itself, too thin and too old to stay the same. Her cheeks and brows have puckered into hollows, taut paper where once she had fat under her skin, but her cheeks and forehead are like mine.

I wonder, for a second, whether I am seeing myself in another thirty years' time. But then I remember all the anger, all the twisting guilt, all the sadness my mother carried until it ate her away from inside. That will not be written on my face: I left it all behind with her.

'Did you come far?' she asks me, a question for a stranger.

'From Clachan, Rachel's house. It's about three hours.'

'Clachan, eh?' says my mum. 'I never went there. Never invited.'

And a part of me is sorry for her; perhaps those rock pools and Duncan's cooking on the barbecue and Rosie constantly telling everyone how clever we were – such *darlings* – might have warmed the edges of my mother, might have softened her.

'We had nice holidays when I was little though, didn't we, Mum?' I say. 'Before Dad went.'

'How is your father?' she asks me, and I remember that she is full of drugs, her frail body has betrayed her and – without this place and its care – she'd be in terrible pain. She's forgotten that he ran away, the prelude to the rumbling and the praying and the holy books, and that neither of us ever saw him again.

My mother is old. Her skin is translucent and her veins are a faded blue inside her. Death, and whatever it is that she has longed for all this time, her salvation, isn't far away.

Spite will only make me sad, pile more guilt on to the bonfire of my childhood that those two books represent.

'I think he died,' I say. 'About ten years back.'

A light switches on inside her; she remembers why I'm here. 'Did Rachel Willoughby pass on my message?'

'Rachel died, Mum. Suddenly, a couple of months ago,' I say. 'It's very sad.' Understatement of the year. Why is Rachel dead? I think. Why isn't it you, with your shrivelled heart, your spidery old body? 'She came to see you, didn't she, Mum?'

'We were pen pals. From when Mrs Willoughby died.' Mum sits back in her chair, lifts her hand a little. Her fingers are tiny, bones with the barest covering of skin, knuckles joined together by webbed twigs. She points to the cake plate with her spider fingers. 'They were your favourite, Joanna, when you were a little girl.'

There is no need to be unkind to my mother: time has already done that. 'They're still my favourite,' I say, and take a pink one.

I sit down in a wingback chair that mirrors hers.

'Was it the drink that killed her? Poor girl.'

'Why did she tell you, Mum? She didn't tell anyone else.' I break the tiny cake in half; it is sticky with childhood memories.

The middle is the soft yellow I remember, the pink icing waxy and slightly melted.

'She told her husband.' My mum stares out of the window.

There is a goldfinch, impossibly bright, on the feeder outside the window. The garden is generously planted and bushy with leaves.

'She did, you're right. But when did she tell you?'

'Poor Rachel told me a long time ago that she drank too much. I said that God doesn't give us anything we can't handle, that He tests us, but He still loves us.'

It fucking killed her, I want to shout, but I'm stopped – arrested by the idea that my mum had told her God would still love her. Maybe that helped. Maybe it didn't.

'Why do you think she told you?' I ask. 'When she couldn't tell me.'

My mum deliberately keeps her gaze from mine. 'Because it's very hard, when you've made mistakes. Rachel knew I wasn't perfect, and everyone else around her was, she thought. Even you.'

My mum reaches out to the tea tray the nurse has put in front of her and her spidery hand trembles.

'Shall I do that, Mum? Do you want milk?'

'It's marvellous that they have decaffeinated tea now, isn't it?' my mum asks me. 'And coffee, you know.'

I think back to the powdered mud she used to drink instead of coffee, bought – in bulk – by her church and sold to the parishioners at a mark-up.

'And I don't judge people, and Rachel knew that. Judgement is reserved for Him.' She nods, definite, a full stop to her sentence.

Instinct makes me move my chair slightly away from hers, away from how far our memories have diverged. When she was younger, rounder, less beaten down, she had judgement enough for everyone – from me to the local Church of England vicar to the man who owned our corner shop.

Try as I might, I can't love her.

'Rosemary Willoughby used to write to me, keep me up to date with where you were, what you were doing. When you first left home.'

I don't point out that I didn't 'leave home' in any conventional sense of the phrase, that I didn't have a sloped graduation into adult life. It wasn't like that.

'When Rosemary died, Rachel wrote to tell me, and I replied with my condolences – my prayers – and Rachel wrote to thank me. Look at that little bird, what is that, Joanna?' The bony finger points at the goldfinch. 'With his little red bits?'

'You taught me my birds, Mum, you know them all. He's a goldfinch.'

'So he is,' she says in her scattergun conversation. 'Rachel said she'd lost the baby – and you'd looked after her.' Her eyes fill with tears. 'And I was proud that you'd grown up so kind.'

I gesture towards the sugar bowl – and she nods that, yes, she still takes sugar in tea.

'I told her that God would bless them with a baby when the time was right.' Her lips soften slightly, tremble. 'I said how He blessed me. How He gave me you when I had almost nothing else – a terrible marriage, a mother sick with her nerves. You were a blessing that turned my life around.'

It doesn't matter how well disposed she was to me when I was a tiny mewling baby, it doesn't matter how much she liked me as a toddler. What matters is that when she had a choice, she didn't choose me.

'And Rachel told you about her drinking, that she couldn't risk getting pregnant?'

My mother nods, sparse tufts of white hair bobbing above a pink scalp. A little old lady serving tea and fondant fancies to her visitor. Benign. Harmless. Full of the past.

I have her chin and mouth, her nose. My eyes and my stature are my absent father's: against her frailty, it feels like he left me something good after all. Even in my late eighties – should I get there – I will still be taller than her, wider. I feel as if I will be more substantial.

'She'd always say that by the time I got her next letter, she'd be teetotal. God bless her.' Her teacup rattles and I reach out to take it from her.

I'm surprised by how easily such a gesture of intimacy sits between us.

'And she started talking to Ben, to the counsellor. We didn't have things like that in my day, you know. There wasn't any counselling, we didn't have those sort of doctors back then.'

She says it as if it's a comment on the times, like decaffeinated tea, but the thought nestles into my mind, disturbs the roots of my thoughts. There would have been help for her, somewhere, at the time, but she would have had no more idea than me of where to look for it.

'Why did Rachel come and see you, Mum?' That small word is strange – like I've eaten a peach and accidentally found the stone in my mouth, rough and hard.

My mum looks upwards, towards the strip lights, the tiled ceiling. 'I had a best friend who I wrote to. Do you remember? Marion? She didn't come and visit often – it was harder to do that in those days. But we wrote to each other all our lives, right up until she died.'

I don't remember, I don't remember any visitors at all who weren't part of the church.

'I told Marion everything. Things I couldn't ever tell someone I saw every day.'

'Did you tell her about me?' I ask. 'About what I did?'

My mother and me, we both know what I'm talking about.

'I did.' Her teeth are small and off-white. A couple are missing at the left-hand side of her top jaw. 'And she replied without judgement.'

I don't bother to ask whether the judgement she generously withheld was for my mum or me.

My mother settles back into the armchair, diminishing before my eyes. With each shuffle she gets smaller, fainter. 'Remember Ann Baker?' she asks me. She raises the pale lines that were once her eyebrows. 'Remember what she did when Satan crossed her path? She used her faith and walked away unscathed. You were not alone, Joanna, God was always with you.' She sits back in her chair, pulls her bony knees towards each other. 'We can always choose His path.'

I realise two things. They are simultaneously shutters that close over my mother and wide-open windows that propel me towards my future.

My mother is – and always was – ill. Her delusion takes all reason and twists it into an unrecognisable knot. It is not, and never was, her fault that she is ill, but – the second realisation – neither is it mine.

'I needed to see Rachel to atone for my own guilt.' She has a tiny coughing fit, as if the crumbs of a crime have lodged themselves in her throat rather than be spoken about. 'I did something wrong – I lied – and I knew I couldn't face Him until I had told the truth.'

'To tell her about her brother? To tell her what I'd told you?'

She shakes her head. 'No,' she says and reaches towards the plastic beaker of water on her nightstand. 'No, not that.'

Instinct, habit, maybe compassion: something makes me stand up and get the beaker for her, hold it to her fragile faded lips.

'Tristan Willoughby,' she says. 'I worked in the Coroner's Office when he died.'

It has never occurred to me before – that my mother would have been the person typing up Tristan's inquest, keeping the tragic notes of his death.

'It was Duncan who changed the records – It was him who—' She stops, lost for words, and I worry that the bird will distract her again.

'What did Duncan do, Mum?'

'They were heartbroken. He was rarely sober before Tristan died, but afterwards . . .'

'Duncan?'

'But they didn't have to behave properly, that class. It was all lunches and golf clubs and – I worried for you, so involved with them.' She peers at me, doesn't say, *For good reason*. But we both hear it.

'I didn't say anything.' She is years away. 'But I knew what they'd done. Duncan knew the coroner well – golf, Masonic Lodge, Round Table. All of it. So when he came and asked them to remove the pathologist's reports, they did it. They asked me to go and get them, then they destroyed the papers.'

My mother's eyes are half closed. She is there, in 1987, listening to the grief of the families, hearing the creak of the car wreck being heaved away from the town centre. 'They were all as high as kites. Drugs, alcohol, three times and four times the legal alcohol limit at least. The Willoughbys didn't want anyone to know that Tristan was using drugs, so they had all reference to the toxicology removed. For all of them.'

'They were all drunk? All on drugs?'

'Four rotten apples, in it together.'

I think of Rachel, of her story going round and round on repeat when she'd had too much to drink. 'It wasn't the brakes. It never was,' I say to her as much as to my mother. 'They all got in the car willingly.'

'I didn't know Rachel thought it was her fault until she got here with the fella, with Ben. I only wanted to tell her about my guilt – make my last confession. I helped the Willoughbys do it, helped them cover it all up. "We're forever in your debt," Rosie said to me. "Anything you want, tell us, anything you ever need."'

My mother looks at her hands, at the empty china cup on her knee, at the hem of her nightie below her dressing gown. 'I asked her to tell me where you were. I knew you couldn't come back: what you did, what I said. We have different beliefs. But I asked Rosemary Willoughby to send me photographs, news, to keep me in touch with you. That way, I never really lost you.'

'And Rosie died and Rachel took over.'

My mother shakes her head. 'She didn't know why, Rachel. Rachel never knew about the agreement. She knew we wrote, that's all.'

The past has exhausted my mother. I can see her fading, the pale light inside her flickering.

'She knew what your operation was, though.' A sudden spite rises from the past. My mother says the word *operation* as if it is made of rotten flesh, as if it has stuck to her hands and climbed, rancid, up her nose. 'And she knew that it had come after you spent time alone, at that place, with her brother.'

I press my fingertips into the fabric of the green chair. My nails whiten at the tips, fill with pink blood.

'She knew you were carrying his child.' She leaves *child* to float around in the vitro of her righteousness.

'What did you say?'

279

'I said you'd said no to the boy, that you'd told me that. But that I'd blamed you, and not him.'

Air gusts out of me like a burst tyre.

'That was wrong, Joanna. I shouldn't have done that, and I'm sorry.'

Some things are too wide for sorry. I nod, and I tuck her words away. I will come back to them in my own time, when I'm not under the pressure of these lights, this over-warm room with the scent of a tropical hothouse.

'Rachel's letters. You said I could take them home.' Our ghosts are being laid to rest, their moans and groans and clanking chains are on their way to peace. The corridors of my teenage years are going to be exorcised spaces, safe to walk in without poltergeist or ghoul or attack from the shadows.

'They're in that cupboard.'

As I stand, she adds, 'I always thought Rachel smothered you, you know. That it was hard to see all of you in the glare of her light. You were a wonderful child, so kind, but people only really noticed Rachel Willoughby.'

A vase of silk flowers sits on the windowsill, the colours of those tiny cakes. If my mother had visitors, if people cared enough about her, those flowers would be real, scented, tiny insects would crawl and buzz across them. They would bring life to this room. The flowers are as dead as the pages of grief that brought her here.

The letters are inside a clear plastic wallet. The sort you might use at work.

I turn back to the bed with the bundle in my hand, my feet stepping towards her even though my head and heart are crying out to go the other way.

My mother is half asleep in the chair, waiting for a nurse to tuck her back into bed for her last hours, last days.

I bend and kiss her powdered cheek. It has the texture of Rachel's dead skin.

'I forgive you, Mum.'

Her eyes are still closed but her mouth moves into a slight arc, her jaw relaxes.

'We all make mistakes,' I tell her. 'It is time to move on.'

My mother is moving on to something new, something she dreamed of so hard that it ruined her life.

And I am moving on too.

Chapter Thirty-two

I'm so glad Meg is waiting in the car. She is the antithesis of everything that has happened in that airless room.

I put Rachel's words on the back seat. Everything we didn't say.

I'm navigating the last of the lanes, concentrating and staring straight ahead. I gave Meg a precis of my conversation, told her what happened in minimalist detail. From then, right up until now – for more than two hours – we've listened to the rest of the seal podcast, talked about what we'll eat when we get home: absolutely anything to change the subject.

'This has put a lot in perspective – about my mum and my dad and me,' Meg says. 'I've been such a dick: things could be so much worse.'

It is not the first time my mother has fulfilled that function, has been the So Much Worse in life. She was my motivation for many things, for enduring hardships, for taking risks. *Things could be so much worse*: I don't suppose it features in many 'bringing up baby' books but, as a strategy, her sink-or-swim model could have gone either of two ways.

I didn't sink. I never have, not even in my darkest hours.

'Are you going to read Rachel's letters when we get home?'

'If there's one after she'd been to see my mum, and my mum had told her the truth about Tris's death. Just to hear Rachel say that it wasn't her fault. In her own words. But I don't think I can manage the rest.'

I will always love Rachel, warts and all – my love for her is unconditional, as I know hers was for me. Her intimacy with the mother who rejected me is a tiny bump in the road of our friendship, not enough to derail anything.

'I'd be intrigued,' Meg says. 'They'd burn a hole in me until I'd read them.'

'Nah.' There is enough of me left for a half-smile. 'I'm going to let the past sleep. Enough damage has been done.'

We pull up outside the village shop and I go inside and buy two bottles of wine.

'Kitchen disco tonight,' I say to Meg, as I stow them on the floor by her feet. 'After one more stop.'

The estate agency isn't the same sort of business as it would be where I come from. This is a one-woman band; she answers her own phone, takes her own photographs, does her own paperwork.

'Just text me from the motorway services or something, once you have an idea of when you'll get back,' she said to me, and that was as formal as the arrangements for this viewing got. 'I'll meet you there.'

Meg and I pull up in the lane at the far end of the village. Beyond this spot there are thickets of low woodland, damp with evening mist and dusty with light. There are one or two more houses further up the lane, but this is pretty much the end of the village – the last of the houses on the main street. Rosebay willowherb blows, long and pink, on the banks beside the road, and the last of the blackberries are shrinking and drying on wild green branches.

The cottage is down a path. All that can be seen from the road is the whitewashed brick back of it, the ridge tiles of its low roof.

The estate agent waits on the other side of the garden gate, her arms leaning on the pickets. 'Watch this gate when you open it,' she warns. 'It's all but falling off the hinges.'

Meg and I follow her down the path and round to the front of the house. It is a tiny version of Clachan, the original one and a half storeys and much smaller, but the same old oak door with bull's-eye glass, and the same scratched window frames either side of it.

The front of the house faces out across a yellowing reed bed and, beyond that, the brown mud flow of the estuary. Two birch trees stand sentinel either side of the path that parts the reeds. The tree trunks are a cracked crazy paving of silver and black, diffusing the low sun around their edges, rippling with texture.

The cottage has the same strip of green pretending to be a front garden: *machair*, the estate agent calls it, and explains to us that that's the Scots word for scrubby pasture growing by the edge of the sea.

'And there is a boardwalk,' she says, 'once you've followed the wee path through the reeds. Only five minutes or so along it to the beach.' And then she remembers, 'Ach, but you'll know that, being up at Clachan.'

'What do you think?' I ask Meg. And we push open the oak door.

'I have no idea what's going on. So no idea what to think,' she says. 'But it's very beautiful. Look at the boards on the staircase. Imagine them sanded, waxed.'

The staircase has bare wooden treads, splattered here and there with paint, dirty with years of neglect. Upstairs, under the eaves, are two bedrooms. The grey, dusty window of one looks out across the reed beds, where the estuary snakes its last few metres towards the sea.

'Almost a sea view.' The estate agent laughs. 'Another twenty feet or so and it'll join the sea – it's only just round the corner. You

284

just need to believe.' I like this woman: enough to know that I'll ask her to the pub when the sale is concluded, that we'll have a laugh together, become friends.

The cottage is Clachan before its big Victorian extension: before the dining room and the wrap-round kitchen. It is ready to welcome someone who could love it, could bring it back to life. A new start for us both.

'I can't stay at Clachan, Meg. It's not my home and there are too many ghosts.'

She nods. 'I guess it's very saleable now – or it will be when I've finished.'

'I'm not going to sell it either.'

She looks up at me, relieved.

And then quickly, and in case she thinks I mean that she should live there, I tell her my plan. 'I'm going to turn it into a business – a high-end catered retreat. People come and stay and I deliver top-notch food to them three times a day. Clear it all away like I'm an elf, so they never even know I was there. People with more money than sense – like Rachel and me used to be. People looking for a beautiful place to hang out and totally chill.'

It doesn't take us long to tour the upstairs of the cottage. The two rooms have newspaper on the floor and smell of old apples.

The bathroom is tacked on the back of the cottage, an after-thought behind the kitchen. The bath is the size of a small boat, chipped blue-white enamel. A copper pipe down the wall leads to a single brass tap. It has history and charm in spades, but it doesn't have hot water. The mirror above the basin has lost its silvered back and I see tiny bits of myself and the house reflected, a honeycomb of possibilities.

'If you move this upstairs,' Meg says, 'you could knock through, get a proper catering kitchen in.'

'Will I get a discounted rate on my interior design?' I ask Meg. I've done up three houses from scratch, and I'm good at it, enjoy it. I could do this on my own – perfectly well – but I don't want to.

'If I get first dibs on the spare room? My own holiday home?' Meg says, but she knows the answer is yes.

'There would have only been this place and Clachan in the village once upon a time,' the estate agent says. 'One each side of the bay.' She is looking in her case for the details. 'They are the two oldest properties in Auchlaggan, as far as I know – and I was born here,' she adds, as if we hadn't guessed that from her accent, from the comfortable way she curls those local words, burrs their soft sounds.

'I've heard great things about what you've done at Clachan,' she says to Meg. 'Could I come and have a look? We get a lot of city people buying down here, spending huge amounts of money to save these old wrecks. Maybe we could have a chat about it?'

'Here's my card,' says Meg, digging in the breast pocket of her dungarees. 'Give me a ring or drop me an email. I'd love to show you round. If that's OK, Jo?'

'Of course it is.'

We walk back out to the lane, leaving the woman to lock up. We take one last look at the little white cottage.

'It's the same house,' Meg says.

'It's not the same,' I say. 'But it's similar.' And that, to me, is better.

◆ ◆ ◆

We turn in through the gate of the sandy car park, and two roe deer, their bottoms livid white like targets, skip into the undergrowth.

Watching them dart away means I don't notice immediately that Ben's car is parked up on one side of the sandy flat.

'OK,' I say. 'Slight change of plan.'

'I can get rid of him.' Meg has her hand on the door, halfway out of the car.

She makes me laugh. 'It's fine,' I say. 'We've got enough wine, and food. Remember your new charitable self.'

She and I walk through the forest. The light is settling in its golden glory, catching on the crooks and knots of birch trees, furring and blurring through the vast needled branches of the Sitka spruce.

My footfall is joyful, connected to the earth, to this place.

Ben is sitting on one of the ancient sun-loungers I left facing the beach.

'Stay for dinner?' I ask him.

He looks at me; his dark eyes sparkle with the light refracted from the water. 'If that's OK?'

'The more the merrier.'

◆ ◆ ◆

I have the music on while I cook.

Meg is upstairs finding out how many houses have sold in the area lately, and what they have gone for. I could tell her that the price of my little cottage was an awful lot more than it would have been a few years ago, that it's going to eat up at least half of what I get for my big townhouse. It was my tenants asking if I might ever consider selling to them that made my vague thoughts into workable plans. I tell Ben about it while we cook.

Ben is doing his best to be useful.

'Beat this, will you? As fast as you can.' Having a strong-armed commis chef for choux pastry is the cook's dream.

'Jesus.' He is puffing with the effort.

'Don't stop. It can't have a single lump in. And then you need to do the same again each time I add an egg.'

He puts the saucepan down on the side. 'I'm genuinely sorry I offered. I'm not fit enough to make pastry.'

'I only make choux when there's a man in the kitchen.' I sound like I'm flirting. 'Sorry, that sounds sexist. It's true, though – I can't stand doing the beating. I end up putting it in the mixer and then it always fails.'

I crack an egg into the saucepan; it slips, jelly and yellow, over the paste. 'Go again,' I say, and hand him the pan.

There are four eggs in the recipe. I'm tempted to add a fifth just because I'm enjoying the company and the conversation so much.

'How was your mum? How did it go?'

History drums on my heart with a rumble.

I give him the precis and by the time I've finished, the pastry is done. I pipe it on to the tray, slide the tray into the oven.

'Now we have to go out of the kitchen. Any loud noises will ruin them. Glass of wine?'

He hesitates. He can't have a glass of wine and drive home – the law doesn't allow it.

'There's a spare room.' I don't look at him as I offer it. 'If you don't mind sharing a bathroom with me and Meg. We're going to take a corner off the big bedroom to put in a shower room, but we haven't done it yet.'

'That would make me feel very much like your guest,' Ben says. 'A formal moving-on from my professional relationship with this house, with its history. Thank you.'

We stand on the beach together, wine glasses in hand, and look out to sea. It's obvious that we're both thinking of Rachel, both still wrapped up in her complications, our losses.

I sit down on a large rock, tuck my legs to one side like a mermaid – although I probably look more like a seal.

I have changed back into Clachan uniform: shorts and a T-shirt, universal, ageless. They are the same shorts I wear most days here: I imagine the pockets full of sand and tiny crabs.

Ben sits down beside me – separate rocks, suitably distanced – and we chat until the kitchen timer rings its little heart out with the effort of telling us the choux buns are ready. The cottage smells like a home, like life has trickled into its corners. Three people make the right sort of noise for a house this size.

Ben is easy company, relaxing to be around, and the stresses of the day dissolve into the tasks of chipping and stirring and icing. The dinner is a formidable three courses, food you'd be glad to eat anywhere, and it feels right that this meal – today – should turn into something of an occasion.

The music has edged up and up while we've been working. I am dancing while I cook, not the full spinning crazy that a proper kitchen disco requires, but moving side to side, shifting my feet.

I reach up to get the plates just as Ben leans into a dance move. We bang together, my arm up in the air and our sides touching from our ribs to our hips. We jump apart but the contact has been made, and it changes the space between us into a trap of static.

'Let's eat in the dining room.' My voice almost squeaks when I say it. 'Can you take this napery in?'

'Napery?'

'It's pretty much my favourite word.' Safe space, change of subject. 'It's one of the first things I learned from them, from the Willoughbys, words to describe things that didn't exist back in my world. The not-posh world,' I add, for clarity.

'So napery is . . . ?'

'Tablecloth, napkins. You never say serviettes – even if they're paper.' I smile at the silliness of it, the rules that laid out their culture. I hand him the tablecloth, the napkins, careful not to touch his skin. 'I was like a little savage. I didn't know that you should only eat soup away from you, either.' I make the movement of holding a spoon, tipping an imaginary bowl away from me and moving the spoon outwards, towards him, then back to my mouth.

'Today years old when I learned that,' he says. 'Fifty-two, and it doesn't seem to have hampered me so far.'

'You'll never know.' I raise my eyebrows at him and he laughs. 'You'll never know what opportunities passed you by because you don't know how to eat your soup properly. Duncan really believed in that, the codes of how to behave that would show your background, your breeding. I guess we know all about it now – the privilege of private school, the connections of the right college.'

'The rigid yet invisible rules of bohemian society,' Ben says.

When I hand him the three silver forks and three knives clutched in my fist, our fingers brush, hot. 'Isn't it weird – alcohol, knowing what to drink when, is so steeped in that. Such a class indicator.'

'But only seen as a problem when it's people with a background like mine.' He has switched to an almost impenetrable Glaswegian accent. 'Aye, right.'

I lift my glass, go to take a sip of wine and then feel guilty. Complicit.

'In between those parameters – there are safe ways to drink,' he says. 'Personally, I find it fun on the right people, at the right time. And in the right place.' He picks up his own glass and it makes me feel more like drinking my own.

Ben opens the door through to the dining room and peers in. 'Are we good in here? All sorted?'

He means have I moved the picture, can I cope with the reminders of my panic attack, of what lay behind it.

'Thanks, all fine.' I add the salt and pepper grinders to the bundle in his arms; he can't carry any more without it toppling.

◆ ◆ ◆

The meal is a great way to spend an evening. Meg is calm and happy, Ben is relaxed and easy – like he fits here, all three of us fit here. I am drawn back to countless Clachan dinners like this: Rosie and Duncan's friends and relatives – vivid, intelligent people full of stories and jokes. People who had travelled, written books, fulfilled dreams. This place was always about making everyone feel welcome.

'You two chill,' says Meg. 'That meal was amazing – but I've got a lot of work to do getting this pitch ready for the estate agent. I'll clear up, then I'm going to carry on working.'

It leaves Ben and me, leaning back in our chairs, in the candlelit dining room. We sit in comfortable silence, looking around the room at everything Meg has done.

She comes in from the kitchen to collect the last things from the table. Everything has gone except the cream jug and the plate that holds the last smeared ghosts of profiteroles. 'That's us now, all cleared up.' She kisses me on the cheek. 'Thank you for a lovely dinner. And you,' she says and gives Ben a peck.

My cheek is warm where she kissed it. So unexpected, and so simple.

'Shall I make a coffee, or do you want another glass of wine?' Ben asks.

I hesitate, slightly at sea in this new world where I notice what I'm drinking, where I'm drinking with a drug-and-alcohol counsellor.

'If it helps,' he says, and he's smiling that wide full smile, 'I'm having wine because if I have coffee now, I'll be pacing the floor till dawn.'

'Wine then, thanks.'

291

'Let's sit on the beach. I'll bring them out.'

It is that hazy phase of night-time, a furred navy blue that has the briefest line of orange at the horizon – like it has been set on fire at one edge. The tide is rolling in: the time when one could neither swim nor walk to the island, the time that the otters run backwards and forwards through the kelp as it refloats off the rocks. Occasionally, if you're lucky and you stare hard enough, their movement alerts you to them and then – once you know they're there – you can watch them for hours, digging and snuffling like sleek little dogs.

I took the two tartan blankets from the sitting room as I passed the door. I've stretched them out, next to each other. I wondered and worried at them, not sure whether they should be touching, or slightly apart. I've left them formal, a six-inch space between them like yoga mats in a crowded class. I have two jumpers from the big drawer at the base of the hallway armoire too. One is a huge cream Aran, cable knit and fit for a fisherman, and it has enough space for my knees when I draw them up.

Ben walks out on to the sand, hands me my glass then sits down on his rug.

'That jumper's for you.' It's a thick brown cardigan, the sort men wore in the 70s, with big fat leather buttons down the front.

'Nice,' I say as he examines it, stretches out his arms and puts it on.

'We look great. Like an advert for pipe-smoking.'

I laugh. 'These jumpers – the whole Clachan knitwear collection – they're the only thing that still makes me feel young. They're all older than I am.' And then I puff my cheeks out, sigh. 'They're all part of what I should be getting rid of, sorting out.

But I mean,' – I hold my arms up and out in front of me, jiggle my long sleeves – 'how could you? They're literally history.'

He does up the buttons on his cardigan. 'It's cold,' he says in response to my laughing at him.

A lazy skein of geese flaps across above us, raucous and late for bed. A last lost goose honks its frustration, left behind.

'I don't think I'll ever go back to the city now,' I say. 'I don't want to.'

He looks out at the sea, mirrors my laid-back position. 'I can't blame you. This place has such magic. Beguiling.'

The moon has risen enough to cast a glow across everything. It highlights the edge of his face, accentuates his features.

When he kisses me, it is picture perfect. The geese have stilled and silenced, the sea is just in the right place – far enough in, far enough out – to provide a soundtrack of the gentlest of waves. His first kiss is gentle, soft as seawater on my lips and seeking permission. The second is the kind of kiss I have missed. A long, exploring first kiss, between people who will or won't stay strangers.

The sea sparkles, the moonlight a shifting pathway, the shadows of the rocks and the island giving it depth in the dark.

'Jo.' His voice is a whisper. 'I didn't expect to find you here. To find you at the end of all this sadness, this' – he looks for the word – 'complication.'

I can't speak. My feelings are rolling around inside me, trying to stay upright while the deck of my mind pitches and swirls, staggers and slides.

'But I'm really glad to have found you, I want you to know that. And I hope, now you're staying in Scotland, that we can see more of each other – be more to each other.'

And when I don't answer, he adds, 'Eventually.'

And my mind slows, slips and clips into place, settles. I know the answer. I know what I want.

I know who I am.

I cover his hand with mine, let my fingers slip between his and squeeze down gently, into the sand between us.

'I'm not here to complete Rachel,' I say, still holding his hand. 'I'm not finishing off her life. I have my own future, and it's more important to me than it's been in decades. That's her gift to me.'

He starts to speak, opens his mouth, but I stop him.

'It's OK,' I say. 'I don't know anyone who wasn't a little bit in love with Rachel. I never have. She was the easiest person in the world to love. It's why I have to leave Clachan, to force myself out of this incredible space and into a life of my own. A new life.'

I move my hand away from his and he doesn't follow it.

An otter skitters on the rocks, drops a white egg that flashes as it slips into the water.

'I don't see you as a replacement for Rachel,' Ben says. 'I see you for you, for Jo. You're a beautiful, able woman and—'

In my interior monologue, that garrulous giggling Rachel points out that I've only chanced upon two men in the last week, that I've already slept with fifty per cent of them. 'Now is not the time, Ben.'

'We've a saying in Scotland,' he says. '*What's for you won't go by you*. That the right thing will find you at the right time.'

'That's how I feel about that wee cottage,' I say, because it's kinder than saying it isn't how I feel about him tonight.

◆ ◆ ◆

We don't stay out much longer. Autumn evenings aren't the same as summer ones; the sun takes the warmth with it when it leaves and tonight is the first autumn night, the first of a long and beautiful transition to winter. To starting over. To letting the old die down to leave room for the new to breathe.

When I'm sure Ben is tucked up in bed and the whole cottage is quiet and sleeping, I take the plastic envelope of letters from my bag. I sit on Rachel's bed, leaning back against her pillows, her headboard, and I let the greasy little felted doll sit beside me. I have sifted out the photos, all taken by Rosie and sent to my mother over the years – mostly here – a montage of us growing up, growing older. Of Rachel, and Tristan, and me.

I don't need to know about Rachel's relationship with my mother, and I have no right to read the other things she said. They are her secrets, that she chose not to share with me, and they deserve to die with her.

I am Rachel's best friend, I always will be, and I will honour her decision. To read them would be like reading her diary.

But this last letter, dated just days before she died, is about me. About what my mother told her about Tristan. About how Rachel felt about it all.

The moon seeps through the bedroom curtains, and I am comforted by the stoic calm of these thick walls, the solidity of their unmoveable history.

I take the letter from the wallet, unfold it, and listen to Rachel speak one last time.

> Dear Val
>
> Your support has been an enormous help to me over the years. You will never know what it has meant at times when I've almost given up, but it's also part of my life as an addict, and that means I can't write to you from my new life.
>
> I am confronting everything I've been hiding from: learning to accept that I can't change the past. I should have let Jo know that she could tell me anything, that I would forgive her anything – even

if there was anything to forgive – because she is the most precious person in the world to me.

I was too young then to know that being silent is the same thing as being complicit. What happened to Jo was awful – what my brother did, then the termination. But the worst thing of all is that we weren't there for her. Now I have time to put this right.

I am making all the changes that I told you I would, that Ben has talked through with me, that my loving stalwart husband has silently hoped for all these years.

One thing will never change, my mutually respectful relationship with the best friend anyone could ever have. I am proud of her every day. We both failed her, but I was not much more than a child. You were her mother and she deserved better.

Jo has been a lighthouse for me, my whole life, the guide to home, to safety. Telling her who I am and knowing that she will still love me means the world. If it is any comfort to you, be certain that I will cherish her and her strength until the day I die.

Rachel

I close my bedroom door so quietly that no one could hear me, even if they were awake. And I take the stairs slowly, missing out the fifth stair, avoiding the creak. The visitors' book is lying – open – on the little oak table in the sitting room. There is a pen next to it that Meg has used to write up our evening with Ben. There are parts of it she doesn't know and my mind glances

296

back to that kiss. I smile at my distant future – there will be other kisses, maybe even on other beaches. Of that I am certain.

The front door opens without a sound, and I walk the few steps to the shore. The moon is huge tonight, another world of opportunity and fortune, another silver promise that fills the dark sky. I sit on the big rock facing out to sea, the book on my knee. It is almost daylight under this moon that belongs just to me, daylight but with shadows, as if the secrets of the past walk like misty friends beside me.

I sketch the outline of a lighthouse on the empty page, draw stripes up its straight sides and a wide beam, searching, almost to the edge of the paper. She was my lighthouse too. She was the yellow light that warmed me, supported me, and inspired me. She was flawed and trapped, but she was mine and she was perfect. And the wonder of human beings, of our intricacy, is that all of these things can be true.

Underneath the lighthouse and in black ink, I print:
Rachel Willoughby. 1968 – 2023
Always her true self here. And always loved.

The sea sings to me, shh, shh. And that part of the core of me that worries – that vibrates with the potential for trouble, for panic – is still.

When I wake up in the morning, in Rachel's room, the smell of autumn on the air is definite, a tang of quietening, of deepening. This is the time of year when Scotland turns from its verdant green to a warm slow red: the birds, the animals, the plants, the glossy lichen – everything takes on that same autumn shade of burnt wine, of almost orange. The tufts of a squirrel's fur, the tail – blazing – of a kite, the sun catching on the shoulder of a deer.

I have one more visit to make before my own new beginning can start.

◆ ◆ ◆

Auchlaggan kirkyard has always been special. A tiny sandy plot, edged in wrought-iron railings that fail to protect it from the sea. Most of its incumbents are from the long history of this village: victims of fishing disasters and drownings; families whose children are listed in a litany of sadness, from infant deaths to the First World War.

There were still spaces in this cemetery when Tristan died – although in the decades since locals have been buried on a safer site, away from the crumbling sandy cliff, the possibility of collapsing into the waiting arms of the sea. Rosie and Duncan buried him here, away from the pointing fingers and the anger of their home town.

The kirk itself is tiny. A white stuccoed building with pews for maybe thirty people inside, another ten standing. I know the inside well, how its tall narrow windows, edged in stone, look out over the firth and the ebb and flow of generations.

I could find Tristan's stone with my eyes closed. Rosie, Duncan, Rachel and I would walk here on Christmas morning. We would attend the service in the packed kirk, sing carols, and wish other villagers a *merry Christmas* and *awra best for the New Year* and then, as they gathered up their families and headed for Christmas lunch, we'd walk round the corner to the grave.

Rosie and Duncan always stood, staring down at the damp sandy earth that covered their only son, while Rachel and I sat cross-legged beside him. We'd loop him into our conversations, more easily than we might have while he was alive: the polite catching-up of news that you feel duty-bound to deliver to a dead person.

We never told him our secrets. Rachel – presumably – because she didn't want to and me, because I couldn't.

When Duncan died – pole-axed by a heart attack as he took a swing on the eighteenth hole – his ashes were interred here. Rosie came just a few years later. Maybe Rachel will join them, or maybe she would be more at peace being near Tim. It's not my call to make.

It would be a stretch to find a more beautiful resting place.

I settle myself down, cross-legged – conscious that my knees don't drop down as far as they should, as they used to. 'I ought to turn up to yoga more often,' I say to Tris to open our conversation.

I lean forward and touch the lines on his stone.

'Tristan Christopher St John Willoughby.

At peace.

1966–1987'

I hold my hand against the cold lettering of the year he died. Tristan Willoughby was not much more than a child.

Who knows what might have happened to him, who he might have been.

I didn't see the Tristan that Rachel disliked, the spiteful boy she had grown up half afraid of. That wasn't the Tristan I spent so long in love with.

My Tristan was the captain of the sports' teams, the winner of the chess tournaments: he had the best records, the most fashion-able clothes, he knew all the film quotes anyone needed to know.

I spent the second day of that weird summer, marooned here as almost-adults, with that Tristan, my Tristan.

I'd barely slept, not knowing how to share a bed with another person, not knowing whether I wanted to touch him or to run. I stared at the ceiling for a while, until the light cracked through the curtains and Tristan stirred next to me.

He turned his head towards me, as unsure of what to do as me.

'Shall I make a cup of tea?' he asked in a parody of adulthood: a child again in this close air, this wrong room.

I waited for him to bring the tea upstairs, stared at the things around me: Rachel's gap-toothed photograph on Rosie's night-stand, Duncan's enormous dressing gown hanging on the back of the door. My mind was a mass of confusion betrayed by my body, my treacherous body that pulsed and fizzed when I thought about Tristan.

I lay back in the enormous pillows, went through versions of the night before. All the years of longing that had led up to it, all the conflicting feelings of having done it. I regretted it, but it was over.

Half of me was devastated by my bad decision, by what my flirting and wishing had led to. The other half found itself in this new world, a world where the large August sun was rising over Tristan Willoughby and me; found the dawn breaking on a day where we had done it, had had sex with one another. Where I would be the envy of almost every girl in my school.

Waking up that morning with Tristan was like eating something so sharp you cannot discern whether the flavour is cripplingly sweet or devastatingly sour.

Tristan brought a tray: toast; tea.

I presumed this was what his parents did at home.

'Are you OK?' he asked.

I didn't know the answer, so I didn't speak. The answer was at once, *I have done something I dreamed of night and day for two years* and *I want to turn the clock back, to have never left my mother*.

'Are you crying?' Tristan asked, his hand on my bare shoulder.

I shook my head. 'I'm fine. Honest.' Giving up my right to protest.

Tristan ran his hand down my arm, reached my hand and took it in his. We lay, side by side, not speaking until the tea went cold and the buttered toast solidified, yellow, under the jam.

◆ ◆ ◆

When we eventually got up, we pulled on our shorts and T-shirts, sat on the shore looking out to the island.

'Are you afraid of the future, Wilding?'

It came out of nowhere. I was eighteen years old; I longed for the future. 'No. I can't wait for it. To go to catering college, to be an adult, to do what I want when I want.'

Tristan had been kind to me today, tender. I could imagine a world in which we pretended last night had been different, in which we told people we were going out with each other, waited until Rachel and their parents calmed down. Maybe even got married in the tiny Auchlaggan kirk, my mother walking me down the aisle – proud at last.

'I don't want to end up like my parents.' Tristan threw a pebble at a piece of driftwood, hit it first time. 'We're different, them and me. I don't want to join the fucking golf club. Sail less and less until I'm the chairman of the yachting club and the only water I ever see is in my whisky.'

He sat up, pulled his knees in towards him. 'Have you seen pictures of them when they were young? Of Rosie and Duncan? Africa, China, India. Motorbikes and horses and boats.' Another pebble tinged angrily against the wood. 'And look at them now. Children, family holidays, office parties. It would kill me, that life.'

I'd seen the photos, the two beautiful young people who went to balls and hunts and week-long parties in castles. 'They probably thought that too. But they're happy now.'

'They're not, I promise you,' Tristan said. He put his face on his knees and exhaled, blowing fragments of his black fringe into the air like it was charged with static. 'They just look happy for other people. He shouts and she cries, neither of them ever stops drinking, and my sister and I sit upstairs ignoring each other so everyone can pretend it doesn't happen.'

He lay back on the sand, his T-shirt riding up across his tanned belly. 'I'm afraid, Wilding, actually afraid of growing up like them. I don't belong in their world.'

And I understood that, how you can live in a house your whole life but never feel like you belong. Never feel like these are your people, like you understand them.

The second time was different – between the high and low tide, between adulthood and childhood. This time it was my idea, my lead.

◆　◆　◆

We lay on the beach until the sea came in as far as our feet.

'You want to swim, Wilding?'

I shook my head.

'Then don't. You don't have to join in. Don't ever let anyone make you think otherwise. It's OK not to want the same things as everybody else.' He kissed me on the mouth, then sprang to his feet, offered me his hands. 'You cook, I'll write the visitors' book.' A mirage of marriage.

'I'm sorry about last night,' he said, just as we reached the house. He stopped me, held both my hands in his, leaned his forehead gently to mine. 'I wanted to ruin things. I'm not proud of it,

302

but that's how it started. I wanted to make my sister's friend mine. To take you away from her.'

I waved away his words, as if speaking about it would make what happened real – I wanted to believe something else. 'Don't,' I whispered.

He leaned against the front door, the back of his neck reflected in the bull's-eye glass. 'But I didn't expect you to be so—' He paused, chose his words. 'I didn't expect you to love me. I didn't expect to be so moved by that.'

◆ ◆ ◆

I can hear the noises of the village across the wind. There is a holiday park behind the kirk, green caravans lined up at a slant, their windows towards the sea. There are morning sounds, a village waking. Ten feet or so below the kirkyard, a woman walks a big yellow dog across the sand. She can't see me, sitting here next to Tristan's grave, but I watch her for a while.

'We had two more days and nights before they got back: my most golden memories of being a kid,' I say to Tristan. 'Before everyone turned up, and you morphed into the Tristan they expected.'

I imagine we're in a restaurant. He is almost sixty now, less taut and slightly rounder, but still extraordinary, still unusually attractive. We are meeting up to talk about our lives and how they panned out.

We kiss each other lightly on the cheek. Tristan is wary, shifty: unsure of how I'll feel about him, of whether we remember all three of those days and nights the same way.

We sit down at our table, smile at each other, and he realises it isn't going to be awful, there isn't going to be a scene. Just two old friends – two survivors – swapping stories. We pick out highlights of our lives: maybe he has grandchildren and shows me the photographs he keeps in his wallet – great-nieces and -nephews who Rachel would have adored; maybe he's as famous as we thought he'd grow up to be and I already know all the things about him. Maybe he and Rachel grew close as they grew older and she's told me his news over the years.

'You shut down the second Rosie and Duncan got back. Stopped: sucked in all your kindness, all the warmth. I was too young – too in your shadow – to even ask you why.' I say this to him, and the grown-up, grown-old version of him covers his eyes with his hands, shakes his head with regret.

And I describe to him, in my imaginary restaurant – after we've ordered our drinks and the waiter has gone out of earshot – how I went to the bathroom with the visitors' book, slit that page from its binding and looked for somewhere to hide it.

I speak softly, not sure how we – how history – should judge those two teenagers.

'It was over. Like a fever dream, like sunstroke. My heart was broken.'

It was the consequences of our actions – his, then mine – that were life-changing for me, not any single one of those three days and what happened there. Three days where I hoped I wouldn't get pregnant, allowed myself fantasies of what would happen if I did.

Where Tristan didn't ask me if I was on the pill and I didn't volunteer the information.

In Auchlaggan, in the reality of Tristan and me forty years later, I reach out to the side of me, snap a few heads of buttercups, a purple thistle running to down. I place them gently on the marble chips of his grave. 'I don't feel guilty about the termination, Tris. It was always the right thing for me. But for years, I carried the responsibility of having ended a pregnancy that was the very last of the Willoughbys. But, you know, it wasn't my responsibility. You or Rachel could have carried on the line, any time, but you didn't choose that route – either of you.'

I turn away from the recrimination, drift back into the gentle now. There has been enough sadness. 'Maybe you never did marry, never did settle down. And you'd show me photographs of all the places you'd seen: mountains and oceans and icebergs. All your adventures, all your travels.'

I look at my hands on my legs, at the map of age and experience, of life, they have become. 'All just because I belonged to Rachel,' I say to him, as if we both – finally – know what a silly motivation that was.

I kiss the ends of my fingers and put them softly to the stone. 'I would have done it anyway, in the end – it was all I thought about. You only had to wait.'

It was him, not me.

I don't stay much longer: I get clumsily to my feet, middle-aged knees, ageing ankles.

'Goodbye, Tris,' I say.

And I leave Tristan to rest: part of the forest, part of the sea.

I walk quietly back to Clachan, to Ben and Meg, still sleeping. I realise that all the colour was hiding in the undergrowth. All summer, pale versions of it hinted at the blaze that would follow when the autumn came. The autumn radiance is accentuated by the clear blue sky and the paper-white gulls – crisp origami shapes against it.

Blue above, red below, everywhere a rich loam peace.

Chapter Thirty-three

It is our birthday, a year on from the day of Rachel's funeral. Aunt Poll is here – in Clachan. Our first visitor, the tester guest.

It has taken this long to get everything done, slotted into place. Clachan is stunning; Rachel would have been thrilled with it. Meg has taken the essence of her – of her style, her charm – and grafted it on to the history of the Willoughbys, of their bonkers habits, their spectacular generosity. And now we are ready to welcome other people here, to the haven of Clachan, to its views and its quirks, its new comfortable beds and extra bathroom. To its contentment.

Rachel's Aunt Poll is the decider: she brought two other old ladies with her – all stylish and interesting, each as accomplished and enchanting as Poll.

I had the tiniest wobble when she told me that one of them trained as a cordon bleu chef after leaving her Swiss finishing school, but I screwed my courage up tight and cooked for them anyway.

It didn't occur to me, when they booked, that the end of their trip would be our birthday, that I'd be with Poll today, just as I was last year.

Getting Clachan ready to earn money has been the priority. I had a spectacular professional kitchen put in my house, glistening in stainless steel and gadgets, before I slept in a room that had plaster on the walls. I was ready to serve fancy dinners when I was still washing in a bucket at night, although I'm delighted that I now have a bathroom.

My house is getting the same quirks and joyful touches that Meg has left in Clachan. I couldn't afford the hand-blocked wallpaper that runs up the stairwell there, so she made a cardboard stencil and painted willowing reeds on to the walls of my hall and staircase, added flecks of metallic gold to the stems where the nodes and rings catch the light.

When the front door is open and the sun shines, my house vanishes into the reedbed, to the bitterns and the frogs who nest there, to the orange-beaked oystercatcher who wakes us every day with his bosun's whistle.

I replaced the old Clachan wheelbarrow with a pull-along wagon, complete with suspension, that folds into the back of my car. It means I can park in the sandy space and decant everything into the cart. I cook carefully, remembering that the panna cotta, the croquembouche, will have to survive a little bone-rattling on the way to the cottage. I have put together a file of recipes that will work, fit round guests' dietary needs, and won't turn into scrambled eggs on the forest path.

'It was wonderful, dear. Thank you so much.' Poll has taken her friends back to the station and then come back here for one last night on her own before she drives home.

I am in the new Clachan kitchen, clearing up the end of their last lunch.

'Did it all work?' I ask. I created precious little breakfasts and picnic basket lunches that Poll and her friends could unpack without me, afternoon teas of featherlight cakes and sweet berries, and then magnificent suppers that I served in the dining room.

'Everyone adored it. They're all booking with their friends and families. It was wonderful. But they were adamant' – she looks at me, her eyes bright in her lined face – 'that you must let us pay or we won't book again.'

'You're my testers.' I stuff the tablecloth into the washing machine, shake the napkins out of the back door. 'It could just as easily have gone horribly wrong.'

'They mean it, dear. So do I. It's awkward to book again if you don't pay. Blurs things.'

I smile and let her talk. We will come to a compromise in the end: I'll give them a hefty discount and they'll feel able to book again.

'Most of all,' Poll says, 'I love how much of my family are still here. I sat in the sitting room in the evening and I could almost see Duncan raise his glass to me. I could swear that when I looked out of my bedroom window, I saw you children running up the beach.' She lowers her voice, a secret. 'I waved at you all, you dear little ghosts.'

'Do you want to eat with me this evening, just a casual supper for the two of us?' I ask her.

'Would you mind if I didn't?' she says. 'There are lots of left-overs in the fridge and I thought I'd sit in the quiet and think about some absent friends. Absent family. But the day isn't lost on me, dear.'

She takes a box from her bag. It is wrapped with tissue and held together with a ribbon.

There are three visitors' books in the stack. The first one is from before I ever came here, before I was even born. The last one is the one I wrote in on the beach.

The one in the middle is mine and Rachel's history. A log of our lives, mostly happy here, of growing up and moving on. Of togetherness.

'Would you look after them?' Poll asks me. 'I don't want to lose my family history but nor is it mine to keep. There's so much more of you in there than me.'

I've put a new visitors' book in the cottage, fresh and clean: Poll and her friends will be the only people to have written in it so far. 'I'd be honoured to keep these,' I tell her. And it's true. I'm more than touched to be trusted to look after this diary of good times, this reminder of each other.

I leave Poll with the ghosts, with the shadows of themselves and their lives, the generations of people who have been born in this cottage, have died or been buried here. She knew so many of them.

It fills me with peace, that idea that you can communicate with the ones who've gone before you – with your lost people – alongside missing them every day.

While Poll will see her brother and his wife, hear them laugh and pour the drinks and fill that house with noise, I will go back to my cottage, to my plans and my future.

I built Rachel into the fibre of my house, the house I would never have bought without her. It is how I learned to carry on when half of me was missing. And how, over time and with the comfort of the changing seasons, the lessons of the leather-hard brambles and the tightly coiled ferns, I learned to love all of Rachel – even the folded-in parts I hadn't known. Even the secrets.

Ben says that grief doesn't only have to be for death, that you can grieve something you've never had, grieve the negative space of it. Accepting that has helped me to add my mother, my teenage years, to these ghosts I live with – as much a part of me as all my best points. Each a part of what made me. I didn't lose my mother to death: I lost her to difference. To a difference in the way we perceived the world, to a difference in what mattered, in where we would find our happiness.

My mother died a few days after I went to see her, and I let her odd little church decide how to bury her. I stood at the back – no one there knew me – and wished for Rachel with all my heart when the choir stood and sang 'Jesus Wants Me for a Sunbeam'.

◆ ◆ ◆

There are new rituals now, with this rebuilt world. No hollering out and no creaking stair, but I am making my own legends, my own marks. Meg painted me a little sign and nailed it to the gate: *Ar Tigh*, it says – Our House. Mine and Rachel's.

Every evening, unless the sea is a boiling ferocity that warns me to stay away, I walk down the planks of the boardwalk outside my house. It only takes me a few minutes to clear the reeds and arrive at the edge of the bay.

Clachan is hidden from here, tucked away in its own little inlet, but I know it's there – that Rachel and I look over the same sea.

I step down at the edge of the walkway, on to the sand, and slip off my shoes. Every evening the sea bubbles up around my toes with that bracing prickle. I only ever put my feet into the water. I am, at long last, a person who doesn't have to swim if she doesn't want to. At last, I can enjoy paddling, enjoy the shallows.

I wave towards Clachan and the sunset. I say goodnight to the Willoughbys and turn away – grateful that they brought me to the place where I went on to build a home for myself.

Tonight is more than a wave – tonight is long loving wishes for our birthday celebration, for the day we will always share.

There were so many people I put forward to Tim when he asked me to write Rachel's eulogy: I pleaded to be released in favour of those who knew her better, who partied late at night in expensive venues, who went shopping in Mayfair with her.

Now I understand that it was this, this peace and past, this settlement of the sands and the renewing of the waves, that meant it could only be me.

ACKNOWLEDGEMENTS

As ever, first and foremost, thanks to Phil McIntyre for smart suggestions and clever thoughts, for always spotting what's going to work in a story. To Sarah Hornsley for being the absolute best of agents, book after book. To Victoria Oundjian, David Downing, and everyone at Lake Union. And to Emma Rogers for this absolutely incredible cover. Thanks to everyone who helped bring this book to life.

To Clare Baker, Janet Lewis, Hattie Douch and Bex Rechter for early reading. And especially to Fionnuala Kearney for reading it about forty times.

To the Mhor Maniacs for being marvellous, and to everyone who's been to Write South West Scotland on retreat or who attends my Zoom classes: you're all inspirational.

Thanks to Prof Ian Hindmarch for his quote from the *Independent* about the human condition: a lot of this book is written in memory of our mutual friend Dr John Kerr, who taught me the tricks that Rachel knew.

My thanks always to my family, to my children and grandchildren, who I was so very lucky to end up with, and to Colin for always believing in me.

And to Jane, always. With love. I miss you every day.

If you loved *The House of Lost Secrets*, turn the page for an exclusive extract from Anstey Harris's *When I First Held You*

Chapter One

For most customers who enter the shop, the thing they most want mending is the past. We can't do that: we can patch it, polish it, we can turn the past into a healthy memory to be built on – but we can't mend it. Once we explain that, they seem happier, content to have an emblem of that time restored, or a memento made usable again. Often, all they need is to talk.

The shop began life as a blue plastic laundry basket outside our garden gate. In it, Catherine would put every single thing that had made its way into our house but that we no longer wanted, or had never found a use for. Magically, every evening, the crate would clear again – as if there were fairies waiting to recycle those flimsy plant pots left after the seedlings had grown, goblins interested in a jumper with a bleach mark on the cuff, or a plastic bag full of plastic bags.

One man's trash is another man's treasure, Catherine would say, when she brought the grubby plastic basket in to fill it up again.

The proof, day after day, that almost anything can be recycled or repurposed led to the bigger conversation that got us here – to the Mending Shop – and, four years after Catherine's death, it's a way to reinvent me. She may have set the whole thing up just to reuse me, I wouldn't be surprised. For an artist, Catherine had a methodical and pragmatic mind: she spent fifty years one step ahead of me and it still amazes me that I manage to live without her.

Usually, the shop is a quiet place – a couple of volunteers beavering away at benches, the occasional customer in from the cold outside, a general air of concentrated purpose. I enjoy the peace in my little office; I have to raise my head above the parapet to deal with a crisis from time to time, but I stay in here with the paperwork. Outside, in the shopfront proper, there are smells of solder, of paint, the occasional whiff of glue as something comes back together, comes back to life. We have customers – although not too many and no money changes hands – and we're all, the volunteers and I, quietly useful.

Today, I am standing by the front door herding cats: the space is filled with people, despite the fact it wasn't designed for that at all. We have long benches across the width of the room, each a few metres apart like school science labs. The walls around the edges are racked with shelves from floor to ceiling: shelves that hold things to be mended, things to be collected, and enough tools to fix anything except a broken heart. The shop wasn't set out for every volunteer, and a number of nosy locals, to all come in at once.

There is an excited buzz of conversation that warms the air and, despite my best efforts to be detached and above it all, makes me tingle with excitement.

'Judith,' a man calls from among the melee, 'could we get you into Make-up?' 'Make-up' means my tiny office. It sits, like an old-fashioned foreman's post, in the furthest corner of the long room. The cubicle doesn't really warrant a word as grand as office: it is plywood thin and the top half of it is glass so that I can look out at the workshop and, which happens far more often, so they can look in at me. There is a door of sorts but it doesn't quite fit properly, and I worry that if it does shut one day, I'll never be able to open it.

'Judith?' he asks again.

'Sorry, absolutely, I'm on my way.' Make-up isn't really my thing but if I'm to be on television, I'd best try and look half decent. Age and the very bright lights dotted all around the shop have bleached my skin enough.

In my office is a nice young woman called Angela, the daughter of one of our volunteers. She has offered to help me look less dishevelled for this morning. Angela sits me down in my swivel chair and just about finds room to squish herself in, between my feet and the door. She puffs powder on to my cheeks from a spectacular box of tricks, foofs and fluffs my hair with her fingers. 'I love your fringe,' she says, almost purring.

'Thank you.' I accept her compliment graciously and try not to think about the nail scissors and the bathroom mirror, the little snippets of grey and white that waft into the basin below as I save myself a trip to the hairdresser.

'Have you been on TV before?' she asks. I am perched on the edge of the chair. She is looming over me, dabbing my face with a silky cloth.

I remember the grainy footage of demonstrations, leaning in as close as possible to the screen during the news, hoping to see myself, hoping my parents wouldn't. I didn't, not until I was in my fifties. 'A placard of mine made it into a crowd scene on a march.' I leave my mouth open, ready to tell her what was on the banner when she asks, but she doesn't.

'Nearly there,' she says, smoothing my hair at the sides. She tucks a few stray ends behind my ear.

'I've been backstage in TV studios a few times,' I say, making conversation while the technical things happen outside the glass sides of the cubicle. 'My late partner was an artist. She did lots of talk shows and interviews.'

She doesn't ask about Catherine either, who she was, what she painted.

'Done.'

The face in the mirror is a pantomime dame.

'It looks heavy like this, but it won't on the screen.'

I nod, I know it's true. I've seen Catherine, painted up like a butterfly, look completely like herself when we watched the programme through later. 'It's great, thanks.' I take a selfie of the pantomime-dame-me, which I'll send to a few close friends later, for a giggle.

The reporter is chatty and encouraging – I don't have time to be nervous.

'Welcome back to *Our High Street*.' The presenter smiles into the camera as he says it, an honest smile, full of support. 'Where we look at all the jobs you could do, if only you knew they existed.' His grin is wide and white and his hand flourishes across the shop. 'Judith Franklin is – right here on the High Street, right in the middle of a traditional county town – the owner of a "Mending Shop".'

The cameraman takes one step back to fit us both in the shot.

'A place where you can have your own object repaired or pick up one already done to replace something of yours that's broken. Is that an accurate description, Judith?'

My throat is a little dry, but I've never had the same problem with public speaking that I've had with more intimate truths, and my voice is strong. 'Absolutely, we exist to keep things out of landfill – first and foremost. We restore things that make people happy, and we turn things that might be thrown away into perfectly serviceable objects that get another life. Keep the plastic out of the sea, and keep people thinking about the planet.' It's a lecture I know off by heart. I've recited it to newspapers, on radio. I've recited it to friends and funders. Once I even had to say it to an angry customer whose beloved childhood pram had its wheels upcycled – by some new and overenthusiastic volunteers – into a go-cart for the youth centre. Our systems are more robust now.

'Why hasn't anyone done it before, Judith?' the reporter – his name is Ben – asks.

'It's a non-profit,' I say, feeling the heat under the powder on my cheeks, glad that it's hiding the flush the huge lights have brought up in my skin. 'No money changes hands here and we can't pay wages or bills in kindness and repairs. I'm sure a lot of people have thought about it, but haven't had the means to see it through.' I don't tell him that I can't find anyone else to take over, that I'm tired of running Catherine's shop but that it's me or no one.

Catherine spent a decade hiding from cancer, dodging and ducking its various attempts to overwhelm her. When, on its last call, she knew she wouldn't recover, Catherine told me to sell the paintings that leaned up against the wall of her studio – the ones she'd finished but not exhibited yet – and put the money to good use: this good use.

'What's the point in holding on to them, babe?' she said. 'You have a house full of pictures, not enough walls, and a crappy social worker's pension. You don't need them to remember me.' She was sitting at the table in our garden when she said it, her feet propped up on a pale-blue slatted chair, a blanket over her knees despite the summer. 'You need money to go to New Zealand, or buy a campervan, or do anything worthwhile.'

Ben cocks his head to one side like a bird. His soft pink shirt is open at the neck and the stubble on his chin – artfully trimmed – grazes the edge of its collar. 'Can you think of an object that encapsulates exactly what you're doing here, Judith?'

The shop is brightly lit, full of people. The old-fashioned gold letters painstakingly painted on to the glass cast an elongated message on the sanded floorboards. The back-to-front letters spelling out 'The Mending Shop' distort as the light floods through them.

A blue jumper sits on the fabric bench, the curls and coils of its wool dripping over the edge like intestines waiting to be sewn back in. On the plastics bench a yellow tractor, large enough for a child to sit on and zoom around these urban streets, waits with its steering wheel removed for someone to fix it. The shop is alive with stories, with other people's histories.

My favourite thing we have at the moment is a snow globe. A glass dome with an underwater scene made of tiny real shells and little flashes of fish that have been pinched out of clay. The work that has gone into the miniature scene is remarkable: the mermaid who sits in the centre of it wears scales so fine they might have come from a real fish, and two modestly placed minuscule clam shells. Over the years, the sea itself has evaporated. The glitter lies, immobile, on the toes of the mermaid, matted in her plaster hair. I haven't decided which bench it belongs on yet. At the moment, she's on the counter – like a talisman – with my laptop and the coffee machine, but I'm confident we'll work out what to do with her eventually.

Whether I will be able to part with her once her bubble has been topped back up and the silver fish are wet again, I don't know. Catherine made me swear an oath about clutter when we first opened the shop. She predicted – from fifty years of knowing everything about me – that I would fall in love with every broken object, need to find a home for every chipped heart. For each year without her, the oath gets progressively harder to keep.

I pick up the kintsugi vase that sits on my desk, not for sale or rehoming. I curl my fingers around its slender neck, thinking of Catherine, of how she took it from the shelf in the gallery in Akita, her gentle nod that said it was ours. 'Sometimes they're accidental breaks,' she said, 'ones that no one meant to happen.' She put the vase down to take my strong hand in her slight and tiny ones. 'And sometimes the vase is broken on purpose – by the craftsman. But whichever way the break happens, the item is always stronger – richer – for being mended.' Catherine smiles in my memory and the solid-silver mend of her in my heart grows thicker, shines more deeply.

I sigh, at once mournful and comforted, and turn to Ben. 'This break . . .' I trace the crooked gold line on the vase with my finger and the cameraman moves closer to me.

'One second,' the cameraman says. 'Can you just turn round a little, rotate the vase towards me?'

'Start again at "This break . . .",' Ben says.

And I do. I trace the jagged line of metal, I show them the vase and how much more beautiful it is for its mend, and therefore for the damage it suffered in the first place.

'And each time an item is mended in our shop,' I tell them, 'it will accrue value, it'll gain a story. Every time we unpack something from newspapers, open a bubble-wrap parcel, the person who has brought it in will tell us about it: where it came from; how it was broken. Most importantly, they'll tell us why it needs to be mended. And then each object will grow, will become so much more than the negative space it would have served in landfill.' I put the vase back down. Everyone in the shop is quiet, listening.

'That's quite lovely,' says Ben. 'And the Mending Shop will become part of the history of the item.'

I nod, beaming. My answer has been even better than the rehearsals I've had in the bathroom at home – saying the words out loud to myself in the mirror, listening to them die away against the porcelain tiles and the silence.

'Each object that leaves here – mended – has another life: becomes something to someone else who needs it. That's at the very heart of . . .'

At the front of the room, behind the cluster of television crew, the door opens and someone steps into the shop.

He stands, undiminished by time, as tall and wide as the frame.

This must be how it feels when you die – when your whole life flashes before your eyes. It takes one click of the brain's mechanism to recognise someone you haven't seen for over fifty years. Another impossible moment to remember who they are and what they did.

Standing in the doorway like a time traveller is Jimmy McConnell.

ABOUT THE AUTHOR

Photo © 2022 Lindsay Fraser

Anstey Harris was born in an unmarried mothers' home in Liverpool in 1965. Now a mother and stepmother herself, she lives in Scotland. She has been inspired by her family history, and hopes to give a voice to the women and children—16,000 a year during the 1960s in the UK—separated from each other by forced adoptions.

Anstey won the H. G. Wells Short Story Award in 2015 and her debut novel, *The Truths and Triumphs of Grace Atherton*, a Richard and Judy Book Club choice, won the Sapere Books RNA Popular Romantic Fiction Award in 2020. Her second novel, *Where We Belong*, was shortlisted for the RNA Book of the Year Award 2021 and she numbers Libby Page, Katie Fforde and Beth O'Leary among her many fans.

Follow the Author on Amazon

If you enjoyed this book, follow Anstey Harris on Amazon to be notified when the author releases a new book!
To do this, please follow these instructions:

Desktop:

1) Search for the author's name on Amazon or in the Amazon App.

2) Click on the author's name to arrive on their Amazon page.

3) Click the 'Follow' button.

Mobile and Tablet:

1) Search for the author's name on Amazon or in the Amazon App.

2) Click on one of the author's books.

3) Click on the author's name to arrive on their Amazon page.

4) Click the 'Follow' button.

Kindle eReader and Kindle App:

If you enjoyed this book on a Kindle eReader or in the Kindle App, you will find the author 'Follow' button after the last page.